The Isolated Mind

By : Clint Ridley

Illustration

By : ShiKage Okami

The creativity, hard work and possibility of this novel is dedicated to my loving and supportive parents, my early life wasn't easy and I went through a lot of troubles but they were always at my side and let me know that following your dreams can come true, you just have to get back on the horse and see it through till the end and when you get the victory it will be sweeter.

Clint Ridley

Prologue

Hello any listeners, look if you have come for a action packed thriller well you're shit out of luck this is just my plain old life story but there is kind of a twist, you see there is some things I need to run across you before we start, my name is not important I am a maintenance worker on a small space station that I'm now currently on. Here is the important stuff this space station I am on is about as big as a two story house it has a Medical room, bathroom and Recreation center plus the main Center Control to the ship and a lower level of tunnels leading to the heating, electricity among other things. This space station was being decommissioned and I was sent to shut the main control down so we could pull it in and scrap it.

Okay now we're in major plot territory as I was heading to shut it down I heard this loud bang, it shook the whole station somewhat like what was an earthquake and with my shocked face and a hint of confusion I stopped what I was doing and heading back to the new ship before I shut this station off.

As I reached the airlock peeking out the window I see the horror that was upon me, the new station was obliterated, on fire and torn into millions and as my heart sunk realizing everyone aboard was now dead I looked passed the wreckage to see the giant asteroid field but it was no asteroid field it is what was Earth now been blown into billions of chucks. I could no longer look at the terror and sunk to the bottom of the airlock sitting there and balling like a baby as I now knew that whatever happened I was now the last human alive and stuck up here in this station.

Chapter 1

Getting acclimated

It had been two months of isolation already, the good thing about these space stations is that they were used as houses so there is like five years of food stored in here for me, I think I've finally calmed from the event now I just have to keep it in the back of my head for the rest of my life and keep my mind occupied. I haven't had much time on this space station to live before so it doesn't help my case that for the past two months I've been pacing back from room to room and rocking in a ball like a baby, the things to do in this station weren't much different from the new one, the only major difference was the technological differences so it can be unreliable at times. What to do first, I hadn't showered in those two months but what was the need to it's just me, there is no social standard, along side that I didn't really have a schedule, we all did have some kind of thing we did that made us who we are, I guess with the tough schooling to be a engineer on the station I had lots of determination and hope, hope for humanity to restart, retry I don't know.

Every morning I would reset the distress beacon hoping someone was still out there, it's not gonna happen I know it just keeps my sanity to think there could be, my life before this isn't of much importance, back on Earth I worked as a engineer on a U.S. Navy ship I didn't have much of a social life and never really saw my family much. The isolation doesn't bother me as much I've always kinda been that way, there would be maybe once a week I'd get human contact other than that I'd be working or with my own thoughts and entertaining myself, I went into a mental shock just knowing billions had died and I wasn't going to get back to Earth, you're all probably wondering how all this happened, I'm gonna have to answer this question a thousand times here's the truth I don't know what happened to the new space station. The Earth though well I assume that the blast from the new station was so powerful if ruptured the core on Earth and broke it into a million pieces, there's really not much more to it, I accept that and I have to live with it, wish the best of luck to me will you and who knows this might not be so bad right?

I've rambled for a while now, seems that I'm the last person I'm going to enjoy it as long as I can, maybe I'll look into the explosion or maybe not, it doesn't really matter at this point, don't get me wrong I'm truly upset about these events I just shouldn't waste energy on something I can't possibly fix, it's not like I'm really putting my energy into something important but you know what they say.

"Don't ask questions you don't want the answer to."

It might be nice to know what happened or why it just also mite hurt to much to know, I feel my sanity would be better off if I never knew, I know what your thinking.

"A whole space station all to yourself stop complaining."

Well it's neat but not all fun and games, it's a lot of work to keep this place running, everyday I have to reset the distress beacon which takes fifteen minutes to do, so if there's a slim chance of another ship out there let's hope I can get its attention. Once a week I have to clean the air so for about an hour out of that day I have to wear a space suit and use about twenty five percent of a air tank, doing the math it seem that I would last long but this station was used for five people to live on it for about five years, I'm lucky that they stocked piled this place to the roof, so instead of me lasting five years or so I'll last at least fifteen to twenty or more.

This is silly but sleeping is harder than you'd think, I'm in space it is hard to sleep period, I sleep fine knowing that I'm in space what bothers me is that everyone's dead and I can't help feeling that I'm being watched, obviously by something not human, it's just in my head though the U.S. went generations without finding alien life as far that I know of, the isolation now isn't completely different from my life before, there's always been story's of people who become astronauts and still get cabin fever. You know how the heads help the people who go nuts, they throw them in space brig, no bullshit they're real yes we do have prison cells on the head station, every human can take in so much in different ways, being alone forever wouldn't be that hard for me I guess I just held out longer than others it help being isolated at the bottom of a war ship before becoming an astronaut, I won't bore you with my personal life to much I just wanted you to get acclimated to my situation.

Why am I even making a log it'll be a blue moon if another human runs across this and I'm not sending the message into space so in order to find this I'd be dead or meet you personally and show you it, if you're still there it seems you're in for the long haul, what does my future hold, people on Earth were always looking to the future and making everything bigger and better, as of the moment there's nothing I can do and I never expect that to change, I'll live for now and make ever second count, I'm the leader of my own world now I do what I want when I want, no rules, no judgment, no expectation, ... no people.

Chapter 2

Keeping occupied

I know I went over the entertainments of the station though there not being much, you see the best thing to do in isolation is keep your mind busy, since I still have to do my actual job I had to keep the station up and running, the station actually isn't that old we just recently updated from it and that's why we were going to put this one I'm on in decommission. The U.S. was going to build a new station with the new blueprints of hardware we made but didn't have the funds to make the final product so due to the debt of the U.S., Russia had helped fund seventy five percent of the station and we're going to run the operation with them.

We did get to make the new station holding ten people, the best thing to come out of the partnership was Russia didn't want train ten new cosmonauts so there was five from Russia and five from the U.S. including me, blah blah blah all the technicality's are on the bottom of my bucket list. Back on the topic I was saying that I hadn't mentioned a lot of the time wasters, we most of the time did testing on life in space and on other planets I just made sure that the station stayed afloat, when we weren't working which wasn't long there were a number of things to do, this station may not have the best technology but it gets the job done, if I had one.

There's four separate rooms a Rec. room with a three seat couch, big flat screen TV, a few gaming consoles, big book shelf, there's the Medical and testing room where we had all kinds of medial supplies and techno gadgets, there was also the pantry room where more than enough food and water was, and finally there is the Control Deck to fly the ship and make contact with Earth. But to the events as of now that seem pointless, oh and there is a lower deck which housed all the set up to keep the station afloat, keeping the air clean and where the back up generator is in case of the power dying of a glitch in the system, That's where I'd usually be all day everyday, but in case of a power outage I really didn't do much Houston fixed that from HQ, I'd normally be looking at the air purity gauges every hour on the hour as well as the main power supply logging them, so I know when to set the air cleaner or start the back up generator in time if Houston couldn't.

This isn't some kind of vacation for me, this isn't a movie or make believe, trust me I wish I was the last person on Earth in this case but I'm not, I'm the last human from Earth stuck in space, I still have to do my job if I want to survive that's just my luck. I'm hungry if you're still paying attention and you know anything about space food it hasn't changed, yep still eating out of a tube or little dry food from a pouch, I'm betting you think cool space food well no it's even worse than army food, It's basically just paste or crumbs flavored like real food, the heads said it's cost effective and last longer in space than actually food, my guess is it's cheaper taste like shit but who cares foods food right. Fuck no I know we're in a lot in debt right now but if you can afford twenty five percent of a bigger and better space station you can buy me a steak once and a while.

What's on the menu today you ask pork shoulder flavored crumbs in a bag and water, god I'd kill for a soda right now, I didn't really have any choice In the matter, I wouldn't expect you to understand, I'd have to say it's not all that bad the food is like a habit you do something for so long it becomes the normal, some of the foods tasted better than others and we always had a set meal plan for the day, that's all out the window now I've got a buffet. Nothing much from eating has really changed drastically I still have to eat and the same amount as I would normally or this stuff wouldn't last long even if it was just me and the food supply was really meant for five, I guess the good thing is I could eat whatever I wanted to but I'm eventually going to have to eat those foods no one likes made the space food way, you know spinach, cabbage stuff like that. I haven't really thought about earth food in a while since I been eating space food for a good two years, I do miss soda, a friend of mine that worked on the station with me did some testing on the Med. Lab to make a liquid to add to the water that gave the impression of lemonade but it always tasted shitty, she never did perfect it.

That's something I could try to do now that I have the time, all the time in the world, well not really I still am to assume that I'll die from old age someday or just do everything I could possibly do till I go stir crazy and end it, god that was dark sorry about that it's just when you are alone for so long you dig into every aspect of thoughts that run through your head, how could one not think about that though the human mind can only deal with so much, It's not something I think about a lot but with the circumstances how could I not.

I'm sorry getting of topic again, as I've said the best thing to do is keep my mind occupied, whenever we got breaks people sleep or do something like watch the TV, get on the computer or play a video game, there is no Earth to send a broadcast from live TV is out of the question. I did play games or search the web a lot but the web is the same as live TV none existent anymore and I would play games but it's not really the same just one player, even though I had probably one of the most important jobs on the station I had quite a lot of free time, Keeping the station stable seems crucial but the heads didn't so I'd be told to take breaks quite frequently since all I did was stair at dials all day. So I guess if the station was going down and Houston couldn't help in time I'd have to beat land speed records to reach the lower part of the station and turn on the back up generator, good thing that never happened, I could spend all day watching videos and playing games but that will drain the power, the power is good for about five years with five passengers with just me and almost no power being used except for a few lights the beacon and other small things I need to survive I should be good for at least twenty or so. Hell I've been through a lot of crap lately not only this but my life before to, it wouldn't hurt to watch a movie, although if I do I'll have to compensate for the energy and not watch another for a couple days.

Boy was I wrong it wasn't the somewhat waste on station energy, It was the paranoia from the movie I've got to be the biggest dummy, cause I just watched the 1979 Alien, who watches that movie while in space and what bigger dummy than me brought the movie on bored, it doesn't help that it's always nighttime in space sort of and that just what makes the station more creepy, I'm acting silly, I'm alone the only reason I'm being paranoid is cause I feel I'm being watched or it could just be my mind telling me there's got to be someone out there. Just let me tell you right now if you're expecting me to find another person it's not gonna happen, the only reason I use the beacon is to give myself a false since of hope, I'm sorry to let you down but the only way I'd find another person is if somehow N.A.S.A. got a ship past our station without us knowing which would be almost impossible. I guess unless they sent out some astronauts from the Russian space launch station which would be highly unlikely, damn I keep getting off point you'd do it to if you had no one to talk to and had billions of thoughts.

Now other than watching movies I decided to play some video games but that's kind of a problem when I have all the high scores and I'd just be doing circles and achieving nothing although what else to do, we also have a bookshelf full of all kind of stuff, most of it is just manuals for the station, when I was on a break we all never really had time to read a book I probably got a hour break out of twelve hours of work and when I was getting rest for five to six hours out of my day I was still on the clock and needed to wake fast if something went wrong. My work was laid back but I always had to stay vigilant, for the other twelve hours of the day another engineer helped , reading is only one of the things I think that helps the most cause with games and movies you get bored or lose games and yeah a movie draws you in with the story as well as a book does but the book typically lasts longer and keeps your attention longer. You see with a game you play it and play it sometimes you win and it's over then playing it again doesn't change your experience, With a movie you sit, watch and listen your minds not as active and it ends in an hour and a half or two plus watching it again has the same effect as a video game it really doesn't change much, with a book every one imagines the story in their own way, that takes more concentration of your mind.

Being a engineer I know all sorts of techno babble, no offense to the science arts it's just that it could matter less at this point, now I'm not saying it isn't important, in fact it's my way of survival now, I'll get into the aspects of the forgotten now erased heritage of Earth. There is a computer in the Rec. room it never occurred to me to get on the internet cause the tower that provided that service offered the internet was on Earth, the only way I get electricity for the TV and to even power this station is cause I have a separate power system that wasn't controlled by an outsource. You know when you're on vacation and take the family in a long car ride hours on end and when you've done everything you can and to keep occupied you look out the window, Ha I wish I could do that, all I can see out the window is endless space and stars. Due to living in space we need to be really active we don't have a running track and the food we eat even though we know we're not suppose to eat it for long periods of time we have to use the treadmill and weights to stay fit and be able to take the living environment, there are of course major downsides to my situation but to live I need to still do my regular job and more I can't just slack off and play games all day although I'd like to, I have to be on alert ever second even when I sleep, if I do at all.

It does hurt me to just ignore the fact that everyone's gone but as I've said if I still want to be around I have to keep playing games, seeing movies, reading. Why are you still listening to me huh I'm just a selfish ass, I mean of course I'm sad and that was my first two months, I can't say I got over it and I never will, a person can only use so much emotion before it just becomes a meaningless emotion, not that I can't feel sadness anymore I'm human. What I wouldn't do for a beer, although that's not a good idea with the big responsibility I have I can't afford to get drunk and screw up what I have left, It's not like I'm gonna restart the human race but till I can, if I can I need to stay mentally well, the irony is that

I need to use my mind to keep my sanity, but in the end it'll most likely be my downfall, I know eventually I'll do everything to keep occupied I possibly can, at that point it's great we as human have no length to creativity.

So what I'm saying is I am in the evolution process as was humans before me millions of years ago, I know what I know and eventually I have to change my game I know that I will outlast the supplies I have, not to get to personal I'm only thirty, when time gets short I'll figure out a plan, may not be the best plan for now but survival is like aspects of a video game in this instant it's trial and error, you try one idea and it might help it might not, the best thing to say is that I hope to make better choices cause survival doesn't have much room for error defiantly not in space.

My game has only begun and I don't even know anymore how long it's from The Big Bang two, though I know it's been just a few months, there's one thing I got to get off my chest something that crucial to my story, I tend to go off topic a tiny bit but with thousands of thoughts going through my head you can't help it, just bear with me I'll try to hit one main topic at a time and stick to it eighty percent of the time the other twenty percent is still relevant just not as important, sometimes, this is getting a little depressing I'm gonna has some major fun, no not a twenty four hour movie or game marathon something much stronger, oh yes much stronger.

Chapter 3

Party like there's no one watching

I'm backtracking the story a little, so for what I'm about to do has reason, okay here we go, I'm the last person in the universe and stuck on a space station, all to do is watch movies, read, or play games, but it's not all fun and games I have to do double time in order to stay alive. I've never been much of a wild guy and now I have the perfect chance, I've thought over the results and I don't care there isn't much to life anymore if I die I die that's the way it was before that's the way it is now, I'm gonna have the wildest one man party ever, I'm gonna get drunk as fuck, high as fuck, eat a shit ton and play the music as loud as I can. I looked it over and I'm right if I survive this party I can survive anything, I may waste some of my precious materials but I deserve this after the life I had and the world ending, I'll tell you one thing once I'm done I'll never be the same, I know I've said there wasn't any alcohol on the station or drugs of course, but we had a lot of medical supplies in the lab so I could just make it.

I know that is unbelievably stupid, I could care less though, I headed into the Med. Lab and busted the lock to all the pills and liquids it actually wasn't that hard to make drugs or alcohol it just takes the knowledge and years of chemical science, it goes against all that I stand in the respect for science, I again say I could care less. I finished mixing the drink then took shot after shot I probably had at least eight of whatever I made then ran to the Rec. room and basted some old rock n roll throughout the station, while flailing about the place I crushed some numbing pills and mixed with some flu goop I mixed up, judge me I don't care yeah it might kill me if I'm lucky.

Then shit got real the music was loud I was spinning like a top, running through the halls in my underwear, dancing to the rhythm of the music and screaming at the top of my lungs, I started to jump up and down on the couch in the Rec. room then bumping my head on the ceiling falling but first on the couch, with my speed the couch fell over backwards, then getting right up like nothing happened I ran out the door but missed hitting the bookshelf head on, I fell to the ground and rolled out of the way before the shelf smashed me, after that I ran it the Med. lab and smashed all the test tubes and other glasses then grabbed a video camera, things got blurry.

It was the next morning and my head felt like TNT was going off ever two seconds, god I got pretty screwed up I only remember few things, I looked around and noticed that I trashed the place, the couch in the Rec. room was overturned and the bookshelf fell over, In the Med. lab the floor was covered in glass. I pulled up a fallen stool seat and sat thinking what in the hell happened, my memory as foggy I remember certain things but what was most clear to me was why I did what I did, would you blame me at this point I could rehash it but it seems so obvious to me and I think we've gotten to know each other so I won't waste your time explaining, sitting there and thinking real hard, what did I do?

My head was stinging like hell, grasping the top of my head I screamed in pain, then I felt a lump on the left side of my head and remembered, yeah I was jumping up and down on the couch that's why it was turned over, the only reason I had for that I guess was my childhood, let me illiterate, you see the last time I think I felt true happiness was when I was younger than ten, I guess I was just so out of what was going on and doing something to remember the good times, acting like a kid jumping on the bed, doing something you know you're not suppose to. I have to admit it was fun while it lasted, childhood and the acid trip I had, I don't want to be but I'm an adult I have more than just a responsibility to do my job and make a living now I have the responsibility to keep the human race existing as long as possible.

Ha me that's a joke but it is and I can't change that, I rolled my chair over to the computer table and saw the video camera sitting there on its side, the video camera had a flashing red light then realizing, shit it's dying it could tell me more about what happened last night. I plugged the charger into the computer to watch it on bigger screen then I open the file and started the video, I didn't know there was more on the camera than just my freak out, there was footage of me and my last crew on the station. I'm not going to go into much detail but it's something I should mention for the moment, being on this station before with four other people, there was a Engineer, Medical /Science doctor, first mate and the Captain.

The video was of us all sitting in the Rec. room talking and laughing watching a movie, it was such a happy moment with friends, I don't remember what we talked about or laughed for, but I was balling to much and blocked out what we were saying. I was happy to see such a happy moment but sad it was over, then the video just cut to me from yesterday, I was in the Med. room, in my underwear ranting at a piece of fruit from the stash we had with the other foods, to tell you in great length what I said would be embarrassing to reveal, trust me you don't want to know.

closing the file and wiping my tears I see a file on the desktop named photos, I knew what it was and I still couldn't pass it by, I knew what I was getting into but something inside me made me click the file, why put myself through this, if anything having pictures of people I knew I won't feel so alone, I scrolled through the pictures and saw a photo of the Medical /Science Doctor sitting at the dinner table holding a glass of water and smiling, I hadn't thought about the old crew for obvious reason. The Doctor in the picture was Julia, she wasn't smiling cause of happiness she was embarrassed, having a look of.

"Don't do that please."

She never was a very social person, I kept scrolling through the pictures and saw one of the Captain and his first mate putting one hand on each others shoulders posing for the picture, the Captain was Duane and co Captain was Carl, the two were the best of friend, they were well into their forties and had been great friends for years so the picture made lots of since. The next picture was of me in a dark corner of the engine room tinkering on something not even looking at the camera, was that really me, well of course it was but was I so anti social throughout my life I wouldn't even pay attention to a simple picture, that was all the pictures really worth mentioning.

There was another crew member that I didn't mention and that was the other Engineer but there wasn't any pictures of her cause she was the one normally taking them, Her name was Wendy, she was a new recruit like me, the biggest difference between us was she was always joyful about being in space and meeting the geniuses that make it possible, I was to it's not like I wasn't trying to get to know others in the company, but work came first and I was always unsocial. It was nothing against the others I worked with I just didn't make friends easy, never really getting to close to people, but Wendy was different, she was more different from me but we still had enough in common, I did make friends, women were always harder to be around, but Wendy and me had that connection.

You know how people say there's someone out there for everyone, I can't say that's totally true but I felt me and Wendy did have something there we just never took the chance I guess my preconceived notion that with being alone in not only in my work but most of my family and social life I convinced myself that no matter how hard I tried it wouldn't work out. If you had as a unlucky and unsuccessful life as me you'd expect to fail you'd think the same way, I know it sound like my life isn't that bad, getting to go to space that's cool, well things do go my way but more of time don't, I sat on my chair with a blank face thinking of nothing then a funny smell crossed my nose, thinking.

"Uh that can't be fire can it?"

Then I start to smell it stronger, I was in the Rec. room a minute ago and knew that the heater wasn't on plus we don't cook anything on the station, also the station was not moving so it couldn't be the engine over heating and if it was the emergency lights would go off and the station would probably be losing its balance. Then all looking in shock to the side noticing the wires to the rewire box were on fire and the flames run up to the box getting bigger by the second, sitting there with a shocked look on my face thinking, "Great just my luck"

Chapter 4

Just my luck part : 1

I lower my head and thought.

"This was just great the first time trying not to be me I actually have some fun then put myself in mortal danger."

It's not like I didn't know this was gonna happen, hell as I said I expected it even in my time of complete freedom I can't have fun, being the last person ever seems cool and it's an idea that's nothing new, everyone has thought what would it be like, you'd be alone I could do anything, how long could I last, well let me tell you in my situation it's no picnic. Why should I assume anything different just because the universe gives me an opportunity to do something important doesn't mean it's a cake walk, every step in this journey is going to still have ramifications good or bad, I'm only giving the impression I'm free of all responsibilities but I'm not, from here on I need to live my life now as if it were before what happened.

Raising my head to see the rewire box engulfed in flames, damn my attention span, needing to act fast, running to the food pantry grabbing a pail and pumped water from a nozzle connected to the giant tank from tunnels below, releasing water into the pail slowly you'd think with all the technological advancements they'd have an easier and faster way to get water, well there's a reason for that.

"Technological advancements."

I'd guess that doesn't apply to the environmental sciences, finishing pumping the water I ran back to the Med. Lab throwing the water on the fire but it had little to no effect. running back and forth two or three times the during then next I throw the pail of water on the fire then just froze, something had occurred to me, there was a fire extinguisher in a cabinet in the Med Lab. See that's what happens with stressful things you tend to have racing thoughts but when you've got nothing but your thoughts you tend to get off topic all the time or be very forgetful.

Pulling out every shelf and making an even bigger mess of things I opened every cabinet, then opening the last one I saw the fire extinguisher and grabbed it pulling the pin, pointing it at the fire and firing the foam to put the fire out but the pressure propelled me out the door and I landed on my back outside the door, I sat up and saw the fire was out and thought.

"Oh thank god, wait I'm not in space."

Okay well I technically I was, but not in outer space, so why did I get propelled, I knew the answer but not at first, you'd think being an Engineer I'd know instantly, doing something for almost my whole life you wouldn't forget a thing, all I can say is that everyone has animal instincts for survival and the more you become an animal you forget who you were, the reason I propelled is because the station was losing air pressure, if the station lost enough it would lose its stationary balance and I'd be spinning none stop through space. standing up then running back into the Med. Lab, looking at the rewire system it was smoking but at least the fire was put out, picking up a hand towel off the floor and using it to pull open the small door on the rewire box and as I did a gust of smoke is pushed in my face, the buttons were fried and sparking.

The box was to destroyed to turn back on the artificial gravity, there was a rewire box near the Captain seat also, if I could find the security code for it I could restore the artificial gravity without using the backup generator, but the Captain was the only one allowed to use it during serious situations. running to The Captains rewire box it needed a security code and I never knew it, there was a folder with security codes I wasn't aloud to know, it was in the Captains lock box but his key were on him when he died on the other station. I went to the middle of the Control Deck and pulled up the hatch to the engine room were the backup generator is, needing to get a smelting torch to burn the lock off the Captains lock box, in the engine room it wasn't that big of a room and had very many small crawl spaces, I saw my tool box was also locked and I didn't know were my key was with the upstairs trashed and losing gravity by the second I didn't have time to look for it, I had to improvise, grabbing my tool box and putting on my tool table and putting the lock on the tool box on a high power vice, I twisted the box with all my mite snapping the lock of the tool box.

opening the lid and pulled out a small smelting torch I ran back up the ladder to the Control Deck, entering the Control Deck I lifted off the air just floating mid air, I needed to act fast or soon the air pressure would go down and I'd suffocate, pulling myself over to the Captain's lock box I turned on the torch and burnt off the lock on the box. Lifting the lid and pulling out a folder with many pages in it I flipped through the pages and saw the codes for this space station, there was at least three pages of codes and I scanning the pages in till I found the right one.

"Ah got it."

Pulling myself over to the Captains rewire system and typed the code, I opened the rewire box and had to turn on the air purification first, then I had to leave the artificial gravity off so would have enough air to reach the rewire box in the tunnel system, that's the only rewire on the station that allows the artificial gravity to be turned on or off. A timer counting down on the screen of the rewire box said five minutes till air purification, I think I've said this before but when doing the air purification I have five minutes to put a space suit on cause after the five minutes a fume is released in the air to clean it and the air I need to be in space suit cause the air pressure is doubled and I need to breath through an air tank if I don't the first breath I take without it my lungs would explode, because the air level was already dropping before starting the air purification I'd have probably two minutes of safe air not five.

I pull myself to the back of the Control Deck were the space suits are and the air lock into outer space, pulling a suit off the rack I stepped into it and zipping it up, next I pulled an air tank off a storage space and hooked it to a valve on my suit, then I pulled a helmet off a shelf above the suits, I hadn't put on the helmet yet befrore I heard the voice box on the rewire system say.

"*Ten seconds till air purification.*"

putting the helmet on I locked it in place and connected the second valve from the air tank to my helmet, the voice from the rewire box said air purification started, I showed a small grin and then sat in a crew chair in the Control Deck and thought.

"Thank god that's over now just wait an hour and I can roam free again."

Then I heard the voice on the rewire box say.

"*Air purification malfunction air level becoming unstable.*"

forgetting for a moment, the artificial gravity wasn't on which is needed to use the air purification, the fuel that's used to clean the air was still pumping into the station and if I didn't fix the balance by turning on the artificial gravity I'd waste the air purification fuel and the computer couldn't tell when to stop using the fuel because of the imbalance and the air it's cleaning could become toxic if it mixed to much with the special gas that allows anti gravity in the station. unstrapping myself out of the chair and pulling open the hatch to the tunnel system I climbed down the ladder, the major problems didn't stop there, I had said before that the engine was pretty much all crawl spaces, my space suit helmet was to big to fit in to the crawl space to restart the rewire box.

Well at the moment I was pretty fucked, here were my options,

1 : do nothing and let the station spin of balance forever till I puke up my guts.

Or

2 : get done what I need to and be the hero I am now that I never was on Earth.

I put my head down and took a deep breath then sucked it up pulling my helmet off and pulling my way to the rewire box, I typed my security code in to get into the rewire box then pressed the button to start the artificial gravity, The voice box said.

"*Artificial gravity will commence in two minutes.*"

At this point my face was getting really blue, I pulled my way back to my helmet and started to feel real faint for a second I was about to blackout then grabbed my helmet and strapped it back on, releasing a big breath I started to breath heavily fogging up my helmet, climbing back up the ladder and sitting in the same chair the voice from the Captains rewire box said.

"Air purification completed all passengers may take off their space suites now."

I wasn't about to trust it yet with the balance mix up and the computer not taking that in account, a couple more minutes went by and I was still weary about taking my suit off, closing my eyes I thought.

"If I die I die I can only blame myself for my moment of stupidity."

I pulled out air tank valve leading to my helmet, opened my eyes and put my hands on the rim of the helmet disconnecting the helmet from the suite, pulling my helmet completely off and held my breath for a second I let out a big breath and breathed in just a little, the air was so crisp and clean I was glad that I could breath easily and I got through this as well as I did, I face palmed thinking.

"Oh great now since this happened and I did the air purification earlier then scheduled I need to do the math to make sure I don't use the air purification to close or to far apart."

The whole reason I've survived this long is because I had almost all of the supplies yet I'm glad I didn't have to resort to the back up generator that would only last me for about a year or two, the only time the crew would have used the back up generator is in bad situations and I'm lucky we didn't need to, if we did It would only take a day for the HQ to help us but if the was some kind of major problem like we lost stationary balance and flew out of reach and it would take a while to get to us, N.A.S.A. made sure that the back up would last at least a little while.

This event may put me back a little but I don't think it hurt to much, I am sad that I don't have anybody to spend the rest of my life with, at least I have more supplies to survive, what's wrong with me that's a terrible thing to say. I know the supplies will be gone before I am so what am I to do then, I really don't want to think about it but that's how I almost died a moment ago, I ignored my responsibilities and I won't make the same mistake it's just that thinking about running out of supplies is similar to having no one with me it's not a light subject and makes me a little stir crazy. I was still sitting in the chair in my space suit without the helmet on, then suddenly I hear the TV in the Rec. room, I knew it wasn't on at the time I was going back and forth to fix the rewire box that was on fire, how in the hell was it on.

getting out of my seat and walking to the Rec. room it was still in disrepair and it was good that the TV wasn't destroyed, the TV was showing a nature show about the jungle, my first thought.

"How was this possible Earth was destroyed it wouldn't be possible there was a broadcast."

I tilted my head and watched the nature show for a minute, it was a bunch of monkeys swinging on vines, Then I remembered.

"Oh yeah the crew recorded hundreds of shows on the TV."

With the torched rewire in the Med. lab that also controls the Rec. room it must glitching some of the sockets, I would turn the ruined rewire off but I don't want to risk another issue. the anti gravity suddenly turned on and I lifted off the ground, at that point I knew something strange was going on I was the only one that controlled the anti gravity and even a electrical glitch would stop at the firewall only to screw around with the password, the pass code used four digits so I'd take a few hours for a glitched computer to get into the more secure options, I had to be fooling myself with the only answer I came up with, could it be possible, no it couldn't, could it.

Chapter 5

Who's there

    I don't know how this could be happening, I'm the Engineer I know this station inside and out not much gets past me although I could make the excuse that I've got to much going through my head, it's not wrong though. floating over to the TV and turning it off I floated to the hatch, going back down and heading to the rewire box but it wasn't messed with at all, I might as well not keep you in the dark but I have a feeling someones in here with me, or maybe it's my mind hoping to find someone that I'm seeing and hearing things, maybe I'm going crazy I could just have left the TV on and not remembered but the anti gravity is unexplained I was for sure it was shut off, opening the rewire box there was nothing out of the ordinary seeming like it hadn't been touched, if it was used it would have been busted open unless someone used my code.

    On the other hand an out source could have hacked into the system and mess with it, that seems very unlikely the only other station near Earth was the Russian space station but it is miles and miles away and it's been decommissioned for the passed ten years, I'd have to check the activity log to see the times it's been used in the past couple days, as the Engineer I wasn't allowed to access those files only the Captain was. switching off the anti gravity it would take a couple minutes, I climbed up the ladder and floated through the Control Deck and then smashed to the floor, the artificial gravity turned on and I smashed my gut to the ground, static from the radio started to play, how In the bloody hell, now I knew something was going on all the electrical glitches couldn't be a quintessence, pulling myself up off the ground and grabbing the walkies on the the radio to connect to the main computer and saying into the mic.

    "Hello, hello anyone please if there's anyone please say something please don't punish me."

    There was no response just more static, screaming into the mic.

"Hey you fucking bastard talk fucking talk please PLEASE !!!"

What the hell was I doing If someone was there they'd be human and respond with no doubt, was going bonkers? It was just my head I wanted to believe there was someone out there, I have to be wrong I know I am, there was no possibly for someone else to be out there.

sitting in the Captains chair I lowered my head and sobbed with my head between my legs, jolting out of the seat and raising my arms screaming at the top of my lungs, behind me I heard a faint noise. I stopped yelling for a moment and listened carefully, then hearing the same noise, it was a soft clang on the outside of the station, I didn't have a clue what it could have been if I was lucky it was a human. I am already setting myself up for disappointment, It was only a hunch but I had to take it, the noise was on the outside near the back left side of the ship, still with my space suite on I went to grab a new air tank, I didn't want to risk using a half empty tank not knowing how long I was going to be out there and with all the pieces of the new space station and Earth could be floating around and if the tank gets damaged or I float adrift I need as much as I can get, it's only a drag I can't bring more than one air tank with me, if only there was a way to swap tanks in outer space.

picking up my helmet I snapped it on then strapped the two valves from the new air tank to my helmet and suit, as I headed to open the airlock to get outside I heard the computer go off in the Med. lab, I heard a video of people talking I knew it was a video I would have known if someone was in here. walking to the Med. lab in my space suite and seeing the computer was on it played a recording of the crew I was with, I knew the person recording was the co Captain Carl he always was, he was filming me working on a computer in the Control Deck while he filmed Wendy watched, I was oblivious to him recording me, he turned to Wendy and she said.

"What are you recording for?"

He chuckled in the background.

"I don't know just cause."

She may have not know why but that was the laziest excuse I've ever heard, the reason he was recording not just this but everything was because he was a survivalist always prepared for the worst, he filmed everything because if he did pass he wanted to let the future generations what Earth had accomplished and they could do the same, why wasn't it him in my situation he would be perfect. continuing to watch the video and saw Wendy just staring at me dazed and Carl was still filming, he had zoomed into her showing a big smile and still looking at me, he asked.

"Wendy you felling alright you got the hots for him?"

Wendy just smiled and gave a little chuckle.

"No stop it."

I stood looking at the video thinking.

"She really did like me I just never had the confidence to ask her out."

Now everything was just screwed up I should have never watched that video but I couldn't look away at her beauty, I didn't think any more about the video turning on by itself It was most likely the technical glitches going on, then again I hear a thud on the outside of the station on the left side. I ran back to the air lock and open the door to the air lock stepping in then typed the code to lower the air levels so I could open the door to outer space, the voice box said.

"Two minutes till air level is at zero."

hearing the thud once again, my mind was racing of what it was out there I already expected nothing special, being on this station for now almost three months or at least I think but more on that later I need to keep my mind clear I hadn't been out to space since before all this happened, I could not afford to make a mistake if I messed up one thing I could get sent adrift with no help, the voice box said.

"Passengers may now exit the space station."

strapping a cable line to my belt to stay close to the station I then pulled the lever on the door leading to outer space and pushed the door open jumping out, I can't fully explain how walking in space it's really like weightless that's the best I can say, I know that's generic but its the most accurate. pulling myself along the backside of the ship around to the left side taking a good look around and it had been a while since I had, I had look out the window once and a while but didn't see much, looking around and seeing bunches of rocks, thousands of them most likely pieces of Earth shattered around, it was good that those pieces weren't moving, if you looked at them not knowing what they once were you'd just think they were space rocks.

pulling myself around the left side and looking up at all the wires and electrical boxes I run my eye up along the surface of the station seeing the radio antenna had crusted rocks glued to it due to wet rocks and mud slamming into the antenna after time. I climbed the outer ladder going up the outer hull and started to pick at the clumped up rocks and mud but it was to strong, it seems kinda of a time waster to fix but I need the antenna clear of all crud to get out a good signal for the distress signal I use, even if it wastes time or energy you know what they say better safe than sorry. I knew it wouldn't amount to much fixing the antenna but as I've said it helps me stay well minded if I still have the unlikely possibility of finding someone, unlikely being the most likely chance. I keep picking at the crud on the antenna but it was to thick and my space gloves didn't give me much grip, I had to go get a pike from my tool box.

climbing back down the ladder and pulled myself across the left side of the station back to the backside, as I did a rock can by my head and missed me by an inch then the rock flew behind me and pinned my cable.

"More like a leather strap which it was."

To the side of the station and I couldn't pull myself any further, pulling my way back to the rock and starting to tug it loose but it was to wedged into a gap in a couple pieces of metal, it was to stuck to pull out, I knew what I had to do but it went against everything I learned in training I was trapped I couldn't wait till it loosened itself I only had an hour of air left and it who knows how long it could take to loosen. I grabbed the belt end of my cable the took a deep breath and unhooked my cable from my belt and clung to the side of the station, I could have found a way to cut through the cable but it wasn't worth wasting a cable though I did have four more inside, I crawled my way to the backside of the station,I had gotten there and pressed the button to open the air lock stepped in and heard the voice box says.

"Two minutes till air level is fully risen."

The door leading to the control deck opened and the voice box said.

"It is now safe to enter the station."

I only took off my helmet and headed down to the engine room and grabbed a pike from my tool box, headed back up and heard a TV monitor in the control deck playing a recorded video of my crew members laughing at the dinner table, I turned to the TV monitor and yelled.

"Shut up, SHUT UP !!!"

God what was wrong with me I always assumed I'd do better in this situation than others but I don't know anymore I just don't, I just had to forget it more than just my life depends on my mission to not only what I'm doing now but what I do with the rest of my life. I decided not to get a fresh air tank I shouldn't be back out very long I did all the usual things and got back outside, pulled my way back to the antenna and started to stab at the crusty rock and mud with the pick, I had to get the junk off and it took some strength but I had to be easy on it or I could snap the antenna. I slowly picked at the crud with the pike after ten minutes or so I pick enough of it away that it was easy enough to pick the rest off with my hands, at this point there was only specks of crud left that it wouldn't make any glitches.

I did all I needed to do to get inside, when I was finally inside and able to relax I pulled off my space suit and helmet then sat in the Captain's chair and just stared into space, not actually I just was so exhausted after what just happened and wanted to shut off my brain.

I didn't often ask but really why was it me who survived I may have some quality's to life the rest of my life alone hell I did for most of my life anyway, was it that I was just the lucky one that lived, was it that it was some kind of ultimate punishment brought to me by the universe or was it god seeing I had a chance to do something great thing that I wouldn't do for myself. But the big question is who am I really who am I ?

Chapter 6

Who am I

I just kept sitting in that chair for I don't know how long it could have been hours or even days with the way things were going I could care less time is something we should never forget but there is no reason I shouldn't expect anything else to change, what kind of life would I live anyway, I make this log in hopes that someone will see it, that's all I have to go on these days hope. It may have been I think only almost four months and to deal with a life like this for the next forty years of my life, it still begs the question who was I? what life could I have at this point after the life I've already had, whoever is listening I've already told you somethings but let's dig deeper than ever before.

I am thirty years old and I grew up in Snow Grass Colorado I was always kind of the smart guy, yes I'd say I was a nerd in school I was always fascinated with building things or taking them apart, science was just a side hobby. I had typical family we just did typical things like any other, I did very well in school but wasn't ever social at really any age, maybe it was I worked to much or maybe it was most people just didn't understand the things I do, I'm no better than anyone else at life but everyone has there advantages but I did not show off or brag I was always was pretty enclosed a lot of the kids I grew up with did different things I should have made more time to be a kid but I had some pretty bad worries always trying to do my best to have a better future, I guess I felt the social aspect of life to me always came second.

It's not like I wasn't liked or no one tried to get to know me, they did I had friends but they never stayed around long due to the typical stuff, moving, divorces or just changing and moving on to better friends like I was old news. So I didn't follow the crowd at the time I was glad to say I was me, at the time I somewhat had the confidence I was just to concentrated on my schooling I make it sound like that's a bad thing, I guess by making my future better I wasn't giving my present the time it needed.

I got into one of the major colleges for space engineering in Texas doing pretty much the same thing I had is my childhood although I had to as much as I worked and did well in high school college was ten times harder, I surprisingly did well and graduated I thought my real life could finally start but even with my degree work was still hard to find. It seem times have changes and new software and other things I needed to learn to get a job in the country and most big corporations used machines to do the important work, none of those options worked for me and I could not believe the first couple years of my working life. I still had a lot of knowledge about space engineering and N.A.S.A. hadn't used many machines to do work that often, it was to costly to make things for them to be in space for only a couple years, I tried to go through the challenges to become an astronaut but couldn't get the job done to survive space, I was well qualified to be the engineer but the space testing wasn't my forte.

After that the best I could get was the U.S. Navy, I passed the physical test with basic smarts about physics and many other factors, I started being a Engineer in the lower decks I never got much social time with other sailors but that didn't bother me, I wasn't well respected cause all I did was turn a couple knobs as they would say. I did that job for about five years and when I was able to take a leave I did, one day during my break for the Navy I had a N.A.S.A. member talk to me about being a Engineer on a new station they were building and they need a new crew but they also had a back log of people that failed the tests the first time around giving people a second chance to get into N.A.S.A., the U.S. Navy was nice enough to discharge me cause due to my new mission with N.A.S.A. it was more important than what I was doing for them, I was lucky I never saw battle I knew I would have died.

When I got to N.A.S.A. there had to be at least forty testers going for the job that only required three people of a five member crew, the fourth and fifth person was going to be the Captain and his first mate, they weren't going to trust a whole space station to a new guy. I spent the first two days doing written tests that I of course passed with flying colors due to my years of learning and work for the rest of the week there was physical training and with the help of my military past I did alright, I wasn't the biggest or strongest in fact I was kind of weak I never had been that tough at all and I don't think I could have been a action hero but I gave everything the best I could.

After a long process of paperwork and painful physical tests I pulled through and finally achieved what I couldn't years ago, after all the years of schooling and letting other life experiences pass by but my work has finally payed off. Earth had given me all my choices and if I didn't take this one I'd be doing some useless job that wouldn't challenge me of bring me to my full potential, the mission I was doing for N.A.S.A. was to just to do testing for space living, I was the one of two on bored Engineers, the other was Wendy. We were set to live on a station that was build all by the U.S. for about five years but after the first two years the N.A.S.A. came up with some new technological blueprints for a new bigger and better station but they used a good amount of funds to build the one we were on so they outsourced the funds with Russia who at that point seemed to now run this new station due to the percentage they owned. Things still seemed amiss at any time any country had just one space station that's all anyone could afford but it wasn't anything new that Russia already had plans to build there own station without source funding so they could help fund the U.S. if they hardly had the money to help after planing to build there own, it was very doubtful that Russia would quit on there idea to help the U.S. with a brand new one, at the time I didn't think to much into it but I should have.

While I was on the station I wasn't much of a different man, it didn't help that I worked for twelve hours a day, I've already told you who the crew was I did get to know them for about two years, the great thing about living in the station was it had five years of supplies for five people so we had more time for work and not getting monthly shipments from HQ. I wouldn't say we were forced to hang out but did we really have a choice, it was like we were all more of a family of friends, we relied and trusted each other always there for one another, we did all the same things that a family would we ate together played games and just socialized, the whole experience opened me up a little, but being alone with them so much we learned a lot about each other it wasn't hard to have more than a friendship feeling for one another, I did feel something for Wendy but I feel with my work and how my life had gone I wouldn't even have a chance In space.

A typical day was waking to my alarm, eating a small breakfast and heading into small crawl spaces that was the tunnel system, watching gauges hours on end then the other Engineer Wendy doing the same even when I was sleeping I was still working in case of an emergency if it was during my twelve hour shift, the other twelve hours were run by Wendy if somehow she couldn't take care of it I had to.

I, what does that word mean, it refers to myself for I while now I have referred to myself as I but the biggest question isn't what happened, what I am to do with my life, what I did in my life, no it's who am I now what kind of person I am, to dedicated to my work, anti social ,smart , but that's who I am on the inside the real question the big question, I've always said I wasn't that important you were just along for the ride seeing the crazy things I've done, I did and will do, I'm the only one to tell my story now and if you are willing to listen that's great, in some way we are connected and my name, my name just seems such a small part but it's not, I am all those things I said I was but behind all that, behind every part of the bigger picture is more importantly that I'm just human.

Chapter 7

What am I

One thing people used to say is we all have a purpose on Earth but more than half the time we all never knew what are purpose was, by that I mean is what were we going to do as humans to contribute Earth, every person had some kind of talent we just had to find it. You now know that mine was engineering but now it seems that the universe has something else in mind, I was always good at my job and I still have to be for my survival. I now ask myself is there something more in my future if I really have one at all, I've said that the isolation doesn't bother me as much as it would others, due to my background I feel I could do well for what I'm doing now, and I have been. I guess not having much of a social life helped me for today, although I do miss the social time I had but everyday I forget there was people, that I knew people, that I had a family. That's the only way I can stay well minded, no matter how hard I try there's always one moment of the day I can't help think about it, the best thing I can do is push on, even with my experience of isolation it was at most two weeks, the human mind can only take so much, I have to admit that I'm not the same person I was coming into this that I am now, in a way I'm stronger but also weaker, you've heard about the crazy things I've done so that's no surprise to you.

I thought back to the night I had the wild party my best excuse is that I was just releasing the built up rage and doing something I never could before, living on the wild side was fun for a night but it got me nearly killed, the thing about digging into your survival instincts is you change from a person into an animal, I feel I need to forget who I was and what Earth was to save myself but in doing so I also hurt myself, I don't want to forget but I have to and that changes me into the animal we have inside all of us, I don't want to become that but I can't stop it, I can't stop nature. As humans we ever evolve getting smarter, bigger, better as a race, I don't know if the chain is restarting with me but that would be impossible it's just me here, there could be a billion different reasons this is happening and I may never know. For now I will live in the moment if you call it living, I often have racing thoughts about everything, about what happened,why ,what to do and who I was or will become.

My mind hasn't totally broken but it's not long off, there may or may not be reason for these things but why do I keep this log that is a important question I don't ask, I think one thing that will last longer than the search for reasons or the memory of what I was along with Earth is my hope, I want to believe I can fix this, I know I can't by having this false hope I get by the best I can. I've already kinda gone a little crazy even the things that happen to me now I got to move on from just keep pushing forward and treat each day as something completely new.

It's not as lonely as you would think I mean yeah it's only me here but keeping this log is kinda of talking to someone, I may not get a response but knowing there's a possibility someone someday will hear my voice helps me. Now I know there was a lot of people who believed in aliens but there was also a lot that didn't, of course when N.A.S.A. did testing to see if other planets could sustain life it could have been a possibility but not in my life time,if there was enough hard evidence that life was sustainable there could be alien life on a planet, but proving that could have been harder than we thought. Even if there was some kind of alien life we could probably never tell the level of intelligence they had, now I'll never know, first of all it would be something that would be a great discovery but by myself and the lack of resources makes it a time waster. I think I settle a lot on some of the questions that are important that are not answered I just remember saying don't ask a question you don't want an answer to, it's not that I don't want an answer it's just I feel not knowing if someone is put there or not, or if someday someone will see this log or even the reason all this happened. That the great thing about mystery's you learn as you go and once it's over the story isn't the same it's the journey that is the important thing sometimes and not the ending.

I wouldn't say being fit for being the only one left isn't that good of a thing, I've said that it would give me a better edge being anti social but everyone needs someone, we're humans it's in our DNA, even if we don't have more than just friendships with people we still need them in some way and when we don't have that we become less human, was I so unsocial it controlled my life, yes I'd say so. My life had ups but it had more downs, there's more I could dig into but it's things I force myself to forget of I would have gone stir crazy on Earth a long time ago and end up dead or in a jail. Let's just says this, I know you guys are listing to my story but it doesn't matter I'm just a small speck on the big universe it's nice you listen and you care but I don't want to get to close, you know how the story ends or at least an idea how.

Hollywood has made this type of story a thousand times and now it's actually happening to me, I've said before the best thing to do is keep your mind occupied doing anything and everything you can think of, being on a space station I don't have a lot of options and the ones I have get old faster than you think so you create something new to do, I can't fully explain how the mind changes it's like asking as a guy that's high.

"what's high being like?"

They won't tell you to the best of there ability cause they can't, I've already gone through everything that really happened with my mental state, the biggest change is not having a crew with me, when I was an Engineer in the Navy I only got one day out of the week to be social ninety nine percent of my week is taken up by work, in the station I had more social time and less work, I did miss the crew but that wasn't must of a change them being gone, the issue was I was only the Engineer now I have to do every job I still have free time today I just have think of survival first all I know is my mind isn't jelly yet and I just have to do what I've been doing and I should be fine.

Chapter 8

Year one

Since the start I thought I would be one of the best people for this to happen to, not that I wanted it, but boy was I wrong, even with my background and all the time I was alone while on Earth I knew couldn't spend the next forty years by myself. It now had been a full year and I was cracking piece by piece and I wasn't going to be the same ever again I had to change I was forced to if I wanted to live, the station had it the worst I was glad that the station was still fully operational, though that doesn't sound like much if you see it for the outside, it was the inside that was the worst and it wasn't just the interior of the station it was me to.

I had a full beard and longer hair, we did have clippers but the new style wasn't bothering me, I hadn't showered in at least god only knows how many months, but the smell didn't bother me either due to the way the station was, my clothes were stained with all sorts of smells and dirt It was such a mess it was more mess then my shirt, but who am I trying to impress. The station and I were just about in the same amount damage each room was cluttered with all sorts of trash, dirty clothes and a muck of other things, I wasn't a hoarder I just didn't have the attention span to throw things out the trash shoot I barely had enough to do things I needed to survive, I didn't get more exercise in the station but with the food I had to eat I wouldn't get that fat, the issue was my body was just weak and wasting away even eating regularly I was losing more weight than I ever had it was also due to the environment I lived in not the space station itself.

Now living a full year with no human contact I fell I still am somewhat mentally well, my hygiene is probably one of the biggest changes, I always flush out my body waste from the station and was glad that the toilet has a rocket propelled release, I didn't have to keep up with social dress code anymore, when this all started I had buzzed black hair and a thick mustache, now I have long black hair that goes to the to my shoulders, thick mustache and long goatee. I hardly needed to go outside but still have to bundle up if I didn't want space to freeze me, I may have over hyped the stations condition at this point, I am a little messy but the real reason I never pushed the trash into space was cause when I do the trash didn't rocket propel out like the toilet waste, it just sits outside the station cluttering the area and I do sometimes still need to go outside and don't want to deal with it, but I feel with time the rubble of Earth would push the trash further out. All the trash I do have or will have goes into the Med. Lab it seems that I really won't need that room anymore, the best thing about keeping trash around in space it that the food that I do eat never molds and I don't have to worry about rats or bugs, it was weird but the space food was made with special chemicals so somehow it didn't mold, also with the food waste never molding or it having the smell of going bad doesn't bother me cause I got used to smelling how bad I was, with not worrying about the social aspects anymore I didn't bother with taking a shower after a while, it may have seemed to be a disadvantage but it wasn't it just means more water to drink.

I shouldn't be putting things lightly but then the story would be to depressing, most people would break after a few months but let me tell you I broke the second this all happened I just slowly let it get to me, day by day I did the things I needed to survive, taking care of the station was to easy for me one of the hardest things is always keeping my mind occupied, we only had around a couple years worth of TV shows recorded but that still wasn't enough, being all alone and knowing the fact I still have a felling someone is watching me, it's just the paranoia pretending like nothing really happened helps but also makes it worse, I haven't reverted to talking to household objects so that's a plus. It helps but the whole reason I'm making this log is to tell others of Earth, what I'm trying to say is I just pretend my work never ends but it never really did before anyway this time I just won't meet with people on a weekly basis, I briefly talked about doing new things when I get bored with what I regularly do, I've watched a good amount of the TV recordings, one fun thing is to mute them and lip sync but instead make the characters say funny things making the moment of the show not match the attitude of it, another is being active I can't just stay mentally active but also physically so at first I'd just do push ups or sit ups but as anything else that to becomes stale.

I thought back to my childhood when I was around ten to think of different toys I had and how fun it would be to have my super ball again, I never deeply thought about it but I did contribute to my anti social stigma growing I have tons of things I could bore you with let's just say I may have done some cool stuff in my life but it was all still pretty much crap, I worked hard at what I wanted to do and not compare to the social status things work out moderately never good but never to bad, the last time I remember not worrying about who I was, what I did, where I was going and every other thing a young teenager to adult would think up was when I was ten. At that time life was just so simple and fun being a child was like being a dog you look to cute to be judged or punished seriously, it was around when I was eleven I had some serious life changing things happen.

What caused my social problems, and no I'm not asking for the doctor answer kind of bullshit I guess the source would be being let down to much having some mental problems that people could only take so much before they just gave up on me, people say I love you all the time to friends and family but that's just hearing it, it's like that it's easier to say than do, I had very few things I truly loved on Earth and I never really got a lot of support, with my feelings a person can only do so much for themselves with a decreasing self worth, I been through so much that I expected nothing to ever work out I wasn't going to get a pointless job that doesn't contribute to the work I wanted to do and I wasn't going to give countless paychecks to a greedy country that used fear and control to appear as a perfect country I may have only been a small fry in the U.S. Navy but I heard things true or not somethings are to solid to ignore.

Look now I'm all jumbled it's not the first and won't be the last time, I was talking about the childhood toys I had, I'd love to have my super ball again, you know I could find something to make a mold for the shape and I could make the liquid in the Med. Lab, though I'd have to clean out a spot to work, see I think one thing is worthless but yet it somehow still comes in handy. I stood out of the Captains seat and slugged over to the Med. Lab, flinging open the door and saw the mountain of trash almost reaching the top of the counter of the Med. Lab counter, as I walked to the edge of the counter I kicked a path out of the trash and sat on the metal chair, I took a second to shiver cause I was in my underwear and could feel the cold metal of the chair touching my bottom, I scanned the counter and saw two ceramic bowls laying on there side, I thought.

"Why are those in here I don't think I intended to throw those away?"

I grabbed the bowls and thought.

"If I can connect these the shape of the inside could make a good mold for a super ball."

I tried to pull open a cabinet but it was blocked by a trash pile so I kicked the pile over then pulled the cabinet open and took out a heavy duty glue gun and glued the bowls together then pulled a laser cutter from another cabinet above me and then cut a circle on the now ball like mold with laser cutter so after I made the rubber liquid I could pour it in to the mold, I then made the rubber liquid and poured it into the mold maker, waited around for about half the day for it to harden.

That was another thing that isn't so easy to deal with day and night, of course it's somewhat easy to tell what time it was I just have to look at where the sun and moon are around the rubble of the Earth, using that way isn't the easiest cause determining where the center of the Earth was is almost impossible. About a night later I woke under a trash pile lunging myself out and flinging trash everywhere my eyes slowly opened and adjusted to the light, I stood and stumbled over to the counter as I did I tilted while walking almost falling on my side, I got up right and after that grabbed a hammer on the counter and cracked open the bowl pulling the gray rubber ball out of the bowl, the ball was around the size of my palm slugging over into the Control Deck and bounced the ball once to the floor then back to my hand then again and again, I thought back to my childhood remembering those super balls used to fly when I chucked them, normally I was outside with this toy but for now that's not an option, I was never allowed to play with it in the house cause of it going off every surface and was hard to stop, knowing that playing with it inside the station could be dangerous but I spent half of yesterday making it so it wasn't just going to lay there. Against my better judgment I let the thought of reliving the fun of my childhood out, I gave a big grin then flicked the ball from my hand, it flew threw the air and bounced off the right side wall then to off the table side by the Captains chair then off the ceiling, it was amazing seeing that little ball bounce off every surface at fast speeds then before I knew it things went to shit like they usually do.

The ball lost control going so fast it couldn't slow down the ball hit the front window cracking a micro hole in it, the purified air was leaking and it wouldn't be long before I lost all air, I was lucky and believe me I know that sounds like an understatement, let me explain prior to the event I had only used two years of materials with four other people and now at the current time the station was three years old and due to the condition I kept it the hull was deteriorating by the minute, I was glad that the glass held as well as it had and that the glass didn't shatter. I had to get the the glue gun and a piece of metal to seal the hole, a oxygen mask and air tank, and finally a heavy duty strap to tie myself to the seat so I won't fly out if the rest of the glass gave way.

Chapter 9

Just my luck part : 2

Once again I did something stupid almost causing the total destruction of this station, the hole in the front windshield was only as big as a pebble so I was losing air slower, I guess I could say that was an advantage, I ran to the back of the station a opened a chest by the space suits and pulled out a air mask and plugged it into a half empty tank sitting there by the air lock door and a security strap on the hooks by the space suits, then ran into the Med. Lab grabbing the glue gun, finally running back to the Captain's chair I strapped myself in and put the air mask on then released the air from the tank into my lungs. Leaning forward into the hole on the front glass and putting the glue gun up to it I pulled the trigger but the remaining glue just seeped to the floor in front of me, realizing that I used what was left of the glue stick I put into the gun, I looked to my side and saw that on the Captain's computer that the air level was dropping fast and I don't know how long I could survive with no air and just this air mask, running back into the Med. Lab I tripped over piles of trash then finally lost my balance, falling forward bonking my forehead on the door frame of the Med. Lab, I turned over on my back and was slowly closing my eyes losing conciseness as my head turned to look into the Med. Lab I see a picture on Wendy smiling pop up on the computer, I lied there losing air thinking.

"No, no getting this glue isn't for me, living to tell our story isn't for me, it's for you it's for humanity I don't care if I have a one percent chance I have hope and to stay human I need to keep that."

My eyes shot wide open and I lunged up from the floor and stumbled to the medical table grabbing the glue sticks and shoved one into the gun, standing there with my back hunched over and head raised without my air mask on and no time to find it I used the last bit of energy I had to stumble to the hole. I glued on the piece of metal then fell on my back with relief, I lifted my head looking back to the space suites and thought.

"Oh yeah I have to purify the air."

So crawling to the Captain's desk and knelling in front of the computer and selecting the air purification I fell to the floor again, the computer said.

"*Twenty seconds till air purification.*"

I crawled pasted the Captain's area then past the manhole tunnel and as I did I heard the computer say.

"*Ten seconds till air purification.*"

I got to the space suits but did not have the strength to stand up and put one on so I tugged at one of the suites pulling it off the hook and sliding into it, as I zip up I hear the computer say.

"*Five seconds till air purification.*"

I grabbed the helmet next to me and snapped it on just in time, the vents started to release the cleaning fumes and I need to connect an air tank to me or I'd pass out and die from air lose, I looked diagonally from myself at the Med. Lab and noticed the half empty air tank I had a moment ago I crawled my way over there and connected the tank to my suit but as I latched the final tube to my helmet my eyes slowly closed and my head dropped to the side of my helmet, I went limp and was passed out laying there in the doorway of the Med. Lab.

A couple of minutes in the darkness of nothing to say I felt a brush across my hair and I woke with a shock to another hand touching my face I noticed I was at the bottom of the engine room in the station, I lifted my head to see that the hand was Wendy's, I looked into her eyes and lunged to hug her it was so good to feel human contact again as I pulled away from her she said.

"What's with you today you just fell down the manhole tunnel and passed out."

As she finished talking I leaned into her again but this time I locked lips with here, for a good long five seconds we kissed and she pushed me off.

"Wow uh I had no idea you felt, well I , just wow."

I just couldn't stop looking at her perfect crystal eyes I asked her.

"How are you here, how did you survive?"

She looked puzzled at me.

"You must have got bonked pretty good, come on let's go eat dinner with the rest of the crew."

I had a confused look.

"The crew but, but how, the new ship and Earth blew up you all died, what's going on."

She just laughed and replied.

"I think you've been down here to long, now let's go eat and maybe I can take that kiss a step forward."

We climbed up the ladder and there was the rest of the crew perfectly fine, I looked out the window and saw Earth still intact, I walked over to the dinner table and sat by the Captain, the Captain patted me on the back saying.

"Alright everyone we only have a few minutes before N.A.S.A. comes to pick us up and put us on the new station, gather your belongings now and we'll get the rest of the supplies later."

I stood there in silence just to shocked for what was going on, I watched my crew run about the station grabbing their personal items and packing the place up, Captain Duane said to me.

"Hey chop chop we can't be lollygagging."

Still standing there with my arms limb and giving them a frustrated look then shouted at them.

"Have you all lost your marbles someone please what in the fuck is going on?"

Captain Duane look at me and seemed pissed.

"I don't know what the hell going on with you today but get your shit together were getting on the new station any minute."

I raised my hands in anger and yelled.

"I'm sorry, I'm sorry but how in the hell are you all alive for the past year I've been here stranded on this station."

The captain chuckled.

"Alright just a little cabin fever but I will deal with you later, now do your god dame job and get on the new station."

I looked out the window by the air lock and saw the new station connecting the tunnel between the station exits, the door from our station leading to the other opened and the crew started to walk through, I walked up to Wendy and grabbed her arm and we locked eyes I said with fear in my voice.

"Wendy please don't go on there, please stay here with me, I want to protect you."

She gave me a confused look.

"Your really scaring me let's get one the new station and calm down."

Her arm slowly slid from my hand as she walked to the exit I grabbed her arm again and yelled.

"Please wait I love you."

She struggled to tug her arm away, as I held on she yelled.

"Stop it you're hurting me."

Then suddenly a loud blast came from outside, we both looked to the door as we saw it get engulfed in flames then as the flames spread into the station burning the walls, the door heated bright red and the bolts holding it in place flung off and the door blasted off the hinges, Wendy turned back and lunged at me for a hug, we grasped each other tightly as the flaming door hit her in the back I screamed and everything went black.

I awoke in a void of white wearing a white dress shirt and dress pants with no shoes, as I looked around there was nothing for infinity, I wasn't standing on anything it was like I was standing on nothing in the middle of an infinity of white, I just stood there with a depressed look thinking.

"This is it I was dead I don't know what just happened, for a while I was the last person in the universe then awoke from it like it was just a dream, but it felt to real and when I was with my crew again it felt to unrealistic the only thing that felt real was Wendy what did it mean did it really happen, was that her could it have been?"

As I looked above me into the endless miles of white a small light descended in front of me, I had this uncontrollable erg to enter the light, as I stepped closer to the light my eyes squinted and I covered them with my hand, crossing into the light and ended up in the dark I could see nothing at all not even my hand in front of my face, I closed my eyes and and thought.

"Now where am I is this hell, all alone in the dark with nothing to do, wait how's this hell there's nothing different I've been doing this same thing for the past year."

Standing there with only my thoughts now, my head starts to sting and I scream with all my might as I hold my head, I slowly open my eyes and again see the light but it wasn't the white void, my eyes focus and I was laying on my side staring into the Med. Lab back on the station. As I lifted my body off the ground I saw blood on the inside of the glass visor, I must have banged my head on the inside of my helmet when I ran into the wall, standing up and limping to the computer at the Captains chair and saw the air purification was done so I pulled off my helmet and zipped out of the space suite, I had been through so much in just the past few minutes or hours with all the endless boredom time seems small to other problems.

I ran my hand through my long hair and it felt so wet, looking at my hand I saw it was covered in blood, looking at my hand in horror thinking.

"Holy shit my helmet was covered in my blood and I had to be past out for about an hour or so and I was still bleeding out."

As I began to feel faint I limped to the Rec. room kicking the trash out of my way while getting into the bathroom, looking into mirror and was very pail and had a big cut on my forehead bleeding out at a slow pace, I pulled out the first aid kit in the closet behind me and stuck an adrenaline shot in my arm grunting in pain I grabbed a towel wetting it and then grabbing the stitching kit and piecing together the thread and needle, I rolled up the wet towel and bit on to it pushing the needle threw the cut on my forehead, pulling the thread through my skin and stitching together the cut I scream in agony and that was only the first stitch, before I began the second stitch I took my bathroom glass filled it with water washing off the exes blood, pushing the needle in again starting the next stitch and I began to bite down harder on the wet towel and moan in pain, as I started the third stitch my blood dripped down my face. Three or four more stitches later my hands were shacking like crazy and as I tide the stitch I was shivering all over, I cut off the extra string and fell backwards into the bathtub and turned on the shower, the water hitting me felt good, I opened my mouth for a drink, as I sat there letting the water wash off my blood and cooling me off I slowly closed my eyes and breathed lightly, as my eyes were closed and I was enjoying the cool feeling of the water and the tub filling up cooling my body I lost conciseness falling asleep there in the water.

Ten minuets or so passed and I was pulled out of my deep sleep by finding myself flailing inside the filled tub almost drowning, I rolled out the tub in my soaked boxers and dried off with a towel on the hook next to the tub, I looked into the mirror and the cut had a lot of dried blood but I was mostly clean. I took a good look at myself seeing the mess I really was, my hair was puffed up, my chest was cluttered with old food and dirt, now that I actually noticed what I had become the worst part was the stench, I smelled awful like rotten milk covered in sweat and dumpster slime, guess just running water over me didn't do the trick, I slid down my boxers and jumped back into the shower, I'm not really the most open person and if you are seeing this I think you should know what a shower is and how self bathing works, well hell who in the world is really going to see this anyway maybe I'll make some alien babe's day so I'll indulge you.

    I was now in the shower letting the water hit the top of my head then squeezing some shampoo into my hands then running it through my hair slowly so I didn't irritate the cut, ha this is so stupid should I really go on I mean seriously there is no chance anyone will see this but the only reason I speak about such a private thing is to humor myself, this is such a joke but let's continue shall we. I washed out the shampoo then grabbed the body wash and softly rubbed it on my chest washing off the crud on my chest, okay okay I'm laughing my ass off I need to stop. I stepped out of the shower and dried myself off and wrapped the towel around my waist, I walked into the Rec. room and pulled out a new pair of clothes from the closets on the other end of the room, walking out into the pantry I grabbed a bottle of water then back into the Rec. room and sat on the couch just thinking.

    "All the times I was in danger was to me being reckless not caring what happened and just ignoring my better judgment, I need to remember that I am in a more dangerous setting and need to work extra hard to survive, but for what, that's a question I can't let get to me, knowing I need to make some serious changes to keep what I have here running it changes my mind set but does it change me maybe I've changed more from the start than I thought, was it for the better or for worse, has anything really changed in my personality or am I just the same person, for now I can't tell what else does the next forty years have in store for me."

Chapter 10

The new me

I sat there sunk into the couch with my legs spread and stomach extended, I unscrewed the lid of my water bottle and sipped it, running my right hand across the right side of the couch I picked up the remote on the side table next to me and pointed it to the TV and turned on a show, I took another sip of my water and thought.

"Here I am again nothing new nothing different, I've accepted my way of survival, but things need to change it's only been a year and I'm bored, what to do what to do I've got it."

I turned off the TV and chugged the rest of my water then stood off the couch and walked out to the airlock and set up a space suite for a walk outside, I finished putting on the suite and opened the airlock and stepped out to space. I floated in place connected to the airlock door, I've been needing to think of new things to do so I went to get some fresh air per say, just floating around with my thoughts, even without Earth the universe was still beautiful, Earth may now be just a asteroid field but everything was still a wonder to look at, it was peaceful somehow my mind was a little more clear. There was no more Earth so I could just explore the universe, Though I wouldn't get far the station wasn't meant for long travel and I don't have a surplus of gas as I do other supplies, I wouldn't know where to go, if I did get that far and it would be more nice if I was close to a planet in case I crash land. I looked at the strap connecting me to the station I was grasping it holding on as hard as I could, there was a latch that connected me to the strap and the station and I thought.

"The only thing keeping me going was my hope things would get better and distractions that help me from remembering the true reason why I'm in this situation, but why do I give myself this false since of hope I know that all other humans have died and through over a hundred years of research Earth never had solid evidence of aliens existing so it could be another hundred years or more before an alien comes across this."

I was still floating there staring at that latch, if I really had no true hope for my future than what was stopping me from ending it, every once and a while I need to ask this question I can't let my distraction of what's going on to completely consume me, it my make me sad to remember but I have to this is my reality now. I thought of releasing that latch and floating away to my death but I'd say the best reason I can't let go is cause it's not me, any person with the right mind would have given up long ago, this first year wasn't a cake walk by any means and lasting that long is saying something even for me, but that's me the first year was total crap and so will be the the rest of my life even with a one percent chance of anyone seeing my story it's something and if I can make it a year what's forty more.

I kept looking at that latch I couldn't help but unhook it, unhooked from strap only staying connected by holding the strap, what made me do it I don't know I can't explain it I didn't want to but did, looking down at the unconnected latch and just seeing me apart from my safety my home even though the strap and I where inches away it was a symbol of being alone more than I ever could be, I connected back to the latch and pulled myself to the airlock door and dragging myself into my home, it may not sound like much but this station kept me safe.

I unzipped from the suite and went to sit back on the couch, that was that I did something different and saw my own opinion in many different lights, the monotony of my everyday life only ever got boring slowly so adding something new to do or mixing things up was a refresher that the universe really is endless and the only thing stopping my creativity is me, people used to say nothing lasts forever, for somethings that are around for awhile tend to stick to the usual and play a safe game but year after year the same game can only be enjoyed for so long before it gets tiring, so people made little changes to what was once a original and simple idea and added their new spin on it that gave whatever it was a unique and new experience while still having some of the stuff we loved about the old way.

What I guess I'm getting at is there are things I do now that won't get old anytime soon and there are new things that still give my life the thrill it needs, I never was good with change though so this process might not take to the effect that you might expect, talking about doing something new everyday is easier than said, a space station may seem like the ultimate place to be stuck but the station can only offer so much so I to have to work extra hard to keep busy and working hard isn't really something I can physically or mentally do, I guess this is suitable though lady luck never was on my side so if I was the last person on Earth I'd be to lucky, there would be so much to do I'd be distracted by ever little thing and not be able to do everything I possibly could have fun with cause I'd die from old age first, but as you all know that's not me and there's somethings that you can't change and just need to settle with.

That's one of the biggest things we had as humans to make choices and our own opinions, I make the decision to give myself a false sense of hope with the distractions I have to keep my sanity, but do I really, I am a man more of science than a higher power, my opinion is that both a god exists and or doesn't exist there can be no one answer both science gives evidence of a non god world but very old testaments and other books and novels give evidence of a god run world, To my point though I do make the choice to give myself false hope for my sanity or do I, is there someone out there caring for me, that could explain the reason I haven't given up even though I really have no reason to continue. One thing people said was there is a reason for everything but is that true, I do believe not, there are tons of things that happened in Earth's history that has no explanation or reason, but the same could be said about if I believe there is tons of times in history there was no reason for things that happened, maybe some higher person would not let me believe there being no reason for things or I simply control my choices no matter what and I couldn't see the reason that was there it was just to hard to believe or find, either way the process of if there is any real choices you ultimately make with total free will can go around in circles for infinity to get an answer to a question that can not be answered without tearing the fabric of reality.

For generations human took many different paths there was no one human like another, there were a set of people who believed or fallowed one thought and many others that had their own beliefs, there were those kind of people that they knew their answer was the right one and there was no other but with the diversity and variations of story's the true meaning or one right answer gets lost in the mix even if there is one at all.

I sat up off the couch and walked to the pantry grabbing a pouch of food, what was for lunch today, yum dehydrated chicken and rice with water, ripping the pouch open and digging out the first bite with a spoon the taste wasn't as bad as I put it earlier, the meal I had was dried rice and sliced pieces of chicken that had a flaky and meat juice taste, as I got to the fourth or fifth bite some of the rice dropped from the spoon and fell into my long goatee, I finished up the pouch and downed it with a bottle of water, I tossed my trash out the garbage shoot and brushed the leftover rice on my goatee off to the floor with my hand and then thought.

"Maybe it's time for a shave."

I walked into the bathroom and looked into the mirror, my long dark hair was frizzed and greasy, there were long strands of hair that looked glued together and others that were wavy cause of all the frizz, my goatee didn't look any better It was looking around the same condition as my hair, no better no worse, smearing some shaving cream on my neck and checks and lifting the razor to my neck but not yet haven't starting to shave I take a deep look into the mirror as I thought.

"For months on end I hadn't taken care of the appearance of the station or myself, when I recently saw what I became I needed a change, but no matter how much I got better on the outside I was always going to be the same inside but never the same from when things started, I did make some small changes to break the monotony."

Was that really changing things though in the end no matter what I do in a different way I'm doing the same thing, frankly I like my beard and long hair changing it doesn't change me, I dropped the razor in the sink, wiped off the shaving cream and splashed some water on myself.

Another week had passed and I have yet to prove myself wrong, mixing things up to bring a new excitement to my life hadn't really changed anything, it did give me something new to think about that would be as you all have heard before being on a station doesn't give me a whole lot of options and I'm gonna be stuck like this for the next forty years and even doing new things to keep my sanity no matter how many variations I make on what I do there won't be enough to keep me occupied. As I finished that thought I was huddled up in blankets and pillows on the couch, watching another show on the TV laying my head on the couch armrest buried in pillows with a depressed look on my face, I needed to spice things up I gave a slit grin then sat up and off the couch walked to the stereo on the TV and turned on the classic rock n roll. As I walked to the Control Deck the tempo of the music rose and I had a jump with my step, now in the Control Deck I was flinging my body back and forth with the music and as the tempo got faster and louder I started to head bang, I was whipping my hair wildly jamming to the song, then suddenly I slipped on a puddle losing my balance I fell forward and banged my head on the counter in front of me.

I felt my forehead and my cut I had from a while back had mostly healed up but now I just split it back open, feeling a small stream of warm blood crawled down my head, The stereo played the next song and it was one of those slow classic rock love songs, I knelled down where I hit my head and started to ball then the computer at the side of me started to fizz and then played a video of Wendy smiling and giggling at the camera she said.

"What is with you and that camera?"

the Co Captain with the camera replied.

"We are not going to be up here forever I'm just creating memory's."

I looked at the computer and yelled.

"SHUT UP, SHUT UP!!!"

Then I threw a jar that was laying on the counter at the computer shattering the screen, Wendy's laugh starts to fade then stop it stopped all together, I crawled on my knees over to the computer rapping my arms around it and still balling like a baby.

"Please no, stay please stay I didn't mean it don't go."

My arms lowered to my side and I stopped crying I was just sniffling now and thought.

"God what was wrong with me, was I really that gone."

I knew it wasn't the real her but that was enough to feel it was, I'd hope to say I wasn't going insane but would seeing her make me the bad kind of insane, no if anything I need to see people even if it isn't a real interaction, of course this was just another way to distract myself but this one thing sounds like it could help more than just doing things to ignore my situation, I needed this, I needed them, but I really needed her.

Chapter 11

It just wasn't really her

The computer in front of me was pretty much destroyed so I had to use the computer in the Med. Lab, I stopped by the pantry and grabbed a bottle of water and banana then sat in the Med. Lab by the computer, opening up the file of all the home videos that the second in command made there were hours upon hours of video I'd say enough to last me about a year, I guess sense the videos were organized by the time they were shot, I'll start with the first one here.

I opened my water and took a sip then started the first video, it was our first day on this station we were all sitting in a circle getting to know each other, The first was Duane the Captain he had thin salt and peppered hair and also a thick black mustache, he wore a checkered shirt with a white undershirt, bluejeans, those yellow type work boots, I know this doesn't sound like a typical uniform but we were going to be living with each other for a while so N.A.S.A. wanted us to be casual. Duane and the second in command were the only two that had been to space before, they were like peas in a pod they had gone three or four other missions before.

The second in command was the one always making the videos so he turned the camera around and introduced himself, he had thin brown hair and a small brown soul patch goatee, he wore a burgundy dress shirt and tan dress pants with black shoes. Next was the Medical Doctor she had medium black hair usually wearing her lab coat and a blue dress shirt underneath and a blue skirt with black boots. Then of course there was Wendy. You probably remember she is the other Engineer on the ship alongside me, she had a bowl cut like blonde hair that went past her ears a little bit, she had these little round checks and such a cute smile, she wore a blue jumpsuit and a white undershirt with red sneakers, she had the softest voice like an angel, though I could be overselling it.

What was it though that I really liked about her, personally I mean, I was around her quite a lot but I never knew if she liked me, I never took the chance I guess cause I hadn't had the best luck on Earth so I was to shy to really give it a shot, it wasn't till after this I really needed her, but it wasn't just about the romance, we did talk often and had many similarity's always taking about our enjoyment of engineering and other personal things, we were more of really close friends the most I could say is she was one of the very few people that I connected with in my life and I didn't want to ruin it with getting to personal plus I didn't have much confidence.

Maybe it's just in my head and the reason I want her to be here is cause she's the only one I connected with on that level, I would hope I did have something there with her and I feel she felt the same way, dwelling on the past isn't the best thing to do right now, it's to late to make a move and second chances don't come around often, though if I was that lucky to tell her how I really felt would I, I had something so great with her already and there's this old saying.

"Don't ask questions you don't want the answer to."

Seeing the videos of my crew brought back some good memory's, I could see it as a bad thing knowing that I could never really have that kind of interaction again but seeing them on video was close enough to as them really being here, I knew it wasn't them, well it was them on the video but it being just a video it wasn't as real as I needed it, what was I to do it was the best I could do and just seeing Wendy's face made me a little more human again and helped keep me mentally safe than anything else could. I finished up eating my banana as the video faded to black and the next one started, the next video was of the crew eating lunch in the Control Deck, the Co Captain was filming once again, Wendy and I were sitting on the floor in front of a counter, I had my lunch trey sitting in fount of me while I sat with my legs crossed, instead of eating I was tinkering on circuit board, Wendy took a bite out of her food pouch then looked to me and giggled, she smiled then said.

"He's like a machine he never stops working, when he's concentrating he's impervious to anything else."

Then she leans into me and kisses me on the cheek, I gave a grin while still working then again she starts to giggle and says.

"You see what I mean."

The video ended and I finished drinking up the rest of my water then skimmed through the remaining videos not really watching any of them, as I kept scrolling the rest of the list I ran across a file called personal logs, these were a daily log that all the crew members taped alone to share anything they felt or just needed to say. We were all required to do this logs so we wouldn't keep our feeling built up and we would feel more mentally well, we weren't allowed to see each others logs, but all of them were kept of file so HQ could help if any personal issues were brought up.

The only way I found them was cause now I have all the codes for the station, the only other person allowed to see the logs was the Captain but only if the HQ gave him permission, there wasn't a lot of security regarding the logs it was more based on the trust system, though if a video was watched it would go into the data banks so if the Captain watched a log without permission the heads would find out pretty suddenly, I saw Wendy's log file and ran the pointer arrow across it but hadn't opened it, I thought.

"I knew this was morally wrong and I shouldn't look at it, it wasn't just to see how she felt about me it was that chance to get to know her more personally and how she felt about all kinds of things, I couldn't do that to her in respect for her as a human I wasn't going to watch them to keep being the human I want to be."

I clicked out of the video file and turned the computer off, then walked out to the Control Deck and sat in one of the chairs with a blank face swinging the chair back and fourth tapping my foot on the side of a file cabinet, the cabinet flung open and a picture fell out from the bottom, I leaned forward in the chair and picked up the picture. It was a photo of Wendy leaning against a tree with her elbow she wore a thin white t shirt and blue jeans, I just stared at the picture for a minute and began to slowly tear up, when we were leaving the station everyone was kind of in a rush to check out the new one so she must have left it behind, I stood from the chair and grabbed a piece of tape from the counter and walked to the Rec. room sticking it to the wall behind the couch, backing up from the picture I leaned on the back of the couch still crying I fell to my knees crawling up in a ball sobbing on the floor, my sobbing got quieter and quieter till I slowly fell asleep.

I woke the next morning still in a ball, I stretched out my limbs like a little puppy would and gave a big yawn, pulling myself off the floor using the couch as a lift I stood there hunched over with my arms limp and a depressed look on my face, I turned to see the picture of Wendy on the wall and slowly lifted my arm to the photo putting my palm to it, my hand slide down the picture and fell to my side. I slugged to the pantry and grabbed some breakfast, went back to the Rec. room to sit behind the couch facing the photo on the wall, I sat on the floor behind the couch with my legs pulled up against my body, ripping open the food pouch and took a bite of the dried potatoes and bacon bits, then unscrewing the top off the water bottle and as I lifted the bottle and my head to take a drink my eyes locked on to the picture of Wendy, I dropped the water spilling it all over my lap, I started sobbing again and as I did I took another bite of my breakfast pouch, my sobbing got louder and faster, my heart just couldn't take the pain.

I threw my food at the wall below the picture and fell to my belly crying on the floor, I crawled my way out of the Rec. room into the Control Deck still balling to heard a faint voice, I got quiet and just listened for a minute and then heard the faint voice say.

"Hello"

Getting up to my knees to see that on the computer that I earlier smashed up there was static and again the voice said with the audio cutting in and out.

"Hello, hello is, is anyone, anyone there."

I stood to my feet and yelled into the mic.

"Hello, hello I'm here, thank god it's another person."

Then the computer went to static and I said into the mic.

"Hello, please don't leave me."

The faint voice came back and started to laugh.

"HA HA HA you thought I was real you're such a loon, you're an old crazy bat, your brains mush."

The faint voice began to yell.

"I'M NOT REAL, I'M NOT REAL."

I sat there in a chair by the computer and thinking.

"How, how things were fine yesterday this can't be my head it can't, I'm not crazy, I'm not crazy."

The faint voice shouted.

"You're gone."

In a loud fast way scaring the shit out of me I violently punched the computer screen multiple times and yelling.

"I'm here, I'm here."

In the process I bloodied up my right hand and got many glass shards stuck in my skin, the computer started to smoke and I knew it would never work again, I walked to the restroom and washed off the blood, there was five or six thick shards of glass stuck on my back hand, sticking myself with an adrenaline shot and wet a towel to bite on, then getting out the tweezers and I tugged at the first piece of glass and started to moan in pain as I pulled it out, god that hurt like a motherfucker. Once again I had to tug at another piece of glass and after two or three shards were removed I started to just ignore the pain, I washed off the exes blood and wrapped up my hand, I stood there looking into the mirror holding my hands to my head thinking.

"No, no I couldn't be losing not now, It was just some random asshole playing a joke they will call back I'm sure."

I walked out back the computer and sitting at the computer looking down under the desk and saw that the computer wasn't plugged in then I finally realized, no matter how long I watch those crew videos, no matter how real they felt or how much they let me remember the good times, it wasn't real, they weren't actually here, those videos help me remember the good times but also remember I'll never have a chance to live like that or have those type of connections again, it not only helps me a lot but it also hurt a lot to, it's sad to say but to remain what I am and who I am I need to remember who they were but also let them go, I'm sorry Wendy.

Chapter 12

Year who's counting anymore

I was wrong completely and utterly wrong, I may have not been the most social person on Earth, I do think I have done much better than most would, I admit I wasn't really social and that it did give me some kind of advantage in this situation but on Earth I did see people I did know people and it may have not been my top priority of my life but I was social and that was enough to say I wasn't meant for this kind of life, no real human is, everyday I lose a little more of myself, I can only be happy that with my endless hope I tend not to forget where I came from.

I couldn't tell you the how long it's been like this, the best I could estimate is a little over two years and I'm back to my old ways, my system of living hasn't changed much and I was back in my boxers, this time around I hadn't bathed in a good few month, my hair got so long it touched my back and my beard was so long it hit my chest, my hair was all frizzed, curled and greasy, my beard was v shaped also frizzed and greasy looking too. I wouldn't say I have given up I just hit a new low but this wasn't a phase that comes and goes I was to far in and couldn't return to how I originally was, the station also went back to the old ways there was so much trash clutter, there was more trash than there was floor, wrappers, water bottles, napkins, towels and dirty clothes not only covered the floor but also the counters. I just didn't have the physical energy or mental energy to do what I could to stay distracted as well during the start, I mainly stayed focused on surviving and doing the necessary things to keep the station in place.

My sleeping wasn't good but it hadn't been for a long time, I had no idea what time it actually was, the clocks on the station were run by computers at N.A.S.A. HQ, but you already know what happened to Earth so it's self explanatory why I don't know what time it is, however I do manually count the days using pencil and paper. Now if I can't tell time and the sun doesn't revolve around the Earth it's almost impossible to tell, the only way I know if a day has passed is because a big clump of the Earth wasn't destroyed and now the sun revolves around that, so having no actual way of telling time I don't know how long I sleep it could be four hours or fourteen hours all I can tell it that I seem to be awake longer than I do sleep and sleeping feels to short, my best guess is it only feels that way cause I can't tell time and it's effecting my brain.

I hadn't gone crazy or anything or really even given up, those videos I was watching of the crew members did still somewhat make me feel more human, I knew they weren't going to last me forever so to make them worth wild I only watched one a day, the crew and I were only on this station for a little over two years and at this moment there were no more videos to watch so I knew then that I had been up here all alone for a little over two years, I'd say that it had now been at least a week sense I ran low on the video count, that was literally all I did for hours on end for days as a time, watching the videos I think helped me more than some random TV show, it's silly to say but those videos really did keep me more human, I may not have the best living conditions, I'd rather live in trash and keep my mind, I saw this coming though I knew that the videos would end but instead of reflecting what to do after I enjoyed the time I had with her.

I'm sorry I meant them well I guess not just the videos but the crew to, I know this sounds crazy but in order to stay well minded I think I needed to lose myself a little, that makes no sense what so ever but what I mean is treating as if the videos are not video and just seeing how they lived helped me, maybe I'm getting a little wonky I knew it was fake, though I wasn't in a lot of the videos so I was seeing these things happen for the first time it was as if they were actually still there, there was still the big question.

"What now?"

It seems I ask this to myself this every few weeks and when I do reality sets in just a bit more each time, I can never forget something that big, distracting myself is only a temporary fix, when I do have these moments I just can't help sitting there staring at the wall thinking of what I've really done with my life, I've learned to accept that I'm defiantly not some kind of second coming, maybe I haven't even thought of the complete obvious, what if I'm really just dead along with the rest of the world and this is some type of personal hell, okay that's enough of that the more I think into this I get worse.

I lunged forward up off the couch and stood there in ankle deep trash covering all the floor, I slowly raised my head from seeing how depressing the station was and pushed my legs threw the trash heading to get some water, pushing my ankles through the trash and turned my head to my right side getting a good look at the room and seeing that the whole room was in disrepair, turning my head back to go out the door my eyes crossed the wall and my heart dropped. The picture it was gone, she, she Wendy she was gone, I never moved the picture ever, in all its perfectness I never needed to, she had to be in this room, she had to be.

I fell face first into the trash floor I dug throwing pieces of trash into the corner of the room, it would be fairly easy to tell what was trash and what wasn't but there was so god dame much every where like some kind of virus. A pile of trash was forming behind me as I kept throwing piece by piece revealing more of the floor, out of the corner of my eye I see a white piece of paper under the couch, my hand sprung for it and pulling it out, yes, yes it was her the picture was clear and clean, I was so happy I started tearing up and held her to my heart, I whispered to the picture.

"I'm sorry I need you, I need you."

I know this seems to crazy to handle but it was who I was now and you can judge all you want I'm me, I may not be the most proud of who I am but this was more than a video, videos end there always the same never changing, so does this picture but it doesn't have a run time and a picture is stuck in place never ending, like me, like me that's what I was something to goggle at I was a freak show, I just can't care about or argue this it is what it is and you think what you want this isn't something that will just end it's me and just me forever I can't ignore it anymore. I don't care how long I last nothings changing for the better and I can't do a dame thing, why try, I have finally accepted my fate fully, but I am still the biggest idiot ever cause this isn't the end and far from it I don't know what it is but some bigger force was telling me hold on but for what I ask the true answer there is no answer. I just hope for something better to come by, I know nothing will but false hope is hope and let's hope that carries me till the end.

Laying on my side behind the couch huddled up holding her still and softly crying till I fell asleep. I woke from my nap, sitting up from the trash floor and looking at the picture in my hands then noticing that the sticky stuff on the tape was worn off and that's why she fell, standing up to put it back in place I looked to my left where the door was and saw the big pile of trash I made to find her, I thought.

"Ah what the hell."

I didn't have much else to do so the next fun thing was cleaning and god knows it needed it bad, I grabbed a water from the pantry chugging it, the whole reason I got up yesterday was to get a drink and I didn't even do that, so doing so I then grabbed a trash bag and started to filling each bag, one by one they added up, having a good ten or more bags of trash, after that I threw them into the trash shoot and went to sit back on the couch. sitting on the couch with my back and head hunched over with my knees and my legs spreed out, I look down to notice my beard has gotten so long it looked like one of those gnome beards it was in a v shape and was black still but with strands of gray, it was just dangling between my legs. I didn't have a reason to shave at this point shaving was a personal preference and I didn't have a problem with it.

Standing and walking to the restroom, looking in the mirror I see the horror I had become explaining earlier the way I looked, explaining any further would be evil. The best I could say was, have you ever seen something like a cave dwelling hermit, I looked more thin last time I remember, if I barely sucked in my gut you could see my ribs. The food up here doesn't change much the same old thing to eat one week after the other, but there is no changing that, being less active than I really ever have, eating the same stuff I have now for nearly four and a half years adds to the monotony, after time of being to confined to be as active as I need to be takes a tole on my body, the human body wasn't meant to live in space for long periods of time, of course at the start my crew and I were to live on a station for five years, we stayed on the station for two years but we all knew that we were all just running tests for space life and we wouldn't be up here for five years. As you've already noticed I tend to repeat things sometimes, I understand how that could get annoying but the benefit is I remember the important stuff easier and these logs I'm making for you or whoever tend to be very long and sometimes jumbled so it's best if I repeat sometimes so you won't get confused about the subject, as I've said if I do get off topic it's normally something that supports the main topic or relates to the topic.

I don't feel like I talk much about how long it has been like this, as I've said that I don't have an actually number but only a best guess I still feel I am doing somewhat okay, though I have to force myself to think that, I know I'm a little coo coo any human would be even with prior training of isolation, as humans we have a wide range of complex feelings and comprehend more that other species of Earth so to answer a long question, yes of course I could go without humans but to do so I must lose the human in me and for now I don't know why my animal instincts haven't taken over but even though knowing I can't restart the human race I could still let whoever is out there who I am. Who am I really fooling I'm bananas, oh bananas I could go for one of those fresh fruits, actually one of the few real foods on the station. For the past few moments I was huddled up with the pillows on the couch again and then I went to grab a banana and sat back on the couch, as I slowly ate the banana I continued my thoughts, as now that a lot of my time goes to surviving and not goofing off as much as I'd like, I try to find ways to spend the time I have with fun and lots of brain distractions, on Earth there were many sayings about time.

"Spend your time wisely."

Or

"Time flies when your having fun."

As humans lived on Earth for generations we had a better understanding of time, as humans there was a typical life span for us as there was for every living thing on Earth, we all as humans knew we were all going to die at some point in life, but just because we had a typical life span doesn't mean we lived that long, humans could have an unexpected end at any point of life, so even with the comprehension did we use it to it's full advantage of having full lives and make those happy moments.

Me not so much but it's something no human can stop, death is inevitable and even now at thirty two years of age I could still die, time is one of those things I should not think about as I am reminded how long it's truly been without others and this is a subject that just makes me worse but in the circumstances I feel for this bio I need to even bring up the subjects that drive me only into more insanity so to not only remember those before me and to also forget the shit I really have to deal with. What drives a man to do the things he does it only boggles me further not knowing the true reason I have yet to give up, I have no way to repopulate no communication with any other life, I know that I will be living like this for the next forty years, alone and bored that is my future so why do I accept it, I may have talked about this topic before and this is a big one as for now I can't answer this question and I may never, even with no hope I have to believe that there is hope and that's the word.

"Believe."

To keep going as long as I have I must believe there is hope, to put that clearer I need to lie to myself about the life I'm headed for in the next forty years. I often did things to distract myself but only for a few moments, as humans we did small tasks to pass the time and many others had main goals something to work at for a longer period of time, but it wasn't work these goals were hobbies or projects that couldn't take just an afternoon of free time, though most of the options for hobbies had a given a meaning in a persons life to lead to some end event or conclusion benefiting themselves or even others, the meaning of life if you asked that question to one hundred people you would get one hundred different answers, I would have had an answer to that at many points of my life along with many different answers from just me alone, this is one of those questions that can't be solved easily, without much detail my basic response would be there is no one right answer each persons answer to life is there own.

As of now my answer is, I don't know, it is just me so what am I to provide for a planet that's no longer living, if I can't help the world I came from I assume it will be a great while till I could help someone other than me so for this moment I live to make sure I stay alive till my natural death or I can work with what ever comes along. To switch topics here, the U.S. did reach great lengths in the technology of space travel, though we never were able to go out of our own galaxy we could have nearly, the advancements of space communication wasn't as great as our other feats but it was possible and that was an accomplishment enough. I sat up from laying on the couch and walked to the wall behind the couch running my hand down the picture of Wendy and giving a slit grin, I slugged out to the Control Deck and sat in the desk chair in front of the video slash radio communicator that I destroyed, there I pulled a small tool kit from a compartment on the desk, grabbing a small screwdriver from the kit and pulling off the cracked screen, inside was many damaged parts and wires strung out of place and ripped. Now I could have used the other computers in the Control Deck but this one computer had better hardware built into it for extended communication uses but those abilities of the computer were only used in emergency situations such as the station losing it's stationary balance and sending it spinning out of control into deep space, the wires in the computers were still live I could have shut off the main power but then I would be wasting the back up generator power and even if I did turn off the main power it wouldn't turn off this computer since it being the emergency computer system.

I stuck my hands in the computer and relined the loose wires, then pulled out a small tube of glue and connected it to a nozzle, putting a dab of glue of the wires to keep them back in place may have not been the most effective way to fix things but I did not have much to work with and this way the wires wouldn't be effected by the glue and they would not scramble around if the station started to rumble. The two wires that had made the computer output video was cut from the indent I made, I got out some wire cutters to sniped off the extra wires exposed from the tubing case it was in, as I grabbed the wire I could not put my other hand in the computer to cut off the exposed wire, I was a technical engineer so I know what to do to be safe, this computer I had not studied as much and it would have been much safer to tear the computer apart to grab the wire and cut it but I don't know the placement of the parts so I would have broken it more, against my better judgment I knew the only way to cut the wire other than pulling the rest of the computer apart was to directly touching the exposed wire without slack from the base of the loose wire. Alright I knew what I was getting in for, I was going to get a small shock ever time I touched the exposed wire, it would sting and in order to not blister my fingers to much I had to touch it as least times as possible.

I took a slow breath and reached into the computer touching the exposed wire, I saw the spark snap at my finger and it stung like hell I gave a grunt then dove in for more, this time I grabbed the wire and held on as I put my other hand in there and cut the wire I keep holding on and gave a loud scream, the wire was cut and I pulled out both my hands to see that my right index finger had a blister on the tip, raising my head to look in the computer and realizing there was one more exposed wire to cut, I then lowered my head and sighed. Switching hands to cut and hold the wire would make this process a lot easier but I'd rather not have blisters on each hand, I grabbed the wire having a pain staking face I held in my screams grunting load under my breath, cutting the wire I felt a sharp pain in my finger worse than any other pain I felt from this, I couldn't bear to watch what I was doing, I opened my eyes and saw the two wires were clean cut, I looked down at my hand and seen that the blister on my right index finger had popped, there was blood stained in the computer but not enough to ruin it, for my finger it was oozing the small bits of left over from the air pocket of the blister. I glued the two wires together and pulled the screen from the computer next to me on this one, turning it on it worked like a charm like I never broke it, there was still one issue though, the hole reason I fixed it wasn't to just fix it.

We did go over this briefly but maybe there is some way to contact other life, human is doubtful unless N.A.S.A. sent some kind of secret mission to the outer reaches of space, here's were this plan gets more difficult, through sixty to seventy years of space travel we never found anything worth wild in alien life, although under contract that for now I no longer need to fallow I can't release that kind of information to civilians, even with the attempt of finding other life the tools I have need work in order to send recordings out farther that earth made them to or I could travel, most people would have thought.

"Aliens wow cool."

Now to say if these aliens were dangerous or not is hard to know but being humans the people running this on how Earth is ruled would see them as a threat no matter what, as humans we destroy each other and what we create, when it gets down to it we where told to not repeat history but that's all we do civilization after civilization failed there always has to be the alpha male at anytime in history there was always conflict, humans can only advance in human life with global harmony. In the alien aspect of this idea as humans we would do something completely stupid to show dominance when we don't need to, it would be a great discovery to meet alien life but I've often thought that we shouldn't so to keep there world safe.

    I stood from the computer desk and walked to the bathroom with a drag in my step, washing off the open blister and bandaged it up, most of the pain was gone by now but it felt kind of stiff and like the blister was pulsating, with blisters you have to put the skin at ease and cool it, I filled a bucket of water and sat it on the couch side table dipping my hand into it while sitting down. I actually didn't lose much blood but due to the lack of physical ability and my diet even seeing blood gets me woozy I just really don't have the capacity to do much manual labor than I need to, now back to the main idea I had, the reason I fixed the much stronger computer was so I could fix it up to get a better signal to deeper space, farther than N.A.S.A. made it to, but to do this I would need to tear apart other computers on the station and use there radio signals and construct something to get a far better signal. Being a Engineer I feel much safer taking apart thing that could potentially save my life so putting it back together won't be a problem, I will at this point only have one computer to send or receive messages from so that's the bigger downside, now I've made it pretty clear I'm the only human so on the off chance I do find life let's hope to whomever these aliens are friendly, now this recording I am making I would assume it would be found by aliens so to let you know if you can figure out how to understand this I am friendly and the only reason I would hesitate to befriend you is due to Earths image of what aliens are, most of the time you all are seen as bad evil things, but I will be opened minded just don't open mine literally. Now I would be smart enough to show this recording to you and hope you could translate it, I wouldn't know though you could not be as advanced as Earth would of hoped, hell having this recording I think gives me the insurance that hopefully one day Earth and I will be learned about by other planets but I could just be fooling myself and if this so called new planet that finds this doesn't find this or can't translate this I'd be speaking babel for hours upon hours.

I looked at my finger and most of the swelling from the blister went down and it no longer stung, I stood from the couch and walked to the Control Deck sitting by the backup computer looking at the screen it was all fuzzy, the screen I put on there wasn't the model it was meant for but it did it's job that's all I could ask for, I stared at the home screen in boredom and with my left hand propping my head up to look at the computer my eyes had slowly closed, as I was about to go into a deep sleep I hear a soft beep, beep beep it went again, I jolted awake seeing the computer in front of me it read.

"Trying to receive message."

There was a little signal bar near almost dead trying to let the message receive but as my emotions brightened with joy the signal died and went away, I sat with a devastated look on my face, that was it I possibly found life and only in less than a minute it vanished, I remembered.

"Wait if the computer can almost receive messages from deep space with the original processor alone than with my update idea it will work no problem."

Chapter 13

A work in progress

I sat at the Captains chair in front of the main computer with a big grin on my face and my eyes wide, only a few moments ago I was so tired and ready for a nap but now all I wanted to do was work on updating the main computer, whatever was sending me a message was at least in the Milky Way Galaxy, the signal point was to low for a good connection so maybe just maybe I can get a better connection with some modifications, even if this was an alien life form it was a living thing, now meeting this thing or leading it to my location could be potentially deadly, but what do I really have to live for so if I am going to be this things test monkey and die in the process I'd be something different in my current life, as my grin started to become a look of grim I thought.

"Wait what if it was in my head like the voices from the computer before."

I mean it's happened before and I thought it was real, I can defiantly say I am not the same as I was years ago I would hope to believe I still can know what real is, it was a tough question what if I was right it was all in my head even if it was fixing the connection with the communicator would help in the long run, that's one thing I can't give up on I can't let my head get to me it is a question I can't answer now but soon, I know I over sold my ability to deal with the loneliness and it's been so long, I'm not completely gone yet I just have to believe that this was real it had to be it had to. I got up from the Captains chair for a bottle of water, swigging about half of it and giving a relaxing ah, even being an Engineer the process of upgrading the connection of the main computer wasn't going to be easy, the parts I would have to use to expand the connection would make me have to modify the built of the main computer, the parts of the rest of the computers were not the same model type and were to small, so I'd need to use more than one tearing up most if not all of the other computers leaving this the only working one.

I started taking apart the computer to the right of the main computer, pulling off the screen and unplugging the inner wires, most of the process was simple all I really had to do was unscrew the bolts to dismantle the main outer parts to get to what I needed, the thing that was tedious was actually taking out the radio single I needed, it was this thin typical green circuit bored that was very fragile and was glued to the inside panel of the computer, in order to get it out safely I had to chip away at the glue and peel it off the panel not destroying it in the process. Having a steady hand wasn't easy due to the lack of sleep, I sat there chipping away at the glue with my eyes feeling more heavy by the minute, I began to chip away at it slower and slower then as me eyes closed I stopped chipping, in a last burst of energy I flung my head to wake myself opening my eyes slightly then dropping the razor I was using to chip away at the glue I closed my eyes again and feel unconscious losing balance and as my body fell from the chair my head bumped against the computer falling to the floor unresponsive laying passed out with my head bleeding.

Who knows how much later it was, I was still on the floor in a ball my eyes cracked open and I felt a warm sensation on my head, this had happened so many times before I knew I busted myself open the cut from a while back was only a wound now but this time I hit the side of my head pretty hard, my hair was to thick so there wasn't much I could do, I really should know my limits I guess I let my excitement get ahead of me, I didn't have to worry about getting things done in a time limit so why was I trying to rush this, the best I could say about this moment is it shows my personality I was always determined to get things done I started even if they weren't successful and even if it put my heath at risk, it wasn't the smartest process but with the hard and long work combined with the time limit there wasn't much room for error, so all in all I still know there is some of the old me in me somewhere.

My head was cut open but after the time I was passed out the blood dried, I pulled myself up using the desk chair as a lift, though I was still woozy I tried to walk on my own but my legs were to wobbly so I sat on the deck chair and rolled into the bathroom, I slide off my boxers and laid in the tub turning on the water with my foot I let the water from the shower nozzle hit my head washing off the dried blood, sitting in the tub letting I let watery blood soak off my body into the drain, when I was done I pulled myself onto the desk chair again and dried off with a towel on the rack and pulled back up my boxers, I rolled back to the computer and took a look at the innards as I noticed that a few wires were cut, I then realized that if I wanted to get the connection board out of there I would need to pull out the wires that were trapping it, this means of course that if I really wanted this connection board I would be forced to shock myself with the open wires to reach it, I could simply forget about this one but there are only two connection boards on the station I'm not using, but I might need to use two in order to get a connection reaching deep space.

I knew I would have to create a new blister in order to get the connection board out, I'd rather not deal with all new blisters, the one I had has healed well but there's still kind of a bump there so instead of creating a new wound let's just screw up the one I already made, I still had the wet towel on the arm rest of the desk chair so I bite on it, it seemed the only way to get the board out was to rip the wires out to, though either way the computer was going to be trash. I took a slow deep breath closing my eyes reaching in and grabbing the wire I then felt the shock instantly but only for a few short seconds as fast as I grabbed the wire I yanked it out faster, I still had my eyes closed and my hand felt like fire but I had one more wire to go so I dove in grabbing the second one and tore it out as I did I felt a warm wet felling on my right hand, I knew I was bleeding again and I opened my eyes to the horror to see that I had three or four blisters on my palm bleeding, my palm was red and bubbly I couldn't bear to look at it any longer, I took the other hand and pulled out the rest of the connection board and as I saw it I felt my heart just drop, it had a giant scratch on the front of it, it was damaged beyond repair, I chucked the trashed connection board at the wall breaking the rest of it. I just laid back in the desk chair with my hands covering my face while I sobbed, all I could do now is pull the other out and hope with only one extra board I could get a better connection.

After some time I lifted my head and wiped away my tears mustering enough strength I stood and slugged over to the bathroom washing the blood off my hand and wrapping the cuts up, limping out to lay on the couch, laid flat staring at the ceiling I began to weep again and thought.

"This wasn't a restart or a test it was a sick joke, that's what my life was reverted to, a sick comedy for some god or higher being to laugh at, was it a test was it, my luck was only depleting, was I meant to survive this, I have no hope, I have no future, any and all good things that I come across just turns against me."

As I laid there debating death I cried blubbering like a baby I raised my head to see the picture of Wendy fall from the air softly on to me chest, I gave a puzzled look and thought.

"That's impossible it was pinned to the wall, there was no wind or any other force to push it off the wall."

My eyes widened in wonder and I thought.

"It couldn't have been, could it, was it a sign, the reason I made it this far was I knew to honer her I had to fight through this, I had to I still have choices I can still make it I wasn't gone and in a way neither was she."

There were going to be tougher trials than this I couldn't give up not now, even in my darkness there is some light as me the human, as long as I can make choices like this I know my human side is still there, for now I'll let you know you have been here this long and it won't get any easier only harder but with you I still have a purpose, forty years, fifty years I don't care my story has only started, I say I don't have much energy left but I have as much as I say I do I tell myself when I give up but now I must have the energy to do what's needed. I flung up off the couch like a dead body rising from the grave, limped with a hop in my step to the Control Deck and plopped into the Captains chair, rolling it to the main computer at the left of me and as I stared blankly into the dark screen I knew if I screwed up this circuit board it was going to be impossible to radio to deep space, there was a computer in the Med. Lab but it was only used for research so there wasn't a voice or video chat on that's all of the computers on the station the main one the one I took apart the one I'm about to tear up and the Med. Lab one, It was my last chance for this idea so I was now wide awake and prepared for the worst.

I grabbed the tools and restarted what I was doing earlier, it was the same exact process as the last one so there's not much to explain without repeating much, though this time I was extra careful slowly peeling off piece by piece as it got to the main event pulling of the most important and one thing I worked so hard for, I dug my hand in there with the razor and very gently chipped at the glue around the connection board, as I was going very slow to make sure there were no mistakes each and every pick at the glue felt like it was taking forever, I finished the edges and very softly pulled the edge of the circuit board with my finger but as I did I knew it wasn't coming off easy, I pulled a small flashlight from the desk and peeked behind the circuit board seeing there was glue also holding the middle of it to. I lowered my head and covered eyes with my right hand and chuckled, I knew the razor I had was to thick to get in there and if I tried I'd bust it, so I pulled a long needle from the medical kit in the desk and gradually picked at the glue between the circuit board and the inside of the computer, after who knows a few hours or so of slowly scraping the glue I peeled off the circuit board and everything went according to plan. rolling over to the main computer, I looked at the innards and knew I was going to have to touch live wires to connect the two circuit boards, I just finished taping up a fresh wound and I wasn't going to destroy the other hand so unless if I wanted to get my cuts infected I had to let them heal first, that was one of the hard parts of this process if I let my wounds heal and finish this later I knew what I was headed for and I just wanted to get this done as fast as possible. My hand already had four or five blisters from the past two times so my best bet was to let these heal and not risk and infection or needing to chop it off to live, you as I well knew I wasn't looking forward to this.

To get my mind off it I stood and hobbled to the couch I laid and dipped my hand in a bucket of water below me beside the couch and grabbing the picture of Wendy that hit the floor as I got up earlier and laid it on my chest as I drifted asleep, one thing I hadn't gone over were dreams, there are two ways to describe dreams, there are dreams that are similar to goals like my goal to work on the connection for the computer, the one I am mentioning is the type of dream you have while asleep. I dove a little into what sleeping was like for me, dreams can be somewhat like life these dreams are most of the time a first or third person view with many different things going on at once, dreams that humans have seem to either be not memorable or to weird making it easy to tell if your really in a dream or not.

Most of the time these dreams that humans have seem to unreal but with the lack of humans my dreams are now only to real that's all I dream about is other human then I wake to this hell hole realizing once again that this is my life, though my dreams actually mimic real life there still pretty weird, I see people I knew and it's the happiest time of the day for me but I'm always still in the space station with these people and few times on Earth, I guess I've gotten so familiar with this area its hard to imagine what Earth was like, I know it and remember it but it's been so long since I've seen or even felt grass. I still can picture what Earth was and I feel that's one more thing that lets me know I'm still human, there are many upon ton of things I can only remember and never experience again, it's been so long I think I don't even remember what soda tastes like, all I've had to eat for almost four years was water, dried camp food and some fresh fruit.

These dreams were welcomed I knew they weren't real but it gave me that false happiness to let me escape from this horror, due to the lack of being able to tell time I never really know how long I'm asleep I can only estimate and it's the same for these dreams, during it slips my mind that it's fake, a minute an hour, twelve hours it's the only time I feel normal, when I wake that's the hardest part having to accept it was fake those are the moments I can't ignore the situation and I take a deep look into my life doing this only makes me feel worse but it's unavoidable.

Now after a night of sleep I stretch myself awake and gave a yawn like a little puppy, I lifted my upper body off the couch and cracked my eyes open allowing my blurred vision to get clearer and as my eyes adjust the the light of the room I see the one thing that lets me forget the devastation. It's that picture of Wendy, it has no reaction it has no feeling but this picture, her she give me the light to start the day. With a smile on my face just gazing into the photo I drag the blanket off my legs and feel the pain return to my hand, my right hand was all tapped up the only good thing was that the pain was not a blazing burn like it was yesterday but today it was more of a bee sting, then my smile goes to a blank expression remembering the reason it was like this and though the pain was not going away any time soon I'd like to have it leave as soon as possible but I knew I was going to have to finish the project I'm working on by touching the live wires, it is something I could just finish in time with the mass amount that I have but I'd like to keep my unneeded pain as low as I can, so to continue my work in hopes there is some type of life out there I must fight through the struggle or more of struggles then just a few. There are things I can do to help my problems but for the most part I have to wait for the answers to come to me if they do at all, it's a long journey with many unanswered questions only with time can these events be solved and that's all I really have anymore is time it may give me a cluster of emotions so it only makes me more human to react normally, I might as well try to distract myself or be happy till something comes along, just wish me luck we're still in for a long ride and I'm going nowhere.

Chapter 14

Time

As I knew the dangers ahead and had dealt with this before now knowing the feeling of burning flesh and being an technical engineer I knew what I was doing was stupid and unsafe but I had no way to protect myself most if not all the science equipment was taken off the station and I could not find any rubber gloves, through all of this I still knew this was the only option I had so it was this or nothing but wasted time, sitting there with my legs crossed on the couch holding my hands to my face covering it. There I had plenty of time to waste, just leaning my hand on my face made it hurt if I did not get the circuit boards connected and let my wounds heal I'd be dealing with the pain for to long, I knew I had to fight through the trauma and get it done, so no matter how weak and tired I was this project was keeping me occupied and giving me less time to be bored. Now that I really think about it what is time, and no I don't mean the meaning of time well kind of what I mean is what's the meaning of time at this moment, the point of time when I was on Earth was to keep track of the day, when to do curtain things and where to be but now here at this current time was there a real meaning to time.

There were things I did during the day but the cycle of my day can be done at anytime of day and this project it was important but it wasn't going to need hours upon hours of work so scheduling time to do this wasn't required, of course I do my regular chores to keep the station up and running, I know I don't go into much details for maintaining the station but it's all just basic stuff and my time is taken up by surviving but most of what you hear is me just rambling or babbling about any and all aspects of my life now, plus a few action packed drama filled moments if you can call them that. I've dulled your minds enough for now as much as I want to just sit here on the couch and waste away forgetting this hell on Earth, though now that saying isn't accurate anymore but rephrasing it to hell on this space station would sound bonkers.

I wiped the small tears from my face and dropped my hand once again revealing my face, still weak and tired I forced my eyes open and flung to my feet, weaving over to the Control Deck I sat back at the main computer desk, hunched over procrastinating my coming pain I saw the file cabinets on the Captains deck were locked still, each of the crew had there own space for personal items, to survive I needed to utilize every tool I had, I knew it wasn't right but I had to check if there was something useful to help me in my journey.

When I was at this crossroads before I respected the personal thoughts of others by not watching the personal daily videos of the crew this situation may be the same but I feel that unknown items could help my cause, I wouldn't say I was really snooping I'm just looking for something to help me, I'd be lucky if I did find something to help me from getting more wounds. I knew the master codes to get into computer files but this file locker took a master key which I didn't have, how was I going to open it and if you are a person that thinks paper clips can get the job done that's all movie magic It never really worked. The worst thing I could do is damage the ship but I would need is a crowbar or something of the sorts to pry it open, my tool bag was in the tunnel system , my body was so weak I knew I could climb down there but back up that I'm not sure of, my diet and physical activity was only getting worse I'll have to set up some kind of work out plan for the future, I pushed my body up on to my legs pushing on the arm rests of the chair with my hands, there I stood with wobbly legs my appearance wasn't any better than it was months before I had grimy looking boxers on my leg hair, arm hair, chest hair, beard and head hair was filled with bits of food, dust and grease, through all that I was so use to ignoring it I was okay with it.

Wobbling over to the hatch leading to the tunnel system and twisting the crank to open the hatch I noticed the hole to the tunnel craw space was pitch black then I face palmed and sighed in distress, the lights leading to the tunnel system were out and I had no extra bulbs so it was out for good, let me explain a little further the lights in the rest of the station were controlled by the generator and won't go out till the generator does but the lights from the tunnel system were individual bulbs to light the area, the bulbs at the bottom in the crawl space were still lit but sooner or later I'll need to use a flashlight to get down there.

I dropped my legs in the hole reaching the ladder, not knowing were the next step was only making my legs shake even more, going down deeper into the hole the less light I had, finally it was pitch black I could not see my hand in front of my face and my legs were now wobbling uncontrollably, my foot slipped off the metal ladder bar and I gave out a yelp. trying to put my foot back on to the ladder was futile, I felt the bar of the ladder with the tip of the foot but with it flinching out of control it slipped off hitting my other foot and as my feet dangled there I also lost grip of the ladder, falling to the bottom of the hole my hands hit each of the bars to try to grab the ladder once again but it was to late I hit the floor of the crawl space.

Screaming in agony not that I hit the bottom if the hole, there was a padded floor in case this happened the reason I was screaming my lungs out was cause due to the way I landed, I tried to ball up so any limbs wouldn't be hit but my right knee wasn't placed right and had hit the wall to the right of me at the bottom of the hole, I looked at my knee and saw it was cut open bleeding out, I could barely lift my right leg off the ground I knew I popped the knee bone out of place and needed to fix it, I leaned my head back looking into the crawl space on my back with my head back my view was upside down, I saw the tool bag at the end of the tunnel, I rolled onto my stomach and crawled down the tunnel to grab the tool bag, I thought I might as well take the whole bag so I would only have to get back down here if I really needed to, as I crawled back to the ladder I thought.

"Well fuck my knee is broken and it's going to be hard enough pulling my own weight up the ladder but also at least a five pound bag would seem impossible."

I flung the tool bag strap on my arm, and grabbed the bar on the ladder pulling my body and feet up to start climbing it, the tool bag was on my back and I was climbing up having to let my right leg dangle while I climbed and again it was dark I very carefully searched for each bar to grab onto making sure I was grasped onto something before I made the next step, it wasn't really a step though, it was pitch black, I had a five pound bag on my back and my right leg was limb so the only way I was able to climb was to grab the ladder and hop with my left leg to the next step and dame I as lucky that I didn't fall again.

I got near the top of the hole and my eyes adjusted to the light, before I stepped up to the Control Deck I pulled off the tool bag and flung it up the hatch letting it hit the floor of the Control Deck, grabbing the rim of the hatch in the Control Deck I pulled myself the rest of the way up and now was laying on the floor of the Control Deck, I turned back and pushed down the hatch locking it in place. I opened up the tool bag and pulled out the crowbar, standing to pry the file cabinet open wasn't going to happen at least for a bit I needed to heal, with my knee out of place I needed to pop it back in or it would never get better, sitting there I scooted over to the Med. Lab through piles of trash, I was now at the floor by the counter of the medical desk, I reached my hand onto the counter and grabbed a vice then placed my calf in it, if I was going to reline my knee bone I needed it to be steady, the vice gripped my calf and I also remembered I had nothing on me at the time to divert my attention or ease the pain.

It had to be done so I slowly breathed and moved my right leg back and forth, if I moved it in the slightest wrong way I'd do more damage, I could feel the tips of the bones sliding against each other and I was so close, as the bone snapped back in place I again was screaming my lungs out and then heard a loud crack, with the bone back in place I felt relaxed, knowing I couldn't put any weight on the leg for a good while that means I won't be able to walk for months, I just had to put no weight on it and keep it straight, no walking and also having no crutches or a wheelchair I would need to butt scoot everywhere I went, still after the day I've had I wasn't giving up for the day I dragged myself and my lifeless legs out to the file cabinet.

I grabbed the crowbar and pulled out the lock on the file cabinet, I sat on the floor and pulled open the cabinet, there wasn't really much just a few documents I didn't feel like snooping in, pulling out the documents there was a little box of junk, a yo yo, some duck tape a small bottle of liquor, a watch and a flashlight, wait a watch I mean I know there's liquor but a watch, a watch, for the longest time I was only able to estimate what the time and date was with basic star reading, I say its been about three years or a little more but this was a watch now I could tell actual time. I grabbed the watch and it was powered off that was a relief, I knew that would mean the battery was still at full power, turning it on it said it was twelve PM and flashing, oh just great I had to reset the time but that would prove nearly impossible other than that little battery symbol was at full. The only problem that I came across was that it said it was had been reset, its been at least three years and a few months from the start so with the help of this watch I'll just say it's three years and four months so about April of the third year, after a while I couldn't remember what the actual date was so I had restarted it from what I call the Big Bang two.

I put the watch away and looked back into the cabinet, as my eyes skimmed the cabinet they locked on the tiny bottle of liquor and as I stared at the bottle licking my chapped lips, just the thought of the bitter taste brightened my spirits but I knew with the lack of medical supplies I could use it to numb the pain definitely knowing there would be more of it. But you know what after the stress I've had today I deserve a special drink, I still needed this liquor for medical reasons I grabbed the bottle it was only as big as my palm so only a sip was as much as I could take, with the bottle in front of my face I licked my lips again and my eyes widened, screwing the top off I could already smell it.

Alcohol at the mass production it was on Earth there were people you drank for occasions and others who drank more than should have, I wasn't much of a drinker only during special events or just a relaxing day was when I drank but now that tiny bottle of liquor was the best treat I could have even with the bitter taste it was far better and different from the water that I've only had for so long. I lifted the bottle to my lips and took a very light sip, it sure was bitter, it was some kind of pure vanilla with a mix of caramel and rough cherry, I shut the lid before I let the lovely taste consume me and I drank it all, the liquid went down my throat and I could feel the after taste, there was about two thirds of the bottle left and then I dropped the bottle back into the small box.

Still sitting lifeless on the floor I looked forward seeing that my right leg had a gash with tons of dried blood all over it, I never did clean up the cut which I should, I grabbed the crowbar and the duck tape, laying them on my lap I scooted to the bathroom but I soon realized I couldn't stand to reach the sink so I could rinse off the cut, so I put the crowbar and the duck tape to the right side of me and reached my left hand up the the sink and turned it on, scooping the water with my hand I splashed it on my cut and washed off the blood. I wasn't able to get into the tub so the blood being washed off was just going to sit there on the bathroom floor and not going down the drain, I washed off all the exes blood and I was glad the gash wasn't that thick so it didn't need stitches. The reason I brought the crowbar and duck tape was to keep my leg straight so not to disconnect the bone again, as I said I didn't have crutches or a wheelchair though I did have some surgical wrapping but I wasn't able to stand so I couldn't reach it on the shelf of the bathroom, the plan was to set the crowbar next to my right leg and duck tape it on so my leg would be formed straight not to bend, the duck tape was the best I could do for now I may lose some leg hair but it's better than snapping my knee bone back in again later.

I pressed the crowbar to the outer side of my right leg and started to peel the tape out in long strips wrapping the the tape tight on my bear skin making the crowbar press tighter to the side of my leg, sealing up the wrapping my right leg was now stiff and could not bend, the great thing was now I could pull myself up to a chair without bending my leg and risking losing the leg, now for the last time I say.

"Still after all this I have to stick my blistered hand into live wires to connect the circuit boards just great."

What else can I say that's what needs to be done if I don't get to it it'll bother me forever, I pushed my back to the sink cabinet then grabbed the rim of the sink with my hands and pulled myself up sliding my back up the front of the sink, now standing with my legs stiff as a bored I hobbled over to the rolling chair in the Rec. room and rolled over to the main computer in the Control Deck, there I saw the two loose circuits, at this moment I spent more than half the day dealing with opening that god dame file cabinet not doing this would keep me up, I don't need this extra pain of opening my old blisters but I will do it I have to.

Sitting there in the roller chair slumped and sunk into the chair, I couldn't take the procrastination thinking about the pain only made my decision to do it wonder, with no thought further I closed my eyes tight took a breath grabbing the loose circuit bored and felt the tips of my fingers shock, I tied the first loose wire to the circuit bored already screwed into the computer, I shouldn't have but I opened my eyes to see a blister on my index finger burst and was bleeding out. Closing my eyes and yelping in fright I grab the next loose wire and put it in place, the connection boards were in place and everything looked right I just had to pop back in the screen and I'd be done with this horrific part of my life.

Screwing the screen back on and plugging it all in I booted up the computer, enlightened to see it turn on and bring me to the desktop screen, it's been a while since I've had this computer on, before I only had one bar of range to almost none and now was really no better this time around I had two bars of range, it's better but still pretty terrible, when the station was more powered from Houston it was always at full bars and we would have been able to receive audio and video at least to the distance of Jupiter, like that was ever needed but it definitely was ground breaking for the time, with the power it has now I'd say I could be able to get messages maybe from Jupiter. Talking about range connections from sending messages awhile back I know I mentioned a alarm beacon it reached out as far as the full range communication would but without Houston's power, it seems like the best option to get notification to other life but it drains power fast so it will always be a last resort, something also I feel I have only talked lightly about is the power of the station, you know the basic knowledge that it was meant to last for five years for five people and I've been on the station for two years with my crew and now a little over three years on my own, during those two years with my crew we used near full power each day but now and since I started living alone I only use less than twenty percent a day so these three years I've spent alone not using the normal power has saved me countless years.

I was in relief knowing that I had finished what I was so determined to do, as I sat there seeing the computer at half bars and ready to receive messages my eyes lingered down to my hands noticing my bloody right palm covered in open blisters, I pushed back the roller chair to see my injured right leg all packed up, then at that moment I lowered my head and covered my face with my left hand fingers crying, but this time it wasn't that I was sad or just some random depression moment, I was happy, I never cried for joy for the past three years and more I've only had very few real happy moments this wasn't much but it was a sign of hope that I was still here and I know I can go on, all I ever felt in the past years were sad and worried. I finally realized that I knew there wasn't much I could do with my life after this but with this victory today I now know that I always have options and this connection bored thing is now my purpose, it might lead nowhere it could take my whole life to complete but this is something that I need to work on it will help me know that no matter how this situation changes me as a person there will always be a human part of me still alive and I have to work hard to sustain my humanity. I knew this was my life now my new mission and I could waste time moping but to honer Earth and humankind I can't throw away the one thing I have been given as a human, a brain that gives me everlasting learning ability and countless other properties to admire, so I must do as much as I can to send my existence out there and show the universe the world that once was.

   I stood from the roller chair and hobbled over to the Rec. room with my stiff right leg and as I got into the room my eyes locked onto the picture of Wendy pinned there to the wall, I wobbled over to the picture and graced my left had over it like I have done every night before I rest, I guess it became some kind of ritual, the picture was the only other thing on the station that imaged a human other than me, having some contact with it made me feel as if I wasn't really losing my humanity and having it up on the wall facing where I sleep is as if she is not only still with me but also looking out for me. After a good look into her I sighed and lowered my head again, I wobbled over to the couch and plopped down, with my right leg in the makeshift cast I wasn't able to sleep on my side like I always do, so I was forced to sleep on my back very uncomfortably staring at the blank plain white ceiling, it was hard to sleep only on my back period, but I had to also stair at endless white while falling asleep and it made me just more uneasy , it reminded me of being so alone that there is nothing there but me just like this white ceiling, as my eyes drowsed and my head tilted to the side I noticed a small gray thing run across the top of the TV, I thought nothing of it I was tired and half asleep I was just seeing things and finally I dozed off, tomorrow was another day and I couldn't wait to know the new fresh hell that this universe will bring me.

Chapter 15

Enjoy, while I still can

It was the next day, during sleep my head must have slipped off the arm rest, I lifted my head and cracked open my eyes letting them adjust to the light, I tilted my neck up to look at my stomach and my eyes were still adjusting, as my vision got clearer I thought I was still dreaming because I swear am now seeing a small rat on my stomach. Okay I know this seems really impossible but I do remember when the crew and I started living here we had four rats to test animal space living but the rats were always getting motion sickness but when they were taken back to Earth one must have escaped, by now the rat was fully grown but looked a little starved, I still was laying there and just had the biggest smile I don't think it really kicked in that there was another being alive with me, looking in the rats face he was just twitching his little nose it was so freaking cute.

I grabbed the little guy and sat up on the couch sanding up my furry fella grasped hard into my skin on my left hand but even though it pinched I wasn't fazed by small pain like that anymore, my walking was no better I had to hobble everywhere I went, each step I took was making me lean back and forth side to side like a penguin, I hobbled over to the pantry with my stupid looking walk and grabbed some packed air dried granola and pour some into a small bowl, after I sat at the main computer and laid the bowl down letting the rat crawl down my arm onto the bowl, sitting there I admired the small creature he was hunched over the bowl nibbling on a granola making soft squeaking noises, It was so cute I couldn't believe my eyes it didn't seem real but it was I sat there with my eyes locked onto him and petting him with a finger.

There was more to this than just the new living thing in my life it gave me a realization to my doubt of this new friend in my life, you see humans are a being of habit there is a normal typical life of a human but based on the choices we make and the challenges we face make who we are and how we act or interact with the world around us, so if there is only sadness and difficulty day after day I and anybody else would have less faith in the chance for happiness. The rat finished nibbling on the food I've given him but still I couldn't stop petting him, it was to much to handle I could feel each hair my finger ran across and again I teared up in joy, was this the universe telling my to continue I did something that will possibly help me in the future and make things better for my life, the computer by fixing it I showed that there is still hope and I do have some purpose and meaning even with little for me to continue or look forward to, was the universe rewarding me for making something good out of a bad situation, I can't possibly know but this makes me happier than I have been in a long time and I need more of that, I look to the computer and no new messages though I know it's a long process there's a saying.

"Rome wasn't built in a day."

Rome was a place on Earth and it's survived along Earth for some great time, so this reaching new life was going to be a slow process and now thinking it could take a while to meet other life I have already been proven wrong just by being given my new little friend, I just have to look up and see the possible good options even in the bad moments of my life. What was I going to do today there wasn't much else to work on for getting myself out there, I feel that for know I need to give my attention to this rat and make sure he is safe, I should find a place to keep him so he doesn't get lost again, then it just popped in my head I knew he need a home like me with this station, there were glass panels in the cabinets of the Med. Lab, the glass panels were to show us what and where something was in the cabinet, I could tear them apart and glue the panels together and make a tank for him to live in.

Walking was still a big problem I could walk but each time it just took to much energy, I put the little guy on my lap and rolled with the chair into the Med. Lab, I was surprised my friend was just laying still on my lap and didn't fidget getting to the cabinets I grabbed a medical bowl to put the rat in and then grabbed a drill from a cabinet below, at this point I drilled off the bolts from the rod of the cabinets one by one, I was glad there was five sides so I could make a open top box for him, pulling off each in tacked cabinet I pulled apart the plastic rim off the glass panels. Looking for the glue gun I noticed the rat was standing on his tip toes in the bowl with his little paws and head peaking over the side of it, he barely did anything but he just made me so happy, he just stood there wrinkling his nose and staring at me, grabbing the glue gun I assembled the pieces now I just had to wait for it to dry.

What to do now I hadn't eaten since yesterday so I rolled to the pantry and grabbed some dried beef space food and a bottle of water, now at the main computer again I was munching on my lunch with the rat on my lap as I looked at the computer while eating I see the a sudden window appear on the saying.

"Receiving message."

Like it did last time, there was this circle on the screen that did loops trying to connect to the message, as this was happening I froze in place only seeing the computer buffering in forever, as I sat there it spent at least two or three minutes buffering but I knew it would never connect the connection was to far and the computer was to weak to reach, my excitement and smile ear to ear changed to a frown and a feeling of loss, I was devastated it didn't connect but as I sorrowed I just as fast realized that there was someone or something out there or I had hoped it always could still have been a glitch, I also knew I didn't have the resources to reach the connection any further, here again the only choice I could make is to wait, it was something that I was forced to put off as much as it killed me I had to. What was the plan now the tank wasn't dried quite yet, I couldn't work on the computer any further and I already had lunch. I looked at the rat to notice all the tiny pieces of dirt in its fur and the horrid stench it gave off, normally I was not affected to my filth cause I got so use to it but this wasn't mine I never came across this smell before, I could have just ignored it but the shocking appearance of the rats condition made me notice mine, I hadn't showered in at least two months and my condition was more of the same a black and slightly grayed gnome beard, long greasy hair, grimy body hair and stained boxers.

It never occurred to me but I really don't want to look like some kind of monster to these new life forms I meet, I knew I was over thinking it but some much good was happening to me maybe I should clean up it might make me feel better and hell I know I don't have to do this but it passes time, the little fur ball hopped onto my lap and we rolled over to the bathroom, It was going to be a hassle getting in and out of the tub but pushing through the pain would eventually make me feel better, I sat my furry friend beside the tub and ripped off the duck tape cast revealing my very dried bloody right leg, my leg was covered in dried blood and few wounds just a little purple around the knee after that I slipped my legs into the tub, then grabbing the fur ball I turned the shower nozzle on with my left foot, the tub filled with water up to my knee I made sure my legs weren't totally submerged. The rat was laying on my chest, I scooped some water with my hand and dribbled it on him, I was surprised he was so calm, shampooing him I felt would be a challenge and I didn't want to get it in his eyes so just a water rinse was going to have to do. I put the furry guy on the soap dish and rinsed my legs washing off the dried blood among other dirt and such, I moved directly to washing my upper body, I know it's weird but I wasn't comfortable naked in front of this animal so I'll just do that part later, after at least twenty or thirty minutes of cleaning and soaking my wound I was fresh and clean.

By now the glue had to be dry on the tank, it was going to be hell getting out of the tub but I fought through the pain lifting my stiff legs out and then sitting on the side of the tub but that was just the start and was easy, next I stood putting more weight on my legs than I should have, as soon as I stood I could feel a unbearable pain on my ankles and just plopped on to the roller chair. I grabbed the rat off the soap dish, drying us both off with a towel I looked into the mirror, I looked like a different person I never looked this bad before, I cleaned up but I still had the super long hair all over, it didn't bother me but it was one of those things that was a big change though I was feeling happier than I have in a long time so I need a new image. I lied the rat in the counter and grabbed a pair of scissors and clipped off most of the gnome beard to a small medium goatee the head hair I felt okay with so I kept it the same, I grabbed the rat again and we rolled to the pantry and got a bowl of granola and a bowl of water then rolled into the Med. Lab, the tank was solid so I placed the food and water in there.

I kissed the fur ball and cuddled him against my cheek, I thought I needed to find something like the message connection to have more meaning in life and I was so silly to not realize it had been staring me in the face all day, it was the fur ball that was my new mission, it was another being that depended on me for survival I was needed more than ever. we sat there nose to nose and the biggest smile I could form, he just licked the tip of my nose and I chuckled, I lied him in the tank and turned the roller chair around to leave, I turned my head back before leaving to see the little guy clawing at the glass he look liked how I've felt, abandoned I just meet him and now I was going away it wouldn't be right if he did that to me so I couldn't do it to him we survived only with each other, so I rolled back to him and put the tank on my lap then rolled into the Rec. room, There I sat him on the floor at the end of the couch then relaxed on the couch myself, I really didn't have much of a day but I've taken enough emotion for a full day I think I'll take more of a nap then sleep, I peeked over the back of the couch and locked my eyes with Wendy and softly said.

"Good night."

Sitting up in the couch I could not lay I was frozen in place looking at the picture, my heart felt so warm, my situation was terrible it killed me knowing that I couldn't change any of what happened, I couldn't forget it or ignore it even with the challenges and trials I face that make me want to end the pain each day but I don't, not for religious reasons not for personal reason but to know It's just me and up to only me to tell Earths story, everyone I knew all of Earth they were gone but they still counted on me to let the universe know we were out here, if I were to release my pain and end it I would fail my life I would fail Earth and most importantly I'd fail Wendy I couldn't do that. There isn't much that makes me go on and that is the big one I just have to enjoy the little happy moments that the universe lets me have, like the fur ball and the picture of Wendy, they help me get by more than whoever can realize.

At this moment I slowly laid back in the couch and again was forced to stair at the blank ceiling till I fell asleep, I've slept one night like this but the feeling of isolation was hard to look at, I just tilted my head to the side and saw my furry friend and he was a lot more help than I let on he was what kept me knowing there was something to hope for, he was just laying in the corner of the tank nearest me, I know I mentioned we needed each other but I think he needed me as much as I him, I slowly closed my eyes while they were locked on him and gave a small breath letting my body clam for the night and then I fell back into my dreamland hoping for more happy moments.

That night I awoke to the painful noise of screeching, I flung to sit up on the couch to see the my furry guy was clawing at the glass tank and making worrisome noises, I got to my feet as painful it was I needed to help him, leaning into the tank I picked him up then checking the watch I found that was now in my right wrist, it was who knows what time but whatever it didn't bother me I was woken out of sleep someone needed me, now I thought I'd never say that but that's right this little guy wanted me and that made me feel so happy. I looked to see that he hadn't drank any water all night, he was abnormally smaller than I thought from when I first met him, oh I get it now he was so small and so comfortable with me when he first saw me, was he a baby, nah he seemed to fully grow, he must have been thirsty, my leg actually wasn't feeling as bad as it was the past couple of days so I slugged over to the Med. Lab and grabbed a rubber medical glove, the reason for this was that he didn't know how to drink from the dish so he must still have been feed by bottle, I also grabbed a pin and poked a hole through the index finger of the glove, this guy must have only been feed milk or water but water was all I had so that was going to have to do.

I filled the glove and tied it up then putting the glove to his face his mouth clung to it and sipped, I yawned as fur ball finished so I dropped the glove into the sink then limped back to his cage and before putting away for the night I gave him one last kiss before I slept, after I laid him in his tank I look to my side and see again and what will always be there the picture of Wendy, I walked over there and did as I always do before I sleep, with my hand in felt glued on the picture not wanting to let go I thought.

"This was only a small start, three years was a long time alone but even with these small happy moments it gave me the power to go on, was it the universe or was it some kind of now unattainable love."

That was the magic of the human mind we as a species can make unlimited free will choices we always have a choice in some way, was it really the universe rewarding me for my small successes in my time of depression or was it the power of love forcing me to tread on and not let Wendy down, that one person it was my biggest regret not getting to know her more, my biggest problem has screwed me over for the last time, I wasn't going to let my stress and worry for my future ruin any more of it, I had dealt with my anti-socialism take the one thing that would have given me the best thing to happen in my life and now I was going to do anything to reach other life somehow it was now and forever my life goal, not for me, not just for Earth, for Wendy she at least deserved that.

Now setting into the couch I look at fur ball for the last time of the night and see he was already fast asleep and so should I because I hope for a happy and busy day tomorrow, my eyes still locked onto the softly asleep fur ball I sighed and closed my easy drifting back into my dreams. I know I did go over the concept of dreams or of what they were now with the lack of humans, as I said they were an escape from the horrors I face but even these dreams of people and feeling normal, it wasn't real and never will be but with the current events it seems that things are changing for the better so maybe my dreams will not be as sad to end with the new happiness the universe has let me have and hopefully more to come, I couldn't tell you what the morning will bring but with the determination that Wendy gives me weather I fight or smile through it I can't wait because that's the thing I thought would never be the truth, hard work does pay off but with the society I lived in there were people who worked hard to be rich and there were ones given it, the more riches you had the more power you got, now with no one to fight over the power or riches the definition has more of now not meant the physical type of rich and more of the moral version, I was rich now cause of my determination, fur ball, fixing the range on the computer among many of other things, to now end a long day I finish saying whatever my future holds it better be ready I'm a new man, not better but new.

Chapter 16

What was real anymore

It has been so long since I've had a calm night sleep, I do mean a long time, I was enjoying the happiness as long as I could and it even made my sleeping better, I typically had nice dreams but my physical being while I was asleep wasn't the best. I loved dreaming of a better life and longed for these moments but it was hard to get to sleep and stay asleep, with just the presence of my new friend I felt more relaxed than ever and as able to feel safe sleeping, when I was sleeping not much woke me but if something was wrong this time I'd be able to hear the rat screeching as I did this past night. These things I just said were within my head while in sleep and now that I think about it I force myself awake by painfully and slowly cracking my eyes open, my morning was like all the rest.

I let the eyes adjust to the light while yawning and stretching out like a puppy, while still laying on the couch I look down to see my right leg less banged up and looking better, I was happy to see that I was able to lift my leg with ease, tilting my head to the side to enjoy the site of my furry friend, I was expecting to see the fur ball clinging to the glass and wanting to be held, what I saw was far worse something that was the last thing I would ever expect just seeing what I saw almost made me snap right there. I've keep you in the dark for to long you want to know what I saw, I saw nothing there was no tank it was gone, that was impossible I hadn't moved it before I slept and the rat could never move it on it's own, the closest explanation I could make was maybe the station lost gravity and spun off its balance moving it, but that wasn't the case everything else in the room was where I left it and if the station lost it's balance the room would be in disrepair, maybe I was blowing this out of proportion I did wake up in the middle of the night and moved the tank but forgot because I was half asleep.

I stood from the couch and walked to the Med. Lab where I made the bottle for the furry guy, I guess I could have taken the tank in there and not just him then left him in there by accident, I open the door to the Med. Lab and scanned the floor and counter with my eyes but no tank to be found, I don't remember taking him into the main deck but it was a possibility, I lifted my head to see the rest of the Med. Lab and as I did my heart dropped, I fell to my knees with a horrific look stained on my face, it was the cabinets, the cabinets they were all still in tack like I never built the tank, it couldn't be possible or maybe I didn't want it to be but it was right there it was real, I just couldn't really comprehend these events I was going through but it was to rough, it was so heartbreaking and confusing, I knew that when I saw that the cabinets were never touched there was something very wrong, but how could have all of this just been fake or in my head it was to long and felt to real.

I crawled with my knees to the counter and started to pound my left fist on the floor in anger while I sobbed and screamed, as I was breaking down I lifted my head and as my eyes widened in realization I now just thought.

"Maybe I was still sleeping, of course that was it the events with fur ball were to real this had to be some kind of nightmare."

I stood and as I was balling, lightly banged my head on the wall and yelled.

"WAKE UP, WAKE UP !!!"

But it was no use I wasn't waking then in frustration I grabbed one of the cabinet doors and with adrenaline strength I ripped it off the hinges and was screaming at the top of my lungs, in the last bit of madness I smashed the glass part of the cabinet into my head and then screamed at he top of my lungs again, the pain was to unbearable so I knew I wasn't asleep, I dropped the cabinet on the floor and started to tear up again falling to the floor myself into a ball. There in the ball I sobbed and screamed in pain, my hands were covered in blood and my hair was also soaked with it running down my face, I could feel the small glass shards stuck in my head and it burned more than I could handle.

I sat up and wiping off my tears, then standing I walked to the bathroom and saw in the mirror my face was covered in blood and my hair with glass shards tangled in and a few shards stuck in my scalp, I defiantly wasn't going to be able to pick out the glass without doing damage to my hair or scalp. I hadn't fully healed from the dislocated knee but it seems it's at the best health it's going to be so I'll have to face living with a limp for the rest of my days, I grabbed a pair of pliers from the cabinet then limped over to the bathroom, there I pulled out the clippers, I knew that there was shards stuck in my scalp so I had to pull them out with the pliers but my hair was in the way so I needed to buzz my head that was now down a little passed my shoulders. I gradually clipped inch by inch till I had barely a couple inches, at that point I didn't have a buzzer so it was as short as I could get it leaving two inches or so, the shards tangled in my hair were cut out and now with the thinner style I could plainly see five small pieces of glass stuck in the front of my scalp, I grabbed the pliers and placed the tips of the tool on the first piece, I thought.

"Oh boy was there going to be blood I just hope one of the shards didn't hit a vessel or something more important, I can lose blood and that's fine but brain blood and to much of it that's a problem."

I took a deep breath and softly tugged at the shard, while doing so I grunted in pain, I knew if I did this slow it would be to much to bear but if I tugged to fast I could spill to much blood, so I softly pulled the first piece and with just the right force it slid out fine. I gripped the second piece and slid it out as easy as the first one, when pulling the pieces out I put the nickle sized shards into the trash can by the toilet, I was glad they were small, thin and were less than an inch, so there really wasn't any deadly damage. I pulled out the other three and as I stood with a bleeding head staring into the mirror I just had an ashamed look on my face, lowering my head I knew I was mad and even more devastated that I now was really losing more of myself than I was before, I can't fully explain why I smashed the glass over my head the simplest reason was that it was a spur of the moment with my mixed emotions.

With my head slowly bleeding the blood from the fresh open cuts were leaking and the blood stream now was falling past my forehead so I grabbed the sink cup filling it with water and dousing my hair all over, I sighed in relaxation the cool water was easing my burning cuts, after doing this countless times I finally started to relax again, the water felt so good I know I filled that cup at least more than ten times, It was something that made feel great but I had to force myself to stop wasting the water, water usage was something I hadn't gone into much but now is a good time as any. The water that comes out of the sink and shower was in a giant tank, when the water from those sources were used they were sent to an equal sized tank that held the dirty water and then was sent back to Earth when filled and N.A.S.A. would send more clean water, but that's not an option anymore so when it's gone it's gone, The only other water on the station was the bottled stash I had there was nearly five years or more bottles worth at the start of my adventure but now I don't really know and with certain supplies being crucial to my survival maybe it is best that I do not know the exact number of things left then all I would worry about is knowing that I may or may not have the supplies I need to live. I wanted the relaxation to continue but I can't waste anymore water and it wasn't worth risking my life, as the water drained from my face I decided that I needed to stay cool, it would let me not have so much tension when moving around so I didn't dry my head off with the towel, my cuts were still fresh and I needed to clean them up better than water the best I could do was to wrap up my head tight in padded bandages then I did so, looking back into the mirror one last time to see my work the bandages were evenly tight and with only two or a little more inches of hair left none peaking out of the wrapping it as almost if I was bald.

I walked back to the Rec. room with my limp and stood at the door, there I gazed at Wendy and teared up softly then limped the rest the way over to her, now a couple feet away from the picture I grazed my hand on the picture as I always do before sleep, all I could think was I failed her today that I was losing myself everyday I wake into this hell, I now questioned more than ever if it was worth my sanity and life to continue this doom, I was now finally realizing that I needed people or pets or really anyone to not only keep myself being me and to show the legacy of Earth, standing there still I let the tears run passed my face and I thought.

"I'm sorry Wendy I only hope I can last to prove my love and dedication but the biggest problem I would ever have to deal with from here and forever was that I was a human, humans were the farthest from being the most perfect species there were more animals on Earth that ran it better than humans ever could have and I was at the bottom of the chain of simple minded humans so even with my anti sociability I still was the worst choice for that last hope for humanity."

My arm dropped from her and my arms were hunched over with my head lowered as I balled once again, limping over to the couch I sat I didn't even have the energy to turn on the TV and enjoy the time I had, I was just to physically and emotionally strained, as I fell into the rest of the couch I once again stair at the blank ceiling, I know I was only up for a little more than a couple hours today but I need a nap and as I said humans can only take so much strain in one day, that was the major issue I was only up for a few hours and with only minutes I felt like shit physically and emotionally.

Laying there I forced my eyes shut but couldn't in my heart I knew I can't ignore my issues and wasting time sleeping was putting a weight on me forcing me to remember that no matter how hard it gets I have to keep on this track or all I've done and worked so hard for is also wasted, I was stuck between a rock and a hard place, was I to forget my mission and do what I can to save myself or was I to fight and put any and all energy into giving what Wendy and all of Earth deserved. I was to frazzled to sleep it was like all the screams of Earth and the last dying breath of Wendy were judging me, I force my eyes to close again and didn't want to think of the horror they all went through as my eye were closed all I could imagine were thousands of blazed and burnt bodies of all ages screaming in pain in the ash of what was left of the rubble chunks of the Earth, it was to horrifying these bodies were nothing but burnt black ash covered humans with red eyes and bleeding all over in a mix of a blood river and the rubble of broken buildings and miles upon miles of ash filled roads and unrecognizable abominations of what were once humans. Laying flat on the couch I covered my ears pushing my hands with hard pressure to stop the screams in my head, it was a horrible scene in my head and out, on the couch I was screaming to myself yelling.

"STOP, STOP."

As my hands were glued to my ears so hard that with the pressure my arms were shacking viciously to stop the pain in my head and I was bumbling like a baby, I had finally had it I wasn't going to be able to sleep till I figured some shit out but with the past tormenting me I wasn't thinking straight, in frustration I took my bum leg and kicked the arm of the couch and as I did I screamed to the top of my lungs in even more pain, now my leg was throbbing and burning as my tears flooded my face they came out burning also, I just need to walk off the pain and occupy my energy to something more productive. Trying to stand I flung my upper body to the side and fell to my stomach on the floor then pushing my body up to stand I was hunched standing and wiping my tears away with my arm, walking into the bathroom again I could see in the mirror that my face was red and eyes were bloodshot I grabbed a pain killer from the mirror cabinet and then hobbled out to the pantry grabbing a bowl for some dry granola with berries and a bottle of water, I sat the bowl on the computer counter and spooned some granola into my mouth then taking a sip of water, I was softly whimpering with each bite I took my mind really wasn't still clear and I could not think of something to give me meaning in life I needed to do more than just stay alive to spread the memory of Earth I needed to get my existence out there but how, that was the issue I had to come over next. I finished the bowl and again wiped my tears off, my head was to out of whack right now so it wasn't going to be easy to figure out the rest of my life, some good sleep would give me a clearer mind in the morning with recent events I really have not gotten hardly any sleep, I dragged my feet to the Rec. room and as always ran my hand down the picture of Wendy and as I did this time I said.

"Tomorrow is a new day I can't be here without you so please give me something to live for it's sad that the memory of you isn't enough to keep me happy and going on but you're a bigger contributor then you will ever know, I fell I've said this many of times but I wish I could have had the bravery I have now to create a better life with you then I had."

Lowering my head and hand I limped back into the couch and closed my eyes much easier this time around, there laying on my back with my eyes closed and muscles loosened I was able to ease into sleep, adjusting my head to the arm rest I had a deep thought look, let me explain further, it has been now about three and a half years since the event and yet with no real human contact or a human voice other than recorded ones I still remember all my loved ones voices. I say I don't want to get into detail about my personal life but I've been talking to whoever for years now so I think you deserve more than I am giving you. To get into greater detail you all know I was never the most social person and with this fact it was hard to not only make friends and love interests it was hard to find work, of course not being a people person there weren't many lines of looking for a person like that. I am opening up a lot more but I still feel it is not that necessary, I won't get into much family details but I can say that my mother was the most help through life, I know it sounds like my life wasn't that bad, I was in the Navy went to collage for engineering and got to go to space, but as many accomplishments I had there were more defeats, I was a loner in school and knew people but never made any long standing friends, except for one he was more of a brother to me and it was the closest best relationship I had expect for my mother of course, these two I knew no matter what I was going through I was always able to look to them for comfort without there understanding and love I don't even know if I'd be here today, is that good or bad well it debatable but none the less they were the best things to happen on my life even far better than achieving my engineering career or going to space.

At this point I was asleep but my dreams were darkness and all I had was my free thought, in this stage I was still fixated on the memory of people I once knew, it has been so long but still I was able to see them as they were unharmed in a peaceful state seeing the grin of my best friend and his chuckle and the long glowing hair of my mother always with her smile with open arms for a hug, this was the scene me and the two most important people to me other than Wendy, it was me and them so happy and joyful greeting one another, this time was different though we weren't on Earth it was nothing forever but darkness and us all standing in a spotlight, as fast as they came they were going faster and as they dissipated for our hug into dust I break down falling to my knees screaming.

"Why oh why."

There once again alone in the darkness sobbing I hear a faint voice, it was heard but I wasn't able to make out the words the voice was saying, all I could see was as far as the spotlight would reach right in front of me but I saw nothing, the voice was getting loader but more of a mix of a soft voice but loud, yet I still could not tell what the voice was saying I just knew it wasn't harming, as I rose my head to the top of the spotlight my tears dropped down my face, I whipped my tears and then saw another being ascend from the spotlight and as it got closer I could see it was Wendy she just had a long white dress on she wasn't an angel but she hovered in front of me putting her hand on my check, we locked eyes and she said.

"I am here for you, I am here with you."

We tightly hugged and as I wrapped my hands around here and as I did she the same she dissipated like the others, but this time I was not sadden I felt safe like she was still there but not, there again I was alone with my head pointed up at the top of the spotlight the spotlight grew bigger and brighter to a point I was unable to see due to the bright light and eventually when the the light consumed me I was back in the real world cracking my eyes open from a long sleep, it was very much weirder than other times I awoke, this dream felt so short but yet it was now nearly a night later I could assume from when I fell asleep, it felt almost instant whatever I guess, now my eyes were fully open and I stretched my arms, all I know is I can't fathom what the universe has in store for me today but whatever it is I have Wendy and I know that, if I forget that I wasn't truly lost I don't know if I am human anymore but I know I have my mission and I'd die for it, I'd die for her.

Chapter 17

Losing the human in me

Awake for the morning I was leaning up off the couch and was going over the choices I had for the day, it has been a good six months or more since I went for a space walk maybe it will give me some inspiration or I could see if there was anything I could upgrade on the radio connection on the main computer, either one was fine. I flung to my feet and stood there by the couch with my wobbly legs, my injury was as good as it could get and I wasn't getting the physical activity I needed, my legs needed more strength but I was afraid if I squatted I'd tear a muscle in my calf, plopping back down on the couch I lifted my legs while sitting, I motioned them up and down to get the blood running and as I did this twenty or thirty times I felt the stiffness loosen and could feel the tension of my legs ease, now with more feeling in my legs I could walk easier, standing again my legs were no longer shaking but I knew this limp was for life, dragging myself behind the couch to see Wendy I looked at the wall and noticed that the picture was once again gone but the pin was still in tact so how did it fall, the floor of trash was still just about everywhere but was better then months ago, I would have noticed the picture on the top layer of trash.

The last time I lost her I freaked but this was a small space station and most days there are moments I don't remember doing somethings and then find the aftermath later, that's how the emotions work with the isolation you do so many things to keep your mind occupied so not to face the truth and dig deeper into the madness, it's not always successful but if there are only so many bad memory's in recent time then what else is there to remember or even expect, if things go in a bad way so often why do I expect it to change any time soon, that there that is the solution I know it is possible to have a somewhat full life with the help of my determination but it will be a slow and painful process, even though I have to fight for so long the hope of redeeming Earth was what lets me have the strength to go that far.

I hobble my way into the bathroom and scoop some water in my hands and dowse my face cooling myself off then I look into the mirror seeing some of my hair peek through the bandaging that covered my head wounds, I peeled off a loose strand and unraveled the rest off to reveal my hair that was pretty short not going past my ears, I was glad to see my cuts were healing up but it was still gross to look at so I covered the cuts up the best I could trying to spread my hair about.

I then dragged my feet out the Control Deck and sat at the left side computer near the main one, spinning the chair around facing away from the left side computer something caught my eye, I swear I saw a shadowy figure standing by the main computer counter, the picture was my top priority but this caught me off guard, I turned my head to the figure and was jaw dropped as what was there in plain sight now.

There was a man leaning on the counter of the main computer, he was about medium height with frizzed brown hair he had on a white skin tight full body jumpsuit, he was spooning granola into his mouth and smacking has lips while staring at something on the counter, you would think I'd be jumping for joy that there was another human but I was so use to this weird unexplained things coming up in my life that I didn't question the sudden appearance of this man, though this wasn't that shocking it was hard to interact with him, it was like even with the tiniest of surprises had my lips glued I guess I really was so shocked I couldn't utter a word hoping he would say something to me, there of course was the possibility that I was getting even crazier and this was just a hallucination. My eyes were locked onto him and saw every breath he took, then as I stared for about a couple minutes I saw his right eye look at me and he paused from eating the granola, I was now just froze in place with his icy stair and could not look away, then in a flash the man chucked the bowl of granola at the ground and yelled at me.

"What the hell are you looking at?"

All I did was flinch at the bowl being smashed but was still froze with the shock, the man then said.

"What are you deaf answer me I'm a human not a monster."

I then spoke.

"How?"

The man responded with a confused look.

"How not?"

Then he grabbed what he was looking at on the counter, it was the picture of Wendy, he looked at the picture again and extended his hand to give it to me and while doing so he said.

"You got a hot piece there."

With that remark my emotions boiled and I unfroze to lunge at the man, tackling him to the floor with flying fists I could not help but smash my knuckles into his face one after the other only to stop after hearing him scream for his life, I rolled off him, he sat up and gave me a mean look while whipping the blood from his nose, he spoke again.

"I was a little out of line but what was that?"

I gave the same angry stair.

"She's a human, dead or not she deserves respect."

He looks to the picture on the floor then back to me with a lowered head.

"I'm sorry for your lose was she special to you?"

"Yeah she was and she still keeps me going."

We stood and shook each others hands, hands locked I asked,

"So who are you?"

He grinned.

"I don't know hopefully human."

I stood in silence thinking,

"Dame that's what I would have said."

Then I replied.

"Uh no, what's your name?"

He sat down at the main computer with his lowered head again.

"I don't remember."

I then asked.

"How did you get in here?"

The man looked up at me with a puzzled look.

"I don't know."

I sat at the other computer and we locked eyes I knew this was very strange but based on all the other experiences I've had I learned not to question things just play along as best as I could, I looked to see the pieces of the bowl.

"I see you've had something to eat."

The man grabbed the bowl and tried to hand me it.

"I should have asked if I could have it sorry."

I grinned.

"No no it's okay I have more than enough here for more than just me."

Then I grabbed the bowl pieces and sat it on the counter next to me, I looked to him again.

"Do you remember anything about the past three years?"

He put his right palm to his forehead and grunted.

"No not much I remember being thrown side to side hitting each wall of the station then an explosion and somehow I was here."

I slide back in my chair.

"Well I didn't let you in I guess you were so exhausted getting into my ship you passed out when you entered and don't remember it."

The men smiled and then stood.

"All I know is I'm here now so I'm better now than I ever was."

I stood to face him.

"I think this moment will help us both more then we realize."

As we smiled he leaned in to hug me, I stood with my arms at my side and just a big smile, I thought I'd never feel the touch of a human again, in the spur of the moment I wrapped my arms around him giving him a hug as well giving a small tear while doing so, we unhooked as I wiped my tears and said.

"Sorry about that I'm just so happy."

He chuckled.

"No it's fine I was close to breaking to."

I pointed to the Rec. room.

"So do you like movies?"

He stood there puzzled.

"Wait, wait you have a TV?"

I smirked.

"Yeah I've got hundreds downloaded to the DVR."

He patted me on the back in excitement.

"Well get the popcorn popping and let's party."

I wrapped my arm around his shoulder as we walked into the Rec. room.

"I only wish popcorn was space food."

As we entered I pinned the picture back to the wall my new friend stood next to the couch as I walked over to sit with him, sitting there he just stood and was staring into space well not literally but I could tell something was wrong. I stood from the couch and he still hadn't moved just standing there like stone, I snapped my fingers in his face but no reaction, okay now this was getting beyond weird I snapped again and then he shook his head in reaction, he looked at me and spoke in curiosity.

"Oh hey who are you?"

I just stood in shock.

"We met just a minute ago are you feeling alright?"

He walked around me and sat on the couch turning on the TV like he knew what to do even though not knowing how to operate it falling into the couch he said.

"So what's on today?"

I slowly slide next to him without taking my eyes away, he turned to look at me.

"Dude what is with you?"

"Is there anything you can remember except what you already told me?"

He was traced by the TV and repeating.

"Seen it, seen it, seen it."

Then I angrily yelled.

"Hey listen."

He turned to see me again.

"I'm questioning this as much as you am I real?"

Puzzled I replied.

"Wait don't you mean am I, meaning me is real?"

With just his blank face I continued.

"And wait what do you mean you've seen all of those shows before?"

He finally spoke.

"I don't know."

I frustratingly leap off the couch and spoke loudly.

"You're joking right after almost three years of you thinking you were the last person ever all you can utter is I don't know."

He tilted is head.

"Three years wow and only a lifetime more to go."

All I could do was slump back onto the couch being baffled by his response, after turning back to the TV he says.

"I've seen all of this anything else you want do?"

I raised my lowered head in my moment of confusion and turned to him again grabbing his collar saying.

"What's your game, why are you toying with me?"

The man then leaps from the couch and starts to yell moving his arms and hands in a motion with his words.

"I don't know what you want, you already know as much as you do"

I looked up at him.

"You mean I do, not you do."

He smirked.

"Do you?"

I growled.

"You mean do I, not do you what is your problem?"

He squinted now face to face with me and poked my nose with his finger.

"Look at it literally without the grammar mistakes."

At this point I was only more baffled.

"I don't understand what your're talking about."

The man was now nose to nose with me and he yelled.

"Are we real?"

I looked even more confused.

"What?"

Then he yelled grabbing my cheeks.

"Are you real?"

I shoved off his hands and smacked my head then yelled back.

"I don't know, I don't know."

Then the man lunged at me grabbing my neck.

"Well get knowing."

I threw him off smashing him against the TV cracking the screen of it, I leaped from the couch steaming with anger, he got up from the wreckage of the TV and stepped toe to toe with me then smacked me on the left side if the face asking.

"Am I real?"

I stood there even madder now holding back as best as I could then he smacked me once again.

"Am I real?"

I was trying real hard to not hurt him I yelled back in his face.

"You feel real."

He lowered his voice.

"I feel here but am I?"

My eyes widened and I finally realized if you and I were real or not I got his game he was, but he wasn't, was I or wasn't I were we real or not was this my slice of hell or was this my life, I cooled down and breathed calmly to respond.

"The answer is I don't know."

The man smiled then grasped my left hand to shake it then let go and backhanded me in the face.

"A more direct answer."

To just stop the craziness and violence I answered his demand as best as I could.

"Yes and no."

He smiled and gave me a hug picking me up and spinning around saying.

"Perfect, perfect."

As he put me down I couldn't help but beg the question thinking.

"If you're in my head I've gone crazy and that option has a reason to be real but if your a real human you're not telling me and just crazy yourself I know I am not that stable myself but I'm not that crazy yet, but there is no solid explanation for you being as there is no solid evidence that I'm a loon so the answer is yes and no I will never get the real explanation."

Standing there the man pointed to the picture of Wendy behind us.

"So Wendy what was she to you?"

I gave him another puzzled stair as I have often these days and asked.

"How did you know her name?"

He nervously says.

"Uh you talk in your sleep."

Well it wasn't much of an answer but I knew it was going to be the best I was going to get out of him, I answered his question.

"She was a close friend, I don't feel good talking about her to you."

He chuckled and said.

"Maybe if I heard about her I could remember something about my past."

"okay you want to wheel and deal I'd expect that from a person like you."

I continued.

"She was an Engineer like me, she was just one of the sweetest of all people great to be around but I was never the most social and getting close to her wasn't easy for a person like me I was to scared but with her and the Earths death my new mission isn't for me to survive it's to let the universe know there was a Earth and she was more than a human, she was my savior."

After that speech I plopped back on the couch and the man spoke.

"Wow that was a lot to take in alright I've annoyed you enough, my name is Taylor."

I covered my eyes and was in deep thought I said to Taylor.

"Wait somehow I know that name I know I don't know you but that name I only knew one Taylor but I can't put a face to it."

Taylor sat back down next to me on the couch.

"I know what you mean I've only remembered so few things after all this it's hard to remember what a good time was when there's so much pain in this life we lead."

I sighed.

"So what do we do now?"

Taylor got off the couch to lean the TV back up to show the giant crack on the screen he said with a laugh.

"Well we aren't going to fix this anytime soon."

As he lets go of the TV it wasn't stable enough to stand on its own so it fell backwards and broke even more and as we heard the screen smash further, Taylor tightened his face hearing the glass break peeping out a sorry and shrugging his shoulders, I stood and headed for the door saying to Taylor.

"You already ate why don't you help me fix up the main computer?"

We both went to the Control Deck and sat at the main computer Taylor asked.

"So what's wrong with it?"

"Nothing's really wrong with it at the moment, unless you want to break it like the TV."

Taylor wrapped his arm around my neck putting me in a head lock saying.

"Were going to get along just fine aren't we?"

Taylor released me and we grinned at each other, I explained the short version of the story about the connection boards and trying to reach someone or something passed Jupiter, Taylor sat there with his hand propping his head up.

"So is there anything else you can do to it?"

"I need extra connection boards but I don't have any left on this station but you, you were on a different station can we get there to grab more connection boards?"

Taylor looked to the ceiling and tapped his finger on his upper lip in deep thought then said.

"It was all really a blur I didn't see my station outside this one, when I woke in here."

"The only active station was this one were you on a escape pod?"

Then Taylor kicked the chair from under his legs and paced in circles.

"Look I obviously took some brain damage I can't remember shit so lay off about it."

I spun my chair around to face Taylor.

"Are you lying again cause you seemed to know your name pretty well?"

Then Taylor paused his pacing and waved his arms in the air angry pointing at me.

"I'm getting real tired our tension, yeah real tired."

Then he ran his hands through his hair, breathing heavily.

"I saw the name Taylor on my suit so I assumed that was me does that answer your question?"

I guess it kind of had to as I said I knew it was going to be the best I'd get out of him.

"Let's calm down, go get a water bottle."

Taylor walks over to the pantry grabbing a water and swigging it down then goes to sit back with me, running his hand through his hair once again and giving a calm deep breath.

"It seems that we have to focus on something different."

"Yeah we aren't coming across any new connection boards anytime soon."

We sat just looking into each other and I broke the silence.

"We could go back to watching TV but you seemed to see it all how is that?"

"I was stuck just as long as you what do you think I did to pass time?"

Then Taylor stood shaking his hands nervously, I asked.

"Are you doing okay?"

Taylor turned his head to look back at me with a tense brow look.

"None of us are really okay anymore."

"I get what you mean."

There sitting at the main computer I was tapping my finger on the counter looking into space trying to think of something to do.

"There isn't really much to do but watch a show or work on the station but the only thing you haven't seen is the logs that the crew made but those are a little to personal."

I stood from the desk chair and continued.

"I won't get much out of your story and I'd rather not reexplain my story so far."

"Reexplain you told me as much as I told you."

"Oh I understand your confusion this station has a video and audio recorder tapping every second of my life."

"I guess that's why I continued as far as I have cause if I can contact other life they may be able to find the recordings and know about the existence of Earth and the fight I made to further there legacy"

Taylor grinned and shook his finger at me.

"That's the difference between us, after all this time you care about others than yourself even if there here or not your a good person."

Then lowering his head,

"All I've done is survive for myself waiting for something to happen for someone to save me but you taught me I need to put my effort in to receive help."

Taylor then plopped on the floor.

"But what can I do I was only one human I'm a waste of your time."

I kneel next to him and raise his head looking face to face.

"That's your problem if you release the human in you it's harder getting it back you even explained the reason I'm here to help you now is because you some how put the effort to find me and I was your reward."

Taylor shoved my hand away and stood now staring down at me he pushed me over with his foot and yelled.

"NO, NO you're the better man and I've wasted my time, why do you keep me around?"

I stood to face Taylor.

"There isn't much choice here I can't just kick you out and we need each other as much as it's hard for us we are all that is left for a reason or not we make the best of it in our own way so stop bickering"

Taylor backed away and patted me on the shoulder.

"You're right it's just hard being hopeful when I've dealt with so much crap in recent years you've just kept it held in so well."

I chuckled and shook my head.

"There's a lot you don't know about my struggle but our timing lets you get to know me on a better day, let's figure out the computer problems later and just relax, you know I have a game system."

Taylor grabs my shoulders and shakes me with the biggest grin.

"You're now just telling me this, I never had anything like that on my station god it's been a good five or six years since I played video games."

Then I grabbed his shoulders and shook him.

"Then what are we waiting for it's been three years grab the snacks and stop lollygagging."

Taylor shakes me again.

"Video game marathon."

Taylor grabs a handful of snacks and water and we head back into the Rec. room and plugged in the game, I had played this same game over a thousand times beaten it and new it from inside out but this time it was like I was playing it for the first time all over again, the game was the same the colors hadn't changed it was all exactly as it always was but with Taylor it was like a whole new adventure, we sat there with our eyes locked on the screen hearing all the sounds of the game, as one of us heard the score go up from the game the energy got more intense and we hopped on the couch in excitement.

It only seemed minuets though it could have been a couple of hours later, I paused the game and look around the room seeing the mess it was still more looking like the city dump then a space station then I look down at my body not questioning that I was still in my underwear more of a caveman than a modern human, Taylor looked at me.

"Dude what's the matter."

"I look like a mess and so does the station does this not concern you?"

"No it's fine I was less or more of the same."

"It's been a few hours and this is getting boring wanna check out the Medical Lab?"

"Yeah I guess a new change of pace would be nice."

I shut off the game that was sitting on the coffee table to see what was left of the snacks that we brought in it was just empty bottles and pouches in fact I had my attention on the game I don't even remember eating any of it, there was a saying.

"Time flies when you're having fun."

Now that was more true than it had been in a long time, I shoved the trash to the floor with everything else then Taylor and I went to the Med. Lab, I hadn't had the need to go in there for so long it was untouched for a while and still was in terrible condition, standing in ankle high trash we took a look around and Taylor asked.

"So what did we come in here for?"

"I haven't shown you this room so I thought once we were in here we'd figure something out."

Taylor walked to the counter and as he walked along the counter he ran his hand across it getting the loose dust and dirt stuck to his fingertips now at the end of the counter he picked up a piece of paper asking what it was I asked him to hand it over so he folded it into a paper plane and threw it at me.

"That's not what I meant."

I picked up the paper unfolding it to see it was the recipe I made for the hallucinogenic drugs I made.

"Oh this is the recipe for the drugs I made it was nothing special."

Taylor walked over to me and grabbed the paper.

"Do you think you can make it again?"

I shook my head.

"No probably not the recipe was jumbled and was more based on luck than a solid mix,plus it's getting late we've had a full day we should get some rest and try it tomorrow."

"Yeah you're right we have a lifetime to figure shit out we don't want to run out of ideas so soon."

"Well you're the guest so I'll let you take the couch tonight, I'll pull up one of the roller chairs."

Now in the Rec. room I pulled in a roller desk chair and sat there watching as Taylor snuggled into the couch, he sat up a little to look at me saying.

"I want to say that today was far better than most in recent memory you could have turned me away but your a good person and that is the greatest quality anyone can have these days so keep the human part of you."

Taylor laid into the couch closing his eyes to sleep but all I could do is stair at his sleeping body I was unable to fall asleep for the longest time it seemed, the last time I fell asleep next to another living being it wasn't real, was I going to make a risk that big I didn't want it to end if it wasn't real but I had to sleep sometime and with heavy eyes I was forced to rest, my last glimpse of the night being Taylor still laying there, was I ready to lose him of course not but what happens happens and there will hopefully be some kind of mercy out of it, all I know right now is this person or thing whatever it is depends on me as the rat did but he sees me as more human and if it or he does I know that I wasn't totally gone yet, getting there but not yet.

Chapter 18

Here to stay

There was now a new thing to wake up to making the journey more fun and easy, well I don't know about more but it adds a new excitement to my hell at least I hoped and that's all I can really rely on anymore is hope it isn't solid and hell even causes more pain then happiness sometimes but that was all I had to go on fooling myself each day that what I was doing was going to be good enough to honer her, even with this Taylor here I feel that my job may never be done I know there's more out there.

Now a little in and out of sleep my eyes where still closed but I could feel this light going back and forth on my eyes and as I cracked them open I see Taylor waving a small pen flashlight in my face.

"Can you stop that, what are you doing?"

"I was making sure you were okay."

"Why wouldn't I be?"

Taylor just shrugged his shoulders.

"I don't know."

Taylor turned around as I awoke and he was shuffling through some papers, I could hear each paper crinkle I then gave a big yawn and felt even more tired than yesterday like I almost never got any sleep but I know I did, Taylor finally turned to face me again to show me the paper he found yesterday.

"I think I fixed your little code this new recipe should work great."

Taylor just stood there eyes bloodshot and arms shaking his hair was also really frizzed.

"Did you try to figure it out today?"

"Uh no I knew if we tried to fix the recipe today we'd be at it till night time so I woke about an hour after you fell asleep and figured it out so we could have fun instead of work."

Sunken into the chair covered to the neck in a blanket I smiled.

"That was real nice of you."

Trying to release myself from the blanket I popped my arms from the sides of the blanket, looking at Taylor he couldn't contain his laughter and fell to his back rolling in his insane laughter, I then threw the rest of the blanket off.

"I don't remember putting a blanket on."

Taylor then sat back up and whipped away his tears from the massive laughing.

"Yeah that was me I tucked you in you looked uncomfortable."

Then Taylor tilted his head winking his left eye.

"Wanna get high?"

I chuckled to suddenly stop and see him eyeing the blue liquid inside the test tube he was holding.

"Wait you're serious you want to get hammered right now."

Taylor grinned.

"Why not there isn't any other excitement anywhere else so turn up the jams and let's get wasted."

I knew the last time I did this it nearly killed me and I learned that my survival was the only way to redeem Earth so I need to do my job, I've done the best I could to try to reach other life and maybe that's an understatement in fact I knew it was, you know what I put my blood, sweat and tears into making the connection on the radio better I may have not found a planet but I found Taylor and he taught me that we all have our jobs to do to live in our current life but that was that those were jobs they were important and we all need to rely on each other for survival but it's our lives and we all deserve a break to be the real us and make new memory's that we can pass down in story's for the next generation so fuck work right now I not only deserve this break I need a fucking vacation.

I kicked off the blanket and rushed to the radio to turn up the 80's hits and as I turn to see Taylor swigged the bottle I didn't even question what was in it I ran over to him and swiped the tube and drank the rest, There in the Rec. room we waved our bodies to the music in a whipping fashion banging our heads in the air and jumping in place, finally the drugs kicked in and as the room was spinning Taylor and I grabbed hands and spun together, then things were getting to fast as I was losing my balance I flung Taylor over the back of the couch and he hit the ground on the other side, Wobbling trying to stay standing I ask.

"Are you all right?"

All I see was Taylor's hand come up above the couch making a thumbs up sign, things were getting a little heated and I feared we'd do something stupid and almost kill each other, I peered my head over the back side of the couch to look at Taylor and see if he was okay then out of nowhere Taylor pounces from the floor with an excited face.

"You know what would make this even more fun?"

"No what ?"

Taylor made the biggest grin I've ever seen him make but this one seemed more evil.

"Zero gravity."

Tyler leaped over the couch pushing me to the ground and raced out the door.

"Where are you going?"

Tyler peeked his head back into the Rec. room.

"Duh zero gravity."

Oh dear god he was serious this man really was a loon I knew that zero gravity might seem fun but mixed with drugs it could only lead to danger, I chased Taylor out the door to see him open the rewire controller on the wall, he grabs the lever that will release the anti gravity but before he does he turns to smile, with a nervous look I beg.

"Please stop you don't know what you're doing."

With his evil smile he pulls the lever.

"Come on let's have an adventure."

As I lunge at Taylor my legs lift off the ground as dose Taylor himself, he floats away in the opposite direction saying.

"An adventure."

I cling to the wall and crawl at Taylor.

"I've had enough adventure in my life so far."

I passed the anti gravity switch while chasing Taylor so I could have just turned the gravity back on but I had told him no and this was still my place I just wanted to smack him, Taylor just floated there making faces at me.

"You just need to lighten up dude."

I kicked the side of the wall propelling my body at Taylor making us clash, our bodies smashing against each other causing us to spin through the Control Deck, now on the other side of the room we hit a wall and I heard Taylor scream from his back being pounded against the wall, Taylor shoved me off making me fly across to the other side of the room hitting my back on the opposite wall Taylor says.

"I was trying to have a little fun so I make the best of the situation and you can screw off."

Taylor wall crawls over to the lever and switches back on the gravity as we fall hitting the floor we both groan in pain I stand.

"There is a difference between fun and deadly."

Standing I hold my the side of my head with one hand and the other hand on the side of my stomach, with droopy eyes and starting to stumble around I almost can't keep my balance, Taylor limps over putting my arm around his shoulder to help walk me back to the couch, as we wobble Taylor starts to weep.

"I'm real sorry I just wasn't ready to take on the responsibility of leaving a legacy for Earth as you were it's just to much to handle for a person like me."

I stopped our walking and look directly at Taylor.

"Stop your bellyaching it's not you it's your mind I know we can still be worth something in this universe, you know that to you just haven't got that through your thick head yet."

Taylor cracks a smile and he continues to limp with me to the couch dropping me there on the cushions, I sit up.

"Wait put me on the chair you can have the couch."

Taylor turns away to sit on the desk chair.

"I can't let you sit here you've done so much for me and I've been so selfish it's my time now to take care of you."

Before I laid back down I smiled at Taylor as our eyes locked and he stood I asked.

"Hey can you get me a bowl of granola?"

Taylor grins back picking up the pillow on the desk chair and chucking it at my head hitting me in the face.

"don't push your luck."

Taylor was heading out the door and I threw the pillow at the back of his head, he made no reaction like it didn't effect him in any way, now laid back on the couch I was once again met with the white ceiling and no ruckus with only my thoughts at this point I could tell the drugs were wearing off and I was felling like my head was pulsating it didn't really hurt though it was more of like I was starting to get back to normal or as normal as I could in this situation. I lifted my head to look at the doorway, a few moments later Taylor enters with my granola, then a new thought hit me why did I look to the door before he even was there.

I mean I knew he was going to return and could have waited till he was at my side to acknowledge him but what had just happened was something I hadn't felt in a long time it was like instinct like I knew he was only seconds away, I don't know I shouldn't think to much onto it, it was a waste of a thought, Taylor now at me side had the dry granola with him.

"I didn't think you would get that for me."

"It's fine what else do I have to do?"

"Thanks bud."

As he holds the bowl over my body to hand it to me I was just about to grab it but he had that evil grin I could see in the corner of my eyes and instead of giving it to me he empty's the bowl onto my chest.

"What you do that for?"

"Come on it was just a joke."

"I might have said this before but I'm getting tired of your jokes."

"You have and they're still funny."

Taylor has his laugh and goes to sit back on the desk chair with that big grin, I sweep off the granola then stood and walked over to Taylor patting him on the shoulder.

"You said you wanted to be more useful and make your life worth wild still so let's get started survival takes no breaks."

"I don't know right now you're hurting man you deserve a break and what could I do?"

I stood there staring Taylor down he was right but to survive you need to fight, my skull hurt from the wounds my limp leg always stung my side was throbbing but I need to forget the pain and let me tell you I wanted to quiet but quieting meant death and there was enough of that, I grabbed Taylor's shirt collar pulling him up on his feet.

"Stopping means death you are a slug, time for partying and moping is over I've had glass in my head, my knee popped out, blisters on my fingers and almost bleeding to death, I survived all that and you made it this far as well that tells me there's fight in you now to your feet soldier slack means stopping, stopping means death, death means you failed Wendy and that won't happen ever."

I release Taylor and we just stair at each other in shock without words, finally I broke the silence.

"Let's get started."

We slug to the Control Deck and sit at the main computer.

"I feel I've done all I can with the connection on the computer, but here's something to think about somehow you got here and if someone was not able to contact through the radio they could see the station but not from a greater distance."

"So what's the plan?"

"Well from a distance the station isn't that visible so if we could tape some reflective thing to the side of the station the glare would be seen at a farther distance."

"Do you have one of those emergency blankets, there made of a foil like thread it would give off a glare."

"Yeah you're right we just need the emergency blanket and then something to stick it to the side of the station."

"What about that glue gun you used to make the rat cage."

I tilt my head looking curious at Taylor and thought.

"How could he know that I swear there's been two or three times he's known a little to much about me."

I responded.

"How did you know that?"

Taylor gave me the same curious look.

"Oh you talk in your sleep."

"Never mind just forget about it."

We stood from our chairs and headed into the Med. Lab grabbing the emergency blanket in the lower cabinet along with the glue gun on the counter, we entered back into the Control Deck near the exit hatch, I sat the supplies on the counter near me, Taylor came up from behind me and grabbed one of the five space suites left, if you do remember one was pretty much destroyed when I knocked myself out in it, I guess it wasn't a total loss I was glad I still had the other four suites, Taylor zips down the space suite to get in but before he does.

"Uh no I think I'll handle this one okay."

Taylor smirks.

"Alright you're the Captain."

I zipped up into the suite, hooked up a new air tank and snapped on the helmet, everything was now air tight and I was ready, Taylor unfolded the emergency blanket.

"This thing is to big we need to cut It in half or it's going to be to much of a hassle to put up."

He was right and I was glad I hadn't released the air into the suite yet I can't afford to waste this stuff, Taylor grabbed some scissors from the desk and clipped the bottom of the blanket ripping it open and then tearing the rest in half with is hands, Taylor handed over the blanket and stood at the air hatch to open it so I could go outside, Taylor pulled the lever to open the hatch and I entered the air release chamber, as Taylor was closing the door I stopped it with my hand.

"This is going to be a dangerous job whatever happens you stay here there's no reason for both of us to die so just wait till I tell you to let me back in, got it?"

"How are we going to communicate?"

"There's a mic in my space suite it's connected to the main computer you'll be able to hear me through there."

He gave a wink.

"Okay you got it."

Taylor rushed over to the main computer the plopping into the roller chair, I closed the door and as I entered the small place between the interior of the station and the dark cold endless space all I could think was.

"This was it, the new big thing to continue my mission and once I step out in the endless void I was getting one small step closer to really figuring something out in my life."

There was a small porthole on the door leading outside the station and I could see many upon many of chunks of what was Earth floating through space, I knew that was something I had quiet a problem with before not being able to predict the pattern flows of the rocks so hopefully I won't get pinned against the outer wall again, I probably shouldn't gloat but I feel I need to tell myself.

"I've had my ups and many more downs but it seems life is slowly letting me get along, I don't really expect anything and don't have many other goals but these little happy moments last and it let's me know no matter how low I go I always will have my mission and in time I won't find the happiness it will find me."

Chapter 19

Are you reading me

This was it the next big part of my life my next step into my mission and quiet literally all I had to do was open the hatch and take the step outside, before getting into all of this I had to remind myself that what I do know to me was something I needed to do for everyone I ever knew and loved, it may not go accordingly or have the effect I need or want but I know I have to believe that this will change me for the better. I stood in the small space between the door to the endless space and the other door to my home, I was stiff as a board I wanted to open the hatch and just finish my goal but this was one of those very unpredictable missions that could go wrong fast and way worse than I could imagine so if I went outside it was finish or don't I couldn't let my loved ones legacy die cause of my doubts, that's what I knew from now on I put all of me into something or give up and fail my whole purpose even if I still have one that was or wasn't intended if there wasn't a reason I lived I made one for myself and the worst thing I could do with my life now was fail.

I patted down myself making sure that my air tank was connected and that the helmet mic was intact, I took a deep breath and closed my eyes for a second then just went for it, grabbing the hatch I slowly opened the door and floated to the outside, I opened my eyes to see such a wonder there was the sun brighter than ever peeking through the rubble of the Earth, the door slid closed behind me as I hooked my line to the side of it, I had the emergency blanket and the glue gun in the pouch the blanket came in, the pouch was strapped to my side as I pulled myself to the outer wall of the station, I spoke to Taylor.

"Can you hear me?"

Some frizz came through the mic then I could hear Taylor's voice clearly.

"Yeah I'm here."

As I scaled the outer wall making my way to the right side of the station I answer back to Taylor.

"I'm on the right side now I'll shimmy my way to the front, you should be able to see me on the windshield."

I could hear a small chuckle under Taylor's breath he responded.

"Alright I'll try to keep my attention, ha windshield what wind we're in space."

I bent my brow and burst out in anger.

"NO SCREWING AROUND!"

"Okay okay, clam down."

I crawled across the right side taking a small step each time as I got to the corner of the front I pulled out the blanket with one hand as I held onto the station with the other, I needed to pull out the glue gun but I had to keep the blanket in place so I had to let go of the station to do so, I was roped to the station but I had never been so far away for the entrance and just floated, last time I let go the strap was pinned to the station by a piece of Earth but I had to grab the glue gun and float it gave be the jitters. I push the blanket to the outer wall as hard as I can so I have some kind of leverage on the station then grab the glue gun with the other hand, pulling the glue gun out I pull my other hand away to grab the glue gun and just as fast pin the blanket to the wall with my free hand that had the pouch around it but with the speed my arm was going to catch the blanket the pouch strap flew off my arm and floated away behind me into the field of asteroids. I didn't think to much into it all I was taking back was the glue gun that I could just carry back in my hand, I pushed the blanket up onto the outer wall and sprayed the glue at the bottom of the blanket away from my hand knowing that I'd be able to feel the heat of the glue and didn't need that injury upon the many others I already had, slowly gluing the rest of the edges of the blanket on then I got Taylor's attention again.

"Taylor I'm finished out here get that door ready to open."

He responded but it was all crackly and I could almost not make out what he was saying, I could tell he knew what I said with his response sounding happy but it wasn't really able to make out many words, The blanket was placed and I shimmied my way back to the door and halfway through the right side I tried to connect with Taylor again.

"Taylor get that door ready I'll be there any second."

Making my way around the right side I felt a small rock gently hit my side, taking a look behind me I could see the pouch I dropped had sent some of the other rocks astray making few of them hitting the sides of the station, turning my head back to get around the corner and back to the door I didn't expect a off course rock hitting the glass of my helmet and as it did my head whip-lashed on the back of the helmet, readjusting my head I clear my vision to see the glass on my helmet crack and I could easily hear the air leaking out, I radioed for Taylor but all I could still hear was more frizz on the line.

"I don't know if you can hear me but get a oxygen mask and air tank ready for me I can't explain now but I got about a minute before I lose air and die."

The hole was bigger than the last crack of the last helmet so I was losing air much faster, I had about a minute to reach the door and open the hatch and enter the station while doing all of this I also had to hold my breath, I took a deep breath and held it, I knew if this glass wasn't sealed I'd have less time to survive so I was forced to drop the glue gun and cover the split of the glass with my left hand and pulling myself to the door using my strap with my right hand, as I counted down the seconds I was now at the door and felt more light headed I pulled open the latch and entered the air lock, The room was light red so this had indicated that the room wasn't air purified yet, still holding my breath I pounded on the door hoping Taylor would turn on the air purification but I only now had less than thirty seconds before I passed out and died so I pushed on the dial next to the door and set the air purification myself, the light turned green and the door latch to the station unlocked the air was fine to breath now but it being able to make it to my lungs and keep me awake was not possible in the time I had the benefit in this situation was that I was now in the station and the fresh air was able to get into my system as I was passed out, I just only hope I would be able to make it to a oxygen mask before I passed out. I pushed open the door and stumbled into the station, tripping over my feet I feel to the ground and smashed the front glass of my helmet onto the floor busting it wide open and glass now spread over the floor, I opened my mouth to let in the air and coughed up some blood mumbling for Taylor.

"Taylor, Taylor you bastard where are you?"

I pushed myself to my knees and see Taylor nowhere in site I yelled out for him but there was no response I knee crawled over to the space suite storage and stripped off my old one now with two helmets destroyed I only had the other three left, I grabbed a oxygen mask from a storage bin below and hooked it to a fresh air tank. Breathing slowly into the mask I was able to relax, some of the blood I coughed up was pretty thick and drips of it stuck to my goatee so as I breathed in the fresh oxygen I was also spitting in and out the blood and getting it caught in my throat making the oxygen harder to go in and out making me cough more, I stood from the ground and limped to the bathroom to rinse out my mouth and hoping to run into Taylor but he wasn't in the Rec. room either where the hell was he, bursting into the bathroom I turned the sink on full blast and scooped the water in my mouth gargling it and spitting it back in the sink, I reconnected my oxygen mask and the air was coming through crisp and just fine, my throat stung and I wasn't really able to speak and knew I shouldn't but I couldn't help yell the best I could to find Taylor but doing so only made my throat throb and sting more making me grasp my neck in pain as I yelled Taylor's name.

I dragged my feet into the Med. Lab that being the last room of the station but he wasn't in there either the only other place was the engine crawl space but I was sure he didn't know about that, I limped over to the manhole and unlatched it open to stair into the deep hole seeing nothing but the darkness then letting out the last bit of strength to yell for Taylor one more time and as I did I felt a sharp pinch in my throat and my warm blood traveling up my windpipe and spitting it up all in the inside of the oxygen mask. Crawling away from the hole I ripped off the mask and whipped off the mass of blood covering my face just smearing it rather than cleaning it, I coughed again and again in small bursts spitting more blood on the floor by my face and I just couldn't take the pain once again breaking into tears and falling asleep, it seemed that was the only way I slept these days either in my tears or my blood I was so exhausted I just can't care about Taylor or really anything else anymore I can't afford a break but I need one, I need a person with me but can't get one I have a mission and don't even know were to begin with it, I laid there only in my boxers on and the oxygen mask hooked up sitting my head in a puddle of blood as I drifted away to hopefully a good dream.

 I woke hours later with my blood crusted on my beard and the oxygen tank all used up I lifted my body to sit up on the floor and there was still no Taylor, I should question it I really should but there's been so many weird things and bullshit that has happened to me in the passed three years so I will just focus on my mission of impossibility as long as I can, it is a terrible thing to say but Taylor's on his own wherever he is and as good as a friend as he could be I just need to move on to the next event and not let it bother me that was the endless battle, I knew I needed to keep my humanity but to survive to deal with the pain and sadness I needed to forget the human me and keep my life simple it was a conflict I will never be able to fully explain or deal with in the right way but as long as I remember what I am honoring no matter how low I go I will always find a way to tread on.

 I stood hunched over while limping to the bathroom once again gargling out the blood and rinsing my face off, I raised my head and took a deep look into the mirror noticing my hair was going passed my ears and most of the cuts where healing up my beard reached halfway down my neck so I was starting to grow out my hear again and hopefully it was here to stay, I exited the bathroom heading to the Control Deck and sitting in the roller chair, I bent my bum leg back in forth to get it back up to strength, it felt like less work to move it so the tissue must have been healing, I looked to the main computer and noticed nothing had been changed like it was never touched and out of the corner of my eye I was happy to see the edge of the emergency blanket peak over the side of the windshield, knowing it stayed intact made me feel more accomplished, as much as this thing with Taylor puzzles me I needed it out of my head I know he was another human being but if I was to focus I needed to let things figure themselves out and hopefully get some answers later and that wasn't the only problem on my mind, I had finished the whole emergency blanket goal but what was next the best thing I could hope for was someone or something would see the sparkle of the foil and try to make contact. I sat there with my head planted into my arms on the desk, hunched over with my face buried into my arms I whimper then raise my head smiling and thinking.

"This was just a set back like everything else I need to keep my spirit up and just keep looking forward."

I chuckled uncontrollably faster and faster thinking.

"There was no real reason for me to keep continuing my life was hell and the roller coaster was never going to stop, I put up with my sorrows and wait for the next small piece of happiness that is only a illusion, these moments of figuring out more things to do to help my situation are of few in a long life of pain, so why try to complete the mission of giving honor to a women I never had the guts to say I loved her, it was a endless battle and will only end with my death there is no finding other humans or other life space was a endless void of pain that taunts me with the false hope I continue to hold into without the answer why and what made me not give up even knowing the way I would end."

Laid back in the roller chair I slowed my chuckling to a stop with my eyes locked on the ceiling, with the nights rest I got I wasn't at really any better health but there was a job that needed done and for real no good reason at all and do it was better than wasting away, I placed my hands on the arm rests of the roller chair and pushed myself up to stand then shuffled over to the pantry to get a drink, as I sipped a bottle of water and looked around to see a lot of the trash from the food and water I already used up, as I have said in the past I can't get an exact number of days it's been since the start but I can safely say it has most likely been almost four years and this station was built to last five years for five people, before the start the supplies was already used for two years already and I am now by myself so the rest of the supplies should last for a great while, I just knew that it wouldn't last my whole life so I should be thinking of other resources to live.

For a couple hours I cleaned up the floor and shot out the trash so I could get a good number in how much supplies I could stretch, with the place cleaned now I reviewed through the food supplies and figured I was plenty good after I counted out thirty or so years of food and water, other resources I hadn't considered was the water for the sink and shower it wasn't recyclable like the air was, the tank of water was below me in another crawl space connected to the one that went to the main power, the water tank was also located near the cooling system, the better situation of having not as much water for showers or the sink was that I'd probably last a good while knowing that I was hardly ever going to bathe and even then if I did run out of that water I could use the bottled I had, although at that point I'd rather stink than die of thirst. I should check the water level, all I really knew about the water was that it was going to be astronomical getting five years worth of water on such a small station so once a couple month we had Earth send up more but now that not being a option at this point it was more of a guess, I really had to think back before all this shit I knew that we hadn't probably refilled it before we were to move to the new station but I was sure it wasn't that long since we filled it at that point, If I remember right we only have the refill for about every few months, I hardly used the water since then and it had been at least three and a half years after that and the water was still running, I'll just have to use it at only the most needed moments, I defiantly wasn't going to check the tank anytime soon with my bum leg but I knew it was never going to be fully healed.

Alright I've rambled on the math and details enough I don't think I know I need a good well deserved break if I can even get that for about a minute before my world implodes and I risk my life staying alive, I grabbed a water then closed the pantry and shuffled my way to the couch, laying down and taking a small sip from the water then placed it next to the foot of the couch and of course once again I was laid flat on the couch staring at the endless white of the ceiling falling into a sweet dream hopefully.

Now with more of the lack in the detail and excitement of my life I was able to remember my dreams more clearly this one was even more unusual than most I stood in a room with no end no exit and a endless color of white, I had my current hair style but instead of the stained boxers with my mess body hair visible I was in a loose fitting white shirt like the ones pirates whore and also white jeans with white sandals. I didn't question the odd things of my real life so why ever question something I knew wasn't real it was just an attire I would never wear, this setting I was dreaming in was as I said a void of white with no end an nothing in site, this wasn't scary to me it was more of what is my current home.

There was nothing but my thoughts no noise at all then suddenly a crack in the floor below me caught my attention it made a loud sapping sound and got bigger by the second as the crack spread below me the floor also lifting from the original level it stood, I was froze with fear not knowing what to expect, my legs wobbled above the crack and I felt as if I was going to fall, now as the floor lifted higher and higher I see a white spike poke from the floor along with a small platform for me to stand on. I stood on the platform and waited for the next unpredictable madness I clinch my eyes shut and could only hear explosions and it abruptly stopped, I slowly opened my eyes to see I was on top of a high mountain seeing the misty blue sky, looking down I see the lower parts of the mountain all sharp edges with deadly spikes, even further down there was a thick layer of mist that made it unable to see the bottom, I hear a soft voice from below, looking to the lower right side of the mountain I see there was Wendy clinging it the tip of a cliff wearing the same beautiful white dress as before, I felt so weak I knew none of this was real but I felt so helpless it wasn't her but I needed to help her but if I moved I would fall off the platform and smash into the spikes below still unable to safe Wendy, she yelled my name for help but I was frozen with fear, I couldn't take my eyes off her and was no help I shed a tear and see her lose grip falling into the mist and I scream her name the best I can past the balling I made. The mist rose and wind blew snow into my face, the temperature only got colder as I stood there nowhere to go shivering in place then as the mist stopped a few meters below my feet I see ice freeze the mountain and travel up closer to my feet, my lower body was feeling more numb and I looked down seeing the ice cover my feet gluing them to the mountain, I wiggled my body to move and broke loose but also lost the balance I had falling forward into the mist and as everything went gray.

I sprung awake from the dream shaking back and forth in the couch I was freezing it was so cold in the station and I couldn't explain it maybe it was my brain playing tricks on me after the dream I had, I grab the water I opened earlier, sipping it I noticed there were small ice pieces at the bottom of the bottle and that was highly out of the ordinary then stepping to the floor I had one foot on the ground and retreated even faster back to the couch the floor was so cold it almost hurt, there was something definitely wrong, it had to do with the temperature of the station obviously, about a topic earlier I had said I wasn't going to check the water tank well the water tank was past the heating unit, my leg was fine for now and I was having no problems with it so the plan was to go check the heating unit and figure out this mess.

I stepped back on to the floor that I swear was an ice rink, standing from the couch I stood straight up and took a step slipping with the first inch I moved and falling back onto the couch, It must have been worse than I thought, the metal floor was so slick from the moister it was going to be a task to get to the manhole I was going to have to army crawl but I also wasn't wearing anything I needed to get clothes on somehow so I could crawl on the freezing metal and not attempt to tip toe then bust my ass, this quest wasn't in my favor, well was it really ever but my point is this was a little overboard and was going to be a bitch to deal with but dame if I won't try, I feel I now have to look at each new mountain I cross I will risk my life and expect the worst to come but there is no lake of fire or sea of monsters I will not attempt to tackle for my mission and sometimes the luck I have blinds me of what the real mission is or if it even really matters for the hell I go through and somehow I come out of the waves of fire and keep a bright smile for the future is that dumb or is it myself letting me know I have more power over my life than I think.

Chapter 20

The new ice age

Fully awake I was thrust into another crazy series of events, I may be over hyping my situation the floor was pretty cold and I could stand the temperature for a bit but moving around was going to be an issue, I hadn't expected this to happen, I left the heat normal for the place and with the lack of social standards I mainly always wore only my boxers, I could walk around bear foot but only for a couple minutes before it hurt, it was like a burn but it was so freezing that to much contact would harden my skin and burn, science was weird like that I just had to make it to the heating unit down the manhole, there was this thick pillow I used to sleep with on the couch it was thick enough that the cold wouldn't get through the threads, it's not like the floor was covered in ice I really shouldn't worry that much.

I dropped the pillow on the ground and then fell chest first on the pillow and started to slide myself over to the other side of the couch on the side farthest from the door, I wasn't going to make it far without proper clothes, I knew the closer I got to the heating unit the cooler it would get, at the dresser I put on a shirt, some pants and socks. Having to stand and endure the freezing pain on my feet of course, now with the proper attire I was able to tip toe to the manhole, spinning the hatch to open it I felt a gust of chilling air blast my face looking down the hole I couldn't see a thing the light for the shaft must have shorted due to the moisture the cold was causing, I pulled open the Captain's personal box to see if there was anything worth using, there in the corner of the box was a mini flashlight so I grabbed it then noticed the small bottle of liquor I was saving for a numbing factor that made me remember about Taylor, it was that time he stayed up all night making the experimental drugs I guess the liquor had slipped my mind, now I think about it the liquor would be a lot better for a last meal.

Okay I know this is a strong subject and really not the time with the current issue but I know it's unavoidable, with all of these crazy problems that no man should deal with was I going to be lucky to live old or were one of these wacky events gonna get me killed, it seemed I do over come the mountains but I'm never the same person after so should I die defending my life against space or end it right now failing everything I worked my ass off for, I have always said that wasn't an option and I need to have some kind of self worth even without one, I think to survive in this world I need to lose the human in me but to keep me and my old life and the remembrance of those I knew I need to have a more logical and reasoning mind but those are two things I need more of these days, never mind about all that right now I wasn't there yet and will do anything to make sure it won't, I may not get any appreciation for the battles I fight but making myself believe there was a greater goal out there to carry on the memories of Earth made me never give up.

Back on topic I turned on the flashlight and waved it around the rim of the hole barely being able to see the bottom, leaning in head first taking a closer look I could see half way down the ladder there was ice covering it leading to the crawlspace door that lead to the heating unit, I touched to the first couple steps of the ladder and it wasn't helping that my legs were wobbling the reason being I was remembering the last time I had to do this, that was when I slipped and busted my knee bone out of place so I am not all smiles and hugs having to come back down here, remembering it only made me shiver more and with the bars covered in ice that was an extra deadly bonus, I just went as slow as I could taking my time.

Reaching the bottom I was still shivering and now my clothes were damped in melted ice making my body more cold, the small door that cut off the heating unit area and the rest of the tunnel was covered in thicker ice then the ladder was, I pulled the lever to open the door and once again being blasted with freezing air but this time also with clumps of ice like snow. I creaked the door open and to see the walls of the tunnel were nothing but solid sheets of thin ice, I hadn't thought it wouldn't have gotten this bad and definitely wasn't going to be able to dress the accordingly for this part, I'd just have to deal with the pain as best I could, the cold was most certainly going to get through the clothes I had on, it was better than just boxers but the water from the ladder already drenched into my shirt, I had a thin work out shirt with some sweatpants and thin socks, I laid in my belly and slid into the tunnel the walls were covered in thin ice but there were some handle bars on the side of the walls to let people pull themselves through the tunnel this made the trip easier that the handle bars were only cold with little water droplets on them and not covered in ice.

Now halfway down the tunnel my stomach was cramping tighter, I grunted in pain looking down the tunnel I see the heating unit and a big red light flashing near the control pad, one thing I didn't understand was that the heating unit was only controlled a few ways, it wasn't connected to N.A.S.A. HQ anymore, you could only mess with it through the manual control pad or the Captains personal control unit, I could have turned the heat up a little before coming down here but I knew this was more serious and I needed to check the manual control pad, inches away from the heating unit I was able to see the unit itself was covered in a mass of ice.

The unit from the view on the inside of the vent looked similar to a typical apartment heater but that was only what you could see from the front, behind the knobs, buttons and the touch control pad there was a bigger steel casing full of wires and electronic boards that allowed the wireless connection to adjust the setting, hopefully the thick ice that engulfed the necessary tools I needed to access weren't flooded with water being trapped behind the ice. I scratched at the ice patch but I only was able to peel off flakes, I had placed my flashlight below me and picked it up again there was a metal rim around the front of the light and I slide the tip of the rim on the flashlight against the ice, it was scraping off better than my finger was. After nearly ten minuets of picking at the ice I was able to see the touch screen that was still intact and usable but only through the now thinner ice I was able to pick at the last of it with my finger. I had expected that there was some kind of technical problem and a bunch of error messages but there was none of that there seemed to be no effect of any mechanical issues it was like someone or something that manually changed it, of course my mind went straight to Taylor, there was no way some one who could have survived in this condition at this range and what would be the point to make it so inhumanly cold, if Taylor was here why would he try to be away from me did I do something wrong, no if this made no since at all there has been unexplained happenings since the start and this was nothing new but the Taylor I knew he was real I think I just ignored that sad fact that something I never could figure out what happened to him and out of curiosity I yell for him.

"Taylor."

I only hear the the cold air blowing through the vents with no reaction in response.

"Taylor."

I yelled again but still no response, if Taylor was out there I would hope he would have answered me, was he avoiding me or was he lost in the twisting vents that were now more than ever a maze, the station wasn't really that big but there is many vents below the station that lead to the heating unit, water tank, waste tank, emergency escape pods and many of other things such as technical supplies and giant radio connection boards that allowed the wireless contact with Earth and the Russian space station. I look back to the touch screen and after a visual analysis it was obvious that there was nothing wrong with the heating unit somehow the temperature was changed without manual or wireless control, the station itself wasn't the top notch technology and building these weren't cheap so there were of course some resources that are better than others, most of the tech we had used on a daily bases was more prone to malfunction with constant long term use but we hardly changed the heat of the station, there was really no radical weather changes in space as there was on Earth so the heater was more for convenience, I guess it wasn't unheard of for it to get glitched but however unlikely I can't waste my mental energy on something I have already decided that it was just a glitch no need to over exert my energy. Looking over the front again there was no damage to the unit which only confirmed my theory more, I pulled my long arm sleeve over my hand and whipped the droplets of water on the touch pad and realigned the temperature to normal, now with the temperature normal the ice on the entrance vent interior would melt and I'd mop it later, I spun myself back around and crawled back to the manhole ladder.

At the ladder I waved the flashlight around to find the first step, doing so the light flickered and then went dead, with my health and being blind now it was going to be a pain climbing back up, the only light in the manhole was the light coming from the Control Deck, I left the hatch open but the light only lite just a little passed the rim of the manhole so I still had no luck knowing were my next step and I knew with my past injury if I fell I would snap my leg and most likely die down here, There was a saying.

"Head for the light."

or.

"Don't head for the light."

This phrase meant that someone was near death or it wasn't there time to pass on, the light referred to a place after death such as an internal happiness called heaven, I'm getting off the main intention of this comment, but what I was getting at was that I wanted to live but to do so I had to head to the light above it was quiet ironic, I've mentioned this briefly earlier but I feel I need to clarify better, I was blind down here, the bulbs that lite the manhole had malfunctioned due to the water from the ice seeping into the wires, the rest of the tunnels below the Control Deck had the emergency lights shut off to safe more energy for the rest of the station, the only light needed down here was the bulbs next to the ladder, that's why I had said Taylor could have gotten lost and if the heating unit glitched while he was lost he likely froze to death and wasn't able to find a way out without the emergency lights on. God, I had thought of going to look for him but I knew my flashlight battery needed replacing and it would rattle me beyond my own mental heath if I found Taylor, he'd be limp, blue faced and cold as ice with dead eyes, I don't know if I could handle that scene it would just be to much, I didn't want to say this but if he was alive he was on his own I couldn't risk also getting lost and if he spent longer than a day in the cold he would have died.

I waved my hand in front of my path to blindly reach for the ladder, my fingers ran across a bar and I knew that was the first step, I felt above me so I knew if I were to stand I wouldn't bang my head on the tunnel ceiling, there was nothing to stop my hand from extending all the way so I knew I was under the manhole shaft, I stood slowly while clinging to the wall using my hands to feel for and climb myself up from the floor using the ladder on the wall, my eyes were open but I wasn't even able to see my hand in front of my face, this climb I feel was going to be dangerous if not the most deadly thing I've done, my bum leg felt heavy whenever I walked and I was never going to run again only a slight jog at best so if I miscalculated even one step it was to the depths with me. It was easier to tell were the bars of the ladder where with my hand but my feet would be a little harder, and I didn't think of it till now but the ladder was covered in water making my grip harder to keep, this was going to be the hardest shit I've had to deal with, another thing almost slipped my mind I still had the flashlight but I wasn't going to be able to hold it and see the next step, I felt this was a life and death situation and it was worth risking the rest of the battery. I turned the flashlight on to see the first step on the ladder and now with my feet and hands positioned on the ladder I put the flashlight in my mouth and looked up, this was better but only gave me enough light to see the next bar above my head, I had to hold the flashlight in my mouth and I couldn't drop it if I wanted any luck so I wrapped my lips around the bottom of it and softly bit down to keep it in place.

I grabbed the next bar and could feel it was still pretty wet, holding tight I lifted my legs to the next step and could feel the water on the bar seep into my sock, I wasn't able to grip the bar my feet were on so if my hands slipped I was done for, I continued this at least ten more times going at a snails pace, as I grabbed the next bar I tilted my head higher up to see how far was left, I was able to see the light from the Control Deck peeking into the manhole closer and closer, the light from the Control Deck still wasn't bright enough to give off anymore light, with my head cranked up I was losing grip on the flashlight and it was slipping farther into my mouth making me lose the grip I had on it, I lowered my head trying to grip it better without letting go of the ladder but as my head leveled the saliva covered on the flashlight and I had to breath through my nose this whole time but with a throat full of spit I wanted to upchuck and I couldn't hold back and my neck re-flexed and I popped out the flashlight and spit up, the last thing I saw was the light spinning around into the darkness and as my vision faded I heard the flashlight hit the steel ground below.

I was now once blind again the only good thing was I was closer to the top and almost out and on the other hand that was the worst news cause if I lost my grip I'd surly die from the fall, I was hesitant but I gradually unhooked my left hand from the bar as my nerves were so tight my hand was fixed in a clinched position and I raised the hand above my head to feel for the next bar, it was somewhat easy to tell if I had a hold on the bar with it being more wet than the wall and I also could feel the curve of the shape letting my brain know that was what I was looking for, my feet though was a totally different story with my bum leg not having the nerves it once had, my best guess was similar to the same way I could tell with my hands but it was only a hunch, as I've said before I was able to tell if I touched a bar with my hand cause of it holding more water and the shape of it but with my feet my guess was that when I step on a bar it feels like a dim puddle and the front and back parts of my foot would feel unstable with some type of thing pushing up on the middle of my foot letting me know I was standing on a bar.

This process was even slower than my attempts only minutes ago, imagine a snail combined with a sloth, my slow pace wasn't the only issue with my nerves tightened I was getting freaked with the dark and lack of senses and that was making me shake, it was like my hands and legs were rock and were trembling with terror it was a mix of solid and loose like an earthquake, I could not count the minutes it took but I knew this section of my journey was longer than it was with the flashlight and after I could assume a little less than thirty minuets I made it to the top. Peaking my head out of the hatch my eyes were squinted and my sight was adjusting to the brightness and I slowly opened my eyes to make out that I was now halfway out of the manhole, I grabbed the sides of the hatch to pull my body the rest of the way out, now with my legs on the floor of the Control Deck and my upper body dangling over the manhole, staring down into the darkness I couldn't see the glow from the flashlight I dropped, the manhole shaft was really not that deep so I could have seen the light if it was turned on, the flashlight was a tool I had to have back but wasn't able to make it out through the void of darkness, it was made of a cheap metal and wasn't standard for N.A.S.A. I knew it could break and I had no doubts of that, best case scenario it just got shut off hitting the steel floor below and the odds as usual weren't in my favor, It was something I wasn't going worry over anytime soon.

I pulled myself away from the hatch before I fell in, I dropped the hatch and spun the wheel to lock it, sitting up I was jittery and propped my leg up to stand and stood hunched over looking at my feet, I slugged passed the doorway of the Rec. room and felt the heat kick on and with only seconds it was getting steamy I pulled off my shirt, then my socks and slipped off my pants walking behind the couch and glancing up to smirk at Wendy, always there as usual, I lowered my head back down and looped around the far side of the couch and threw my body motionless onto the couch, again as I ended each day I was greeted by the endless white ceiling that showed no character or any variation only looking more dull as the days went on. My body was weak my day was over I only did one thing and I was a wreck and need to replenish my energy, it was sad real sad it seemed with the long stressful and body wasting tasks I did to continue my survival it gave me less energy in the long run risking my heath and more accident pron only endangering my life more.

I closed my eyes into my dream hoping for a better day than most I had this was the cycle and it needed a changing real fast or I'd waste away doing the thing I needed to do for my survival, it was a hard cycle to quiet and as the events that occur do help me they hurt me more, and now I was back to square one what was the next event what was the next pain and would I be able to trudge along evading death one more day, the answer to the question could only be answered or close to figured out as the event aspired. I was to tired to give an aspiring speech tonight you get what I give you and now I wasn't only physically strained but also emotionally stressed beyond any level I thought was humanly possible and I hate to say it but was all of it really worth it well hell no it wasn't, no human can or should lead my life and it was becoming to much I wasn't giving up but I had no mission anymore, I loved Wendy I missed my loved ones but even if I find a better life I could not and could never get any appreciation for the hell I traveled, I will do the necessary things to stay alive but if a new life is out there it has to find me. I know this was a drastic decision and I wasn't okay with it but I had to be or one more of these insane missions would be the death of me, now I guess I wouldn't quit on it forever I just really need a vacation, time to heal my wounds and my emotions, it may be a endless venture with no real reason, as I said one of the few things continuing my life was attacking the next event, for now I must relax taking ease with my wounds, I mean look how far I've come and if I gave up after all I've accomplished.

"Thought it not being much."

Each struggle I made took a piece of me with it and I won't let the madness get me now, the greatest tragedy would be me letting go of all I work for and failing everyone that ever was had been or could have been on Earth, I deserve a break but I won't let myself fail the most important thing of all I will use my last dying breath to make it happen I'm sure of it.

Chapter 21

There is no day off

I woke for another day into the ever continuing madness, but before I start the descent I feel I need to get off topic to clarify a common theme that may be misunderstood, this log I make it is intended to tell the hard work I put in to let whoever is out there the legacy of the Earth and my struggles, I hope to be lucky enough to show my work in person, whether it be an extraterrestrial or somehow another human. I hadn't thought about it much but I do take a lot of liberty making this log since it would hopefully the majority of it being seen by a alien that most likely would not understand a word I say, if they're smart enough to travel trillions of miles I'd hope they may be able to translate my words, some of the quotes I mention are said and understood by humans so that's why I explain them more and that's the most detailed I get about human dialog, if I were to get aliens to understand every little thing I've done up to this point I'd be teaching them the English language and what every word means and my story's long enough so they have to deal with not getting it. Back to my main subject I was saying that I woke, on the couch I laid on my side with my arm laying under my left side and I rested my head on the back of the couch, the particular quote I was wanting to mention earlier before I went into the side story was,

"I need a vacation."

This was a thing people said as a joke after an exhausting event as I did, their situation was nowhere near my exhaustion or stress and I was more worn than most that quoted this, the plan today was nothing, I was going to sit on my ass, eat and watch TV, it wasn't much and benefited no one other than me and that's what was needed right now. I leaned over nearly tipping myself over the edge of the couch trying to grab the TV remote on the coffee table, then sinking back into the seat I turned on the TV, I had mentioned before that we had hundreds upon hundreds of shows on the DVR I think I nearly had seen them all after this much time, one of the many cool things with the TV was that we hadn't gotten cable hooked up but we had many empty channels that I was able to hook up a good number of shows to them, that made each empty channel have one show playing, making it feel as if I was watching live TV, I flipped back in forth on the list of around fifty or so channels then finally picking just a random one, I sighed deeply rolling my eyes and laying the remote back down, I pulled my blanket up covering my chest as I was sunk into the couch with my head adjusted on the pillow. I knew this felt like a bed day, it was one of those day where you wake up and as you are up for the day you spend the first two or three hours of your day still in bed, not sure how common that is but I've had quite a few of those moments.

I sat there mesmerized by the TV with my eyes locked on the screen and with my attention unhooked from the sweet relaxation of something so simple it felt like a once lost happiness that was now found, mind numbing but also something that gave me a feeling of doing a normal everyday thing, my eyes glued to the normalcy of such a simple object was interrupted by the groins of my stomach, that was nature for you my body let me know.

"Hey dumb fuck I'm hungry."

Lifting my body to sit up, I felt the blood moving back into my left arm from sitting on it for so long, humans could relate to that tingling sandy sensation that came with this feeling, I did the same that was now becoming the usual, I pushed down in the couch with my hands to lift my body up to stand with more strength that a human with my body type would need, with all the mental and physical stress made my thirty three year old body seem more like a fifty year old one, my legs were also just as stiff and I moved with only a few feet each step as I limped slowly out the door and into the pantry grabbing a bowl of granola and a water, I couldn't even barely keep my arms held up and had the granola bowl and the water hanging from my hands as they swayed while limping back to my throne. That thought made me chuckle a little I was glad I could still know the feeling of laughter, the whole throne nonsense it was only a couch but it was far better than the desk chair any day, it was the most comfortable seat in the universe of that I now so in a way it was a throne.

Back on the couch I sat up as I pushed play on the remote and resumed watching as I sat hunched over sitting in the middle of the couch, very slowly I scooped the granola while my eyes were still glued to what I was watching and with some time the food entered my mouth for me to chew, I wasn't really watching anything important and frankly I couldn't remember the scene as it passed I was just glad I was doing anything else than risking my life, there has been plenty of times I could have come in here and watched TV so it wasn't that miraculous but it was different enough. After two or three more super slow bites I did the same process with my water, clearing my last bite with a swig of water I couldn't stop myself I chugged the water feeling the stream of refreshing crisp water travel down my throat and not being able to stop such a good feeling I finished it to the last drop and then let out a reliving.

"Ah."

I lowered the bottle to look at its bottom rim to see I hadn't drank all of it leaving only a small puddle at the bottom, I was still hunched over holding the rim of the bottle with my fingers and still eyeing the TV not moving an inch, this would seem like the best situation, I was so distracted from my worries I was almost oblivious to my surroundings, that was till the new mini disaster took place which I always expected but not so soon.

I was interrupted with the abrupt darkness, the power going out had gave me a scare making me drop my water, I could hear the remaining water spill onto the floor and hit my bear feet, this wasn't like when I was in the ducks there I at least had a small light with me only somewhat blind, I could have been underselling myself I had lived on this station for about five years so I knew the layout fairly well, but of course not perfectly, I was able to feel around and get an idea of where I was like in the manhole, without the light I didn't know where the main computer was and if I typed aimlessly on it I could screw up the settings of the station and make this place a death trap, the only safe option I had was to go into the lower tunnels and turn back on the lights manually, if you could call it safe it wasn't but it was the best I could get at the moment. It wasn't like the total power was shut off the station it was just the main electricity, I'd be in even more trouble if the total power was shut down, that would mean that the stations gravity would fail and the station would either plummet to the Earth but since that wasn't an option it would likely spin out of control aimlessly at world breaking speeds into the endless space, my best option right now was to make my way to the manhole travel down grab the flashlight I dropped earlier and head to the back end of the station and switch the power back on, there was another saying.

"It's easier said than done."

That was more true now than ever, some people memorize or just know any amount of things so well it's something you'd never forget, like a first pet name or you first phone number, there either things you use or are around for so long or remember fondly that you could never forget it, what I'm getting at it that this place has been so much part of my life I don't even remember what Earth really felt like, god I've got to be seriously damaged if I can't even remember what grass felt like. No matter how well I knew the station I had to use different seances to find my way around, for someone that was blind it may be simple but with someone who didn't rely on touch I'd have more trouble than I intend, I feel I must oversell myself on this situation I knew the layout pretty well but a lot of the surrounding surfaces were similar to one another so I could be walking in circles, the time for talking was over actions were only going to get me moving forward.

I could still feel the water puddle that my foot was dipped in, standing like I normally did pushing my body off the couch I was standing but was froze in place with the fear of what the next step had waiting for me, this wasn't just taking each small step in the dark to get going, it was about taking that step that moved me into the next event of my life and even in all the pure darkness I was able to mentally see the light that I knew was in my future and if it wasn't I'd make it be, In the dark I lowered my hand to touch the couch that help me lead myself to the wall next to the exit, feeling there was no more couch left my arm dropped from the end of it and I was now out in the open darkness only being able to reach in front of me till I hit the wall. Mentally I knew that I was facing the wall and the exit was to the right of me, since I hadn't turned while walking from the couch I was for sure I was correct, traveling my hand on the wall as I walked to the left I hit another surface and I had assumed this was the door frame, taking to hands and spreading them out I hit a surface without fully extending them both so I was sure that I was in the middle of the doorway, maybe this was easier than I originally thought, exiting the safe Rec. room.

"If you could call it that."

I was now in the open darkness not able to feel out far enough to touch any surface, based on memory I could estimate I was near the main computer and only a few feet passed that was the manhole, if I was to find the manhole I had to feel on the floor to reach the hatch, it was weird not knowing how far from the ground I was and falling to one knee felt more like falling off a cliff without my vision. Placing my other knee on the ground I then lowered my hands reaching for the floor feeling the cool steel, feeling the chilling ground I grinned thinking it was better than doing it with the frozen over one, on my hands and knees I inched slowly with my head tucked in hoping not to bash it against something, my tensions were high with my fingers twitching as I crawled, I knew if I was to find the manhole I was to grip the wheel hatch on top so I needed to take bigger steps with my hands, with my twitching fingers and the cool floor my hands were sweating almost gluing my palms to the steel with my warm sweat. I lifted my hand moving it forward farther out till it couldn't extend any farther, I wiggled the tips of my fingers hoping to touch something but as I leaned I lost balance and slipped on the cool steel smacking my face on the floor.

Grunting and lifting my head I positioned back in place and felt a sharp pain on my nose, slowly bringing my hand to my face I felt a warm liquid seeping out, oh just great I had a nose bleed, there was nothing I could do about it now, for the moment I had to focus on one thing if I was to stay alive, back to the same game plan I kept inching with one hand held out and the other planted on the floor sliding it as I went, after a few steps I felt the blood from my nose drip onto the hand I was crawling with, it was moving slow and stop fairly quickly, after smashing my face and a snails pace deadly blind journey across the room I could feel the wheel hatch of the manhole, just repeat what I said a moment ago over and over in your head that sounds insane doesn't, how could going only a few feet across a room be so pearling, there was to much to not believe to go into but these days the smallest of things could kill you.

My sweaty hands gripped the hatch, I twisted the door open lifting it up in place opening the manhole tunnel, I know it seems I shouldn't have to worry I mean I've done this before but on the way up so it's nearly the same, nearly, I put my extended hand onto the ground inching it up the side of the manhole cover then slowly reaching into the tunnel, it was then I knew I was at the right place, sweeping my legs around and placing them in the tunnel I dangled my feet feeling around then I hit my heels on the ladder, this wasn't something I was taking lightly getting in the tunnel was harder than going down it, I slid my legs as slow as I could manage into the tunnel while I grasped the rim of the manhole, halfway in the tunnel my legs felt weightless as they swede, I pushed them against the wall placing my feet on the bars of the ladder, then I slide my hands down the surface of the wall grazing the bars level to my head.

I now was steady and clinging to the ladder, the best thing I could come up with was that I was halfway through my current hell, that was a bigger accomplishment than you'd think I may have walked across the room blind and put myself onto a ladder but this environment was the worst to be in with even the slightest disadvantage, the motions I took down the manhole were identical to my passed attempts there wasn't much out of the ordinary, I feel explaining this travel would just be me repeating myself so for the benefit of not being repetitive I will say it was smooth I was nerved racked and twitchy as usual that's as basic as is was. At the bottom of the manhole I ran my hand across the steel ground to feel for the flashlight, my fingers hit what I knew was the flashlight as I turned it on my vision became clear, the light was dimmer than it was the other day, I knew the battery was weak and would last me about ten minutes. I had to use my time quickly it would be hassle to lose the light again and get lost, I'd be afraid I'd never be able to find the manhole. I shook the flashlight hoping to get a better brightness but it only made the light flicker, staring into the light I see a drop of blood hit the middle of the lens, my nosebleed wasn't to terrible it had slowed but I didn't really have anything to plug my nose so I had to let it drip and dry up.

I placed my thumb on the lens and whipped off the spot of blood letting more light get through, the light was dwindling and I knew time for dillydallying was over I needed to make my way to the electrical system in about less than ten minuets and back or I'd surly die, glancing the light to my right I turn into the near crawlspace, slowly pacing down the tunnel my travels had also mimicked the same way as they did when I was heading down the ladder, with the light dimming I was only able to see a few feet in front of me, though there wasn't must to worry about I knew the general direction I was going.

I had not elaborated on the structure of the tunnels a whole lot, it was as straight forward as it could be, there were really no twisty turns each path had a lead off to another important machinery, but without the light and how well I knew the layout it would be a task getting back to safety. Though the heating unit vented up to the main deck the tunnels were fairly cool staying at a neutral temperature, to get anywhere down here it took a good couple minuets, there was five areas in the crawlspaces.

the first I mentioned was the heating unit, it was not in a smaller closed off room like the others, I had already stated this before but it's always nice for a refresher, the heating unit was just a medium sized board fitted on the wall that was covered in loose wires and a manual touch pad, down the tunnel from that was the water and waste tank they were in a closed off room from the tunnels but there was a small hatch leading to them, on the other side of the tunnel system was five escape pods used for only extreme situations, if something was to occur the escape pod were always in a ready state.

At the time N.A.S.A was working on long time living in space there was always the worry of a malfunction and a need for a quick escape, the escape pods are quite different than most expected, they were quite bigger than escape pods used in the Navy. These ones we designed were meant to head straight back down to Earth but the testing wasn't perfect so the navigation unit connected to its communication network was nearly perfect but as everything else it was glitched, that's why the design we made was a large pod so you could stand in with a lounge chair and behind it a pantry with a months worth of food along with the rest of the technical nonsense. The last room in the tunnel system was where I was heading, the electrical system was similar to the heating unit, it had a bored and touch pad same as the heating unit but that was just the front there was a hatch behind the board that lead to a smaller room with the massive electrical system, all this entailed the control of the lights on the whole station and tunnels, the on and off switch for computers, TV and other random tech, there was really just to much to list at the moment.

I didn't have a map but I knew the tunnels like the back of my hand, it wasn't helping that the light was dwindling and I could only see a few feet ahead, this had forced me to take a slower pace making sure that hadn't passed my destination, I felt I was about half way there, the crawlspaces were big enough I was only hunched while walking my way through and in combination with the lack of light and moving slow it almost was no better than being blind. Taking each step farther I could feel the air getting more cool, it seemed very unusual if the heating unit was acting up again I would just go ballistic, the last thing I need was to backtrack and fix the heater to. I drew even closer to where I was headed and as I did I could feel the air getting more crisper as I eased a breath out I could see a small air cloud form from the breath I made, at the moment I knew something was up and as usual the universe wasn't playing fair, I had no time to get to both places now so I had to just get the electricity fixed than recharge the battery on the flashlight.

In this dimwitted moment I was having it occurred to me that if the tunnels were getting cooler the heating was working still, on the lowest percent of power the only thing that was always forced to stay working was the stations gravity stabilizer but now I knew there was at least a affordable amount of energy being used to power the heating. I guess someone could have theorized that if the station was on lowest form of power for long the station would get cooler but only after a longer period of time at least power, so this cool feeling down near the electrical system was not caused by that and if not what then? Now at least two thirds the way it was getting even colder this was a strange situation, continuing to make my way I catch a stench of something vulgarer, it wasn't like fried wires that would be the most explainable, as I step closer to the smell I look to the floor and my light catches something that was like a blue substance in a puddle.

I raise my light to reveal what wasn't just another travesty this was much more, my heart wasn't sunk or broken it was my brain, it was an unimaginable site something that made my brain pop not only fear, sadness but also great anger. The blue puddle was frozen blood leading to the body of Taylor, pail blue stiff and brittle with a expression of no emotion just a blank face no frown no tears just a look of boredom. I couldn't stair another second I turned away looking back to where I came, as I came to a small whimper, it ran through my thoughts that the body was in my way I wasn't going to be able to step over it and I of course just wouldn't leave him there but I needed to grab his freezing skin and bone moving him hoping not to snap off an arm. I turned back to Taylor, in reaction I fell back in the shock of what aspired.

There gone, there the body had vanished with no trace, no blood, no ice not even an imprint, this was a little to much to handle I pounded my fist to my temple hoping I was dreaming, how was I suppose to react or do, this was out of my control even out of my reality, it was unexplained and frazzled me beyond the comprehension of these settings. The coolness eased to normal and I had no choice but to tread on, only this time I wasn't going to forget this, I couldn't. Stepping onto the spot I saw Taylor felt to weird, at first I knew I had to just leave it behind me but my first step was hesitant, stepping there gave me this guilty feeling like somehow I was hurting him, but I jolted for it getting across and continuing. Still crawling my way through the tunnel system, I was shacking my head in disbelief of the event that aspired, if it was some vision or hallucination then where was the real Taylor, where else could he have been but in the tunnel system.

My light was flickering and dimming even more as I tried to shake the flashlight getting more juice my vision was dimming even more, with the light fading away I could see less and less in my path then being able to just see only my hand in front of my face the light abruptly brunt out. In the darkness I was faced to the direction I needed to go, I was back to inching every step not wanted to bump into something and hurt myself, it seemed for any endless void there was nothing but the darkness. Faced in the right direction I could see a dim blue light illuminate from a far, as long as I did travel and knowing there was no working electricity I knew this light was the back light of the touch pad on the electrical system, this was a brightened moment.

I grinned keeping my eyes locked to the light and stepped forward to it turning the next corner and and there was the electrical system, at a first look there seemed to be nothing physically wrong with it, no broken knobs, no cut wires, it seemed the problem might have been a inner working of the technology. Typing some random testing patterns it also seemed the hardware wasn't hacked or tampered, it was very weird there was no trace of a disturbance all I needed to do was turn the whole system back on, doing this was uncomfortable for me I would only normally turn on the power I need for the upper level but with no light to travel back I would need to use the tunnel emergency lights, I just hope the ice from the heater malfunction didn't defuse many of the lights I relied on. The plan now was to head back up, charge the flashlight than get back down here to shut off the unneeded power till then was still the mystery as was the rest of time. I lived in the moment dealing with the hand I was given it could be a royal flush or a total bust, that was another Earth reference so you won't understand if any of this at all but that's beyond the point.

I won't bore you with the same back and forth story of traveling to the Control Deck, so let's just skip to there, I will however tell you I was lucky that most of the emergency lights along the tunnels were mostly intact so I had no trouble making my way back. With everything taken care of I was able to just relax, I could have taken the long nap I deserved but I was afraid if I did fall asleep I wouldn't wake in time by the time the flashlight would be fully charged, if I wanted to use the least energy as possible I needed to head back down there as soon as the light was ready, for a while I thought that what I needed to do to pass the time was to keep my mind occupied with the stations entertainment but it wasn't just that, what seemed to be the typical day was planing what I was going to do but it to be interrupted by a life and death situation, it wasn't as straight forward as it seemed but things just got more hard to deal with and at a point I expect it not to get only more harder but it would happen more often and get worse as time went on.

I have mentioned that these events do at times damage me in a physical way, like I know due to the dislocated knee I will forever have this limp, I not only worry about the physical injuries I mite indoor there is also the mental ones. Now I know this was a conversation that is well over due, I mean the site of Earths destruction would put anyone over the edge and don't get me wrong it did me but as sad as it was all I can really say.

"It was what it was there was nothing I could do."

It was as I said before this was something I think I could never really find out, my mental condition would never be the same in a good way or not, humans are kind of like clay, just the smallest change there was no way it could ever be in the same form as before we all change but as much as we work at our inner self we help our self esteem the best we can but are always different in the end. What I was trying to get at before is I went into something much bigger than me was that the best excuse I could make for my actions, reactions and reasoning was that I was human, we are an imperfect being, we can only take so much and it just builds and builds, it's not like I have some type of therapist up here I can't just unload my stress and get advice I was stuck with it all bottled up, in a way this log was therapy it gave me some kind of false hope I was actually accomplishing something.

For now I could assume a couple hours pasted I was slumped into the Captains chair with this dull face stained in my expression, I swayed in the roller chair side to side giving an icy stair over at the flashlight, the light was plugged in and there was a smaller orange light at the bottom of it indicating it was charging and with every second passing the charging light only made me more irritable, after so much time of the same old thing I was focused on waiting there to shut off the unneeded energy. Eyes locked on the charging light waiting for my life to continue I tapped my finger on the table slowly at first trying to take my thoughts off the irritating process but I was determined to get this over with. There was plenty I could have done to pass the time by but for what I deemed good reasons I wanted to only focus on the main mission, this let me know I guess I could still have a focused mind and haven't lost my morals.

My fingers tapping at a faster pace it felt like the orange charger light was burning into my soul toying with me, you know I waited and waited, I wait for years to make a life I deserved, to get into a good college, to get into space, this was bullshit I shouldn't have to appease something so menial as even time itself. I've gone without so many unexplained events, occurrences with no reason or logic if these oddities could happen to me why can't I change even the simplest of logic why was I as a human still confined to the rules of life I knew, if life wasn't fair now why was I still forced to play by its rules as if they were still established or mattered. Still gripped onto the orange light I felt the fire build in my head and in a moment of rage I pounded my fist on the table screaming for a second grasping one hand with the other then smashing the hand on my forehead for my moment of stupidity but that made my hand sting even more.

With my thoughts focused on my bright red hand I see behind it the flashlight battery light turn green indicating it was fully charged, my mind was racing I was fooling myself thinking somehow the universe was trying to toy with me, that was the main key to really all of this, I was just over thinking things and letting it get to me, but you see there was no way I could stop the deterioration of my mind all together I just had to slow its pace the best I could hoping the day I went bad shit crazy wasn't any time soon.

Once again I am needing to head into the tunnel system below I hope not to bore you with me repeating the same tasks over and over but it's all that's going on, but I can understand if most people won't want to hear of my travels in the crawlspaces for the umpteenth time, just be kind enough to let me take a brake from the story will you.

Alright I'm back it was as the passed few times the same typical story I went down there and did what was needed everything taken care of all fine and dandy and hopefully nothing unexpected to arise in the future but with me even mentioning that I already knew even without saying something to jinx myself that life was hell and I'd be a bigger fool not to expect something to go wrong. I am not trying to purposely repeat myself but these pass couple days or really however long it's been I've lost track by now, but it seems with all the similar and repetitive event it's felt like I have not slept in so long like everything was just one big day due to the matching tribulations I have dealt with.

Normally after something so stressful I'd want to just crash crying myself to sleep but found myself unable to get to sleep I was a little drowsy, I don't think it was that I couldn't get to sleep it was something more, kind of a gut feeling as if something was already amiss. I was there back slumped into the Captains chair looking side to side, nothing out of place all as it was left, then what was it, it wasn't as if I felt something was physically wrong with me or the station it was just a weird explainable feeling I guess the simplistic way to put it was like I felt I was being watched. In the chair stiff as a board I feel this cool sensation on my shoulder, peeking my head around to see a little behind me I could feel my back was chilled and glaring up behind me I see a small vent blowing cool air directly at my shoulder blades, I know I know your're going to say.

"Don't over react it's something simple don't get freaked."

It just wasn't as easy as that I tell you it wasn't I know good and well I only left on very little energy so this vent blasting the cool air at me would be hard to convince me it was a simple technical glitch and for such a tiny and unwanted inconvenience it wasn't going to bother me that much, it didn't use up much energy anyway, if I was going to head back down there I'd be for a dame good reason, theses days it seems I'd be better off just living down there. These passed moments have dragged on for a little to long but as in a good story in life there sometimes are no real good stopping points so this time around and in a long time I hadn't ended the day in a ball and tears flooding my face, for now I wasn't going to bed but I wasn't doing much now either, this may be an expected recurrence, I may have made this reference before but you know me by now I'm a broken record, life is like a roller coaster there's fast paced action putting me on the edge of death and then there is the slow climb to something bigger so I bet not long from now shit will hit the fan, so let's just have fun while we can and hope for the best on the other side.

Chapter 22

The future is cold, The past was chilling

Back now to a unplanned time of day I was not bothered by a life and death situation but waiting for the moment to find me, in the mean time I was still relaxed into the Captains chair, not being able to sleep and needing something new in my life other than video games, eating, space walking or watching videos there wasn't much I could do and the well was running dry. Fed up with the monotony I jolted out of the chair onto my feet, I flicked my head into the direction of the pantry thinking if I was really hungry or just bored enough that eating was now a thrill in my life, in some ways it was and I was glad I had quite a bit to last. In fact using space food and some fresh fruit as the primary diet wasn't that ideal, it was neat for a while but as the original mission up here was to test space living it was only ever temporary same as the space food, it was good enough to eat for at least a couple years but it being used as a regular life diet would prove to be unstable.

We perfected the space food well enough for a small amount of time as a diet but now with no other food than this and a few fresh fruits the effects it could take on my body development where unpredictable you have to remember at this point I was in my early to mid thirty's after now dealing with all this for at now three and a half years. After all this time with the unstable diet my body showed no unnatural changes other than the physical injuries I indoor due to my own stupidity, I did appear to be lankier than before but I was an average weight then anyways. I wasn't middle aged yet and I felt the effects of the diet worked slowly but with another forty years of it I couldn't even start to explain the possibilities the outcome could be, standing in place with my expressionless face I wore thin white boxers, no shirt and no shoes, my hair had grow faster than expected, my beard was medium sized and the wounds from the glass being stuck in my head healed nicely and my hair was able to grow a little passed my ears.

I glance down looking at my arms to notice that they were more skinnier as well as my chest and abs, with my lack of a normal diet and physical activity my body was deteriorating slowly. I've been meaning to mention more about the testing we've done, one of the more over looked aspects of the everyday living test was the exercise. To even get into space we all had to pass the mandatory physical drills, the living conditions we set for testing where in very early stages and for a larger population to live in space was going to be a chore, just not everyone was suited for the balance of this life. Living a life on Earth our bodies tear down after time of aging combined with many other factors as diet, exorcise and living conditions, if I wanted to live to be seventy this diet was only going to make my body worse over time but I had no other options so it had to do, the best I could do to counter act this was work out the best I could at a regular bases. It was a new experience that was definitely needed, still standing stiff this new idea broke my concentration of nothing.

I lifted my hands balled up into fists and took a deep look seeing the scars of my past, it tells the struggle of my journey and makes me what I am today good or bad that wasn't such a concern anymore I at least knew that with these complex thoughts I still had some form of my former self. I snapped my left hand out throwing a punch into the air than also did the same with the right arm, I could feel the adrenaline rush though my muscles as if each punch as a small burst of negative energy being expelled from my body. Standing straight up I threw more punches each one more powerful than the last, after who knows I'm just gonna say ten minuets of doing this I could feel the burning in my arms, I let my arms drop to dangle from side to side, the little energy I did have not being able to sleep was now wasted.

I yawned walking back to the Captains chair easing myself back in, I knew with the unnatural diet forcing my heath to deplete slowly that exercising was something that was going to be a daily thing such as all the others I mentioned, if it didn't I'd probably die by the time I was in my mid forties.

Giving a bigger yawn I hunched over in the chair staring at the computer, I tend to briefly bring up the testing missions N.A.S.A. was working on and in more detail of the mission my crew and I were doing. As if it was really classified anymore, I don't need to worry about being taken to federal prison, that's beyond the point what I am getting at though is there is a fairly good reason I don't speak often or in greater detail of what entailed the mission we were sent on.

The reason is mainly cause it is something not to dwell so much with other crap always arising to deal with and it tends to lead to a depressing subject knowing the outcome, planted there with drooping eyes trying to keep attention to the computer I knew I was tired and could have just ended what I was saying but I still felt my day wasn't really complete yet letting out another loud yawn my eyes felt more heavy, I moved the mouse of the computer around clicking onto some of the mission files, I have told you most of the basics and there wasn't much to the story, you could call this repetition but I call it human I was thankful enough that I was able to remember this as well as I have. The basics again were it was N.A.S.A. was able to get the funds to build a long running station though not the most technologically advanced it was made for a five year space living test facility and I think the best anybody could really hope for was it to last three at best. Now with being up here alone for a little over three and a half years and at least two with others from now on was going to be uncharted territory, back to the story though, the crew was two engineers that was Wendy and me then there was the science officer and of course not to leave out the Captain and his second in command, you know there actually wasn't much to the beginning to start with we barely had time to train and there wasn't much explained to us more than we were going to live our normal everyday lives but in a space setting, I thought looking through some of the files on the computer I would find more answers but that proved just a waste.

There in the chair I wasn't even hunched over now it was more like I was using the counter as a bed with half my body in the chair and the other half laid out on the counter, I was weak and just wanted to pass out but the position hurt more than let me get to sleep, I raised my hand to prop up my head but only on its side not straight up I hadn't even had the energy to lift my head but sleeping in a desk chair was going to get me bitching about the pain tomorrow. I pulled my hands off the counter letting them droop to my sides swaying, my neck was hunched trying to lift it the best I could I felt so exhausted, lifting my head straight up my eyes feel heavy and slowly closing them I catch on the computer screen before they are forced close,

"Attempting to receive message."

But it was to late my eyes felt glued shut and my body became weightless the last thing I could feel before passing out was my body falling from its sitting position and as I fell I banged my forehead on the edge of the counter. Now I was curled into a ball eyes shut slowly breathing and could feel the warm blood seep down my head as I laid whimpering like a puppy falling asleep for the night.

It was the next morning adjusting my eyes was harder, in a ball I raised my hand to feel my face while trying to crack my eyes open, doing so I felt small pieces of crust on my eyes, my eyes burned a little and my head felt warm I had a light sweat dripping from my forehead. Lifting I feel a sharp pinch at the side of my chest, grasping my side I groan in the discomfort. Sitting up now I see that the top of my chest and chest hair was drenched in sweat, I pulled my legs closer in to get on my feet to only be able to be hunched over, I wasn't able to fully stand attempting to gave me a sharp sting in my lower back, I feared if I walked to far I'd just topple over with my pain. In the Captains chair leaning back the sweat rolling down my skin began to become irritating along with the sweat seeping down my forehead falling my eyes making them burn even more, I couldn't just sit there and ignore it, it wasn't that I was weak I was just sore trying to stand.

I tip toed my way to the Med. Lab hoping to find what was left that could help, near the Med. Lab I was still hunched walking there and at the doorway I cough into my hand, my stomach stings again and clinching my side I lost my balance having to rest myself on the door frame of the Med. Lab, staring down at the floor I feel my stomach churn I bend even farther over falling to my hands and knees and spitting up all over the floor. At this point it was worse than I had expected, it seemed unlikely that I'd get the common cold up here in space, then it really hit me. I understood my curiosity of the situation it wasn't the common cold but a similar form of it, earlier I had mentioned the food I was stuck to eating for my regular diet and as it wasn't stable or tested enough for those reasons I should have expected.

I got to my feet again stumbling to the counter in the Med. Lab, pulling open a cabinet I grabbed one of the few basic stomach relaxers that was left in the stash, I hobbled back into the hall entering the pantry, I knew that the majority of the food that I was going to eat for the rest of my days was the space food so there was no getting around that, but as I said the food was only a temporary solution and after time the formula would suite or settings with changes in the style it was made or prepared, I stood there looking around the pantry checking out what was all left, the pouches that are the space food were in little packets about the size of my fist and there was still enough that they were still stacked in piles higher than me, other than that there was at least eight big potato sacks full of granola and the first bag was only starting to get almost empty. I need to learn other ways to conserve food as well as energy, not just the stations energy but also my physical energy, the packets didn't have a designated expiration date but we tried to do the best at making them last at least a little past five years though it was never established how long they really survived so I had to just trust in lady luck, the granola on the other hand would last a great while it took decades for it to expire and a mug full of it would be a meal, also the bags were so big that it would take at least more than a year to finish a bag along with also eating the space food.

There of course seemed to be a problem with the food now it wasn't know if it was now expired but it could be a factor other than that maybe my body just wasn't meant for this diet, it seemed to work fine for the past couple years and if only now the food was having a negative effect was unlikely even that was the case I had no choice but to eat it, the space food did keep me going and gave the energy I needed but now it was causing some sort of stomach issues, I did take the stomach relaxer and there was quite the stash of it but as everything else it could run out and what then. I was leaning on the door frame of the pantry, lifting my hand to wipe the sweat off my head I look at my hand and see small pieces of red bits covering my palm, then I remembered that when I fell I hit my head on the counter, I must have cut open my head a little not noticing it when I woke it dried over. I went over the numbers of the supplies a thousand times but it's always good to be accurate, you know that the pouches of food would last for a good while still and the granola would last longer though the fruit by this point was trash, the main problem was that I need to save the granola the best I could, which this means I must almost never eat it, but it seemed that the pouches over time caused more stomach problems and the stomach tablets would help but I only have enough tablets to last a couple more years they were a resource we assumed would rarely be needed so once they're gone they are gone and it would prove to dangerous to eat the pouches with the consistency that was needed at a safe manner.

I limped no more than usual back to the Captains chair, going back to looking through the computer, I was trying to explain earlier about the N.A.S.A. mission my crew and I were on, there wasn't much to the story for one thing the computer I was getting the info from was the Captains computer and it was the only functional one due to the changes I made for the message receiver, in the corner of my eye I notice and icon telling me about a dropped message I couldn't receive, I may have mentioned before but the only other close station near mine was the abandoned Russian station.

The Russian station was out of use about two years before we started production of the station I was using currently, the station that the Russians used was far more advance than the one we even built to replace this one, the reason it was decommissioned was cause after nearly ten years of service it was getting to costly to maintain the power and technology could surpass what U.S.A. could build but with all the work needed to run it just got to big of a hassle, all the power was still intact and could be turned back on but after now at least twenty years of service the circuits would be deteriorated and possibly with the right tinkering it would work again. Whenever I did visit the Russian space program there were always rumors about the abandoned Russian station booting itself back up like some technical glitch but those were only rumors, the Russian station was pretty much on the other side if the world or you could now call it the other side of Earths rubble.

I struggled out of the chair moving into the Rec. room, it was stupid of me but I forget to mention the fact there was a wide port hole next to the TV or what was the TV, I stood next to the broken TV seeing the screen was cracked but other than that there was no further damage so it was fixable, I look out the port hole hoping to get a glimpse of the Russian station but there was thousands of rock in the way it was almost like a wall, it would have been impossible for someone to reach the Russian station before the blast so my hopes of another human out there was just crazy, the best I could hope for was that the rumors were true and the Russian station was glitching trying to send a distress signal out, with the years of deterioration on the circuits the signal for the communications may or may not be able to reach me but without seeing the system myself I couldn't make that assumption, it would be nice to know there was another working station out there but it being much older than mine if I was somehow forced to move from this one to the Russian station it wouldn't be any better in fact with the faster paste aging of the Russian station it would almost me a death trap of course it's better than drifting in a space suite with limited air supply.

I am now remembering some other details I hadn't mentioned but before that I am sure I had mentioned that the U.S. was to far in debt so that's why Russia helped fund the majority of the station, I had also said something about a third party helping with the funds but most of it was also rumors there was no official documents about a third payee, this falls in line with what I was getting at a minute ago. When I was accepted by N.A.S.A. after finishing the basic training for space flight and living they sent the crew the five of us that were to be sent up here for five years were sent to the Russian space program to meet with more advanced and trained cosmonauts. That's where I heard the rumors about a third payee but there were many of nights of drinking after we trained with the Russians it would relax our muscles, over there their training was ten times harder, another reason that would have supported a third payee would be the nationality ratio, I wasn't able to meet the other five Russians that were sent up with us for the new station but it would be fairly easy to tell if there nationality was amiss.

Still planted into the Captains chair I was aimless in what the future held, that wasn't anything new but most of the time I had something that occupied me in a fun but more often a deadly way, but at the moment I had no current issues, well other than the stomach problems the food caused, that was something I needed to figure out sooner than later knowing if I was to put it off it would bite me in the ass later. For a while now I felt stuck to the Captains chair, sitting there leaned back with my legs spreed out, this chair had been my main location on the station for at least the past couple days, but it felt longer. It was my life lounging around doing what was needed to survive but I could picture it now my end would be me never being able to find any other food source by the time I was fifty and die here in this chair and after another fifty years I'd be a skeleton glued with my brittle bones here.

It was a life I think people could imagine the concept of being the last person was explored and thought out in many different ways but in order to really understand the trails and emotional turmoil you had to live it, but you can't this was my burden and in a weird way I was glad it was mine to bear I could never wish this life on anyone even my worst enemy. You could say that the life and death situations I deal with are the hardest part, and don't get me wrong they are but the one thing that is equally tough is waiting for the terror to occur, it's not like I am warned before hand but sitting bored makes my life tougher than trying to keep my mind occupied. It was going to be harder than the past few years since the TV was near broke, the screen was cracked and still working but it was only a matter of time before time took its tole as it did with everything else, and life was going to be a bitch with my bum leg, as I said I was forever going to have a limp with my step but that all happened a while back so after time also I think it wouldn't bother me the limp would be part of my everyday life as it has been and I'd soon not notice it. That was the deal the universe made with me, there would be the hard times and I'd use all I have in my human spirit to get through the troubles and in the aftermath more would be wrong than good but with all the troubles this causes there is always something to keep me going letting me know if I tackle the next challenge with my all and got through it I'd be hurt but I'd learn from it and be better off than I could now realize, it's all kind of a twisted moral but there is some kind of lesson in there somewhere.

I was getting sick of remembering the good times, in a way remembering my past life was helpful and gave me happiness but also depressed me knowing I'd never have it again, the hardest part of remembering the past is knowing I have to remember it in order to keep who I was, but that was the issue with my continuous survival, even in my past life every experience good or bad changed me as a person and even now with these experiences I was forever changed. On to a lighter note I was draining my life away sitting there living in the past, one thing I had mentioned before was the personal logs the rest of the crew made, I try the best I can to stay with the central topic but with the racing thoughts it's not easy, the issue I could say I was worried about at the moment was my attention span it wasn't that I am distracted it was that there wasn't much going on and after so long there would be less and less, the concentration I had was dwindling and was the biggest problem I will always have, the lack of work my mind was using is only going to get worse if I didn't keep my self occupied it would and already has been worse than any physical hurt I go through.

Back to the personal log, I've already decided that I was to good of a person to invade the privacy of my friends even if they were gone it didn't seem right. Things change though I won't take advantage of Wendy's personal thoughts, I turned to look at the computer and scrolled over the personal logs, Duane the Captain of the station was a person I wish I could have know a little better, I always felt the real reason we were friends was cause we were struck together here, if we worked on Earth together we many not have hanged out as much, I hadn't gone into much detail about Duane but now was a good time as any. You all know Duane was the Captain of the station, at the time he was around his mid to late forties, he was not a new recruit like me, Wendy and the Science officer, Duane and his second in command had been on more than a few missions to space so N.A.S.A. wasn't of course going to let a bunch of rookies run a space station.

Duane's back story was similar to mine he was a war veteran, there was really to many things to go over about his war story but in short he went through hell and came out to emotionally distressed he was honorably discharged after being the only one of his group to come back from a surprise massacre during his last mission. He got the job from N.A.S.A. after they heard his story, he was able to pass the physical challenges with ease but there was always the concern about his mental condition, space was dangerous but it wasn't a war zone so he was capable enough. Still there at the computer I clicked onto the personal log for the Captain but a password indicator popped up so I pulled open the Captain personal locker a grabbing the notebook of his important info, after finding the code there had to be around five hundred videos, you have to remember the whole crew did these videos at least once a day, so there was a lot to go through but I think as anything else it would get tiresome so I wasn't going to watch each and every one.

I opened the first video with hesitant not knowing what to expect, I clicked the play button and there sat Duane on the Rec. room couch, I guess that was something I forgot to mention about the personal logs when they are done the person was put into the Rec. room alone to video tape as long as needed, back to the video the day the video was taken was about a week into the first year of our mission, I could tell he was distressed about a minute in, he said nothing only sitting there moving his hands through his hair and covering his face, he breathed deeply and sighed after this he looked straight into camera with his dead eyes then finally spoke.

"I don't know what to think about this I know it was fake it was a dream but it felt so real like a memory more than a dream."

He then covered his eyes and breathed heavily again.

"It was the dream I couldn't get over that but it wasn't once I had it again the next day but it wasn't like the dream repeated it was like I was watching a TV show it was a continuation."

He lowered his head and shook it in distress.

"The dream it was me all alone in some kind of train car there was no entrance or exit I was just stuck, I was only asleep for six hours at best but the dream felt like it went on for weeks."

He raised his head with his dead eyes again and continued.

"The weird part was having the dream continue for many other nights, I was just sitting in this train car with no human contact I can't remember much else than that I wasn't sure if I was kidnapped or it was some kind of government experiment."

Duane's face got pale and he had this depressed looking face.

"This was just beginning to be to much hopefully it was just some weird shit and it would be over soon it's just that every night I dreamed it seemed to get worse and more real I didn't know how long I could take it, I'm done I'm just done for now I'll pick this back up tomorrow."

The video ended and I was sent back to the Captain personal logs I clicked the next one and sat back while I listened, there in the video was Duane again sitting on the couch this time he still had that distressed look and his hair was a little frizzed, it also looked like he had just got done crying, he never took his eyes off the camera as he stared with a now blank expression then he spoke.

"It wasn't stopping the dreams felt to real it was so unexplained why was I having these dreams why were they happening more than once?"

I paused the video and thought.

"What is this he was having all these problems but none of the crew never knew there was more to this story I knew it but did I want to continue with his terror that was so similar, did I want to fallow his madness of course not but I felt I needed to and maybe I'd get some answers."

Chapter 23

What was there to unfold

Starting where I left off watching Duane's personal logs I knew something was wrong from the start, It wasn't enough in the first video I saw all he could talk about was these strange dreams and they continued to the next, what the most curious part of his stories were they are about him being stuck alone for long periods of time, and that to him they felt to real, even weirder is that the dreams seemed to pass along to the next night. I continued the video seeing Duane with a pale face and stressed look he went on talking.

"This was beyond anything I was ready for, I had heard of dream that are recurring but this felt more than that."

Duane covered his mouth and closed his eyes breathing out slowly then he started again.

"This sounded crazy but I was suspecting these were more than dreams, when I woke I felt the same emotion I had in there like I really was living it somehow."

Duane placed his hands on the sides of his head and sighed then continued.

"Talking about it was to painful I just can't right now there's really nothing else I want to talk about I'll update this story tomorrow."

Duane stared dead eyed into the camera and started to water up his eyes but the video went out before he let it out, I need to know more I didn't even question my actions I was to connected to this and felt uncontrolled to see what happened next. The next video started and there was Duane once again in the Rec. room this time he had this deathly ill look and blood shot eyes, he laid back into the couch and let out a slow deep breath then lifted his head to look into the camera while still laid back to say.

"And again as I guessed the dream kept occurring, these dreams seemed to be longer than I was sleep."

Duane dropped his head back again.

"There really seemed to be no reason or since to make out of the events there was little variation to the surroundings but I could easily tell each dream was a different day, each day that went on in the dream would make my vision more blurrier like I was forgetting a distant memory."

Duane lifted his body to sit up and get a more direct look at the camera.

"All I could really make out was I was in a train car there was no exit but there was some small hole that gave over food, I wish I could say more but I just couldn't remember much and as each day passed I knew less of what was going on."

Duane rubbed his eyes.

"I can't go on talking about this even the most smallest of facts and remembering the terror, I'm just going to end this log and see what the next day brings."

As the video ended I had the same dull look as Duane did in the video, I placed my hand over my mouth in discomfort and sighed, I was learning about these strange occurrences but I felt with this new information I was only more lost and had more questions than answers. Was that it Duane's dream must have been some crazy parallel and I was hoping for more out of it than realistically needed, I mimicked Duane's actions from the video as I drifted into the back of the chair and thought.

"I wasn't getting anywhere with these videos it seems with each one reveals a little to his story and what was the connection to mine in this case I had just gotten myself excited hoping for answers and as there really where none the events he went through were unexplained, did I dare to see what was next as the same as Duane seeing more to the story only made me fell worse the major difference was that I was living it and he felt he was his eventually ended mine never will."

I hunched back over planting the upper half of my body on the counter with my head propped by the counter and my hand lied beside my head, I inched my hand to the mouse and clicked the next video, I did so unwanting but I knew if I took the pain and just got it over with I'd be a stronger person in the end. As always there was Duane back at the couch, this time around he appeared normal but still had his soulless eyes locked on the camera, about a minute in of staring into space Duane smirked giving out a small chuckle after, he seemed to be a totally different person since last, there was no frizzled hair or bloodshot eyes then he finally spoke.

"Last night was different I can't exactly remember what I dreamed about I just knew it wasn't the horror that I experienced the days before."

He let out a relaxed breath and continued.

"I have felt more relaxed this morning than others, the passed few days were just so strange I couldn't make out much of what I was experiencing the dreams were faded and felt like memories but not recent ones like something I haven't lived in for so long but what I could make out all the being alone stuck somewhere like a prisoner but I've never lived anything close to what this was, other than the time I was the last member of my group fighting in the war and was evading capture but that's a story for later."

Duane rubbed his face trying to wake himself then went on.

"I can't say the worst was over and maybe the dreams would return all I know is living in space was never going to be easy I wasn't a rookie and it could be just as simple as it all being in my head, I'll let you know."

Another video ended and I was still without answers, it was a fool of me to latch my thoughts to a anything that gave me a since of hope, that was a hard thing to let go of I needed to be hopeful but it seemed the universe didn't want me to be and I shouldn't expect things to be hopeful in this situation. I fell bored with this media as all else did, I clicked off the video files there was no use to continue I was learning nothing new and only getting my hopes up, I could say I didn't have time to waste on watching more I did but even with the new information things were done and there was going back the final result would only tear me apart knowing there was nothing I could have done.

Still laid back into the chair it seemed my whole life was this chair, as if I was melted into the chair and was now part of me it sure seemed to be, for the past three days or two or one hell I don't know anymore, I'm just calling it two that's the end of that. I sat up sniffling my nose noticing that the stomach stabilizer I took was wearing off, I hadn't eaten in a while but I knew since the stomach pill was losing its juice the effects of the space food wouldn't be noticeable, the last meal I ate was already digested so there was nothing to screw with my health, but there lies within the problem, I could see the effects of the pill were dying out and I was feeling weak but I couldn't remember the last time I ate and was hungry, I couldn't waste the granola so hopefully the space food and its after effects wouldn't be as bad as I'd think.

I struggled out of the chair with my still feeling like I had been sitting there for hours and probably have, slowly pacing over to the pantry I grab a space food pouch and as I spooned it in me I couldn't stop eyeing the granola sacks. I'd rather have those but I needed them for the long run for now though I needed to tough it out with the possibly deadly space food, I added up the numbers almost a billions times I bet but I can never remember the final numbers for the space food, you know having racing thoughts, trying to keep occupied and being not able to remember the most crucial things is kind of redundant. By that I mean I have to remember where I come from but that hurts and even trying to keep going and not lose my past but still deal with the terrors of today I tend to want to forget things and time will to that alone without the help of the rest of the nightmares in my life.

Done with my pouch I throw it to the side, looking down I noticed the disrepair of the station it was no worse than usual there were wrappers and junk strung about, propped up in the pantry door frame I ran my hand through my hair noticing it was back to close the length it was before I was forced to cut it, then running my hand down the side of my head and down my beard I could tell it to was back to its length before. Turning to look back at the computer I know that I was sick of getting nowhere but I wasn't done with the issue, I knew there are just somethings better left unknown and in life there was no rhyme or reason to the issues we all dealt with, life was just a bitch and its next target was at random. I knew the long hard journey ahead I had been living it for the past almost four years all I had was time, I knew the heart ship it could cause, it could shed some light on the subject but also bring a shadowy darkness.

Stepping into the Rec. room I grasped my lower back, it had felt stiff needing something more comfortable than a desk chair, tip toeing my way to the couch I peer my head to the wall and see Wendy there well her picture that is, in a long time it felt I smiled I hadn't been in here for a while and seeing her again just the site of her brightened my day even at its lowest moments. Earlier I had mentioned a vent between the Rec. room and the Control Deck that was blasting cool air, I had thought it wasn't going to make much of a difference and it didn't really but I could still notice it was a little cooler in here than normal, it wasn't as bad as it was when the heating was malfunctioning so that is the good side I could look to, what I was getting at is that there was more of a chill and I needed more on than boxers or sweats.

Slugging over to the clothes I grab a thin white T shirt with a pocket in the front, dragging myself back behind the couch I lock eyes with Wendy extending my hand to grab the tip of the picture, I peel it off the wall to lowered it by my side and I stair down at her then bring her to my eye level, I crack a smile and look into her smile. Feeling the connection I tear up a little with a bigger grin, I grab the other side of the picture with my free hand and now cradle her, I rub my thumb on the corner of the picture and have the biggest smile I've had in a while, bringing her up to my chest I hold her up to my heart and then place the picture in my shirt pocket holding my hand there on the pocket for a couple seconds more. I wipe away the tears and tip toe to the couch easing myself into the couch this time than usually just plopping down, I was laid out there and was not really tired and wasn't falling asleep drowned in my sadness like other times.

I was unsatisfied with the progress I made on Duane's logs and I'll try to be hopeful the best I can but I won't hold my breath, I didn't know if the day was over it didn't seem like it was I was dull minded at the moment not knowing what to do next just waiting for time to throw its next horror at me, the only issue I could foresee was these stomach problems, I ate the space food a minute ago after the stomach stabilizer I took wore off so as soon as the new space food I ate starts to digest there would be some issues but I hadn't exactly knew if the old stomach pill was finished I could only guess based on if was showing sickness but it was nowhere near accurate it was more of an alarm letting me know.

"Hey dumb ass take another soon if you don't want to puke guts."

Though still all I could say is that the effects of the last stomach pill I took was only starting to wear off and taking another would be worse than letting the space food take its effect, if I took another stomach stabilizer now I would feel more drowsy and with the unstable outcomes and a bunch of theories wasn't solid enough to almost accidentally kill myself so I had to tough the pain out for at last another couple hours and make perfectly sure the pill was out of my system.

Laid flat on the couch I was greeted to an old friend, it was something that I hadn't felt in what feels like a long time, it was the white void in the ceiling, but this time was different I was only physically seeing the white beyond of no end but as a human I have an imagination I can change the world around me to what I wish, not in a physical since though but I could imagine a better scene, and as I stared into the white void I no longer saw the emptiness of the room that mirrored who I was and how I felt today, being an imperfect human as all really were having an imagination was what made me the strongest but also the weakest, it made me feel better but I always knew it was and never could be real and after time I would be forced back into my hellish reality.

As I had said this night was different I was easing into a sleep and with eyes locked onto the white void I imagined a better scene, this night was better than most in the past months, I grinned no longer seeing the void and started to see purples, reds and pinks as my heart warmed and I feel asleep with a grin and tears of joy this time around, and before my eyes feel heavy and my body forced them closed I place my hand on Wendy and let time takes its course, now in a long time I slept well knowing not just Wendy but also Duane and all the people I loved were never really gone they couldn't be and with an awake mind I knew their memory would never be gone even if I couldn't avenge them or leave a legacy for Earth they all were still real with the existence of me.

It was the next morning and I could still feel the smile on my face like it hadn't left since I had fallen asleep, I sat up to see the picture was still in my pocket, I probably should have covered up last night I felt more chilled than yesterday though it still wasn't that bad I just need to cover up more. Stepping off the couch I slug over to the clothes and put a thicker shirt over the one I was already wearing and then stepped out to the Control Deck, I could feel the cool air blasting out of the vent above the doorways, I turn back to get a look at the vent and I see small ice crystals forming onto it and have that oh great thought, it didn't seem to be anything to serious and it wasn't something I needed to worry about now I wasn't going back into the tunnels until I felt good and ready, I felt I was stuck in space.

"Oh sorry no pun intended."

I just stood there in the middle of the Control Deck with a blank face and I knew I needed a change of pace, I've already decided I was going to look more into the back story of these events but for now I needed something new, but what that is the question I will be repeating to myself for the rest of eternity. I stood there kind of loose with my still blank expression and after a few seconds of dim mindedness I sneezed. This was no normal sneeze either when I sneezed my body involuntarily hunched back with my neck and letting out the sneeze I bent forward letting out a loud noise and instantly after my stomach churned and I felt a sharp pain in my side, then I remembered,

"Oh yeah I need to take another stomach stabilizer but if the pill had nothing other than the pain to counter act, so if I didn't want the pill to make me pass out I needed to eat more of that poison."

You all probably think the lack of real air is screwing with my head and you question why I still eat the unstable space food, well the main reason as you know is I need conserve the good food and if I take the stomach pill with the space food it could counter react the negative effects of it that's mainly it so there you go I don't think I'll need to mention it again.

So I did as usual grabbing a pill and pouch of food from the pantry, I walked over to the exit hatch and looked through the port hole into the endless space, I thought back that it had been quite a while since I had stepped out there, maybe no fresh air would do some help, I won't explain it but you would laugh if you understood that joke, I weaved over to the door hatch and grabbed a air tank, I had thought for the moment that I was pretty sure I had plenty enough air tanks for me to last me a lifetime, you should remember we needed nearly five years worth of air tanks on the station but it wasn't like we space walked everyday, and I barley ever went out so the air I had could probably last me a lifetime.

I struggled into a space suite connecting all the little latches and ready for my exit, I had no real reason for going out there but just to float about. I unlocked the air hatch and stepped in to start the air suction and open up to my way out, standing there my body felt loosened and almost weightless, it was because my body was weak and even standing was beginning to be a chore, a red light flashed and the over the intercom the computer said.

"Air decompression hatch is now stable you may exit the station now."

A light on the hatch leading to outside was green indicating everything was safe, I placed my hands on the wheel lock and tried to turn the door open but it proved to be harder than usual, I wasn't that the door was stuck I knew the issue was my body, I didn't get a lot of exercise and with the unstable diet my body was only going to deteriorate slowly after time and only be able to have some type of acceptable muscle mass for me to live if I worked out more. I guess that was the next thing on my list I know in order to really stay safe I had to counter act the effect of the space food with fixing my body, after a few minutes of tugging at the wheel lock it had loosed with my weak power, the door creaked open and I could peek out seeing not from a far this time was the asteroid field that once was Earth.

I floated out but with very little space to move around, the rocks of Earth moved in less than inches after such a long time, and were now just passing by the station, the other rocks that passed by the station were regular space rock and were of normal size so they had no issue moving faster, the rocks that were the Earth are to large to move at faster speed there wasn't much space weather to push them any faster either. Now out here I tried to get a view of anything but passed the asteroid field of Earth anything there really was to see was the endless space and the giant nova that is the sun, people have said for years.

"Don't look into the sun."

But I was far enough away I could look at the sun but not for to long and there wasn't much else to stair at other than the moon, just a big gray rock nothing to special to see there. with the moon and sun you could see specific features that made it different than other planets. The moon was what look like a big gray rock full of craters and the sun was almost like a painting a masterful piece of art, the sun was a giant ball of fire full of lava and magma hotter than anything in existence there was no way humans would be able to step foot on the sun, it was so powerful we'd burn to nothing before even getting close it was so hot.

Floating with no worries letting space drift me out while I was hooked to the station, I leaned my head back and relaxed I closed my eyes and moved my arms around me in place, it was a better sensation than just sitting on the chair but here I could imagining a better scene, it was one of the best and worst things about being a human I was able to some what get away but was always pulled back into my hell. I open my eyes to see that there is no change every rock in the same place as if I never closed my eyes, I say these rocks were Earth but if any other person took a look at them they'd just look like regular space rocks there were no special indications of the appearances of the rock like the moon or the sun or really any other planet in the Milky Way Galaxy for that matter. I was tethered to the station so I wasn't going anywhere, I made extra sure this time I was good and latched to the station, trying to stay calm and relax the best I could with time I had in the day, but as it's said nothing lasts forever I also never got a break with the next life and death situation right around the corner, and to speak of the devil I catch something in the corner of my eye behind me, I turn around to notice a light flash on the backside of the station, you mite remember earlier I had set up a shiny emergency blanket to attract attention and you mite think.

"Well why in the Sam hell didn't you just use the flashing lights for the same purpose."

The reason I don't use the flashing lights on the outside of the station is because they use to much energy, the vent blowing the unnecessary cool air was bothersome already but if these lights continued for a while the station would be at critical energy, the least I could possibly have on was the station outer gravity stabilizer so the station wouldn't spin into infinity out of control, if I left nothing but that on would mean I'd be living in the dark with none of the needed technology, that was kind of a contradictory I needed some of the tech to survive but there was some that I couldn't turn off if I wanted to make things more easier on myself, either way the energy will die out after so long so I'd rather it be later than sooner. I turn back and ignored the questioning lights to get one last look at the beauty of the sun before I went back inside and as I did a small rock about the size of my head flies at me hitting my helmet, and thank god it didn't have enough force to smash the glass of the helmet or even make a crack I was lucky. But with the reaction I flung my head back and banged it against the back inside of the helmet, doing so I felt lightheaded and felt my eyes droop as I pass out.

Chapter 24

Suffering for what

Knocked out I was in a dream state, inside I cracked my eyes open to see I was floating in clouds wearing only my boxers, I could feel a cool breeze that chilled my skin giving me goosebumps, I was there in a void of endless cloud and blue skies feeling weightless. I didn't know what to think my first thought seemed obvious to humans, was I dead was this heaven I questioned, you see after a person passes on or dies there are many people that believe an afterlife that sends a good persons spirit to a place in the clouds called heaven, this is where the true and good warmhearted people go from Earth into the afterlife.

I wasn't much for religion but all this felt real kind of a dream but not really, I don't know how to fully explain it, it was like a vivid dream a dream you could control, I was able to swim through clouds with ease, but there was nowhere to go nothing for miles and miles. If my hunch was right and I was dead or this was heaven then where were all the other people, in curiosity I spoke up.

"Hello."

"Hello anyone."

There was nothing no response all I could hear was the echo of myself, then after a minute or so my voice traveled on and it became dimmer till the silence was back. I stopped flying about, as I floated there among the clouds things were quiet I had no thoughts and nowhere to go, not knowing what was going on, an through all the silence I somehow hear a faint bell from behind, I twist around only to see more of nothing there was nothing to make this sound, then the bell got louder it got clearer and I could make out it sounded like bells from a church. I could hear them behind me again and I swerved back around seeing more of nothing, and again the bell got louder and it sounded like more than one but this time around they sounded off all around me, I twisted my head left and right, up and down I didn't know what to make of it.

It was giving me a headache and I tried to block it out holding my ears with my hands, it became to unbearable and I was screaming in pain then the bells stopped all together, again there was only silence, I lowered my hands and opened my eyes and as soon as all was clam I hear a ear shattering alarm like an emergency siren and I go back to covering my ears. The sirens get louder by the second, I look around hoping to get out off this mess but as I try to float away all the clouds around me burst into flames and the blue skies turn red, I lose my power to float and now am falling, while falling I see a river of fire below screaming my head off in fear everything goes dark.

Then suddenly I awake in my space suite still out in space floating there, I see and hear a red light on my helmet flash and the computer voice say.

"Air tank low air energy at critical level you have one minute before empty tank."

I shake my head to wake myself more and get a bearing on what's going on, the best I could say was that I was glad I didn't crack my helmet I didn't need another useless piece of junk laying around, I spin around to grab the rope connecting me to the station and pull my way in grabbing the hatch to the door and opening to entering the air lock chamber before I enter the main Control Deck, I lock the exit door and press the air valve release in the air lock chamber so I can get back into the station and as I do the computer voice in my helmet says.

"Thirty seconds till empty tank."

Then the computer voice in the air lock chamber says.

"One minute till you may enter main station."

This was my day it was going great if I didn't want to pass out in the airlock chamber I needed to hold my breath for thirty seconds, then I hear the computer voice in my helmet say.

"Five, four, three, two, one."

I take a deep breath and hold it in as I see the timer on the touch pad in the air chamber read at now twenty seconds then ten and at this point I was getting more lightheaded, as I see the timer get to five seconds I grab the hatch leading to the Control Deck, I feel my brain getting lighter and my eyes more drowsy then the timer hits zero and I pull the hatch with the little energy I have left to push open the door and with the door wide open I fall to the floor unhooking my helmet and letting the stations air fill my lungs.

I laid on my back huffing and puffing letting the air travel through my body as my muscles relax, I was sweating through my space suite and felt I was over heating making it harder for me to get air in and out, my body was so weak after this, I think I finally had to accept the fact that no matter what it is that I am doing even relaxing it will be hard. I slip out of the space suite but it was more of a struggle than usual I felt so weak it hurt to sit up so I slid out of my clothes peeling off my shirts while still laid flat, I pull the picture of Wendy out of the shirt pocket holding it there in my left hand while on the floor motionless, struggling to lift my arm I grunt as I pull the picture to my face and I crack a smile knowing she was still there for me.

I struggle to lift my upper body off the ground and now I sit there at the entrance of the air lock with my body hunched as I sit, my throat was dry so I did my best to pull myself across the floor, as I pass the Captains chair my body can't take the pressure and my body weight pulls my down and I smack to the floor arms out and head flat, I try to fight my pain and not just quite and rest, I peek forward and see Wendy's smile I let out another grunt and push myself back up as I scream in pain as I crawl to the pantry I never took eyes of that smile, I was now at the doorway of the pantry and again smacked to the floor in agony with Wendy in front of me I huff and puff as I crawl completely flat and I raise my hand to grab a water bottle on the bottom shelf unscrewing it and dowsing my face. I sigh in relief and cough a little cause I was stupidly water boarding myself, at this point I was just to weak and needed more rest but I was even to weak to crawl to the couch or Captains chair I had to sleep there for the night, but before I slept there were some stuff I needed to mention.

I had said before about the vent that yes it did use energy but hardly any and it was an acceptable amount to cold so it didn't bother much, the light I saw on the outer hull of the station though used more energy than the vent but not by much, though the numbers are only going to add up so when I do get my strength back I needed to venture back into the tunnels, I was surprised that those bulbs on the outer hull were still functional after all this time but they were also rarely used. The second thing was the exercise I need for the current diet I was using, I needed plenty of rest for tomorrow cause that was my mission for that day, if I wanted to head down the tunnels again I needed to be at my peak if with all the stress my body and mind has been through if I didn't take some resting time the best I could I'd never make it to the electrical system and back, let's just hope that the universe thinks I deserve a break and these next few hours would be on my side, I would say I won't hold my breath but I already did and that also sounds to cheesy for the moment. I lifted my hand to my face and get a last look at Wendy her smile still gave me that glued grin on my face, I placed the picture on my chest and closed my eyes taking a deep eased breath, my eyes got heavier and I was settling in for the night.

The next morning rolled around and I cracked my eyes open unwillingly, I was still laid flat and was forced awake because I was sweating a lot, my limbs felt more light and I was able to move my arms up and down but my head and body where drenched in sweat I was warmer than the other day and I felt my fever was getting worse it seemed that the stomach pills helped my digestion problems but didn't stop the biological issues. I struggled to lift my upper body off the floor but it sill wasn't as bad as last night, sitting up now I needed to take another stomach pill it would help the fever but I wasn't going to be able to eat the space food today, I feared if I did I'd be even worse later the best I could do for now was take a pill and drink some water other than that I needed to work out a little today and build up my body muscle so I could resist the pain for continuing this diet, the worst of it was that with the energy I had at the moment I couldn't do much exercise today without overexerting myself.

    I raised my hand up to grab a water noticing the picture of Wendy still in my left hand it was a little wet with my sweat damping the picture but there was no damage it was just a little sticky like it was glued to my hand, I peeled it off my hand and carefully placed it next to me on the floor than went back to grabbing a water and chugged about half of it. I slowly stood after and was breathing small bursts of breaths, standing I leaned over and picked up the picture and walked over to the Rec. room not picking up my feet more like sliding my feet along with each step, inside I pinned the picture back to the wall and hobbled over to the bathroom. I was hoping the stomach pill would help some but all the sweat would make the exercise more uncomfortable, turning on the sink I splashed my face with the water, after doing this about two or three times I notice the stream of water was smaller and this told me there had to less than half if the massive tank left so to conserve the water the tank uses less as the tank drains so it lasts, I turn my head to the shower and chuckled I knew that I had already taken my last shower, I couldn't take another shower ever if I didn't want waste the rest. I do somewhat remember mentioning the functionality of the water tank I can't say if what I did say was completely accurate it was a piece of tech I hardly deal with so I didn't fully know or remember the way it worked I just knew that water was replaced after a few months but that was for five people and this time it was only being used for one and hardly ever so it wasn't surprising it was just now running out, the best I could guess without actually seeing the tank was that the water went out a shoot and evaporated it's just one of those things that slipped my mind it wasn't that important and worst case scenario I would have to use water bottles.

I looked back into the mirror seeing how fast my hair grown back like I had never shaved, my head hair was now to my shoulders, my beard and mustache were formed into one and nearly reaching my chest. The water stream was smaller enough but I turned the power on low damping my hands and splashing my arm pits and chest rubbing my upper body down and drying off, now more relaxed I was able to breath clearly, I look back to the shower and see the metal bar above the shower holding the curtain up, I had thought that I'd be able to use the bar for my workout so I pulled it down and hobbled out to the Control Deck. In the Control Deck I look through the Captains file cabinet and there was a smelting tool and some hooks, I picked up the hooks and reached to ceiling trying to glue the metal hooks to the metal ceiling, and as the power was turned on the sparks fell into my face, in pain I drop the tools and cover my eyes, temporally blinded I scream in pain and weave over to the bathroom again splashing my face with water, now with my face at ease my eyes were blood shot and I smacked my head repeatedly due to my moment of stupidity as I screamed in agony.

"Why, Why, Why?"

I hobbled back to the Control Deck and grabbed my metal working helmet as I should have and fitted it on getting back to gluing the hooks in place, done with the job I place the bar on the hooks pulling down on it making sure it stayed in place, I let out a big breath and go grab the water bottle I had and chug the other half with each drop. I walked back out to the bar looking above seeing it was at least a couple feet above me, looking down at my arms I could tell my muscles were weakened, the reason I put the bar up was for exercise there was this move on Earth called a pull up where the person would grab a bar above them and pull there body up making there head go above the bar, doing this was to improve many different muscles, I took a deep long breath and it was time to start, I gripped the bar warping my fingers around it and tapping my fingers then finally gripping it tighter, I raised my head and pulled my arms upward feeling my feet lift but not fully off the ground, having to do this not even one full pull up I could feel my arms throbbing.

I went for a second try and lifted again, this time completely off the floor but only by inches, I repeated the process three or four more times getting no more higher and it was the best I was going to do, maybe this was a little to advanced for now, I wasn't ready to give up yet and in a burst of extra energy I lift higher than before with my neck way passed the bar and not able to handle the weight I loosen the grip and slip letting go and falling to my back slamming myself on the metal floor, I groan clinching my stomach and curling up as I roll on my side. Okay so this wasn't what I needed now I should start on something easier, I thought it out and sat up grunting with the pain and I could see my stomach turn red, as I sat there spirit broken I didn't know if there was much else I could do the normally least painful work out I could think of is sit ups, that's where the person is on there back and sits up and that's something I've been doing for days now, but with the strain on my stomach I didn't want to blow chucks so that was a no for now.

I feel the only exercise I could do today was to use my full body, it did occur to me that I could use the anti gravity or gravity balance system, this way I could make my body lighter and not use as much energy to do the pull ups, I grabbed the counter of the main computer and pulled myself up to stand, then weaved over to the rewire box and change the gravity. With everything in place I only took away enough gravity to make me feel lighter but I wasn't floating off the ground unless I had jumped, slowly tip toeing over to the bar knowing if I had taken a big step I'd lift off the ground, in place I gripped the bar and lifted my legs noticing I was almost weightless and now it was much easier to pull up past the bar not using to much energy only really having to lift about half my weight instead.

Doing the same process as earlier I was not as exhausted after around three or four more minutes of this I felt a rush of adrenaline and picked up the pace getting faster and faster, then all the sudden I feel a bigger weight pushing me down as I lift up and lose control and with the fast pace I lunge up losing my grip and letting go flying up near the ceiling and flipping backwards then falling chest first hitting the main computer desk and falling down the side. I laid in a ball as my stomach was red and had a big bruise mark across it and I screamed in pain and balled like a baby then through the screaming I groan and cough up some blood all over my chest and the floor, I laid there broken and in shambles it was just to much to deal with I had thousands of thoughts racing through my head, my stomach was in agony and I couldn't sit up I turned my head up to see that the gravity was back to normal and it just was to unexplained all these technical mishaps the station wasn't in that much disrepair, the vent, the lights, the water and all else to much to count it was obvious the universe was done with me.

I struggle to get the energy to sit up and as I do hunched over and head lowered I knew as I always had this life was never meant for me or any human for that matter as good as I could have done I think I did my best but I was just prolonging the danger and punishment it wasn't worth it I was trying to make some kind of purpose for my life but there was no good one the reason I currently lived wasn't to leave some kind of legacy or log it was to be a higher powers rag doll and as far as I know I still had my free will and I had enough. I stood the best I could and was off balance wiggling my legs and the blood was dripping from my mouth down my chest, I limped over to the deck holding my stomach with one hand and the other dangling, this all was just to much and I was working to nothing and getting squat in return living a sad hurtful life with no love, no happiness. I limped the rest of the way to the Rec. room and pulled the picture of Wendy off the wall then limped back to Control Deck, standing around in one hand I had Wendy and with the other I grab some rope from the supply kit by the space suites, slugging back to the bar I throw the rope over it and tie a hang knot, stepping up on the desk chair and fitting the rope around my neck these were my final thoughts.

"Wendy I am truly sorry I love you with all my heart I am only human and I tried, I tried for you for the world I nearly killed myself everyday and doing this breaks my heart more than any other regret in my life, I knew this wasn't really you and I felt you there but you are my greatest regret I only wish I could have confessed my love earlier then and now you made my day and kept me going I am again truly sorry."

I kiss the picture and stair at her with her perfect smile and for the last time I crack a smile myself seeing the imprint of my lips on the picture, I shed a tear while staring deeply into Wendy's eyes thinking of all the good times we had, my heart warmed and tears rolled down my face as I smiled at her, I dropped the picture and my eyes fallowed its movements as it drifts to the floor and ever so lightly I inch forward knowing what was to come.

Then ... out of nowhere something outside bangs into the side of the station and rattles the Control Deck I lost my balance slipping out of the knot and onto my back, I flail in pain and thought.

"Whatever that was wasn't an asteroid it was to big to be one, a simple asteroid wouldn't shake the station like that."

Out of a last bit of adrenaline I stand and hobble to the air lock hatch, looking out the part hole I couldn't believe my eyes this was impossible I knew I was going crazy there it is in plan site it was a site to see, I rubbed my eyes in disbelief it was it was ....

A small space shuttle like an escape pod parked right outside the airlock. The outer door slid open and revealed more of this space shuttle it had a bulb looking door and as it opened up into the air lock fog flooded into the area, I opened the inner airlock door and let the fog engulf me and as the smoke cleared I was just in total shock there in the cockpit something I thought was unimaginable, impossible either I've gone loony or I'm the luckiest son of a bitch ever, either my luck was changing or this was the next worst thing to happen the best I could say was there's something always new on the horizon but how long could this last, all I knew was I couldn't pass this up and this had to some kind of sign that I wasn't done and needed to tough it out but not for me for Wendy, I almost failed her and even if there is no goal that wasn't me it was the sickness of depression, I am strong I am me and I am only human but I'll be damned if life will get me down my only downfall will be my own stupidity I can beat this and the next time hell comes for me but frankly I just don't care anymore so let hell freeze over I'm ready for it.

Chapter 25

There was always something next

I thought I had seen it all I thought I had been through the grinder, death was in my face each and everyday, I was broken, weak, sad, I went beyond my limits testing my brain each day, testing my will, I went farther than any human would I questioned the logic, I questioned my purpose but through it all I came out the other side only more broken I wasn't stronger I only got weaker, was I stupid not to end things sooner or was I a visionary.

Standing in all the questioning all the unknowing all the madness I was truly lost now, or so I had thought I had no idea anymore, everything was a guessing game I didn't know what I was seeing what it really was if I was insane but I think I knew the answers to these questions all along, though I could still kid myself and say I was still here. After the shock of the current events I could no longer take the sight in, I turned and leaned on the airlock door sliding my back down it to sit, all my brain could function was to hold my hands to my head in disbelief, I shook my head vigorously hoping I was still awake and wasn't in some crazy dream.

An alarm played through the computer intercom and the airlock door behind me slide open and I fall back hitting the airlock floor behind me, cringing me face in pain I stair up seeing a figure appear through the fog, it looked so small, I lifted my body up and turned around to see a figure about the height of my knee. It just stood there motionless, I cleared my vision to make out there was an American flag patch on the shoulder of this small thing. Then it really hit me I didn't know how it was possible but this thing was a Capuchin monkey that was used by the U.S.A. for testing, I got on my knees and motioned the Capuchin to come to me, the Capuchin grabbed and took off its tinted space helmet and now I could definitely see it was what I thought it was. the Capuchin waddled to me and extended his hand for a shake, still in shock I felt uncontrolled and shook his little hand, I had the biggest grin as so did the Capuchin. We lowered hands and the Capuchin turned around showing me a small backpack he was wearing, the Capuchin pointed at the pack and made noises, I think he wanted me to open it. I unzipped the pack and pulled out a small notepad and written in red on the cover was.

"CLASSIFIED INFROMATION."

I open it up to the first page but before I start reading I see the Capuchin dash back into the shuttle he came in, I looked in confusion and after a few seconds he waddles back out with two mini bananas, he sits and peels the two bananas from each other then offers me the second one and smiles, he peels and starts to eat the banana and I get back to reading the notepad. Before I started I was flipping though the pages and seeing there was like fifty pages of writing so I started of course on the first page.

"Hello reader this may seem fake due to all the experiences you may have had by this point but let me inform you that you have not gone bonkers this is real."

"Let's start with the Capuchin, his name is Tang he was a Capuchin monkey we smuggled onto the new space station the U.S., Russia and us a third party where building, in case of a mission failure my group will be unnamed, also in case of interception of this message I won't go into much detail for the safety of my companions, to you the test subject what you know is true if the test worked you are the last."

"You may wonder why the Capuchin wasn't placed with you but if we did that would defeat the purpose of smuggling."

"I wish I could reveal more to this story but I fear if the mission does fail war will break out and my country is the first to die, other then this the rest of these notes is medical information and care for Tang along with the mechanics for the pod he came in."

That was the end of the first page, this all was still a little jarring but at least I did finally get some incite on this subject, it wasn't much but at least I knew there was some kind of third party fund and it was hidden from the U.S., if they had known there would be no deal made, and before we place blame it would be highly unlikely Russia would do anything against use, all of what was made wouldn't be possible without them, not to mention Russia's technological advances in space travel were years ahead of ours so they would do nothing to jeopardize our friendship they're to good for that.

I closed the notepad and Tang stood grabbing the banana from my hand peeling it open holding it up, I smiled and asked.

"What are you doing little guy."

Tang leaned forward and smashed the unpeeled banana in my face making it all mushy, I chuckled and whipped my face off eating the mushy banana off my hand, Tang extended his hands out wanting a hug, he steps near me and places his arms on me and I take my hand patting him on the back as we hug, I can say this was all to much but not in a bad way as I would normally mean, in a long time I did feel a forgotten feeling, it wasn't happiness or some kind of false love this was real it was, this love I was feeling felt to real I knew I wasn't losing me I was just picking up the pieces, I teared in joy as I cradled Tang in my arms. He releases his hug and looks in my eyes lifting his little hand to whip my tears away and I chuckle again, Tang leaps away from me and motions his hands upwards wanting me to stand, I struggle to but I did it for him, as I stood there legs wobbly he puts out his hand wanting me to hold it, so I grip his small hand and he drags me along to his shuttle.

The shuttle he was in was a standard escape pod meant for a human there was a chair big enough to fit me and next to it was the control system, the chair swiveled around to a door behind where there was air tanks and food lasting a person about a couple years, these escape pod had enough space food for a couple years some bags of granola and some fresh fruit, this begged the question its nearly been four years and with all the extra trash in the cockpit I could tell someone had stuffed more food in here than protocol standards so that somewhat explains why Tang lasted this long, but even that begged a bigger question. The third country funding the new station wasn't America but somehow who ever it was got a hold of an American Capuchin space suite and was able to set all this up but how in gods name did they train a random Capuchin to do shit like this.

Tang lets go of my hand and rushed over to the Control Deck computer and sits on the counter motioning me to come over and sit, I slug over picking up the instructional notepad and then sit with Tang, laid back in the chair Tang just stairs at me and I continue to read from the notepad.

"On to the care for Tang, there wasn't much needed to be done for him the past care takers made sure he would be self working needing no help, he was trained to pretty much control everything on the escape pod and has been taught to hack into other security systems messing with heating, lights and other energy sources."

It had then occurred to me that a while back I had been seeing something was attempting to message me but wasn't, Tang's pod must have flown to far out and lost contact so he traveled back to were Earth would be to get my attention, that still doesn't explain why he couldn't just message me but it does explain all the weird technical glitches that nearly caused my death ten times over. I lowered the notepad and shook my finger at Tang, his response was lifting his hands and arms in a confused look like saying.

"What did I do?"

Tang grinned big and climbed onto me up to my head and there he was patting on it, I turned to look at Tang's pod and I had thought there was more good out of this than I had knew, I had Tang and that was great but there was also the pod that Tang had so if things got shitty I'd be able to get out and there was also the food that he had brought so there was more to eat and last me longer but there was also the five other escape pods below the station I was just glad to also have the extra supplies. Tang climbed back down my arm and sat on the counter just sitting there emotionless with a blank face, in fact it was a little creepy, there was something I had glanced over but I know I need to speak more about it I really would hate to.

Look there are moments I may get gullible and seems like I'm losing like what happened with the rat and that one guy, yeah that one guy what was his name again, god this is really going to bother me I could place a face but not a name it felt like so long ago and frankly I can't remember when it really happened if it did at all, it was weird I really don't even remember some of the things about the story, why was he gone what happened all I remember is him being here than gone no explanation but I don't know how it got that way. Alright I was getting way off topic, what I was getting at was the reality of things I could feel Tang was real it felt to real but so did a lot of things, I guess I shouldn't get to comfortable and wait for what times tells was I being rewarded or was I being punished I couldn't tell.

I look back to Tang and still he was emotionless, as unsettling his reaction was how could I blame him he was and had dealt with all the same situations I had, being human I felt I probably had more of a concept of what was going on and how to deal with it so I was surprised that Tang's brain wasn't mush by this point at now nearly four years. That was also something I tend to gloss over, there wasn't much of a process to record these logs, well really they weren't much of logs as they were more of a life video and audio recordings, I didn't sit down at a camera and mic there was video cameras placed all over the station with video recordings I only mention what I feel is needed so of course you haven't heard each and every day and buy now I'd say it has been at least four years, when I was placed on this station it was almost six years ago then I was twenty eight now I am thirty three. I broke my concentration and look to Tang again and he shook his head breaking his staring into space, after I had thought about how long things have been I wondered all of what Tang had been through it's not like he was able to make logs on the pod so there wasn't much to go off of, I picked up the notepad from the counter hoping for answers. I flipped page by page and saw there was more written about Tang, it said.

"Tang being a Capuchin they typically live to be fifteen years of age at best, Tang was already five when he was placed in this pod."

I closed the notebook and placed it back on the counter, What I had read the best I could assume was that Tang was nearly ten, and I may have mentioned this before but I feel I need to be specific, I know now that the pod with Tang was to ride by the side of the station so that I could let him in later but somehow the rubble of Earth could have bumped into his pod and sent him adrift. I stood up and started to walk to the Rec. room but about half way there I hear Tang whine and I turn back to see him there on the counter still whining, I motioned my hand telling him to come with me but he just raised his hands like wanting a hug, I walked over him and he jumped on my arm clinging to me, I smiled at him and remarked.

"You lazy ass."

Tang grinned and I went on my way back to the Rec. room, there I pulled Tang off me and sit him on the couch I walked over to the entertainment center and to my dismay it was utterly shocking what I saw, it was the TV, the TV was intact like no damage was ever taken to it, like a total repeat of the rat cage I made out of the cabinet doors, but I wasn't going to let it get me down I shouldn't have but I brushed off this unexplained madness. I turned on the TV and switched to the video games now that they worked, I pulled out the controllers and sat with one and placed to next to Tang, I didn't know what to expect but I thought it would be funny to see how he reacts. Tang only looked at the controller, then I showed him the one that I was holding and pressed the a few buttons on it, he stared at my actions and mimicked what I did, I don't think he fully understood what he was doing and what it meant. Another question that I had wondered is what did this guy do for fun on the pod, I mean I knew he knew how to control the pod but when he wasn't working what did he do. I waved my hand getting Tangs attention and as he looked to me I pointed at the TV and pressed the buttons on the controller, Tang also looked to the TV and mimicked the moves, then he started to chuckle, I didn't know if he was reacting to the game or the bright colors of the TV.

I tried playing the game with him but it wasn't as successful as planned and I shouldn't have expected it to, I stood from the couch and walked over to the TV to shut it off and I look back to see Tang raise his arms in question. I then walked over to the speakers and turned on some music, I see Tang turn his head in wonder as I jump to the music and he stands on the couch jumping along with me, Tang jumps down from the couch and jumps beside me with a big grin, we danced around for a few songs and after a while it got tiresome, I couldn't explain my refreshed energy it was like this good feeling gave me more to live for, in a way giving me more energy, but the events were draining me quick, working up a sweat I stop dancing and limped to the pantry as Tang fallows behind, out the door of the Rec. room I turned into the pantry and I could feel Tang grab my ankle while we walked, in the pantry I grabbed a bottle of water and started to drink from it then I feel Tang tug at my pant leg, I knew that the water bottle was to big to give him one so I chugged about have of the water and then handed the rest to him.

I limped out to the Control Deck and look back seeing Tang suck on the bottle then I look back to the pod limping my way over to it and opening the pantry behind the swivel chair, I see that in this crawlspace is most of what I saw earlier, there was more than the standard amount of food and other things, also the water bottles were smaller than the ones in the pantry on the station so that answered that question. I exited the pod closing it up and entered back into the station. Yet another thing I may have glossed over, the pod was connected to the exit of the airlock, if I wanted to go for a space walk I would need to take the pod and move it down under the station near the others, but I have never driven one of the escape pods and wasn't taught so I'd have to take at least a month learning from the drivers manual and that's only to start and moving the pod around it'd take more months to actually learn all the other functions like temperature, speed upon many many other things to count. It was something I knew was in my future and so was heading back down the tunnels to switch off the exterior lights and that vent slowly freezing the Control Deck but for now I needed more relaxation and I hope the universe agrees.

Breaking my stair at the pod Tang pulls at my pant leg and sit in the Captains chair bending over to lift him up to the counter, Tang was there sitting with his bored expression but what we could do was pretty much done, there was plenty of work still needing to be done and in the mean time we'll figure something out. I spin in my chair around in circles seeing Tang's head follow my actions and as I forced stop the chair from spinning to look at Tang's grin I kick the side of the counter feeling something hit the tip of my foot, I peek down to see a small round looking clay ball almost like putty, it did bring some curious thoughts up, it looked like some sort of bouncy ball but I knew N.A.S.A. would never let someone bring that on bored, and it wasn't like it was in a locker or cabinet it came from under the counter as if someone meant to hide it. I pick up the ball and get a closer look noticing the deformed shape and what reminded me of a super ball I had as a kid, this ball somehow felt familiar not a memory on Earth but up here I just couldn't place it. Tang grabbed the ball grasping it with both hands and shaking it, I swiped the ball back giving him a stern look.

"We won't be playing with this toy it's to risky."

Tang reached out his hand air grabbing for the ball and whimpered.

"No, we can find something safer to play with."

Tang stuck his tongue out and gave me a thumbs down in his disapproval, I brushed it off and opened Duane's personal cabinet below me and dropped it in there, I think we both had a big day and the energy I had left was strained if there was any at all after this day I was surprised I didn't faint and I didn't know if I was strong enough to even make it to the couch, it wasn't like my body was tired and with some relaxation after my workout did replenish me a bit, this time around I was more tired after the emotional track I was on and using the little power I had to move place to place around the station was just to much, that's got to be the worst thing to hear, that just after simply walking around I was so ready to end the day. I struggled out of the seat and Tang jumped to my arm, I grunted feeling the pain like there was a lifting weight on my arm and with the discomfort on my face Tang could tell I felt hurt and scaring him with my groan he clinched my arm tighter, with the pain on my arm and struggling to even stand with my wobbly legs I limped into the Rec. room and before I plopped into the couch Tang jumps off my landing on the back of the couch as well.

Laying flat I only had my thoughts and I feel Tang fall from the back of the couch onto my stomach and it felt like someone sucker punched me, I groaned and lift my head to see Tang lay on top of me stomach to stomach, today was full and I knew some of the future would be busy too I would take me a great while to learn from the owners manual of the pod and I still knew I needed to get back on the horse and try this exercise thing before I tackle going back down in the tunnels and what of Tang if I were to venture through the tunnels I couldn't have him fallow I needed him to stay safe, it was all running though my head and with racing thoughts I was mentally stressing out having a mini panic attack but before my top popped I feel Tang's breath pushing his stomach against mine and as I look up I see Tang fast asleep breathing in and out with his hands wrapped around my stomach. he was just so darn cute, I placed my hand on Tang's back and sigh with relief, as I eased into my sleep I had a last thought for the night.

"These passed few years I have rarely had a okay nights sleep and this was one of the few, I planned for the next days or weeks hoping the next horror wasn't to much to handle and I felt it was time to realize I wanted to do things for the next days, weeks and years waiting for the next bump but that wasn't possible I was glad I lived past today and that was the best I could hope for, plan for now and if I was lucky to make the end of the day with few scars it was a win and as the events destroyed me they built me stronger and ready for whats to come I change for the better and worse every battle ripped me apart and glued me together, parts of me will forever be gone but the new me became tougher than I ever thought was possible, this was the major question was I a human or an animal what chunks of my past were to last and what parts of me would form into the animal I become each day, so I can't ask what the future held the most realistic I could ask was what did tomorrow hold."

It was the next day as usual only this time my eyes didn't ease open they shot open I couldn't remember if I had dreamed something my sleep felt instant like I only closed my eyes for a second but I had a full night of sleep, I peek my head down to get a glimpse at Tang and to my discomfort he was gone, at this point you might think I'd be freaking out and having a bitch fit but my mind was racing and all I could think was.

"Fucking shit what the hell was happening this couldn't be happening."

I didn't know what to feel there was so many emotions rushing through my body the suddenly I hear a screech from the Control Deck and I sighed in relief and I know that sounds terrible for me to say but at least I know this wasn't some kind of freak dream I knew I was awake and this was all to real so Tang was really out there. After just repairing my body I take my burst of energy and speed to the control room getting to the door and slamming against the door frame, I hobble the rest of the way to Tang and see him swaying back and forth then noticing the small liquor bottle in his hand, this was just great it was obvious he was drunk, but fright not there was about half of that small bottle left so with the size of Tang it wasn't surprising he couldn't handle his alcohol and there wasn't enough left to do any real damage. I pick Tang off the floor and sit him on the counter taking the empty bottle, now that I think about it that could have been a good last drink and that was its original intention if I wouldn't have used it for medical reasons.

Tang sat there pounding on his head with his tiny hands and I grabbed them stopping from making it more painful and to make matters worse there wasn't anything on the station to help hangovers, I knew he must have been looking for that ball and saw the liquor. I didn't know what to do was Tang a bud or a child, we were getting to know each other but I didn't want to piss him off by disciplining him, I shouldn't think to much into it there was no need to punish him he was just being curious. What now was the normal I had no question about my habits as I sat in the Captain's chair, Tang was still sitting on the counter with his drowsy eyes and there next to him was his notebook, then I had a recollection.

"Oh yeah I needed to start reading that owners manual for the pod."

At this point I need to get things done as soon as possible not knowing how much time there really was, I was already slumped into the chair and didn't feel like getting up and I knew my laziness would be the death of me but all I was doing was rolling a chair not going to war though based on my luck I might have as well been, I rolled the chair over to the pod opening one of the side compartments and pulling out the manual. I turn back and see Tang pointing at me and laughing, then I had thought.

"You know it would be much simpler if he could just tell me what to do, what were the odds his owners would had fully taught him all the mechanics or if he could really even understand that much."

I rolled back to the desk opening the book to the first page and of course I wasn't going to go over each and every detail and this manual was like four hundred pages, I wasn't going to go over all the lessons of the book myself only what I needed the only issue was I know it's going to be the most time consuming thing I've done in a long time and it wasn't something I could do I one try I needed to study over the details like a test for school only if I got an F I'd die, yet I still needed to fix the vent before it froze the Control Deck and the outer lights before they drained the stations power and as you've heard I needed to fit in my body workout.

Not even into the first page I hear Tang screeching and I sit down the book to give him attention, he was swaying back and forth his drowsy eyes then suddenly I knew he was losing his balance and then he fell off the counter hitting the floor.

Chapter 26

There was only today

Okay, okay it was now freak out time, I hopped out of the chair to reach for Tang and picking him up and laying him back onto the counter I felt his chest feeling his tiny paints that he made, he was breathing but as I said there was nothing on the station that could have helped him. The only medicine on here was the stomach pills but those wouldn't do much and I needed to save as many as possible, the only other medicine was the stash in the Med. Lab but a lot of it was used for experiments so I'd think almost none of it would be useful although it was worth a try, Tang was breathing so it was okay for the moment to leave him be while I looked through the medication, after this I needed to keep him cool and let him get his rest, I wasn't going to be able to move around the station in just the chair so against my comfort I struggled out of the chair to stand there wobbly and limp my way to the Med. Lab.

I hadn't been in there for quite a while I hadn't had a reason to look around in there, entering the Med. Lab I stayed stood up by leaning against the door frame, getting a full view of the room it had also been quite a while since I had cleaned out the Med. Lab let alone the whole station. There was a thin layer of trash that flooded the room with the floor still visible, hobbling over to the counter I pulled open the cabinet to see most if not all the bottles and jars of medication were either empty or almost none left, standing there in disbelieve I was just to baffled how could something like this happen, these medications were rarely used when the one station medical doctor was in work and I wouldn't know what to do with half of this stuff. It was at this moment I felt as if this occurred more than once, I couldn't tell you how the medication got this way but somehow the reason was on the tip of my tongue and once again I was always left with more questions than answers, I was wasting time and Tang needed me, rushing back swaying back and forth I picked up Tang off the counter and hobbled over to the Rec. room laying him on the couch and sitting beside him. I knew I was overreacting there was no serious damage done I just had to let his pain pass and make sure to keep an eye on him, then I had thought how hard it was for me to recover from past injuries I've taken on the station and to be blunt I wasn't even now over some of the past injuries there were even some that would stick with me for life like my bum leg, to think about it I know it was only a few years ago but I can't recall how it occurred all I knew is I was being a dumb ass most likely and caused it but most of it was a blur.

Not to mention but with the slowed pace of my healing and what seemed to be my body aging faster due to the environment I didn't know how this all effected Tang, at this point he was middle aged with his normal life span and with the past years living in space how could that effect his health, I had an idea of what was going on with me but barely and Tang I feel it would take to long to even come up with some kind of estimated health effects in his current state and if I did somehow it would only be a best guess and wasted time. Tang was snuggled in the blankets getting some sleep, he looked eased enough but I thought some lite classical music would help and against my better judgment I lifted my almost worthless body off the couch to turn on the stereo, the music played and it felt like it was moving through my body it was so soothing as I made my way back to sot on the couch, sitting up I see Tang still panting and I lightly pick him up laying him on my lap so I could pet him, as I stroked his fur Tang breathing eases and he lets out a long sigh beginning to breath normally again.

It was sad but I have said it before I'm sure, this is what life is now each day gets shorter and shorter my emotions can only take so much I just woke up to today's horror and I already need a nap, it was complete crap but I knew the day wasn't really over I just needed to tend to Tang and hopefully this afternoon will be better but with all these worries it seems I don't even have time to be hopeful, it was bad enough I only lived for today now I was afraid I could only have to live for the moment and hope to pass it in one piece. I sat there moving back and forth rocking Tang in my arms all I could think was.

"I know that I just had this recollection about not worrying about the future and take each day one at a time so not to over think my work load, but now it wasn't like these events were only happening every other day or once a week now there was something to stress out about everyday big or small no matter the size the terror even the tiniest amount was to much to bare."

Okay I was really letting it get to me and that's what a sickness dose this wasn't a normal sickness it was more, a mental sickness not having the confidence, power or hope to make something out of such a tragedy, I thought I was at my lowest the other day and was ready to let go but even at my worst somehow the universe lets me know there's always more to a story you just have to take that next step. My mission may not have been to leave a legacy for Earth or avenge Wendy, for now my mission was to be there for Tang as he was for me, what was his real mission, I can't answer that but as a story goes on it only gets bigger with more things to question and if you're lucky some type of answer, to end this passage the most cliche thing I could say is your future wasn't set it is what you make it. I couldn't really believe that either though, I felt I did control my actions but was there any real free will, I couldn't control the weather or any other disasters that happened but I could control how I dealt with them, or do I, there was more convoluted theories that I could explain but I'd be only talking in circles. My thoughts on this matter tend to change more than how often my life is ripped apart, at the moment I could say I did control my future but I also didn't, this idea wasn't to common but it explains that nothing was real and everything was real, in fact there were just to many details to go into and shockingly this bored me.

I was now in and out of being awake and wasn't rocking Tang anymore, I could hear Tang snore almost like a purr from a cat, it gave me a warm felling inside giving me reassurance that I knew someone was still there for me in some way and that I had to be there for someone also. Tang being here raises more questions than one of course but one puzzling thing I didn't gloss over was him being actually used for space, you see the Capuchin were mostly used for testing in the U.S. very few ever went to space, the environment was a bigger gamble, we could assume and test the best of our ability to make human life in space a possibility but for monkeys the testing could be done it was just harder to conclude a statistic without a normal verbal response, we would have to make the best assumption for monkey space living by body, diet and x ray testing so even with the most trained and most apical test subject there could still be issues with the effects of space to a monkey. Don't get me wrong the same could be said for humans but the testing is more solid and hard to find inaccurate data but it was possible.

Sitting back I was unable to sleep and it had been at least a hour, or I could guess really it was now nearly impossible to tell time but I could estimate the days easier, and frankly it was a waste of mental energy to dwell on something so small. I had racing thoughts about all my curiosity at the moment but I also needed to keep an eye on Tang, god I'm just a dumb ass sometimes, earlier when I was talking about the probabilities of a Capuchin living in space I completely forget the fact that Tang came from neither the U.S. or Russia, there isn't many other countries that tested with space travel than maybe China, Japan even if England could have had the funds to start a space program but there were to many variables to go over not to mention any country with enough money could train a Capuchin for space. I had an idea of what was going wrong with me, you see with these racing thoughts there are so many worries that not everything I needed to take care of and everything I need to prepare for doesn't always get done and some of these mishaps lead to fighting for my life, that was something I needed less of in my life, the best I could assume was with all the stress and mental hurt I was suffering from premature memory loss something I wouldn't have to deal with till I was seventy or eighty, and now that I was thinking of all the imperfection in human space living it was totally possible that the body stress, unnatural diet and living environment could age me faster. On Earth there was a saying.

"Time flies fast."

I may have said this before but to remind you and me this would mean that time around you seemed to pass by faster than a normal pace, there were plenty of things I'd never get to in my life there was only so little time to focus on one thing we all had a life expectancy, I would hope to life to be seventy or eighty, at the moment I felt like dying sooner but to adapt to this life there were going to be some drawbacks I'd be lucky to make sixty.

With to much stressing my mind I let out a big sigh finally drifting into sleep my eyes had been closed for a while and now they felt real heavy and just as I felt like I was asleep I hear a small yawn and I feel Tangs hand graze my stomach, as I fling my head up waking to see Tang stretching and yawning like a little baby, he wakes to open his eyes we look at each other and he gives me a big smile.

"I guess I've got to get up too right."

Tang just continued to smile, then he rose off my lap to sit up then jump to the floor, then waddled back out to the Control Deck and in discomfort I let out a hurtful sigh thinking.

"Oh great he's back to action."

Against my comfort level I needed to keep an eye on Tang, you wouldn't think I'd have to based on his age being almost nine he was old enough to learn to use that pod, I painfully stood staggering to the door seeing Tang back to what seemed full health he was doing flips and running in circles, it was surprising how well he bounced back from what happened I can only imagine what he had to deal with alone and what was really going through his head. It was to bad I couldn't give him any medication for his problems and even if I did the medication wasn't tested for a Capuchin and I could make him more worse than help, though it was only just a half a bottle of liquor so rest was good enough for now.

I was leaning on the door frame knowing with Tangs replenished energy the day was to start, I continue into the Control Deck and feel a harder and cooler bast of air hit my neck and peeking behind me to see the vent the ice was thinker and spreed farther out I knew it was becoming a bigger issue if it got any worse the vent would get clogged with ice and it would be a bitch to clean. I am still not ready to make the travel down the tunnels, I may have said this earlier and with my loss of thoughts probably many other times but I was the most bright when it came to working on the main computer so all the functions weren't that straight forward to me and I already had to take months out of my life just to move the pod down to the others I didn't need more time taken off to learn every program in the computer it would be faster to gain my health back the best I could and defy death yet another time at least I hope to say that.

For what seemed to be the passed week my plans was to exercise and make the trip to turn off the cool air and external lights but every step of the way there was another hurdle for what seemed the next was taller than the last. Tang slowed taking a break in his hopping around and turned to face me extending his arms then grabbing the air like wanting a bottle, for being almost nine years old he was such a baby but being a nice guy I hobbled over to the pantry and grabbed a water drinking about half and handing the rest to Tang, it was kind of silly that I needed to drink half of the water in order to give Tang some, I guess I didn't really need to but he couldn't have a full bottle or it would burst his stomach. Holding and sniffing the rim of the bottle Tang was displeased and then threw the bottle to the floor spilling some of it, I slowly bent to pick up the bottle and shook my finger at Tang.

"Hey that's all your getting there's no more liquor and even if there was you wouldn't get any got it."

I handed the bottle back to Tang and he took it with a mopey look and sipped the rest of the water out, I laid beside Tang sitting straight up on the floor getting ready to finally exercise, I think earlier I was overestimating my power and the pull ups were a little to advanced after the tole space living did to my body, it was time to start something much simpler like sit ups. I did need to strengthen my body but couldn't waste time after time the power of the air conditioner and outer lights would build and build giving me less time to live safely on this station, so I did have some time to delay before things got critical, I feel the best I could do was at least a couple of days before I wanted to make the trip, either way I would be safe for a while like a couple of years before the effects of my laziness would kill me, and that of course wasn't gonna happen I was going to figure this stuff out in the next couple of days.

So you are not lost I mentioned sit ups they're nothing like pull ups and much safer, sit ups are as simple as they sound you just start flat on your back and then raise you upper body to, well sit up, enough jabbering time was of the essence, I laid back straightened flat then sat back up, then again, and after around twenty more times I peek to the side seeing Tang was still standing there next to me with his head tilted in wonder. Going up and down a few more times I see Tang jump beside me, then as I pause Tang climbs onto my belly as I was laid flat, I thought I'd still be able to do the sit ups with him there but when he started to jump as I lifted off the floor I felt a sharp pain he continued to jump, grabbing Tang I placed him back to the side of me as I held my side grunting and yelling.

"Fucking hell Tang you can't be doing that."

Tang frowned and walked over to the bottom edge of the desk to sit, I continued my process moving up and down but Tang kind of mashed me up good, each movement was only more grueling but I fought through the pain and finished up the session doing about twenty more. Sitting up exhausted I panted looking at Tang being all pitiful and I said to him.

"Don't give me your pity party."

Tang stood with his head lowered and a sad look extending his hands for a hug.

"Oh alright I can't stay mad at you."

Tang raised his head to reveal a big grin and he ran to me with open arms and we connected for a hug, it was a nice moment of happiness but I needed to stay on topic so I sat Tang to the right of me and I was getting tired of doing the exercises not physically I just had other things to think or more of worry about, the list for this time around was only having myself deal with even more dire situations. I needed to build my physical strength to make the tunnel travel easier so I could shut off the outer lights on the hull and also shut off the vent by the other rooms so the Control Deck doesn't freeze over, then there was also need in to move Tang's pod to the lower level with the other pods but before that I would have needed to learn from the drivers manual, now I think it would have been easy enough to drive the pod, the basic controls such as its flight was already taught to the whole crew I was with just in case they were ever needed, so I guess needed to learn about the heating, lights and to many other functions of the pod weren't needed just to move the darn thing, though I guess it wouldn't hurt to give a small read.

I lifted my body from the ground struggling as usual and feeling a small burn on my lower back and as I stand there I grasp my lower back grunting in what was the normal reaction by now, I feel Tang jump to my arm as I had my hands placed on my lower back trying to reline it. Standing straight and stiff I feel Tang crawl up my back and onto my shoulder, I walk to the airlock hatch opening the main door and then now facing Tang's Pod I open the hatch to it leaning down by the arm rest to pull the drivers manual that was in one of the side compartments attached to the chair, I head back into the station to sit in the Captains chair and as I lean back to open the manual to the first page, Tang while still on my shoulder I feel him jump off landing to the floor at my feet and I simply just ignore his actions. I read from the first page.

"Hello new operator and welcome to the world of space travel."

I gave a small grin and thought to myself.

"What is this an introduction to preschool why so preppy."

Then my thoughts were interrupted by Tang's howling so after hearing him screech I peek my eyes over the top of the manual to see Tang jumping in circles then suddenly stop to hobble back and forth almost losing his balance and as he gets his footing he looks up at me and smile. He just wanted attention and there were more important things on my mind, of course I understood that he went through the same turmoil I had and wanted to relax, there will be time for playing but the work load only got bigger and deadlier so I really needed to keep my mind cleared, focused and on task. I got back to the manual, reading the next line.

"Okay new adventurers the first thing you need to know is making sure the pod is ready for your flight."

This was already starting to bore me it wasn't like I was doing this for fun and most of what I was seeing that needed to be read in the beginning of the manual was stuff I already knew, as I said I knew where everything was placed and needed to be and how to move the pod itself. The rest of the other things I needed to know were random applications and I need to look further into the manual to find that specific information, and for now I realize there was nothing else I needed to keep up on if I was just to move the pod, this current task seemed to be more of a waste of time than anything else and as if there was such a thing as a waste of time these days. I knew there were dire things at hand and you'd think every second counted but my views on the subject seemed to be thrown back and forth there was just to many passing thoughts that keeping track of every little idea wasn't easy to get around to and most are forgotten or put on the back burner. Uh I keep forgetting some of these sayings could be taken in the wrong way even if you could possibly understand a word of me but what I was taking about was.

"Putting something on the back burner."

This meant that a thought of mine wasn't my first priority and could be taken care of later if at all. God this was life was getting to one second I was reading the manual then a second later I was explaining the human language, I seemed to be only focusing on one thing but even that was to much for me, I already knew reading the manual was an unnecessary task and there was five other pod under that station so if I wanted to read it I had plenty of other chances or so I had hoped. I laid back in the Captains chair rubbing my face trying to keep myself awake and as I whipped my eyes they widened to a realization and with no verbal response I start to smack my head with my hand, let me explain I don't mean to self abuse myself more than I already have but this realization was that there was only five places that the pod could be placed and all where taken up by the pods that the station came with so that means there was nowhere to put Tang's pod, can you believe this whole reading the manual and waiting for the right time to move the pod was just a giant waste of time, how could I forget something so simple as this, the plan always seems to keep changing and it wasn't like I was going to be able to keep the sixth pod.

The plan now was that I needed to unload the supplies from Tang's pod then just unhook it from the airlock letting it go afloat into the deep reaches of space, and as I swiveled in the chair another jarring fact occurred, Tang's pod was the first thing I was going to be able to send out to the rest of the universe it would be a great chance to send out a message but really I wouldn't know what. I guess before I was to unload the rest of Tang's pod that could pass as a good time waster, I needed to figure out what would really be a good thing to send to alien life. To not get ahead of myself I didn't expect anything in return and what where the odds that this message would reach that far in my own lifetime, and in fact I knew it wouldn't the pod even at its own lowest power would move at a snails pace it would be like a couple months before it left site from my station and to reach an alien life could take millions of years who knows if at all, but that was my biggest mission I needed to send out some kind knowledge that there was evidence of Earth and all the work I put in, it wasn't like I could send all of what I was telling and had told you I had to use something simpler.

I hopped from the chair, well it was more of a jolt flinging out of the chair like a fish out of water but either way I was standing fine, then as it came to be a known recurrence I feel Tang jump to my arm as I stagger to the door of the airlock. After a minute of thinking of what to put into the ascending pod my plans changed again as if I do this as often as I breath, I couldn't decide what I was going to send out and I thought it could occur to me as I was clearing out the pod, that seemed to be the way things went I figured the plan out at nearly the last second it wasn't an easy life and hell there's no excuse I just had to take the time to prepare for the worst, and that was something I remember people from N.A.S.A. taking about they'd say.

"Anything that can go wrong will go wrong."

The hardest part of that statement was we prepared for hundreds of possible things happening.

"Nothing like this."

But either way there were so many unknowns that we couldn't have predicted and been ready for every disaster, alright alright enough talking I almost feel I talk to much but if I rarely or never talked you'd be even further in the dark, oh wait.

"Further in the dark."

That was another saying on Earth, wait wait I'm rambling again I'm not here to teach language skills. At the airlock I turned to wheel to unlock the airlock door, entering the airlock I pull up on the pod door to reveal the rest of it. I stepped into the pod then feel Tang drop from my arm as I turn around to sit in the pod chair and swivel around, now staring into the back of the pod I thought to myself that the pod looked smaller on the outside, I hadn't really gone into detail about the build of the pod but it wasn't anything to wild. There was a large swivel chair that had a back that looped around the person kinda like the shape of half of an egg, then on the sides of the chair and under the floor there was random storage and waist side there was two panels of random controls, in front of the swivel chair there was a big thick window that had a touch pad control and between the two there was the steering wheel, the only other place was the storage in the back of the pod. It held the more important supplies such as food, medical stuff an extra space suite and many air tanks, I had said before that this pod seemed to be over stuffed with more than regulation would allow so the person would know that the driver wouldn't need to survive the stranded amount of time that a person was meant to be in here.

For now it seemed I had a good amount of food, I knew the pouches I had would last me almost my whole life, the fresh fruit on my station and this pod was mostly trash by now the only other food was the granola, I had started with eight sacks and was finally down to seven and I was sure glad that most of the time the crew and I stuck to eating the pouches. Taking a deeper looking into the numbers of the supplies on the pod I could see that normally there was only one sack of granola needed for the standard pod but there was now another two sacks added to the pod, the standard amount of pouches were three pouches a day for about a month so there should be who knows how many left but there seemed to be at least a couple hundred thousand of what was left since Tang made his travel back to my station.

That was another question I have yet to ponder over much, I did wonder how far Tang went out and why he hadn't just gotten onto the station after the event. The event had been at least now a little over four years so if it took that long for Tang to make it back to me his pod must have been hit by the blast so hard it hurdled him to at least passed Mars, that was the best I could estimate since I knew well enough that it would take a maned ship at least three years to reach Mars. The funny thing was that with ever question there were only more questions to be presented such as with how long it took Tang to get to me and how he was thrown through space, the other question that I stupidly hadn't asked till now only thought of was how far was I also pushed out, well I could still see the sun and the moon close by and what was left of the rubble of Earth so I couldn't have been pushed out to far and really I do have to think back, though I didn't have to think that far back it felt like forever ago, all I could remember was the station was rumbling shaking all over but I could say I remember it moving forward.

God, always getting off topic that's a regular thing and get used to it that's just how it goes one second I was reviewing the inside of the pod and another second later I was doing the math of space travel, getting back to my work I spent a couple minuets flipping through the pouches of space food, counting the numbers there seemed to be more trash of the pouches then there were of the pouches, there is usually one sack of granola but in this case there was three, Tangs eating habits mimicked mine there was only the surface of the granola gone so there was plenty left over, as it looked now with the food most of the pouches were eaten but there had to be at least a few months of them left. With the other supplies such as medical and technical supplies there was more than enough, it looked like the air tanks were almost never used and there was no damage to the extra space suite, though I didn't expect there to be I knew it wouldn't fit Tang and he was always wearing his own so it was in perfect condition. The medical supplies was in the same condition also it seemed very little was used, all in all I'd say this was a score, alone with the supplies I had was more than enough for two but with Tangs added it was an extra bonus so I guess there was more good out of this new discovery than thought. It didn't take long to clear out the pod and as I carried the food and other supplies to there needed places each and every time in and out of the pod and into the station I would get a turned head of curiosity from Tang, what of must been going though his mind, and no that wasn't just a joke statement.

I knew that Tang could never be able to fully communicate with me but of course I was curious about his travels as he probably was experiencing the same travels to, it was the best situation to have someone with me as I had wanted for the longest time but what made it a drag was that I really wasn't going to be able to go more in depth in my dialog with my new friend, and frankly you most likely wouldn't understand why as anything else I saw for that matter but you see on Earth us humans had many different languages to speak to one another as so did animals but humans and animals couldn't verbally talk with each other, that's kind of the irony in this situation, I needed someone in my life but yet it was a Capuchin an animal that I wasn't able to fully communicate with, I would be able to at least attempt to tell him things and make him understand some stuff but not on the same level as a human conversation.

Finally carrying the bulk of the pod into the station most of the work was done, taking another trip into the pod I got onto my knees checking all the little storage spaces and other crevasses, most of what I pulled out was what was expected just some random unused medical supplies, taking it in and placing it with the other stuff Tang tailed me along the way like a shadow. Then a thought had hit me, there was plenty of things I did for distractions on the station and I mentioned most to you but I do tend to pass over taking about when I do the more important work like actually keeping the station stable, a lot of my work was repetitive so you would get bored of it quiet a bit, though as it seems I've had to venture down in the tunnels so many times I'm betting hearing about that gets tiresome and those adventures are not quite over yet either.

Okay okay I'm rambling again but what I was getting at was that I did things to keep the station afloat that isn't always mentioned and I could get into more detail later but what of Tang, putting away the medical supplies I plopped back to the Captains chair finishing my thought earlier. You see Tang was at least trained somewhat in order to function the pod, now most of pod was automatic and normally they were used as a escape pod launched back to Earth but obviously this ones destination wasn't Earth and even with a short extended time of stay on the pod there was maintenance that went into keeping the pod safe. I guess you could say it was a surprise that Tangs brain wasn't mush,

Capuchin monkeys could learn to an extent but to deal with what I was going through, even as a human it was to much and could Tang comprehend what was going on? Well he survived this long so I guess he knew something about working on the pod though myself I haven't had the training to work with the pod to his extent, I really shouldn't worry myself with the details of his journey it'll only drive me more crazy.

There still in the chair I pondered lots of things, I knew I still needed to workout more and figure out what I was going to put into the pod, standing from the chair I loosened my body shaking my arms and legs then right before I was about to squat Tang jumps to my shoulder sitting on the back of my neck. Then I start to squat going up and down, I wasn't sure how Tang was going to react but doing the motion many times there was no response from him. While doing my workout I had thought back to the events today and as I would usually say that I hadn't done much I guess I really hadn't, I wasn't emotionally strained or that physically exhausted but as I continue my workout I felt my energy depleting fast, I felt I could have done more than I thought but as I tire I stop then stagger back to the Rec. room with Tang still on my back and as I fall to the couch he jumps to the top of the couch.

The exercise did tire me out and faster than normally, though it seemed there wasn't much that went on today and as my concentration dwindled it was getting harder to remember this morning all that well and keep my eyes ajar feeling more heavy, the day felt short and I knew most of mine did feel shorter than normal, I had a feeling today was different I didn't know if it was longer though my body was more weak today than others from not doing much physical activity and for some reason even though only a day had passed I could only remember fragments of the day. With all the rambling and taking in circles in my head I was quickly slipping into a dream state and in a last moment of concisencess I could hear Tang sliding down the top of the couch then landing on my chest, he lied there breathing slowly falling asleep as well and now almost completely out of it before I couldn't feel what was going on outside my body I could since Tang was also fast asleep and breathing extending his stomach pressing against mine.

Chapter 27

Back down the rabbit hole

My eyes opened into a small dark room, there wasn't much light at all the light that there was very dim I couldn't almost make out where I was, well I actually didn't know I knew I was asleep I mean of course I was, the dreams at the start where like any other as humans dreamed then as the time went on instead of the unnatural style that was a human dream started to mimic what was real life, seeing people I knew doing normal things but as I woke each day to the horror knowing it only ever could be a dream and I descended into madness my dreams got crazy again, not like the weird, like a typical human dream was though I don't think there was a standard that was human dreams. The dreams of recent months where far from what I was used to and with the strange events I mentally Indore had some kind of underline of subliminal meaning.

In this dark place I could easily tell I wasn't in a void like other times, I knew I was in a very small dim light room with no markings on the walls telling me nothing more than I could see. This room was cool but not freezing, this itself wasn't alarming but what was that the room was light dim though I couldn't tell how the light was getting into the small space, I could not see a bulb or a stream of lights, what there was seems to be the light coming from the cracks of the walls, though it didn't give much vision to view the whole room I could see only right in front of me with dark points at every angle from myself. I could only stand there motionless with the curiosity then I hear light footsteps growing slowly louder but only to a normal sound of noise, as the footsteps continued I listened closer wanting to hear if there was anything else.

Why was this such an importance right now it's not like this moment mattered this was a dream and I could wake soon, though there wasn't much to do till I woke so I was so to say stuck with it. As the light footsteps continued it became a bother I knew that this room was to small for a person to walk as far as I heard the steps going, in the anticipation waiting for whatever to come from the darkness my mind flooded with the possibilities and I began to shiver with the nervelessness. Abruptly the steps stopped and I eyed back and forth checking each direction near me, then in front of my I notice a human foot step into the dim light, as I lift my head to see what was connected there was a silhouette of a man only revealing his lower foot to the light, with my twitching body I gulp to say something.

"Who are you?"

As I stared in wonder I could see the mans lips move to speak.

"Have you forgotten me already?"

I couldn't respond I didn't know what to think or say and in the moment of silence I see the mans lips smile then his body move forward to reveal more of himself, that was when my heart had dropped, not in a bad way I was overjoyed I wanted to scream to the mountains I knew it was fake but it was something I hadn't seen in so long I feel I may have really forgotten him, it was Duane he stood with the biggest grin while in the dim light only a few feet away from me. Duane stood there half in and out of the light revealing very little of himself, I didn't know what to say or how to respond, as I had said I knew this was fake and most of the time if a person from the past appears in my dreams these days there seems to be an underline meaning but hell if I could understand half of what they were getting at, though that's how dreams are they're not meant to be that simple. Standing in the silence I finally choke something up.

"Is there something you could help me with?"

Still there barely visible Duane said nothing only with the same reaction as before just him with his slit smile and a cold stair, we where both frozen not moving through the whole experience, in the awkward moment I thought of the next thing to say.

"So could you explain the whole ordeal with your personal logs?"

He didn't answer, he continued standing with that smile of his and after more than a few uncomfortable minuets of his stair that smile began to seem more sinister. Then in a fit of rage I flung my hands out and screamed.

"Are you here to help me at all?"

As usual he had no response but this time around he stepped closer into the full view of the light and I could now see all of Duane, his smile was gone and now was emotionless with dangled arms and his head was straightened with his eyes directed at me, but not like just a weird stair it was like he was taking a deeper look into my soul. Then out of nowhere Duane hunches over viciously coughing then as fast as it starts it abruptly stops and he stands back up to an expressionless state, fully visible I see Duane's face turn pail , his eyes turn bloodshot, his lips and skin look dry and start to crack, his hair grows out fully within seconds then his mustache, beard and head hair turn completely gray. Duane looks deathly ill and the site was sickly, Duane raised his hand touching my cheek with his dry bony concrete like skin, I try to look away but feel to drawn to the horror and as we had locked eyes I see a piece of his skin from his cheek fall off to reveal the bloody muscle underneath.

Duane grabbed my hand to shake it but this was all to weird, I tried to pull away but my hand felt glued to his and as I could see his skin crack more and more pieces fell off I could see the bloody muscles pulsate and all Duane did through the event was smile back at me. I tugged harder trying to get away but it felt useless and with a burst of energy I tugged harder pulling myself off, looking down I see I was disconnected from Duane but thick gooey strands of blood were connected to both are hands, in fear I shake my hand trying to break from the gross glue like blood.

In a fit of rage screaming as I pull my hand back breaking the blood strand I look up to see most of Duane's face has deteriorated and hair in pieces than with his weakened arm dangling I hear the joint snap and his arm fall from his side to the ground, Dallas then reaches with his left hand at me opening his mouth letting out a deathly scream like a scared little girl and as I could not close my eyes in the fear and my nerves were tight from the tension making me frozen I could not look away or run I just stared at his body falling apart and when his scream were dying I see his jaw loosen to break and then fall to the ground as well. Now Duane nothing more than what a zombie would be lowers his hand and backs into the darkness almost non visible, broken from the fear I yell at him.

"Why are you doing this to me, what do you want?"

Duane has no reaction as if I could tell with nearly half of his face gone, Duane raises his left arm again to point at me, then as I reach for his hand we touch our tips of our fingers and suddenly his hand turns to dust then spreads to the rest of his arm, I brake into tear as I see his upper body crumble away into dust as well as his legs and he becomes nothing more than a pile sand sitting on the floor in front of me.

I fall to my knees sobbing with my eyes locked onto the pile of dust, I scream as I feel the tears seep down my cheeks, with my hands in the air I bring them down to pound at the pile of dust then fall forward smacking my head on what I could tell was a metal floor with what was Duane covering my midsection, balled up I huff and puff crying myself to sleep the best I can. I knew I was already in a dream so falling asleep in a dream was the least weird thing about this all, as my eyes grow tired they were also burning from the tears and I couldn't keep them open much longer but as I look at the crack of the light being let in at the bottom of the wall I see two pairs of feet walking and before I close my eyes I hear from the outside of what was this room.

"What tests are left for this prisoner?"

As I closed my eyes in the dream I awake in real life, my eyes slowly crack open and as I lean forward I notice as usual Tang wasn't there, he must already have been onto his schedule as if he had one. I rise from the couch felling better than most days, I turn to the side to a warm welcome from the picture of Wendy, walking around to the back of the couch I take a good long look into Wendy's eyes, I thought that the picture had made its place on the wall behind the couch but after time it seemed to be not the right place for such an important piece of my life. I peeled the picture off the wall and the tape with it, walking the Control Deck with my limp and the picture at my side, in the Control Deck I see Tang sitting in the Captain's chair scooping food out of a pouch one bite after the other almost inhaling it.

"Hey take a breath."

I joked, Tang lowered the pouch from his face to look at me with a big grin, while limping my way over to the Captain's chair, Tang placed his pouch of food on the counter then faced me raising his hands grasping the air wanting me to place him on my shoulders, so I picked up Tang and he crawled up my arm to the back of my shoulders as I sat then I taped the picture of Wendy to the corner of the computer. I sat back in deep thought only wasting more time than I should have, earlier I had thought I had all the time in the world per say then had to live day by day hoping to make it in one piece to the next moment, for now I didn't know what to think there was a list of goals I needed to get around to but I get winded so easily and the emotional tole takes a bigger chunk out of my ability to move around. I've been feeling a lot physically better then weeks ago so maybe I don't really need to work out as often, though I feel that could only be a temporary break with the possibly deadly diet and lack of physical activity either way I'll need to build up some kind of bulk or I'd simply waste away.

I guess with working out being put off for now I needed to focus onto finding something to put onto the pod to send out into to void of space and as repetitive as it is I still need to venture into the tunnel system again to shut off the external lights and the vent blasting the cool air, I swivel the chair around to see the vent noticing the ice was spreading farther out, I know I mentioned my many of adventures in the tunnels, you may have wondered why I just don't flip some switches on the main computer to turn off what I need done and I may have explained it before but it's as simple as not wanting to read through the manual for the pod, I knew how to drive the pod but if I was to stay live in the pod at some point I'd need to know every aspect of controlling the pod, it's the same with turning the unneeded power off with the computer up here instead, since I did most of my work in the tunnels I never used most of the functions on the computer and it would take more time to learn it than I feared I had.

I remembered back to my past travels and how when the ice engulfed the station there was sheets of ice in the tunnels and I needed to wear warmer clothes but this wasn't as bad as that, the ice was spreading farther past the vent but the damage shouldn't be as bad as before and would most likely be cornered to the area it was coming from, at the moment the two things I was most focused on was turning off the unneeded energy and figuring out what to put in the pod to send out.

Wasting enough time I needed to head down in the tunnels, I wish I could clear up this whole pod mess but my mind felt frazzled and with all the wasted brain space I wasn't going to come up with an answer anytime soon, the best thing to do now was work on what I could and worry about that later, I wasn't going to go for a space walk anytime soon so the pod blocking the door wasn't a bother, though if I needed a quick escape the pod wasn't filled with the necessary supplies and hopefully I'd get to lower pods fast though it wasn't like I'd be heading back to Earth and there was only a months worth of food on those pods so I'd surly be doomed.

Alright that's enough of that I needed to prepare for my travel, turning the chair around to stand Tang jumps off the counter to fallow then the thought occurred to my.

"What was I going to do with him?"

Walking into the Rec. room I put on some regular clothes just in case, but what I had said was something I need to look over, I knew that Tang wouldn't feel easy if I left him up here though I didn't know how he would react to going with me. Making our way back to the desk I pulled the flashlight out of the Captain's safe which was probably about half charged so that was at least good enough for the journey, though I was fully prepared there was still the issue with Tang, if I did leave him up here he would probably freak out, and not to sound anymore crazy than normal I had a fear that when I returned to the surface Tang could be gone, though in the moment I don't know why that would have been a concern I just felt if there was a possibility he was fake this could be an opportune moment for the universe to hurt me more.

I guess that answered my questioned I had to take Tang with me but another issue was that Tang was to small to really climb down the ladder himself and I didn't really want him doing that either way, there had to be some way I could carry him down with me and then as we where at the bottom he would have to walk in front of me along the way, I thought maybe there was a way I could cradle him so going back into the Rec. room I grabbed an extra shirt looping it around my arm and neck I made what resembled a pocket hanging from my neck, this way I was going to be able to fit Tang in the pocket then climb down the ladder without having to carry him.

With the flashlight in one hand I spun open the hatch to the tunnel system climbing in feet first and halfway into the hole Tang waddles over to me with a curious face, I click the light on and then pick Tang up holding him under his arms like a baby then place him in the pocket, he fidgets around a little but finally calms as I start to take a step farther down I held onto the ladder with the light in my right hand and Tang dangling from the pocket. This trip down was a lot better than most and I was down at the bottom with ease, now in the crawlspaces I sat upright taking Tang from the pocket and placing him in front of me, I waved at Tang to get his attention pointing forward saying.

"That way."

Tang looking directly at me pointed where I was pointing then stepped farther into the tunnel, I crawled up to where he was and motioned my hand forward wanting him to keep going, as I got closer to him he walked farther in, as we crawled our way deeper into the tunnels I of course was worried with all the things that could go wrong but I tried to not let it get to me. The light was charged enough to make the trip so than was one less thing and with the light I knew exactly where I was going so hopefully everything could go smoothly, thought that there was a problem within itself, if I had thought there was something that could go wrong it usually did. Continuing our way I pushed Tang along turning a few corners and then finally reaching the heating unit then in a realization this trip wasn't going to be that simple though nothing really was, you see this was just the heating unit and I was going to be able to shut off the vent blasting the cool air but if I wanted to shut down the external lights I needed to head over to the electrical unit, it may be farther into the tunnels but it needed to be done.

Scooting forward to the heating unit I opened the touch pad fiddling with the controls while Tang was at my side, I lowered the heat at the specific vent needed, a message popped up.

"Power in that sector is low redirecting power for significant usage, rebooting system, system back to normal response in ten minuets."

I placed my face into my hands I knew that if the system was rebooted I'd be without heat for ten minutes, that wasn't the issue really, the issue was that I had let that vent destroy itself, not only that but that vent was also connected to the air being distributed to the Control Deck, Rec. room, Med. Lab, bathroom and the pantry so from now on if I want heat and cool air to reach those parts of the ship I need to use less heat and cool air everywhere else to compensate. Looking back at the touch screen I see another message.

"Reboot will begin in ten seconds."

Then as the timer hits zero I hear the sound of the big fans kick on and feel the floor rumble a little, I had done this process one or two times before so I was used to the feeling but Tang on the other hand he was probably more confused than I could understand and I doubt he's been through stuff like this, so when the floor was rumbling and the fan noise got louder I could see Tang was only getting more frightened. Tang was shivering, in the crawlspace we could hear the gears of the station moving around and the heating unit booting up again, all kinds of clangs and dings sounded off and Tang seemed very afraid not knowing what was happening, and suddenly everything went silent then as we heard a dial up sound there was a loud bang afterward like someone was smashing two pieces of metal together. I knew the sound was normal and part of the process but it even made me jump and in my reaction I see Tang jump to, when landing back to the floor Tang starts to screech then spin in circles and in his fit of rage he bolts off out of site into the darkness of the tunnel, I call out for him.

"Tang NO!"

I lifted the light aiming it down the tunnel but could not see him, I called out again.

"Tang get back here."

There was no response, I couldn't hear him yelping and his footsteps on the metal floor, I now had to find Tang among all of this mess and hopefully the battery lasted on the light to make the rest of my trip, the heating unit would have been nearly done when I got started working on the electrical system, when I would have been working on the electrical system I'd hope it also wouldn't need to reboot the plan for that was as simple as flipping the right switches but with Tang off on his tantrum he was more important and the rest needed to wait longer.

Tang ran off back in the direction we came from so backtracking wasn't on my to do list and it would be a chore to get back to the electrical system, making my way back I slowly paced down a long tunnel calling for Tang but there was no response, there was a couple turns leading back to the manhole and taking the first and peeking around the corner I shine the light down the rest of the tunnel. It was the most quiet than it's ever been for a while now, I was alone for so long that I got used to the silence and with the warm welcome of Tang things weren't as quiet as before, with the abrupt silence my tensions rise and began to feel more uneasy then out of the dead surroundings there was a faint voice, I turned my head in all direction wondering where it was coming from, it sounded human but I couldn't make out the words as it surprised me beyond belief, as the voice grew louder to a normal volume my eyes widened in shock as I recognize the voice was myself, I mean it wasn't me but it was the voice was mine but not like I was hearing my own thoughts this was somehow my voice outside myself yelling and I could hear it.

I know this sounds bonkers but it was true I was hearing my own voice outside my body without me saying a word I could hear myself per say call out.

"Taylor, Taylor."

I was frozen, was it fear not knowing how to fully explain this was it the unknowing of what events were to come, I don't know but as I was there crouched in place in the crawlspace not moving I could hear what seemed to be my voice keep shouting.

"Taylor, Taylor."

There puzzled with my hand dangled and the light hitting the floor only wasting the precious energy that was needed I could only think in deep thought.

"Who was this Taylor, why was my voice yelling for him what did all this mean?"

I didn't want to hear the insanity anymore, I pushed my hands against my ears trying to block out the voice as it got louder and louder till my hands couldn't block the noise and with a red face I ball my fists banging the sides of my head, the voice only got louder and faster with no stop.

"Taylor, Taylor, Taylor, Taylor."

It was insufferable and my face was turning blue, I lowered my hands still balled up and pounded the metal wall at my side and with the pain I scream then throw my head against the wall trying to get the voice out of my memory but that just hurt worse and looking to see my left hand was dripping with my blood then feeling the warm blood seep from my head and down my face.

With all the agony the voice suddenly stopped and I was back into the silence hoping to hear Tang screech but there was nothing and I was just there hunched in the crawlspace with a headache, a busted forehead and a bloodied fist, you thought that was hell that was nothing compared to the years of other crap though you already know this, to make matters worse there was always something next bad or good there always was and as I get a better look at my banged up hand in my other I notice the light start to dim. I knew I didn't have the mental or physical ability to deal with this situation another day also I needed to find Tang and if I put this job off another day who knows what could go wrong if it wasn't finished it could mean life or death, the light was dimming but it wasn't to low yet I still had a good amount of time before I'd be lost in the dark, I just had to brush off the unexplained voices there was to much stuff like that going on and dwelling on it was a waste of time.

Making the next turn I shined the light around looking up at the ceiling and on the left side wall I could see the ladder and the light above the manhole coming from the Control Deck so I knew I was on the right track, stepping closer to the ladder I could hear a clanging like metal was softly hitting against each other and as I get next to the ladder I shine the light at the first few steps and see there was Tang clinging to it and shivering with fear. Tang had a ring of metal on his wrists that were part of his space suite so that was what was the metal making the clanging noise when he was shaking against the ladder, I extended my hands letting Tang grabbed my finger with his small hand and I pulled him closer to myself and Tang then clung to me, we sat there in the tunnel as I cradled him with one hand.

But the horror wasn't over yet and we needed to trudge along and as I turn back around and head in the direction of the electrical system and before we even made the first turn Tang was freaking out, he was distressed but more in a calm way, somehow he knew what we where headed in for and as I paced farther into the tunnels Tang started to whimper, as I continued down the tunnel I petted Tang trying to calm him then getting to the heating unit the touch pad message was.

"Reboot complete, power redirected, attempt success."

With that complete we headed forward finally reaching the electrical unit, this process was actually quiet simple it was just flipping through some menus and pressing the right buttons, at the electrical system I place Tang on the ground and letting go of him he grabs my shirt not wanting to let go, he motioned his hands wanting my to pick him up again but I had to focus on the electrical system, Tang tugging at my shirt wouldn't let up and needed my attention, so before I messed with the touch pad controls and screwed something up I picked up Tang once again and seeing the grin on his face I smiled back then placed him in the custom pouch I made earlier then got back to work.

Focused on the pad I see many different control options that read.

"Gravity stabilizers, Outer hull stationary gravity, Interior station lights."

Ah there it is the outer hull station lights, clicking it open I was brought to another page with all the outer hull station lights options, there was just as many functions as all the others, there was lights on about every lining of the outer hull but now none of it was necessary and just wasted energy, so with no needed for using any of those functions the best thing I could do was shut off all the lights in the outer hull. Most of the outer hull lights that we did leave on was the back and front lights just so we would have something to let other travelers know there was something in the way but there was also lights on the sides of the station and a few on top and bottom, if you remember I was on a space walk and the outer hull lights turned on and that was before I had meet Tang, then I had leaned from the notes that Tang brought that he was trained to use the functions for the pod and even knew how to hack into other things so the outer hull lights turning on could have been a glitch or Tang could have hacked into it as he neared closer to the station.

Now with the outer hull lights shut off, Tang snuggled around my neck and the light only getting dimmer I turned around heading back to the manhole ladder, when making my first corner I could hear Tang snore in the little pouch and looking to my left hand I see the flashlight was dimmer then earlier and I wouldn't have but five minuets before it would die, while I stared at the dwindling light I notice the dried blood from my hand then I had remembered I bashed my fist and head into the metal after what seemed to be a mental breakdown, I lifted my hand up to my forehead and feel the crusted blood peeling off small pieces of it out of my hair. Don't get to worried I've really been through worse and this wound was only a small puddle there's definitely been more blood then this seeping out of me at one time, hearing Tang snore gave me this warm feeling inside, I didn't know how to fully explain it but I know it felt like someone loved me, like someone was there and could make everything much better, normally even with Tang being here the only time I could tell I wasn't alone was if Tang was jumping around and yelping.

Making that second turn I had the manhole ladder in my sites and now at the bottom of the ladder the flashlight starts to flicker, I shake the light trying to get more juice but that was no help and the light weakened with every passing second. Tang was still fast asleep as I gripped the sides of the ladder and started my ascending journey, taking the first few steps I was off the ground holding the flashlight in my hand against the ladder, I was able to see in front of my face but that was about it, the light didn't reach upwards for me to see more than two or three steps but as I continued to climb I looked up to see it was near the top and the light from the Control Deck light only the first few steps down the manhole. Nearing closer to the top my flashlight begins to flicker rapidly, with my tensions high each step up became slower as the next step my grip hardened, a sweat breaks down my head and as I inch to the next step the light in my hand burns out.

For what now what seems to be such a recurring thing like waking in morning or breathing I somewhat got used to the darkness, I was so dark on the inside and a lot of my outside life was to not as black as my mental turmoil. I look up staring at the light from the Control Deck and lifted my hand from the safety of the ladder to feel for the next bar, then I had remembered that this wasn't as hard as I was making it out to be, though it may be exponentially harder for any other person but if I remember right I've done this one or two times before and with the memory that I've conquered this evil before and I even with my horrific experience I was broken but also a little stronger in a way and with the memory telling me I know I could do this and I have, this wasn't going to stop me and I've been though to much for such a menial thing to let it get the better of me. With the recharge of positive reinforcement I grabbed for the next bar and the next till I reached the rim of the manhole tunnel hatch and reaching the light I squinted my eyes as I adjusted to the light, pulling myself out to sit on the floor of the Control Deck I look down at Tang to see him cracking his eyes open and awaking to the sudden brightness then giving a small yawn, I stand to pull off the custom pouch and then place Tang on the Captain's desk.

Standing there looking over Tang I peek over to the Captain's chair, not to be repetitive though you know I can be I know this chair has been one of the main setting points of my past challenges and crawling through the tunnels I wasn't ready to lounge anytime soon, looking behind me I see out the porthole of the air lock and there still was Tangs pod. I thought there could be some use for it but there was nowhere else to move it on the station and I wasn't up to taking a space walk soon anyway, then there was that whole trying to make a message to send out hoping other life could take notice of my existence but I never could make that kind of big decision. For now I couldn't think if there was something I needed to do, though I guess you do have those times, there are times where I really have nothing to take care of or tend to so I'd have to wait for the next terror to confront me as it usually does and always will. But what kind of life was that and that was a stretch of a statement this life I was living was no one person could live but only deal with and fight against it, now at this time the best I could estimate was that it had been the mid to late of the forth year it more felt like a lifetime and there isn't much I could hope for in a life like this but I have to believe there is some kind of silver lining reward after all the trauma I've gone though, there just has to be I know it.

Chapter 28

The fight is still on

Only moments after I was still standing there with a blank face staring off into space, and in this moment I realize in my boredom it was the first time in a long time that I wasn't overly bothered or stressed about current events, this at first wasn't alarming but normally there was always to much going on and with this moment of seldom I didn't know if it was relaxing that I wasn't presented with a life and death situation or if I should be afraid that things were to normal than they where before even if I could make a statement like that. I mean is that what my life has come to, where there's just so much shit to deal with that any kind of at ease moment makes me think something was very wrong.

Looking back to Tang he was laid on the counter fast asleep, I didn't want to wake him he seemed to be so peaceful and he had the right idea, after such an adventure we both needed a nap but I was still a bit frazzled from the tunnels and even emotionally drained so though sleep was the best solution I felt there was something more that could have been done today, what may that be I don't know I just know that I was a little drowsy and bored out of my mind. A while back I did mention trying to do new things to keep occupied, you know well enough that based on my location there can only be so much reinventing, really thinking it over I could have done many of things, like watching more of the personal logs I have yet to go over, I could go for a space walk if I really wanted to put the work into releasing Tang's pod, other than that all I could seem to manage was standing there with my thoughts and my blank face.

Feeling limb I wrinkled my lips as I could tell they where chapped and my mouth was dry, I broke from my gaze and limped over to the pantry getting a drink of water. I moved over to Tang, looking down at him and sipping my water I thought to myself that I knew I had been though hell not only for the what I think was now the five years I've been up here but most of my passed life to. You see no human can handle my current life and I may make it sound easy but you guys only hear a fraction of what really goes on, I don't try to keep you guys in the dark but its more note worthy to mention the horrors and tribulations that I over come than listing to me drone on about using the air purification or doing other menial tasks to keep the station afloat, I guess I should go over some of the loose ends but first I needed to get comfortable.

I sit the water bottle on the counter next to Tang then plop down onto the Captain's chair and sinking into the seat I feel the chair slowly lower and then hear the spring underneath me snap then the chair lowers to the ground, with the Captain's chair broken my upper chest was the only part of me that reached above the counter, there it was that's what I was waiting for. As I had said earlier it was unsettling that nothing was putting me into a uncomfortable position and though that shouldn't be a normal thing not being in a life and death situation was out of place so no matter how big or small the inconvenience was there always has to be something that makes life just a little harder it was a expected recurrence and wasn't slowing down so why should I assume much to change.

But back to the main subject, I know I've been though hell and a lot of it, for what sounds like I may be intact I'll tell you I haven't been for a long time and I've been in shambles being broken down only farther with each challenge, so in a short answer no I was far worse than I could ever let on than you'd understand, with all the challenges I broke more and more. The other tasks I did during the day weren't worth mentioning but I guess knowing more would hopefully answer some of your questions, I still had to use the air purification every few weeks or something like that and the mess I dealt with about the airlock kind of screwed with the timing of the air purification and that made the safety of the situation iffy but I've been lucky so far.

Another menial task was checking dials that showed the track of certain power levels in many different parts of the station, I had mentioned this one before it was the main job I took care of when this was a five crew station, the switches, gauges and dials were the core of my past job, they told me the increase and decrease of the power in all parts of the station and if something needed to be pushed up, pulled down or redirected, then I also took care of many of the repairs that where needed. I had said before that in the past I nearly lived in the tunnels as I worked down there and I was constantly on watch waiting for something to work on, but if somehow I wasn't able to see or get to the dials in time there was a virtual version on the main computer that the Captain could check on and if needed could inform me of the changes for me to fix.

Now that I was nearly doing the work of a five man crew by myself I couldn't stay in the tunnels and even when in was working there wasn't much to be on the fence about so I thought if there was some kind of issue I could catch it on the computer then head down to fix it. There was other things that the crew took care of that was no longer needed, like doing experiments for finding other life, testing non human life stability and extended human space life stability, I think I can safely say I've already done pretty well with that last experiment and if you remember this station was to last five years but all together I've been up here for a little over seven years and a little over four of those where me all alone.

The other to mention was testing the radio connections from the station to the many space organizations on Earth such as N.A.S.A., the Russian space program and the Japanese Space program, all these different test where done each day and took up most of our work time, but a lot of the hardest work was maintaining this station. The station that I am currently on was the first time the U.S. wanted to make attempts to send humans to live in space for more than a year at a time and finally when we can up with the plans and funds, it didn't produce the most up to date version but it was sustainable for our testing limits, that was what made it a drag to life up here, this station needed daily work done by more than one and though I may have made it passed the testing schedule meaning we must have done pretty dame well making this bucket I just had to keep up the work load and wait till the station plummeted or I killed over.

Sitting there in the broken chair I placed my hands on the counter pushing down to lift myself out of the seat, Tang was still asleep and if I was going to try to get rest I needed something more comfortable than a desk chair, passing through the Rec. room and into the bathroom, gazing into the mirror I can see that I was back to my old ways, my head hair was near my shoulders, my mustache and beard morphed into one and the length reached to the middle of my chest, my skin was pail with a few small red blotches. Looking down I could see the abundance of hair all over my body, I was only wearing my trunks and looked like an ape, looking up into the mirror again I knew it was me or at least a form of who I was but that was it I was forever changing in both good and bad ways, while staring into that mirror though I knew inside it was me and this image of me was what I had been for so long, I couldn't remember the last time I was clean shaved and off this station. I didn't what to say this was me and it wasn't it was who I had become, we talked about having choices as humans but my options seem to decrease with time and there was no going back.

In the bathroom standing loose with my eyes locked on my own back in the mirror I was frozen in my stance with my thoughts my mind was temporally blank, as I looked deeper in seeing only myself it almost felt there really was another person in the room though I couldn't kid myself and had to realize that dream was never going to be possible. I had Tang and that should be more than enough but as my human instincts where boiling I needed human contact, slowly lifting my hand to touch the mirror my reflection matched my movements and as I made contact with my mirror self for a moment it really felt there was another person with me but as fast as the feeling came it depleted away and the look of happiness turned to pure hate not only for my situation but also myself.

My mind flooded with the memories of my past, I never got to have a steady and successful job, I couldn't find my true love and when I could have I chickened out, I lived paycheck to paycheck went through hell with family stress and social issues, though don't get me wrong I did do many things most humans don't get to it wasn't easy and being the last man in the universe most humans couldn't deal with the stress and would kill themselves after all I have gone through up here but the most painful thing of all to realize was that I didn't need to go through this from the start I shouldn't have to kill myself up here being the last human I should have done it back on Earth with the pathetic life I had.

In my disgust and anger I could no longer hold in the pressure and with a burst of adrenaline I pulled back my fist then flung it forward at the glass mirror making a divot into it, dropping my hand I look at the mirror seeing the smashed glass in the center then looking down at my right hand I was lucky there was no shards stuck in my hand but it did burn like crazy and with the pain having a late kick in I feel the full effects pulling my right hand closer to my chest and cradling it with the other as I screamed my head off in the pain, I lifted my hand up to get a better look and I was all bright red, grasping my right hand wrist I continued to scream shaking my hands forward and backward and as I could feel the muscles in my hand pulsate the skin turned white again then the burning turned to a light throbbing.

Looking into the mirror I could see parts of my face in the smashed glass like if somehow my face was shown to be in shambles and tore apart, I just couldn't bare to look at myself any longer so I lowered my head and made my way back to the Rec. room. As much as I wasn't tired I felt that I had been though to much drama today and needed to try to get some rest, before I went to lay on the couch I peeked out to door to check on Tang knowing I probably woke him with all my screaming and to my curiosity he was still passed out on the counter of the desk, at first I had a grin seeing Tang was sleeping with my worries then slowly it occurred to me that with my hooping and hollering Tang would have surely woken, I limped over to Tang to pet his back hoping to get a reaction and as I continued to pet him his eyes peeked open and he gave a calm yawn wanting to get back to sleep. Knowing he was fine was reassuring but him not waking during my whole ordeal was still in the back of my head but it was useless to drive myself crazy on something that may not be anything.

Sitting back in the Captain's chair I decided that I needed to keep an eye on Tang and I'd have to sleep in this desk chair for now, leaning back in the chair I feel myself falling asleep, looking up one more time I glanced at the picture of Wendy pinned to the computer then my eyes get heavier and as my vision blurs the last thing I see before I pass out is Wendy's smile.

I cracked opened my eyes and as my vision was still a blur I was leaned back taking a look around the room, it looked like I was drunk and confused about my surroundings then my eyesight became normal and in shock I see that Tang was no longer on the counter, I twitched my body forward turning my head and body in all directions to see where he could have been. I was still a bit drowsy and in a soft voice I called out.

"Tang, Tang where are you?"

I then had thought about how I was still a bit tired and remembering how when I was sleeping I hadn't remembered dreaming anything, normally I dream quiet often and I tend to remember a lot of them because I am able to truly get away for this hell for a few moments but this time was different I had no dream what so ever everything was blank and dark, telling time was always a hassle so I didn't know if I was asleep for five minuets or five hours, I was more drowsy when I did wake so maybe I just got less sleep than usual.

I tried shaking my head trying to wake up faster but that only made me dizzy and in the distance I could hear a soft crunching, leveling my head my eyes widened and I could hear the crunching again but it was very faint, it sounded as if like someone was chomping on wood. I lifted myself out of the Captain's chair only to stand with wobbly legs then fallowed the sound to the pantry seeing to my delight that Tang was there sitting in the open potato sack of granola scooping up pieces of the granola into his mouth, I couldn't help but scold him.

"Tang no bad stop we need to save that stuff."

Tang stopped playing with the granola to acknowledge me, then he climbed down from the bag and clung to my leg, I knew I shouldn't have been that mean but the space food pouches we had where decreasing and the food needed to be planed out, I reached to the side grabbing a water bottle to drink. Limping back to the Control Deck Tang was still clinched to my right leg, I lightly shake my leg then he jumps off and we eye each other, Tang grabs at the air wanting me to pick him up but I just chuckled responding.

"You can get up here without me?"

He whimpers and repeats the action.

"Okay, Okay you big baby."

I roll my eyes bending over to grab Tang as I could feel a sting in my lower back then grunted as I lifted Tang to my chest to hold him like a baby with his head on my shoulder, I started to lightly hop hoping he would fall asleep but it wasn't working and the pain in my lower back was starting to cramp, I placed Tang on the main computer counter and he gave the same look as before and wanted to be held then I got a better idea.

I gave a big smile back and then started to hop in place barley getting off the ground, going up and down repeatedly with a big smile Tang began to screech and grin back then with his arms in the air he fallowed my actions and hopped with me. We where having all kinds of fun and it was a happy moment that was long needed and with my decaying heath I needed the exercise, of course this didn't last long and I was huffing and puffing in no time as the pinch in my lower back becomes unbearable and I tumble over laying on my side on the floor as I have my back bent backwards and I grasped my lower back in the pain. I had a light sweat and my face turned red but after a few seconds my muscles relaxed and I was able to lay flat then looking up I could see Tang peeking over the counter wondering what was going on.

Picking myself up off the floor I moved to the Captain's chair and as much as I hated to and even though the day had just started I needed to relax, this chair has taken up to much of my life already and I needed a move, I go to stand again able to keep myself on my feet but I was straight up and my back felt stiff and like peanut brittle so adding pressure wasn't smart. Tip toeing to the Rec. room Tang jumps to my arm but misses the landing and dangles from my arm by his hands, in the Rec. room Tang jumps off my arm to the arm rest of the couch as I loop around the side to fall back and sit in the middle seat then bringing my legs up to the right seat so I could lay flat on the couch. Leaning to the side I pick up the remote for the stereo turning on some classical music, I feel the music flood into my system and as I lay still I imagine moving to the tempo and the calming tune eases my pain letting my body and mind relax then I feel Tang grab the tip of my foot and wiggle one of my toes then again and again so I look up to respond to him with a groaning tone.

"What do you want?"

He just sat there and continued to shake my big toe, I knew what he wanted, he wanted me to get up and move around and I knew I should it would be better for my heath plus he was already bored and wanted someone to play with, but he just kept at shaking my foot faster and faster like he was saying.

"Get off your lazy ass sleepy time over get to work."

I lightly pushed my foot forward then Tang let go of me, I pulled my body up and sat with my upper body a few inches off the couch looking forward to respond to Tang.

"I'm up, I'm up."

Sliding my legs off the couch I sat straight up but now leaned back on the couch seat, Tang began to frown then jumped to the seat next to me and pounce up in the air screeching he wasn't to happy, I let out a disinterested groan thinking that this was unexpected. I knew that I hadn't dreamed anything and that was amiss and felt just as tired now as I was when I went to sleep like I almost got none, I can't explain it, it's probably just my body reacting to all the stress I've been through in the past few weeks, but the brighter thing to see about this was that I wasn't really alone and I had Tang and he depended on me, it may not be my dream reward but it was a living thing and I had someone to take care of other than myself. To my disliking I nerved the strength to push my body off the couch with wobbled legs as I stood but that didn't matter to Tang we was looking for the same wanting contact that I had craved for so long I was just glad that deadly work didn't seem to be on the agenda hopefully only playful fun if my pains would allow it.

Leaning over I grabbed the remote to the stereo turning off the music, then slowly limped over to the Med. Lab with Tang, I had thought since I hadn't been in there for a while there could be something I could find to pass the time, entering the Med. Lab Tang was behind my right leg while we stood at the door and we could see that the space was quiet in disrepair though now that wasn't such a bad thing since making scientific discoveries wasn't my top priority. I hadn't stepped in this room for months and

I could see the effects, most of the cabinets where flung open from times I was looking for things, there was random tools for mechanic and medical reasons strung about the floor and counter, then there was also few empty food pouches and broken glass from bottles, beakers and the inner frame of one of the cabinets. Oh yeah it's kind of coming back to me I do somewhat remember that, I knew that a while ago before Tang there was a reason I smashed the glass part of that cabinet against my head and had to pull out the shards and cut my hair but the memory only adds more mystery I can't for the life of me remember why I would have done such a thing I just knew it was connected with a bad event.

Tang runs passed my leg to near the middle of the room and on top of a small pile of trash, Tang bent over to dig through the trash pile, I leaned against the door frame seeing Tang on the trash pile with a piece of paper in his hand waving it through the air, he then slammed the piece of paper against the floor. Relaxed on the door frame I chuckled at Tang he was acting so silly and only destroying the place more, I should have stopped him but he was having so much fun and we both needed it. It wasn't like the Med. Lab was going to go to any important use so trashing it more than I already had seemed like a stress reliever so I joined in, we didn't mess it up more than it was before we most of just took the trash from the floor and spread it throughout the rest of the room. We weren't doing anymore real damage and we where just mindlessly tossing trash about but it seemed to keep Tang happy and seeing him smile and yelp it was something we both needed for a long time, after about five minuets of playing with the trash and jumping in circles I slowly stopped and was at a loss of breath then was hunched over panting in and out with heavy breaths, Tang caught on and ran to me to pull at my pant leg, I rubbed the top of his head and assured him that I was okay.

"I just need a break buddy."

I limped out of the Med. Lab to the pantry for a drink with Tang fallowing behind, finishing my drink I look to the wall of food pouches and notice that there definitely was less now than there was during the start, I mean the crew of five did eat nearly two years worth and about another four was eaten buy me but only the portions I needed plus there was the amount that Tang brought along but still I could tell there was less than I last remember taking count, though that was no mystery all the food that was gone was the ones I or Tang would have ate. I looked down behind me seeing the bags of granola and as it irritated me that I wasn't going to eat it for a good while now it was something I had to deal with if I wanted to conserve correctly so the disliking frown and growl I was showing fit with my inner emotion. Facing forward to see the pouches again my faced turned to a blankness, I hadn't eaten yet today and maybe that was the reason for my decreasing health that and the untested long term effects of the food pouches but if I wanted my life to last I needed to eat sparingly to make it count.

I grabbed a pouch and we moved back into the Rec. room sitting on the couch, turning on the TV I watched some kind of nature show, I'm surprised this hadn't hit me before but these nature shows that where prerecorded where almost like being there back on Earth, I hadn't touched grass for such a long time and the shows gave me something that was long forgotten and in a way will keep me more human knowing that I could remember all the good times there was of my past life and I wasn't some kind of kook lost to my situation but still it also gave me a hatred for knowing the real feeling of Earth was something I'd never have again, but that was that and I've learned it's not smart to ponder on something you could never fix.

Spooning the food down you would think that dried crumpled ham and beans would get old after awhile but surprisingly it doesn't though there are other flavor so it's not totally routine, about halfway though the pouch my mouth was dry and I regret not taking another water bottle, scooping in a few more bites I could feel the chunks of food not going down easy and getting stuck then I began to cough lightly. The coughing continued in small bursts getting louder and faster, I sat the food pouch down on the table as I was hunched over sitting there on the couch, my couching wasn't stopping then there was Tang sitting by me pulling on my side wondering what was happening himself, I couldn't force the coughing to stop and then I could feel a large gap of air travel up my windpipe making me give out one last big hack, I brought up my right hand to hack into and with the coughing abruptly stopping I looked down to see small spots of blood in my hand.

"Oh shit that's not good."

I knew exactly why this was happening, there had been a few times where when I had eaten I didn't take those stomach stabilizers I had mentioned though I didn't think just missing a few would lead to such a screw up but with continuous consumption of the untested food it would do more damage without the right steps taken to keep my organs safe. Then of course you would question if this food was slowly killing me why put yourself through that self torture knowing there where many other things still trying to kill you, well I could dig into the granola but as any food it goes stale, the granola would go stale faster than the food pouches and the pouches would last longer than the crew would have been up here and they'd last longer than the granola, we did have some fruits but those only lasted a couple years in this environment but now there was no way I could replace the fruit and the stuff I didn't eat was thrown out the garbage shoot.

Getting up from the couch I slug to the door and behind me I hear Tang screech, I turned around whipping my face with my hand showing a discomforted look then I motioned at Tang.

"No you stay I'll be back."

Tang just slid back into the couch while not taking his eye off me as I entered into the Med. Lab to get a stomach pill, I had said before that I hadn't gone into the Med. Lab for months but really I had only gone in there for those stomach pills so I was only in the room for a couple minuets nothing worth to mention or be in there for any other reason since most of its purpose was now wasted. Near the counter I gabbed the pill bottle from the cabinet and popped on in my mouth swallowing it dry then exiting the Med. Lab I leaned into the pantry taking a water and as I leaned on the door frame of the Rec. room I sipped the water and see Tang stand on the couch to smile then start jumping.

Taking a deep breath I swig another drink of water then wipe my brow to feel a small sweat, it was kind of a sticky hot feeling, I take another drink then run my hand through my hair and could tell it was stiff but yet greasy, if I'm not mistaken I had met Tang around a little after three and a half years alone, as I had said many of times it had to now be at five years maybe a little longer if my math wasn't right but I didn't feel like staring at the rubble of the Earth for hours to get a good estimate. What I'm getting at was that it's been probably around a little over a year since Tang showed up and I hadn't taken a shower that whole time, to social standards going out the window you know I don't really care about keeping myself clean, you know I have always been looking for something to pass the time and as I was feeling icky a shower could ease my tensions. Hobbling over to the bathroom I peeked back to the couch realizing that oh yeah there's Tang I couldn't leave him unattended for so long, I needed to keep an eye on Tang but wanted to relax in the shower, I guess I could take him in the shower with me but I'd have to keep my underwear on but it's not like I was going to use shampoo or body wash I was just going to let the water hit me.

I limped over to the table by the couch to set down the rest of my water then motioned Tang to follow me, we walked into the bathroom and I stepped into the shower, I couldn't have Tang be outside the bathroom not knowing what he would get into and I couldn't trust him to stand outside the shower curtain he might find a why out the door if I wasn't looking. With my underwear still on I leaned over to grab Tang then placed him behind me in the shower, closing the curtain I peek behind me seeing Tang was in the corner of the shower standing there, I turned the nozzle lightly to let out a small stream of water only letting a small amount of it pass me hitting the wall by Tang. Bending forward I drench my long hair in the water stream letting it soak my boxers as well, I peeked behind me again seeing Tang slowly moving his had to the stream of water and as it made contact he screeched moving his hand back to his side, I chuckled responding.

"Oh you big baby."

Tang looked up at me screeching again, he wasn't angry he was just displeased and wanted to be somewhere else but I still didn't trust him, turning my head back to the nozzle I sighed in relief as the water hit my scalp and seeped down my forehead then my neck, I ran my hand through my hair and let the water roll down my back. Standing there in the center of the shower my head was lowered and my hair drenched in water as it was also flat and weighing my head down covering my eyes from seeing much, this was a moment that I needed for a long time my body was always in stress and a shower relieved my tensions letting my muscles loosen, but of course that was never enough and I stood there loose feeling each drop of the water hit my chest though my head was still lowered as if I looked ashamed.

I should be enjoying myself but with any event I slowly get back to realizing the hell I'm in, the issue I guess was all the wasted water, it's not like I ever had to shower again I didn't but this helped and was something to do but normally the time when the crew took showers was quick and speedy, we only got a couple of minuets to shower and the tank that was in the tunnel system would be refilled every month or so plus the water was used for not just showers but also cleaning our hands after medical tests or when my hands got all grimy from working in the tunnels.

Looking up I stair at the shower wall in front of me seeing the water seep down hitting the rim of the wall and the floor of the shower and while I was gazed at the traveling droplets the water from the nozzle was directly hitting me in the face, I bring up my hands to whip off my face then pull up and back down the top of my head flipping my hair back. From behind I hear Tang screech again then I start to feel little water drops hitting my calf, peeking back there was Tang splashing in the water smiling and flinging the water in all directions, when I was peeking my head around I could feel the water from the nozzle hitting me in the ear and it tickled a bit making me smile. I was chuckling at what Tang was doing then with the cool water hitting the side of my head my ear began to feel numb but suddenly I could also feel the pressure of the water drop, the nozzle had two settings full blast and soft, most of the time we had kept it on full blast since a shower would take forever on the soft setting but the only time the shower would auto switch was if the tank was running low.

As you could assume this wasn't good if I ran out of the water from the tank I'd have to use the bottled water and losing all the tank water this soon only made the situation more troublesome, leaning down I shut off the water and bring my hands up again to whip off my face, stepping out of the shower Tang fallowed and clung to my foot as I grabbed a towel from the bathroom closet behind me to whip off the rest of the water and the same for Tang. Letting Tang climb up my arm and onto my shoulder we head back out to the Control Deck and sitting Tang on the counter I needed to check the computer for the water levels in the tank, I had mentioned earlier that the water tank was in the tunnel system and for now I wasn't going back down there for a long time hopefully, clinking a few buttons I found the right page and was seeing a virtual map of the water tank room in the tunnel system, the percent bar said that there was now less than one third of the water level left, I turned off the screen and leaned my head against my hand as I look at Tang.

"Can you believe this?"

I don't think Tang really understood my discomfort but he turned his head to the side in confusion so at least he was emotionally connected with me, standing from the Captain's chair I was tired of sitting there and I was equally tired of laying on the couch all I could think to do was pace back and forth in the Control Deck, I probably did need sleep but I was sick of laying on the couch and the Captain's chair they where beginning to be old locations and that wasn't something light to say with knowing I was still stuck in here for at least another forty years and in my pacing I paused holding my hands to my head realizing.

"Wow I'm now thirty three, I've been up here for six and a half years and four and a half of them alone, well for the exception of Tang though but even as great as it was it just isn't the same as another human but it will do and with the normal life expectancy of a male being mid seventies on Earth may I add so with another fifty years at best it felt like I've already lived a lifetime."

With my rambling thoughts it brought another issue, it was Tang, I think I've had Tang around a little over a year now though the math could be wrong but my point is when we met Tang had to be around five or six and most Capuchin live to be around twelve so he only had another six at best and the idea of that scared be beyond thought and with these dark thoughts as I was pacing I started to lightly tap my hand against my head, it was just something I didn't want to talk about.

Still walking in circles Tang was there on the counter calmly sitting, the shower did relieve some tension and with a cooled body it did help but I could still feel a slight heat under my head, I wasn't burning up but I knew I was starting to get sick and there was no doubt if I had something or Tang did we would infect each other, and to add onto that if I remember right I can't recall any of my crew getting the common cold during our journey, the only sickness that was most recurring was motion sickness but that also was very far and few, we did have all kinds of those medical pills if those events ever rose so they where easily fixed and tested in rarity.

Bored as always with the situation I just needed to redirect my thoughts, once again as always I plopped into the Captain's chair giving out a huge huff in my disinterest thought of the same location after same location, I chuckled a bit out loud thinking.

"If only there was an interior decorator lost in space like I was and could run across like I did with Tang."

But that only got me thinking more about other things possibly being out there in the deep reaches of space well knowing finding Tang was a one and impossible chance it was most likely we could be the only living things for parsecs, I chuckled again thinking.

"Ha in joke references, you nerds will get what I mean, god I miss good movies."

Then staring back at Tang he had a blank face and I returned to my original thought, as I was saying before Tang and I where most likely one of the few living things left in the universe as of what I know and I may have mentioned what I'm about to explain before but this time I want you to understand the math behind it.

You see when the event began it had been at least I think three and a half years or so before I met Tang, he was in a standard escape pod that was used for the new space station I was getting on before the event and if Tang was in near proximity of the blast he would have died as well, I can also assume that based on the design of the pod he wasn't blasted into space before the new space station was in production so he must of somehow been connected to the new space stations escape pod system and been sent off to make a safe distance away before the blast could happen. But there was still one big unanswered question, if Tang's pod was sent off before the blast it could have only gone less then a mile of distance out before the auto stationary kicks in and then drives itself to the preset destination course, most of the time those preset destinations are Earth but with Earth gone the GPS had nowhere to find it and knowing that Tang got to me almost four years later after the event that must mean his pod being so light weight was sent hurdling all the way passed Mars because we did theorize it could take up to three years to reach Mars with a maned ship but if he did travel that far out how was it possible?

Spinning around in the Captain's chair I peek over to Tang's pod that was still in the airlock hatch, that got me thinking about the memory logs that where recorded on Tang's pod, if you remember I had mentioned that there where all kinds of cameras around my station recording every second of my life, I had also said that I've been up here for at least four and a half years or so before I ran into Tang and it also was theorized it would take three years or more to get to Mars where I would assume Tang would have started his travels back to me. I was thinking that maybe I'd be able to answer some of these questions if I looked at the memory banks of Tang's pod.

Getting up from the Captain's chair I stumbled over to the pod opening both the airlock hatch and the door of the pod then sat in the pilot chair then bringing down the door I was able to pull up the computer menu of the pod. I hadn't talked about much of the technical aspects of the escape pod but they were fairly small so there wasn't much but the main computer system was some of the most advanced tech we used for something so small, there wasn't much room to move about in the pod, the only way to stand was turning the pilot chair around to the storage space in the back of the pod there was the only place someone could actually stand. The shining glory of the escape pods was the main central computer, the screen of the computer was within the glass of the door of the pod it was also a touch screen and some of the most impressive tech we got and a spectacle to see.

Situated in the pod I opened the computer screen searching through the tabs of the system then finally running across the video and audio files, to my dismay for the past year there was very few logs reported though I did know why, Tang had been with my for the past year and the pod was connected to the airlock and was only turned on and recording when Tang or I entered it. The video logs that where cataloged from the past year where just of me moving stuff out of the pod among other small times Tang ran into the pod to grab something, earlier than that was the three and half years or so that Tang was alone, but there was one questioning thing I did notice about the video logs, they all seemed not to be twenty four hours around the clock taping like my station does.

This fact alone probably begs a question for you, you all know that I try to save as much power as I can but having as much video logs seems to be a good thing to me plus it doesn't take up as much power as multiple computer though I guess I could have turned off the camera when I was sleeping, but back to Tang's video logs now. I had doubted if Tang was trained to turn off the pod camera so the best I could assume was that the pod was set up to use a movement based function, so let's say if during Tang's travels and around ten minuets after there was no movement within the pod the cameras would go into sleep mode and then if Tang was to move again the cameras would boot back up and record, that was only reasoning I could come up with for the shortened video logs.

My main reason for searching through the logs was to see what happened to Tang right after the event but looking at a few others wasn't going to hurt, watching a few made only a couple months before we met I was surprised to see how self officiant Tang was, there where videos of him searching through the pantry, using the air tanks when the air was being recycled and cleaned, he must have been through some grueling training to be able to comprehend what he was supposed to do.

After a few days in the life of Tang videos I scrolled down to the video logs from the beginning of his journey, the log I was currently watching I was able to see the brand new station right in front of Tang's pod so this was before all the terror this had also meant I was right about Tang's origin, at the point of this log the pod was recording Tang inside the pod and also the aftermath of the new space station but this moment I was viewing was a little before the blast. Looking down on the lower left corner of the outer pod recording I could see on the new space station that not only was Tang's pod was set adrift there was two other pods that where attached to his and being also dragged along with him, so that also did raise a question.

"Where were those other pods?"

Though I didn't want to relive this horror I was forced to put up with seeing the blast again but from the eyes of Tang, knowing what I was about to see was heart shattering enough but also having to wait for what I know was going to happen killed my spirit even further, then it happened I see a thick blue beam shoot from the new space station and head right for Earth and as the beam dies the new station starts to rumble and you could see the metal tearing apart then there was an explosion on the new station that engulfed the then rest of it starting to tear apart in all directions.

The camera of Tang's pod peeks to the Earth and you could see the biggest crater that you could imagine this hole was about the size of Europe and deep enough to hit the core of the planet and with enough damage that was taken from the core the Earth began to shake and tear to pieces, this was no fast death though maybe for few it was but the rest of the planet was to wait till the core broke apart further till it dismantled the ground level with the atmosphere becoming ripped into nothing and there was no chunk of land that had a breathable substance and these now piles of Earth would become nothing more than space rocks.

The log only had a few more minuets left and I knew that this nightmare was only the start of something bigger, with only a couple minuets left I continued to watch the travesty and suddenly as the Earth was torn to billions of chucks the core was visible with its bright glow and was the rocks pulled away from the core there was nothing keeping the core in place and stable, as the core shook and the waves and radiation and magma rippled you could see a blue orb form in the center of the core itself then as the core glowed brighter and brighter almost impairing the view of the recording the blue orb began to expand taking over the other substances of the core and as there was nothing left of its original form there was the blast the rippling circle matter flattened and widened expanding farther out like something you would see on the fourth of July.

The ripple of blue matter stretched out for miles and miles then hit Tang's pod sending it deeper in space but this was no simple nudge it was like somehow this explosion wasn't hitting the pod it was pushing it at what seemed to be light speed and as the pod slowed the blue ripple faded and in the distance in the video I was shocked to see there was Mars though it was tiny and Tang was a credible distance from it I knew somehow this blue matter sent him as far as in between Mars and Jupiter then the video ended abruptly and I was to assume with the camera movement function on that the blast must have knocked out Tang.

With the video ended I was laid back in the pod staring blankly into the screen and as my head lowered I start to sob and let the tear drops roll down my face, it was as if I relived the event all over again and even though I only saw the aftermath of the destruction then I did feel the effects and now seeing the event first hand it only made me feel worse than before as my face now was wet from the crying and the top of my chest hair was damp from the tears rolling down my neck and chest. I pushed open the pod door to see there was Tang standing with a curious look then Tang extended his arms and ran at me to hug my legs, I still wasn't sure if Tang fully understood what all was going on but as least he knew I was feeling terrible, Tang let go and scurried back into the station then I pulled down the pod door again and shut off the computer, I don't think I could bear with anymore despair I'd come back another day and watch more of Tang's travel.

Opening the pod door once again I was going to head back into the station but I could feel a sharp sting in my chest so I leaned back into the pod chair taking deep slow breaths then I could feel a burst of air travel up my throat making me cough, I covered my face with my hand and coughed again but harder then again and again with each cough getting more heavy then it seemed I was hacking but as I slowed and my breathing was back to normal I open my eyes to see my hand I was coughing into was covered in a small splat of blood.

I knew this couldn't be good and I didn't think that the stomach stabilizer pills I was taking weren't having the needed effect, I needed to eat the space food since it was the only thing I has mass amounts of but it seemed to be slowly killing me plus even if I was to eat the granola first I would eventually have to eat the space food and it wouldn't be long till I was back to eating the space food anyway. Laid back in the pod chair again my neck was bent back and I was staring at the ceiling of the pod, feeling the blood from my hand seep off and onto my legs as my hand was resting against my belly. Normally after such a stressful moment (Basic definition of my life) I make some kind of life realization or a heartfelt speech and though the day was short as most seemed to be the time I was awake was nothing but stress and bad memory and in my sleep I was able to dream a better life but I always awoke back into my real life. Look this was the case today I was just to warn and needed to revert my attention and as much as I need to tell myself there was a silver lining and hope for a better future it was a lie I had to swallow with my pride, even if it was false hope and there was no chance there was true happiness I still had to believe there was some kind of good life out there to live even if it was impossible stranger things have happened.

Chapter 29

Sick of life to what end

Alright, alright I know I was clear about the time pacing a lot but I feel it's not totally easy to explain and I can hear your sarcasm right know.

"Oh there he goes off again about how long it has really been."

To tell you the truth it's not easy and never will be, I can only guesstimate so knowing about Tang's past let's me know it's been at least more than three years and I am fairly sure I've been with him at least a year so to be fair I'd say it has been at least around five years after the event and seven all together. Though it seems like some events I tell you about blend together there are some moments that happen a few weeks to a few months forward, and that's enough of boring you with that, though I should mention that it has been a few weeks since I watched Tang's pod memory banks.

I awoke another day on the couch with Tang demanding as ever, really I have no need to complain I know pets are hard but I was happy enough to wake each day and say I had him but still it wasn't enough and I think even if I fixed most of my problems it still wouldn't be. Leaned up on the couch I was wearing a shirt so that was a change and as I look to see Tang he wasn't jumping for joy like most days and in fact he hasn't been being very active in the past week though I couldn't imagine he got nearly any physical activity in that pod, as we stared at each other he did look a little more slump and just worn, but I guess that came with age I think he had to be probably nine years old so he was passed middle aged.

Sitting up on the couch I pulled the picture of Wendy out of my front shirt pocket and gave a large sigh and a look of boredom, then I could hear a soft screech from Tang and as I lowered the picture to look at him he was slowly pacing to my leg placing his right hand on my left pant leg, I knew it was time to wake and think of better things, I lowered my arm for Tang to crawl on but in return he just raised his hands only wanting to be held and I couldn't say no. Picking him up we left the Rec. room and headed into the pantry for breakfast and same as usual there was still plenty of space food pouches, ripping yet another one open of what seemed to be an endless supply I gave a disinterest look into the pouch itself, though I should be happy I had still a ton of food left I couldn't be a chooser knowing I wouldn't last long without this stash but the worst part was I knew this food was slowly killing me and the stomach stabilizers where the only pills on board to help with it but they seemed to have almost little to no effect.

After getting food for Tang and I we headed into the Med. Lab for the food stabilizers, I as a human needed to take one full pill but Tang was smaller so I had to give him half of one and as sad as it is I think Tang never took those pills when he was on his own so his health was decreasing faster than mine, though another perk about meeting Tang was that since he was smaller he only ate also half of the space food pouch than a full one so the food all together lasted even longer but the unpredictability of its effects was still a issue.

Back in the Rec. room we where finishing our meal and sucking down some water, breathing in relief I finished my last drop then peeked down at Tang seeing him finish is water too and as he laid his water bottle down next to him he to release a big breath but then he starts to shake his head faster and faster then he stood to hunch over and cough again and again. I hopped off the couch and sat on the floor next to him and started to pat him on the back thinking he might need to burp and as the coughing stopped I heard nothing from him, no screech no sounds nothing, he was still standing, he turned his head back to look at me and to my shock Tang's lips where covered with spats of blood. I pulled the picture of Wendy out of my front pocket and placed it on the floor so I could then take my shirt off balling it up and then to wipe off Tang's mouth, I knew this wasn't good and it didn't look like it would get better anytime soon the best I could do was make sure he took more of the stomach pills more often than he ate but hopefully whatever the bug was would move on, I patted him on the back lightly and assured his safety.

"You're all right, it's okay, you got this little bud."

Tang lightly screeched and placed his hands on my stomach to give me a hug, I picked him up lifting him to my shoulder to hold him like a baby and then began to pat his back again. We sat back on the couch and though we just woke I think today was going to be a lazy day as Tang needed to rest from his illness and I needed to watch him every second, with Tang still cuddled up on my shoulder I lifted from the couch and headed out the Rec. room to grab supplies, there wasn't many times when someone from the crew got sick and I could only think of one instance, at the time all we could do was send the sick person to the quarantine area in the tunnels of the space station, so it wasn't a possibility to send them back to Earth it wasn't cheap getting people in space.

Now in the Med. Lab I grabbed a handful of stomach pills and a few of the pills that help with fevers and stuffed them in my pocket of my fresh shirt then I hobbled over to the pantry grabbing a couple water bottles a few pouches of food and to my disinterest a cup of granola, I know I should save the good food for now but I needed to regulate Tang's health and that wasn't going to happen if I kept feeding him the space food and he wasn't getting any younger so for now he would have to eat healthier and get the bug out of his system and he'd only have to eat the granola for the next week so he could get back on track.

Back at the couch I placed the pile of supplies on the table, I needed to keep an eye on Tang for awhile so having the supplies at hand was going to make this easier, laying back I could feel Tang lightly breath and he was kind of half awake but I needed to get those good juices flowing so hopefully drinking more water would help him. With Tang laying on his back on my legs I leaned forward to grab a water bottle unscrewing it and feed Tang like a baby and I was happy he sucked about one third of the water down, placing him at my side he was balled up and sleeping, he sure did get to sleep fast I'm thinking maybe he didn't get much sleep while I was sleeping so with my attention on him he was able to fall asleep. It was a good thing today seemed to be pretty chill and there was nothing serious to take care of though I shouldn't count my chickens before they hatch oh and by the way that means I shouldn't assume anything knowing what could go wrong at any moment.

I leaned forward to grab the radio controller hoping if I turned on some smoothing music it would keep Tang asleep longer, Tang was sleeping well without the music and hopefully it would help him stay in deep sleep but I was feeling the effects to and as my eyes drooped I knew I just woke but there wasn't much to do and if Tang needed me I could hear him screech, I let the soft sounds flow through me and it eased my tightened muscles and as I loosened to relax while sitting back on the couch I let my head fall back as my heavy eyes seemed to glue shut as I take a nap.

Though the experience was soothing nothing ever lasts and what seemed to be an instant I could suddenly hear Tang screeching while I was slowly waking, I was in and out of it and with my cracked eyes I peeked around the room trying to adjust them to the light again, it was weird I felt more tired now than when I fell asleep. Looking down to my side there was Tang where I left him and with my eyes blurred from waking abruptly I try shaking my head to wake further then as my vision fixes I turn to my side and see Tang looked like he was still asleep but he was flinging back and forth and screeching like if he was having a bad dream. Sitting up I leaned over to him and lightly shook his arm not wanting to scare him, this wasn't working and Tang was just laying on his back on the couch, his eyes where clinched and his body was balled up as he twisted back and forth holding his sides, most likely he was having stomach issues and needed a pill, shaking his arm again I called out to him in concern.

"Tang, Tang wake up buddy, wake up you need your medication."

Tang's screeching got softer then slowed to a stop, then his body loosened and he laid flat to open his eyes and look to me, as we locked into a stair Tang gave a soft whimper and held his belly then flipped over and stood to face me, he continued to whimper and hold his belly, I leaned over to the table grabbing a stomach pill and broke it in half for him and as I turn to face Tang to feed it to him his whimpering was droning on then suddenly I see him spit up some brown gunk all over his space suite and it sure did smell like shit almost to unbearable. Motioning the pill to Tang he tried to shove away my hand and screeching in disinterest, I pulled Tang's hand down to his side and tried to feed him the pill again with a stern attitude.

"Tang no you need to eat this it will help."

With hesitance Tang swallowed the pill and sucked down some more of the water bottle, grabbing the shirt I used to clean Tang's blood I also tried to whip off the puke that was on the collar of his space suite but only the top surface of it came off and what was left was a wet patch and the horrible smell, I mean I can't really complain I never kept the station all that clean or showered but I've gotten so used to my own stink that seeing Tang's was getting pretty sickly, whipping off the stuff the best I could I smiled at him and chuckled.

"Alright bud we've got to get you something else to wear this stuff stinks."

Tang almost was like a little baby and taking off his space suite reminded me of what was like changing a diaper, I zipped Tang out of his space suite and threw it aside and then as Tang was standing there looking drowsy it had occurred to me this was the first time I was seeing Tang naked, normally I would change clothes maybe every couple months but for Tang there was nothing else he could wear so this space suite he was in he had on for the past what is now five years. It was kinda weird having Tang not wear clothes but there was nothing else I could put him in and I don't think I'd be able to get the smell out of his space suite though he was a Capuchin so it's in his DNA to be wild I guess he'd feel more comfortable without clothes.

After a few days of more relaxing I was shocked to say there was no notable issues of survival and with Tang just lounging around he finally seemed to stabilize the bug but that's all the pills did, the pills didn't get rid of the bug from the underdeveloped space food it just laid low till it built up and infected the person again, it wasn't the most safe and working out the sickness was stressful but at least the full effects of the bug didn't take very often. During Tang's sickness he mostly slugged around but now healthy again and being able to move freely without the space suite he was all kinds of jumpy, he looked to be more active now than he was before the illness if that was possible. Hunched over on the couch Tang was running around the Rec. room getting his daily exercise plus if he wore himself out now I wouldn't have to later, something I had kept on the back burner was what I said about what happened if one of my crew ever got sick, Tang had gotten the worst that I've seen of the bad space food but there was no way I could have quarantined him it would be torture to leave him isolated I wouldn't want to do that to him and I'd want to believe he wouldn't do that to me, so I knew I would eventually get his same sickness since I was on the same diet but the bug in my system was probably speed up after being around Tang.

In fact just sitting on the edge of the couch my forehead was feeling kinda warm, I already ate my meal with the stomach pill and stayed hydrated with more water than usual but my mouth was still dry, my head was still warm and I did feel a small pinch in my lower stomach, looking up Tang was bouncing around and screeching for me wanting to play. I wasn't really up for it but Tang was happier than he's been in a long time so I wanted to see him enjoy our time together, I pressed my hands down on the couch lifting my but off it only a few inches though before my hand and balance began to loosen and my grip falls as I plop back down on the couch, my lower back and thighs hurt with a sharp sting. I let out a painful grunt while hunched over sitting on the edge of the couch and I could feel my stomach start to churn like someone was squeezing my stomach and not able to hold in the pain I barf a puddle between my legs on the floor, Tang screeched and tip toes slowly to him but I motioned him away knowing it was a bad idea if he was near me, I had no doubt that I caught what Tang had and I wanted him to keep his distance the best he could so this wouldn't be a endless cycle. Tang was a caring soul and wanted to help me, he tip toed closer and I moved my hand trying to shoo him back.

"NO Tang, no you stay there."

Tang stood in place accepting my command but he screeched for my attention and started to thump his food, I just shook my head at him but I knew I needed to clean my mess and had to fight through the pain. After the mess was taken care of I laid back on the couch and there on the table was Tang waiting to hear from me.

"Just leave me alone for a minute buddy I need to relax."

I laid on my side on the couch and tried to get a cat nap before Tang got to active and wanted to play, my eyes ease and I could feel drowsy and as I fall asleep I last see Tang laying on the table in front of me also taking a nap. I woke similar to the last few times and it was getting a little unsettling, you know that normally I would have some kind of dream that imaged what life was like or at times I'd get to see loved ones, I knew they where never real and it killed me a little inside but they where a welcome edition to my situation, though recently my dreams have been blank and in total darkness not lasting that long like almost as soon as I feel asleep I woke only moments later. Slowly waking I stretch out and yawn, I feel a small drip of sweat travel down my forehead then as I sit up on the couch I feel around my neck to noticed it was also drenched in sweat and there was a ring of sweat around my collar.

I could tell I wasn't getting any better, I also felt a cool feeling at my legs, it was weird my upper half was sweaty and hot but my lower half was freezing. I stood from the couch, feeling wobbly I stumbled my way to the bathroom almost losing my footing and at the sink I look into the cracked mirror seeing my face was pail and moist with sweat, I scooped some water from the sink and splashed my face hoping to cool myself off and I could see that the stream of water coming from the sink was thinner than usual so I knew I was still running pretty low on water in the tank. If I was going to survive this I needed to get some more stomach pills and something to get this flu to go down, hobbling out the bathroom I looped around and headed to the Med. Lab, in the middle of the two rooms as I exited the Rec. room and entered to Med. lab I turned to see there was Tang sitting on the counter of the Captain's desk messing with the keyboard. I paused my steps getting Tang's attention as I shook my finger at him.

"Hey you, I'll deal with you later."

Tang shrugged his shoulders like he didn't know what I was talking about, entering the Med. Lab I could feel the sweat seeping down my head and my legs felt frozen, about half way to the cabinet my legs where shaking and I began to lean to the side then in a second I could feel almost weightless as my whole body leaned and with wobbly legs I lost my grip and fell to the floor hitting knee first. On the floor motionless I screamed with all my might as my face turned red and my bum leg stung like a motherfucker, the throbbing slowed but it still stung quiet a bit, sitting up I pulled myself to the counter gabbing one of the lower cabinets and then pulling myself off the floor to lean against the counter. I continuously grunted with pain as I pulled open some of the cabinets getting what I needed and limping my way out the Med. Lab I then grabbed a water bottle from the pantry to take my pills, I then moved out to the Captain's desk wondering what was going on with Tang, I stood in front of him and the blank computer screen and then patted Tang on the head.

"You just playing around?"

Tang smiled at me then I could hear a bell noise from the computer and looking at the now light screen there was a message that read.

"Message contact range has been extended."

I couldn't believe what I was seeing was this true could Tang have done something like this, I mean it seems he wasn't trained that vastly when it came to using the pod but either way whatever he did was kind of a help.

"Do you even realize what you have done, you're such a good boy."

I patted him on the head again and then took his hand letting him climb to my shoulder, we both headed back to the Rec. room and I placed him on the table in front of the couch as I laid back down, I wasn't going back to sleep but I knew I needed to still recover for a couple of days and it wasn't going to be easy trying to keep away from Tang and we probably both shared this illness so what was the point of trying to contain it, it would eventually go away on itself.

Laying flat I turned on the classical music hoping to relax my tensions, wrapped up in the blankets and laying on my side nothing changed much, my body still felt hot on the upper half and freezing on the lower half though these pill always took time. Laying around for at least another couple hours I wasn't able to get a nap in and Tang was getting bored throughout this time as I could see him on the table leaning against his hand and a stained look of boredom. After moving around I couldn't find the right spot and I've got to tell you sleeping on a couch for the past five year was tearing my lower back apart, as you should know there was a couple sleeping pod that stood upright but I never got used to sleeping standing up.

Getting annoyed with being so uncomfortable I began to involuntarily shaking my right leg not being able to get it to stop, this was alarming but I felt it could have just been some kind of muscle spasm and needed to let it work it out on it's own, at first the shaking was light and more of a wiggle but as the seconds pasted it got faster till I felt like my leg was some type of vibrator then it wasn't just the one leg after a few minuets it was the left leg also. You'd probably think if you're so cold turn up the heat but that wasn't all, it was a mix of my flu, being cold and a muscle spasm, the pills weren't going to take effect anytime soon and with the heat situation I needed to save as much station energy as possible and these blankets weren't getting the job done.

For at least a couple minuets both of my legs where shaking uncontrollably and then I with my legs freaking out and feeling cold I feel this burst of coolness rise from my thighs and raise up to my head and as it overcomes me my teeth start to chatter as I feel every uncontrollable bite I make, the sound of my teeth clanging was like someone was smashing glass plates together, grasping the blanket tighter my whole body was shivering now and I began to breath heavier through my mouth as my teeth chattered louder and my body felt more like I was almost jumping on the couch. My body was feeling the full experience of whatever this was and I thought that the worst was over but I needed to find a better way to warm up with out using to much station energy, the one basic couch blanket wasn't cutting it I needed more clothes on and the emergency blanket then abruptly the shaking stopped and my muscles eased and slowed the shaking to nothing.

I slide my legs off the couch and with my upper body still on the couch I was faced up while somewhat still laying down, fighting against the pain I lifted my upper body to sit straight and grunted in agony with the sharp pinch from my lower back, just sitting there my legs where lightly shaking while I had the blanket half on and off. With equal amount of pain from sitting up I lifted my body to stand but my legs where still just as wiggly, as I tip toed to the door from behind I could hear Tang screech so I turned around to respond.

"No you stay, stay there I'll be back."

I couldn't even say I was walking my way out I was tip toeing and each step felt so small, my legs where wobbling faster and I had the basic blanket around my bear shoulders all I was wearing was some boxers but I need to head out to Control Deck and at the storage below the sleeping pods, as I exited the door my legs shook faster and I lost my footing slipping and falling knee first again like last time, on the floor I was knelling hunched over and tried the best I could to lift my body up and start to crawl. Looking down at my knee I could see that my bum leg was a little back and blue, standing again I was more hunched and raising my head I could see there was the picture of Wendy taped to the corner of the computer monitor, for a second behind the view of the computer at the surface of the front glass of the Control Deck there was something shiny hooked to the corner of the glass itself.

Limping forward I got a closer look then noticing it was the emergency blanket, at first glance I was a bit confused, I don't remember what it was there for or how it got there but I do somewhat remember there was something going on that seemed to be in my head at the moment that made me do it. Straightening out my back I grunted again but as I eyed the unattainable emergency blanket all I could do was chuckle at my stupidity and now I had to turn back around to grab more clothes and hopefully that would help my situation more.

Back in the Rec. room I put on a couple of shirts, some shorts and longer pants over those, feeling a little warmer I was still shivering but not as bad as earlier, as I had said this wasn't really all such a coolness it was a weird combo of cold and hot though my body was chilled my head still felt this kind of icy hot, medication wasn't going to help any further and I'd be afraid if I took anymore it would hurt more than help. I was sitting stiff on the couch hunched over with small shivers and with a burst of strength and a painful grunt I lifted up to stand the best I could, there in the middle of the Rec. room with the extra layers of clothing and the blanket wrapped around my shoulders then covering my front I knew I had to be more hydrated so I headed my way out to grab more water talking each step at a snails pace with my wobbly legs like I was a toddler.

Now with the water and back on the couch I took a good long sip and sighed in relief knowing though it didn't seem like such an accomplishment but getting the water and getting back here put my heart in a good place, I mean last time I slipped on my ass and hurt my bum leg.

"I shouldn't have to risk my life every time I want a drink."

Unwrapping some of the blanket I take a look at my leg hoping I was playing it out worse in my head, I hurt my right bum leg and all I could see was that it had a few purple spots but other than that it should heal in a few weeks, taking another big swig of water I sighed again then poured a small bit in my hand to splash in my face. Lowering the water bottle there was Tang on the table smacking his lips eyeing the water, there was about one third of the bottle left and frankly I don't think I should worry about getting him sick or me more sick things tend to just pass anyway but I smiled at Tang giving a small chuckle.

"You lazy ass you know you can go grab your own."

Tang just screeched and grabbed for the bottle so I handed it over and as he sipped the last of it I petted his head and smiled at him.

"You're such a moocher but I love ya."

Tang placed the empty bottle to the side and smacked his lips again and I knew that was as good for him as it was for me, seeing his enjoyment in such a simple thing gave me that warm feeling in my heart, you know there where so many things that have gone wrong, will go wrong and could go wrong but though there are those things to drive a person and Capuchin crazy in the future, some of the best moments to remember where those small happy moments just taking each day as they come and enjoying the small victories as well as the big ones but that's what has changed the aspects of a life now there where such simple activities like drinking water that a human on Earth would shrug a shoulder to but here in the moment it wasn't only relaxing but somewhat a reassurance that we where still alive and kicking through all the hell we deal with.

Laying back in the couch I sat still wrapped up and in front of me there was Tang lightly jumping in place and he sure did make a recovery from his sickness, he was a ball of energy and frankly it was a bit of a shock knowing the struggles he has gone through he still has the emotion to jump and play, thinking about it I think that was the beauty of it, Tang was an animal that was taught amazing things for an animal of his kind but I don't think he fully understood the situation and it's implications he was like a baby there was always some innocence to his manner, the ball of energy was still hopping about and with his big smile he leaped at me hitting my chest as he landed, coughing and groaning as he crashed into me Tang wrapped around me to give me a hug, as I looked down and my gut stung I couldn't be mad all he wanted was contact as anyone would.

Patting his back Tang stood on my belly as I was laid back and then he started to hop, I wasn't having it and it hurt like a motherfucker, I grabbed his sides to stop his motion and he sneezed at my face then gave out a cough, I began to worry instantly because this wasn't some one off where he goes back to doing whatever, he continued to cough in small spurts so I laid him back on the table as he kept on with it, this wasn't a normal cough either it was almost like a smokers cough and with one big last burst Tang spits up this yellow stuff all over his chest.

"Dammit Tang now I got to wash you off."

Tang sat on the table giving me this sad look.

"No, no buddy I'm not mad with you."

This gunk was stinking up the place and it wasn't going to be to easy to clean off, one thing was that Tang didn't like the water so much and really I needed to use as least water as possible, if I used the tub I would waste to much water but I don't know how well Tang will take to the sink, the water came out faster in the tub than the sink so it wasn't the best choice. I stripped the blanket off myself and was no longer shivering after about an hour covered up, I still had the extra layers and was warm enough, picking up Tang off the table I could see that the yellow gunk was just a small spot right below his chin but looked to be very thick.

Holding him out in front of me like I was carrying a baby with a dirty diaper I paced over to the bathroom and placed Tang in the sink, standing at the sink and Tang in the center of the bowl I grabbed a towel placing it next to him, the water was going to come from behind at Tang and I knew as soon as the water hit his backside he'd have a bitch fit.

"Okay Tang I'm going to clean off your chest so you're going to have to get wet got it ?"
Tang frowned shaking his head back and forth and whimpering, I smiled and giggled.
"Well it's not like you have a choice in the matter."

I picked up the towel with one hand then turned the knob on the sick with the other, as a small stream let out I dabbed the towel in it and as I could see the sink start to fill with the water then it hitting Tang's back, Tang screeched lightly but I assured him it was okay and shushed him. Taking the damp towel I pressed against Tang's chest and lightly whipped at the yellow gunk, the gunk was thicker than I thought and was hard to scrub off and through the whole thing Tang was whimpering, doing the best I could I got most of the gunk but the spot was still wet and slimy. Putting the towel under the water again the stream was getting thinner then finally stopped, that was when I knew I was dangerously low on water in the tank, I scrubbed off the rest of the gunk on Tang and used the dry end of the towel to finish up.

Grabbing Tang from the sink I place him on my shoulder as we head out to the main computer, with the sink not working all that well I needed to check the water levels, at the computer Tang jumped to the counter and I fiddled with the keyboard bringing up the page, on the screen there was a diagram of the water tank and the digital dial next to the map of it said ten percent so that wasn't good. If I am remembering right the tank held almost two months worth for five at best and with just me for a while I guess it's safe to say I've used up the water better than expected, normally N.A.S.A. would replace the water after a few months and now it looks like the water level was near the rim of the bottom which we never let it get that low before so I could assume with the redirected power I'm using and the low pressure that the pipes don't have the energy to pump the rest out to me.

I turned the screen off not wanting to look at the disappointment, there on the corner of the screen was the picture of Wendy and even just the presence of the picture itself still brought the light into me, though there was a bright side I did still have a good amount of the water bottles if I really need to use it for that purpose but I probably took a shower once a month even if that and other than cleaning myself there wasn't many times I needed to clean a mess.

Tang still on the counter was steady and quiet and that wasn't his normal self expectancy not recently, seeing the look in his eyes I could tell he was bored but there was something more to it I knew this sickness was kicking him where it hurt and the same goes for me, we both had been through the grinder mentally, physically and emotionally but this sickness was a mystery it came in patches, one day we could feel fine and over it but another day it was like we were being sucker punched, the medication was what I thought was a temporary fix but the effects of the space food was faster than the medication, maybe I was being stupid maybe we needed to dig into the granola but either way one was going to be gone sooner or later so should we deal with the shit effects of the space food now or when there's nothing left to eat but it.

In a deep look at Tang we both just sat there like statues motionless and in a way I think he understood more than I was giving him credit for, our faces were blank and unsettling so I gave this giant cheesy smile hoping to get him to laugh but there was no reaction.

"Really Tang, really?"

He sat there with the same expressionless look so I leaned back in the chair and began to spin around in circles one after another faster and faster, at the edge of my view I could see Tang still on the counter and as my eyes feel heavy I get a bit light headed then stop the spinning chair. Back to a still mode I turned the chair one eighty to view the counter and Tang hoping to see a brighter reaction but to a shock he was gone, whipping my head in ever direction I couldn't see him around the Control Deck, whistling for him there was no reaction and the station was silent, in a fit of rage I yelled.

"Tang you get out here right now."

There was still no response and my head began to race as I worried and my hands twitched, standing I was swaying a little not recovering from being dizzy from spinning in the chair, stumbling I walk to the Rec. room and there was still no sign of Tang and then turning back I check the Med. Lab but still no sign, it wasn't possible he went into the tunnels he wasn't strong enough to lift the hatch plus I would have heard it open I just only hoped he was okay but where. Exiting back into the Control Deck I ran back in forth the room looking in every small space and feeling my heart race I yelled again.

"Tang where are you please?"

Running my hands through my hair and breathing heavily I could feel my heart thump fast and I began to hyperventilate as then I fell to the ground and balled up crying, abruptly I felt something hitting my chest and opening my eyes I was in the Captains chair and there was Tang pounding on my chest trying to wake me. I stopped him and we connected for a hug it was then I realized with my declining health I must have passed out when I was spinning in the chair and what I was experiencing was just a dream of sorts so that was more hopeful, Tang calmed and sat on my chest I brought up my hand and scratched at his head assuring him I was fine.

"It's okay bud I'm okay."

Tang laid on my chest and feeling his breathing against mine put me at ease knowing we were both okay for the moment, still laid back in the Captains chair Tang had his hands wrapped around my chest, I closed my eyes just to rest them and trying to relax I could hear Tang softly whimpering. I think today was stressful enough and we needed a nap and I know it seemed like we just woke and I wasn't doing much at all note worthy but as neat as space life sounds if I told you the everyday events shit would get boring fast, for now I just wanted to relax so we'll wake in a few hours. I felt less sick after cooling down but now I think after wearing these extra clothes I began to lightly sweat and needed to take off a layer, pulling off Tang I placed him on the counter again then took off my extra shirt and pants leaving on a thinner shirt and shorts.

I peeled off the picture of Wendy from the computer screen and placed it in my front shirt pocket, I then picked Tang back up and we made our way back into the Rec. room to lay on the couch, laying flat my muscles could relax feeling the soft couch under it and as I shut my eyes I could feel Tang was there spread out on my chest laying on top of me, as I could feel my mind drifting off I could hear Tang softly snore as his breathing extended his belly pushing against mine, this went on for a few minuets till I was in a deeper sleep and my brain began to ignore my surroundings, my last awake thought was that I could hope for a better setting to dream in and at least momentarily I could be at peace.

A few hours later I was still in deep sleep my eyes seemed glued shut but asleep I could easily hear Tang's whimper, I didn't know if it was part of a dream but the feeling I had was like hearing a baby cry the connection I had with Tang was like father and son I never wanted to see him in pain and if he was ever hurting I was always there for him. Hearing the whimpering continue I couldn't ignore it and tried to force my eyes open and pushing myself out of the deep sleep my eyes finally cracked, I was half awake and groggy my vision was all blurred and I felt lightheaded trying to stand but after getting my footing I was okay. With squinted eyes I peeked around the room to notice for some reason the lights in the Rec. room where turned off and it rare that I would ever turn in off, peeking around the rest of the room I couldn't see the light from the restroom or the Control Deck and I hoped it wasn't some kind of blown fuse that means I'd have to reset them manually in the tunnels and that's the last thing I want to do, during all this I could also hear Tang's faint whimper coming from the Control Deck.

The area was dark but still visible the main lights where shut off but in the case of a malfunction the emergency lights came on, these emergency lights barely light the place due to the fact normally if there was malfunctions it can't be known how long it could take to repair it and with the unknowing the station had to be at its safest so the lowest amount of power was used and if it got to that point almost nothing would be functional not the water, heater, computers, radios or standard lights. With Tang's whimpering droning on I was getting worried and fallowed the sound of him, his noises lead me to the dim lite Control Deck and in the middle of the room near the tunnel hatch there was Tang faced away from me just standing there and softly whimpering, I rubbed my eyes clearing my vision and tip toed over to Tang getting to his level and reaching out to touch his shoulder.

"Tang buddy you okay?"

Tang had no reaction to my appearance and stood stiff, I pulled at his shoulder and turned around for him to face me but with the dim light I couldn't see his face very well but I could somehow feel he was staring at me and with our eyes connected the whimpering stop and the room was silent.

"Tang what is it, what's wrong?"

The station was abnormally silent I couldn't even hear gears moving around it was like the whole station was shut off then suddenly all the lights turned back on and to my shock my face was frozen with fear as I could see Tang was still motionless but I could not look away at the horror of his face.

He had no eyes, I mean he had eyes just no color it was all white and his mouth was dropped open, my arms lowered to my side and stuck with fear I didn't know how to react, I couldn't understand what was going on and as his body was stiff and brittle in an instant it seemed like his skin and fur was deteriorating in a time lapse, after a few seconds he was a scary statue the next he was bones in a dust pile. I covered my eyes with my hands and cried uncontrollably sitting there and rocking like a baby then pulling at my hair like I was going crazy.

In the middle of the Control Deck rocking in a ball screaming and crying I start to feel lightheaded and feeling my eyes get heavy I fall to the ground passing out and now in a void of darkness with no end I stood there hearing Tang's whimper grow louder and louder till the noise is unbearable and I cover my ears in pain as I clinch my eyes together in reaction, the whimpering continues but begins to slow and I slowly open my eyes to notice I was on the couch in the Rec. room and everything seemed to be fairly normal. The lights where still on and things were where they needed to be but as my vision clears from a deep sleep I could still hear Tang's soft whimper from the Control Deck, I was very confused what happened earlier must have been a dream and it was very unsettling knowing that most of my dreams before took place on Earth and mirrored what was a normal life but now I dreamed about being on the station so when should I question what was real anymore.

Tang's whimpering droned on and it was like glass piercing my ears I was just glad before was a dream and he was still alive, I guess you could say my motherly instincts kicked in and I shook my head trying to wake myself then I lunged off the couch and sprinted to the Control Deck slipping into the doorway as I turned to corner, getting back up grunting in the pain I held my side and limped into the Control Deck to see there was Tang in the middle of the room standing next to the now open manhole tunnel hatch. This was questioning enough but I was more worried about Tang, he stood there motionless and as I called out for him he turned his head to face me and I could see a look of sadness and hurt, I responded with worry in my voice.

"Tang, Tang it's okay let's get some medicine."

Tang continued to whimper and let out a loud painful screech as he grabbed his stomach and hunched over to puck all over the floor, I reached out my hand and called to Tang.

"Come on buddy let's go relax."

Tang started to stumble around and as he lost his balance he fell backwards into the manhole and I could hear him screech all the way down, I tried to lunge out and grab him but I was to late and as I fell near the manhole reaching in trying to catch him with no success I laid there in my failure sobbing but that wasn't the worst with my body weight slamming near the manhole, the manhole itself came down and smashed against my right ring and pinkie fingers. I screamed in the great agony while I was sobbing over what happened to Tang, taking my left hand I manually opened to manhole hatch again to reveal that my right ring and pinkie finger where cut clean off, the metal edge of the hatch was like a knife cutting against my trapped fingers, as much as I never wanted to go into the tunnels again I needed to save Tang and his life was on the line so hopefully the blood loss wouldn't kill me first but before I made the journey I took off my shirt wrapping it around the stubs of my fingers.

With the hatch open fully I stepped into the ladder and made my way down slowly, I guess since I had to redirect the power earlier the station power system decided that the emergency lights of the manhole where worth keeping on so I was glad I didn't need to bring along the flashlight, being careful where I stepped near the bottom where there was Tang lightly panting but still alive, I gently picked him up and there was no reaction out of him and also there at my feet was my two fingers, you probably have heard about being able to reattach fingers after they where cut off but I really didn't have the right supplies and even if did reconnect them they would most likely have dead nerves and would still never move again so there wasn't a point to take the risk of wasting supplies.

Climbing back up was harder but possible, it wasn't easy I had to use one hand to climb and the other damaged to cradle Tang the best I could and climbing out the top I stood from the floor to place Tang on the counter as I sat in the Captains chair. Hunched over the counter the shirt covering my bloody hand slipped off and I was now sobbing into my bloody hands, trying to whip my tear away just spreading more blood and tears around, in front of me there was Tang still panting, his eyes were shut and he seemed to be barely hanging on, I felt it would be futile to try to feed him more medication he just wasn't awake enough to swallow it and if he slipped under he would go into a coma I just didn't know what to do. He was in pain and I didn't know if he could come out of this easily and if he did recover what would change about himself it would be safe to assume that if he came out of a coma he would lose a few brain cells due to the smaller size and lack of brain activity, I whipped my eyes again and started to pet Tang on the head but there was still no reaction.

"Tang I'm so sorry this happened to you please if you can hear me be okay."

But there was no change he laid there almost lifeless and continued to slowly pant with his eyes closed I knew there wasn't much else I could do but watch him slowly die, breaking into tears again I knew what I had to do and though the thought killed my inside it was for the best, I patted Tang on the chest and gave him a kiss in the head as I sat there sobbing. Looking away I stood from the chair and limped over to the sleeping pods and disconnect one of the sleep compression tanks, grabbing a mask from the pod and putting the tank under my arm and limped back to the counter and sat down feeling broken. Placing the mask over Tang's face and connecting it to the tank I just couldn't push myself to press that button, I whipped my face again and slowly teared up as I ran my hands through my hair, with messy hair and my face and chest covered in tears and blood I felt limp not wanting to do anything but die, but staring at the motionless body of Tang was worse and I couldn't let his suffering continue, I pulled at the dial on the tank and pulled up the level of how much was being released into his system. Realizing what I have done my heart sunk and I began to blubber crying and screaming.

"God why, why now, take me you motherfucker, take me."

I could hear every slow breath Tang took and though it was quiet and soft they felt as loud as a horn and pierced my heart, his painting got slower and I couldn't watch the pain anymore I covered my eyes and after a minute it was total silence. Sitting there with covered eyes I quietly sobbed hearing nothing but my own grief, I felt like my heart was in my throat and it thumped hard as it also stung, he wasn't human but he was here he was my life and now I was more alone than I could ever be and it just wasn't worth it anymore I felt like my heart was going to explode and I've dealt with more than enough death it was time I put myself at ease and forget the worries that faced my future because I wasn't going to live for my future I was going to fight to survive and that wasn't a life worth living anymore. I stopped my crying an there was nothing no sound or anything it was like those dark voids I have in my dreams and opening my eyes peeking around there on the counter was Tang's lifeless body he was finally gone and focusing on him the only thing I could hear was the gas seeping from the tank as it was being wasted, it hurt me to much to stair at him and I then unplugged the tank not wanting to waste anymore.

Laying my head on the counter I just didn't have the energy to end my suffering after I just killed my best friend I didn't care and wanted to waste away starving myself to death, I closed my eyes and sighed I was just feeling so much but somehow almost nothing and numb, I was sad, angry, bored and to many to count but with all the emotional distress I was numb. In my dead state I was alive but didn't move feeling limb I just felt out of options and wait for death but something drew my attention I thought there was nothing more, I wasn't happy but I was curious there was a noise there was a sound coming from the computer then the computers voice said.

"Receiving incoming live chat."

I opened my eyes and lifted my head from the counter to take a look, this wasn't some malfunction it was real but how could it be, the computer message went away and a fuzzy live feed appeared on screen and to my shock I was flooded with emotions I didn't know how to feel I was flabbergasted like the gears in my head snapped and I just couldn't respond to her, and yes her. There she was my heart and mind couldn't take it and she said something but the video feed was scratchy I couldn't make it out but it was really her the real her, it was Wendy somehow somehow she was alive then as the quality cleared I could see everything perfectly and she spoke again.

"Taylor is that you, is it really you?"

I stood unbelieving not knowing if this was really real but frankly I didn't care it seemed to real I was overcome with all kinds of emotions but unable to speak but then I feel my heart thumping uncontrollably I feel my face droop and body become limb and my eyes feel heavy then I was weightless I couldn't move but I could see myself fall to the side and hit the floor as I jolt uncontrollably and lose my awareness as I pass out, I was having a heart attack.

I was again in a black void unable to move or talk just standing there but somehow I knew I wasn't dead I don't know how I knew this but it was just some feeling it's like an instinct I couldn't explain it I just knew. All I could think was that it was what it was and my body would have to work though it no matter how long it took I just somehow know I would wake again and all I had to do was wait, but through every struggle and pain I was torn apart and destroyed physically, mentally and emotionally but though all those troubles the best thing was I was alive and pushed on after all of it.

this wasn't my end but till my next visit I'd have to say one of the most important things I learned was though humans are some of the most imperfect things one of our best qualities is our spirit, we always get knocked down but always stand back up and after a few times we may be a bit beaten but the will power of humans can't be unmatched we just try and try and though we fail there are ones that give up but there are also always few that keep fighting, so all the struggles and death defying I do I just have to remember even if I'm dead wrong that there's always something next and life goes on and I'll see it through till the end of my time or something finally becomes to much and kills me in my attempt but that's my mission.

It's not leaving a legacy or reaching other life that's life my life even if it can't be defined as a normal life it's mine and I need to continue not for anyone else but me because I know once it's my time to leave I know I can finally tell myself I did what I could and came out knowing my life was worth something to me. Standing there in the void all I could do was wait but the pain was worth it because I knew even it if was real or not I could possibly be back with her, Wendy she was the next thing to give me the strength I needed and I was fine waiting however long it took because I knew my life would and will continue, so just remember if I can do this why can't humans before me do less of a challenge so if you're struggling there's always something around the corner to change your life for the better you just have to find it so good luck and I will be back my hope will live on.

About The Author

When growing up there was a few things that Clint Ridley wanted to be such as a pro wrestler, professional mascot, working with tech or writing for comic books but as each of those things where an idea at the time writing stories was something that was always around, from when younger than ten Clint made parodies of favorite cartoons, at the age of twelve he wrote a seventy page book in a notebook that he still currently has, the book he made when he was twelve was based about a young boy getting stuck in a video game it was unoriginal but a big step in the young authors future love of writing, his best advice it that no matter what type of media you work in you just have to remember there will always be people who like your work and don't but the only true opinion that matters is your own and if you think you can do better you can because if you ask that question your not doing your best and that's what your fans deserve because your fans are always the best fans so only give your best if you want to be the best.

Next in the Isolated series
The Isolated Mind : The Box

If you were enthroned with this adventure come back for the next adventure in the series for "The Isolated Mind : The Box". Remember those dreams that Captain Duane had, was there more story to those events? What is there really to unfold ? Read the next journey in a prequel following Duane during his last military mission that had him become a prisoner of war in the Congo jungle and leave the military to be trained by N.A.S.A. that leads to his ultimate fate, but what of those dreams, were they dreams? Find out next time in the new chilling war slash thriller story

Made in the USA
Coppell, TX
08 October 2022